I0670405

The Glove of Shadows:

A Tamalarian Tale

Joshua T. Calkins-Treworgy

BooksForABuck.com

2009

THE GLOVE OF SHADOWS: A TAMALARIA TALE

Joshua Calkins-Treworgy

Copyright 2009 by Joshua Calkins-Treworgy, all rights reserved. No portion of this novel may be duplicated, transmitted, or stored in any form without the express written permission of the publisher.

Warning: The unauthorized reproduction or distribution of this copyrighted work is illegal. Criminal copyright infringement, including infringement without monetary gain, is investigated by the FBI and is punishable by up to 5 years in federal prison and a fine of $250,000.

This is a work of fiction. All characters, events, and locations are fictitious or used fictitiously. Any resemblance to actual events or people is coincidental.

Published by BooksForABuck.com
ISBN: 978-1-60215-095-9
April 2009

Also By Joshua T. Calkins-Treworgy:

The Tamalarian Tales
Damnation of the Realm: Freedom or the Fire Volume One
The Dread Knight's Redemption: Freedom or the Fire Volume Two
A Hunter and His Prey

The Amelia City Stories
Roads Through Amelia
Wraiths of Formuth

Bob the Zombie Tales
Motor City Shambler
Forward, Shamble!

Non-series titles
The Last Days of Freedman High

Dedication

To my wonderful wife, who gave me the idea for the Headmaster of the Hoods in the first place. At least, one aspect of him.

Before We Begin

Greetings and salutations, readers. Welcome once again to the realms of Tamalaria. I come before you now a little older, though not too much wiser. Insofar as wisdom goes, I still have a lot of catching up to do on my mother and father. Hell, I've got to catch up to either of my older brothers yet.

However, it gives me great pleasure to know that I have at least attained the wisdom necessary to realize when a good idea needn't necessarily be my own. The tale you're about to read is largely here thanks to a handful of innocent ideas and comments my wife Audrey made during a role-playing session. There are several characters herein who are almost entirely her creation, not my own. However, she did always say from the get-go that if she ever gave me an idea that I liked, I was free to run with it.

Writing this was like a marathon in that regard. I hope you enjoy.

The Glove of Shadows

Prologue

Shadows stretched and loomed away from the oncoming company and their hefted torches. The heavy, metallic scraping of armor boots and greaves filled the air, and the dust they kicked up clung to the hundreds of small cobwebs all around the company. The air available to them ran dangerously low, though none yet felt the fatigue or onset of oxygen deprivation. At the front of the group, a young Elven man, brilliant crimson hair flowing halfway down his back and covering a healthy portion of the plate armor, ducked his head low to avoid striking his forehead against a brick set too low in the ceiling.

"Careful there, lads," he said, speaking over his shoulder to the Knights and Clerics who joined him on this expedition.

"What is this place, lord Reynaldi?" one of the Knights, a pale Human gentleman in silver chain mail, asked from behind two or three of the higher-ranking Knights ahead of him.

"Not entirely certain, young Townshend." The Elf turned to face his company.

To say that the Elven Paladin was handsome would have come as a severe understatement, particularly to those Human women who had fallen for his dashing appearance. His cheeks sloped along his face smoothly, in the genetic tradition of deep forest Elves, and his eyes hosted a limpid, alluring quality all their own. His smile shot straight and sure across his face, slightly raising the boyish dimples that could barely be seen except by a close observer or long-time acquaintance of the Paladin.

His silver full plate armor gleamed with polish and lack of use, for each time Archibald Reynaldi, High Exorcist of the Order of Oun, went into the realm of Tamalaria to perform his duties, he took with him a completely new set of armor. Each commissioned suit had to be blessed individually, depending upon the circumstances of his quest. After all, a set of plate armor enchanted against vampiric powers would do him precious little good against a Lich Lord.

For his current quest, he had received reports from a nomadic tribe of wandering merchants, known as Wayfarers, that strange noises had issued from the earth near a hill in the southwest. The report had been taken by a Knight in Fort Flag, rebuilt since the time of the War of Vandross, and summarily sent on to Fort Annassi, where Reynaldi served during the second half of each year. The descriptions of the noises and sights led him to one conclusion—Gheists.

Now that his party had arrived, he sensed no such undead spirits or creatures. "Gentlemen, I am at a loss. Do any of you detect anything sinister within this tomb?"

The Clerics, devout believers in the wisdom of Oun, could normally detect undead spirits for miles in all directions.

"We sense nothing, my lord," Father Flauri, one of the Clerics, said quietly. "However, something does seem off about this place."

"Explain, Father." Reynaldi set his torch in a handy bracket on the wall.

"Well, lordship, as you have just demonstrated, this place was clearly once used by people like you and I. For what purpose, I know not. We have not come across any rooms or corridors with anything more than barren floors and cobwebs. Yet, something remains in this place. A spirit, or an object, or some great power."

"An artifact, perhaps?" asked the highest-ranking officer, a Knight by the name of Charles Hayes, one of three sons born to James Hayes, a member of Byron of Sidius's entourage. "Tombs like these often hold artifacts from another age, imbued in part with the spirits of those who last wielded them. My father once wielded an artifact weapon of just such a nature." He lit a fresh torch—one of the rapidly diminishing stock. They had been scouring the man-made structure for hours without discovering any source for the Wayfarers' claims.

"It is possible," said Reynaldi. "However, all we have yet to search is the room we could not enter. There was no handle or knob, just a thin slot."

"I still say you should have let me tear that door down." The brash young Jaft, Helios Warik had never had much use for puzzles. This whole damned place looked and smelled like a puzzle to him.

"Now, now, Helios. You must learn the Third Guiding Principle of the Order of Oun: 'Patience is key, despite being difficult to attain.' If you ever wish to pass the trials and become a Paladin of Oun, you must remember your lessons." The handsome Elven man turned to lead the company back to the door with no handle.

Small rodents and insects scurried once again at their approach, their tiny tracks and those of the intruding exorcists the only indications that anyone, or anything had been through this place in centuries. Here and there, traces of former occupants could be barely detected; under an inch-thick layer of dust, a crumbled bone. Stuck in a decaying chunk of concrete, a strange coin of some sort, eroded to a translucent state.

Once again standing before the door with no handle or knob, they saw another sign of some sort—a partially preserved corpse, wrapped in rotting leather armor, rusted and ruined thief's tools in a belt around its waist.

At first glance, one could assume with some certainty what had happened. A tomb raider had come down about fifty years earlier, tried to get into the chamber beyond this slotted door, and suffered some grizzly fate that involved a sharp blow to the head. The enormous cleaver-shaped hole in the skull suggested nothing less.

But Archibald, returning for the third time now to this odd door, realized that the corpse was facing away from the door. Not only that, but no tools had been in the thief's hands at the time of death. Instead, a shattered short sword, still relatively unfazed by the ravages of time, lay just outside of its grasp. The sword appeared to be mythril, a very sturdy and lightweight material that could withstand any amount of time. However, only a few other metals in all of Tamalaria, or elsewhere, could destroy mythril. Whoever had access to that sort of weapon had intruded, and this corpse had failed to guard the door.

"My lord, you may want to take a look at this," said Father Flauri.

Reynaldi turned away from the corpse to see what the Cleric wanted.

The older Human gentleman swiped at a set of letters etched into the stone with a small brush, one that Father Flauri kept for these expeditions into the ruins of a time gone past. *Always, always, always,* he would think as he prepared for the journey, *there's some set of vital information carved into a stone or a piece of wood, and nobody will find it except for me, because nobody thinks to bring a small brush for just such a situation!* "These markings are an old language of some sort, clearly used by the former inhabitants of this stronghold. With a little time and Father

Revas's help, we may be able to decipher this message." He looked into Reynaldi's eyes.

Ye gods, Flauri thought. *He's already approved. Such a patient man.* "It may even have something to do with how to open this door."

"Do it." Reynaldi moved away, setting yet another torch in a wall bracket. "All right everybody, let's take a quick count of how many torches we have left."

Everyone in the company settled in, seating themselves along the corridor walls and taking a look at their supplies.

"We have six torches, my lord." Charles Hayes delivered the report to their leader.

The faint whisperings of the Clerics behind him gave Hayes pause, but he continued on with his report. He felt a drop of sweat running down his forehead, and his lungs began to slightly cramp. "We are most likely running out of fresh air, my lord. We shall have to abandon this place soon if we make no discovery, my lord."

Reynaldi looked up at the corridor ceiling some ten feet over his head.

"I know, Charley, I know. My chest is starting to hurt, too." He lowered his gaze to find his armored hands, clenching them into fists. "But you heard Father Flauri. There's something down here, something that doesn't sit well with him. I trust his instincts, Charley."

"As do I, my lord, but we are low on torches, food, water, and air. We have a few hours, that's—" Hayes never got the chance to finish his objection. A loud, grinding, clattering noise swept out from the Clerics, who presently tore at a section of the concrete wall with their metal-tipped staffs.

"Here, lordship," Flauri cried over the din of his own efforts. "The trigger to open the door is behind this section of wall."

Helios Warik smiled wickedly at his commander.

Reynaldi nodded and rolled his left hand in a 'go ahead' motion.

The Jaft Knight calmly placed a hand on each Cleric's shoulder, moving them easily aside. Warik cracked his neck, the sound of popping bones filling the air like rapid drum roll beats. A moment later, as his right hand crashed into the wall panel that Father Flauri had identified.

The stench of concrete dust mixed with the acrid aroma of his Jaft flesh to give everyone a vague feeling of nausea. He'd removed his glove to throw the killer blow, a technique he'd learned years before joining the Order, and his odor had been released with the removal of the glove. Lord Reynaldi respected his skills, but found his odor too offensive for words. The enchanted glove had been an effective measure to keep him along.

Still, Reynaldi thought as he peered at the red lever behind the hole in the wall, *he has his uses.*

Grasping the handle, the Elven Paladin pulled it toward himself. To his surprise, the handle came easily enough. The door that previously could not be opened slowly began to slide into the wall to its left. Shortly thereafter, the grinding of stone on stone ceased and the entire stronghold sat silent.

Archibald Reynaldi stepped over to the doorway and peered into the hollow chamber beyond.

In the middle of the chamber, an altar sat in a depression in the floor.

There appeared to be no guards, no traps, but the Elven Paladin knew better than to walk in blindly. "Father Flauri, do you sense any magic protections here?" His eyes fell on the object atop the altar. It appeared to be a simple glove, constructed partially of leather and partially of metal. But he knew it could be no ordinary glove to be so heavily guarded, and to remain intact after decades or centuries.

"No, lordship," the Human Cleric whispered next to him. "I sense no magic, or spirits here. There is, however, something coming from that glove. It is an artifact, of that there is no doubt, but its intended uses, its powers and abilities, are presently beyond my ken. I would have to get closer to it to identify it."

"Your knowledge of artifacts is well appreciated, Father." Reynaldi inched into the chamber. He held his hand behind him to stay his allies in their position. The room had been checked by the old Cleric, but if there were a problem, he would not sacrifice those in his command. "Stay well back, gentlemen, until the nature of this object is known."

Finally, he stood before the strange glove, and sensed what it must be.

A small smile of triumph worked its way across his face as he snatched the glove off of the pedestal, and placed it swiftly in his rucksack.

Smiling to himself, Archibald Reynaldi returned to the doorway and his waiting crew.

"What is it?" Father Flauri's voice was a reverential whisper.

The Elven Paladin looked down into the cleric's wizened face, and leaned forward slightly, speaking in a whisper of his own.

"Good father, what we have found here this day shall be taken to a safe place, until I find a way to destroy it."

Flauri eyeballed him quizzically for a long moment.

"Father Flauri, we have found the Glove of Shadows!"

The Glove of Shadows

Chapter One
The Deus Family

Annabelle Deus, called Anna by her friends and loved ones, strolled easily from the Gnome-engineered gas stove to her seat at the kitchen table. In an hour or so, her husband, Harold, would be home from the market where he sold his simple wares and homemade jewelry in order to hold up his end of expenses.

As she sat, she wondered how safe he was. The city of Desanadron treated all of its residents the same—meaning that everybody ran the risk of being assaulted or mugged on a daily basis. If you owned a business, you most likely paid protection money to somebody. And you knew who would be attacked at your front door if they crossed into unwelcome territory.

Resident gangs, Guilds, and individual bullies made up a good quarter of the city's population. Harold, being a simple, naive kind of fellow, a trait she'd always loved in him, simply didn't hold with the idea of paying for a bodyguard. He didn't feel he should have to pay anybody in order to have a successful business, except of course the tax collection agents. In addition, Harold believed that a smile and a civil tone could take care of any situation.

Anna knew different, but she allowed her doting husband his thoughts on the matter. *After all*, she thought with a smile, *the 'boys' are keeping an eye on him.*

A timer in the kitchen went "ding," and she slowly stood. "Better get to those potatoes."

She moved with a speed and grace through her kitchen that spoke of a very domestic sort of woman. Strangely enough, few men ever realized that a woman moving like Anna through a kitchen, looked a good deal like an agile fighter on a battlefield. "The boys will take care of things."

* * * *

Harold Deus pored over the small notebook he used to keep track of his sales. His long, pencil-like pointer finger ran down the sheets item by item, the total price of the product kept next to a running total.

None of his merchandise sold for much—Harold came from a long line of merchants who never got a building for themselves due to something they kept in their hearts. That particular thing happened to be called integrity, a term mostly foreign to the tongues of businessmen in Tamalaria.

His standing policy was 'sell for only two times what you paid'. In this way, Harold managed to make just enough money to feel he kept up his end of expenses at home. He wished he could make more, so that his loving wife, Anna, wouldn't have to put in so much time for the Councilors' Committee. However, he knew it would be impossible for them to survive on his earnings alone. Between his sales and her earnings, the couple lived comfortably.

Harold put his pencil to the paper on the third page, and re-checked the numbers one final time. "Well, not bad all-in-all," he said aloud, smiling toothily.

Someone behind and to the left of him cleared their throat meaningfully, sending a small, familiar wave up Harold's spine.

"Oh no," he whispered to himself, swallowing hard as he turned around to face the throat-clearer.

Before him two men stood, dressed in the simple, tattered clothes of folk whose lives have been supported by the earnings of others. The shorter of the two, a Human, leaned on Harold's cart with a small knife in his left hand. He cut a slice off of a green apple and popped it into his mouth. His hair, kept under a blue cloth bandana, crept out on the sides of the rag in curls of oily black.

While the Human's demeanor caused Harold to swallow hard and think of escape, the other gentleman, the one looming over the merchant's miniscule frame, made him want to scream.

Standing easily at around seven feet in height, the man had the blue skin and the faint stench of a Jaft. Looking up, Harold spied the craggy face and bald head typical of the Jaft Race. He also noted the standard curved, serrated short sword hanging limply from the Jaft's hip.

He noted the details absently as he wondered how to talk his way out of being mugged.

Behind the Jaft's massive frame, Harold saw the Human, his long, black sleeves blurring with the speed of his movements, pocket something from Harold's cart.

He thought over the inventory of his cart, and realized that one of his most expensive items, a bracelet made of pure gold, had been hung from one of the hooks at that end of the cart.

"Um, ah, ha ha, that's six gold pieces, um, sir." He pointed at the Human goon around the Jaft's left side.

Huge, gnarled hands found purchase in Harold's tunic shirt, hoisting him against his own cart.

He hit with an audible 'thud', the wind wheezing out of him so roughly his vision blanked for a moment. Then he found himself once again looking into the Jaft's cliff-like face, the brows knitted tightly in barely contained violence. The difference was in perspective. Now he was held in front of and over the Jaft's head.

"Um, then again, you look like you're good for it, sir," he murmured rather lamely.

"Glad to see ye be thinkin' straight, bucko." The Human thief chuckled. He tossed the half-eaten apple aside, and produced the bracelet from his shirtsleeve, eyeballing it carefully. His moustache curled up along with his lip as he grinned at the jewelry piece. The trinket may have been labeled six gold pieces, but it could be pawned for twice as much.

His day's work done, the thief turned to his right and prepared to saunter away.

He managed two steps, not looking up from the bracelet, before he bumped headlong into a well-toned chest covered in thick, crimson fur. Those chest muscles tensed visibly in front of his eyes, and a deep, primal growl escaped the throat of the creature before the thief.

Looking up from his treasure, the Human spotted the thin straps of the open-chest vest worn by the Red Tribe Werewolf, a simple patch on its right side.

The patch indicated that the hulking Werewolf was a member of the Hoods, one of the two large thieves' Guilds in the city of Desanadron.

"Here now, I think I'll just, ah, put this back," he managed, placing the bracelet back on its ring hook.

"What the fuck're you talking about?" The Jaft turned his head slightly to look at his companion.

For a moment, the Jaft felt a tiny, tiny impulse to drop the merchant in his hands and run. An animalistic instinct screamed from the pits of evolution at him, *flee now!*

Whereas most of the humanoid Races tend to listen to such warnings from within, the Jaft Race still lacked a great deal of civilization and enlightenment. They looked at such instincts as a sign of weakness, and no Jaft worth his weight in salt showed weakness.

"He's a Hood, Jeff." The Jaft's partner backed away from the Red Tribe Werewolf.

Jeff laughed scornfully, dropped Harold roughly to the ground and squared his body towards the Werewolf.

"So what? He doesn't look like much of a thief to me!"

"I'm not." The Werewolf cracked his huge, knobby knuckles.

The sound reminded the Human thief of the noise his brother's spine had made when he had fallen off the roof of their house a few years back. Certain doom surely followed that sort of noise.

"I'm just an enforcer. You will leave, or you will pay for the bracelet, if you want it. If you opt to do neither, then I shall visit great bodily harm upon you." The Werewolf, let his arms hang limply at his sides. His fingers twitched and curled, his whole body resonating an aura of terrible violence.

Having seen and heard too much for his own taste, the Human thief turned and put as much distance as he could between himself and what would surely soon erupt into a battlefield.

Disgusted by his partner's lack of spine, and the fact that the Werewolf didn't seem at all intimidated by him, the Jaft loosed a battle roar and charged his opponent, lowering his head and putting his right shoulder forward.

Hmph, the Werewolf thought. *Such pathetic form, even for an amateur.*

As the Jaft connected with his bull-tackle, the Red Tribe shifted his weight, wrapping his left arm around the Jaft's head and throwing his lower body out.

The combined weight and momentum resulted in a roughneck, wrestling maneuver commonly known as a DDT—the Jaft's face hit the cobblestone street at high speed.

As soon as the Werewolf sprang off of him, he got to his hands and knees, spitting out a shower of teeth and blood. Jeff wobbled a bit as he got to his feet, only to find that his opponent had already assumed a fighting stance.

"You're good." The Jaft put his own hands up and approached cautiously.

"You're not," the Werewolf retorted.

Damn him, Jeff thought. *How can he be so calm?*

He lunged forward, throwing a jab-cross combination that the Werewolf easily patted and blocked aside.

He's mocking me! He threw a volley of wild, roundhouse punches, each knocked aside more forcefully than the last.

Finally, the Red Tribe Werewolf made his own offensive move. The crimson combatant shuffled forward, throwing a low-line kick at Jeff's shins.

The Jaft saw it coming and moved his hands down to block. But there was no force behind the blow—a feint?

The Werewolf whipped his leg up from the forced block, crashing his muscular lower leg into the side of the Jaft's head. The impact made a noise similar to raw meat smacking against a metal slab.

As the Jaft tottered back and forth, stars flaring in front of his eyes, the Werewolf shuffled forward and launched a vicious jab-cross-uppercut combination that broke the Jaft's jaw and fractured his faceplate.

His vision blurring to darkness, the Jaft toppled over onto the street, bleeding and battered.

Harold, who had been watching the fight in stunned silence, clapped along with the crowd that had assembled. In Desanadron, it doesn't take much to make the mob stand up and take notice. The Red Tribe, barely breathing heavy, glared down at his fallen opponent.

To Harold, and the crowd, which included several merchants who had already been shaken down by the two bandits, he was a hero. To the city guards, his display might make him seem a menace. Before Harold could even thank the man, the Werewolf was off and running. Within a few minutes, he was out of sight.

* * * *

The Red Tribe Werewolf darted down side streets and alleyways until at last he planted his feet in the dirt and skidded to a halt a few feet away from a suspicious-looking Wererat. The Wererat wore the black leathers and belts typical of a man of his profession, looking part road agent and part pirate. He leaned easily against the back wall of a tavern, one leg crossed over the other, cleaning his long claws with a thin dagger.

The Werewolf looked at the ground, and found the Wererat's tracks had only been made a minute or two before his own.

"Real nice of you to help out." The Werewolf cracked his neck. "Remind me again why you came along, Flint." He addressed the Wererat in a low growl of thunder.

Flint chuckled softly, shaking his head and letting the point of the dagger droop until it pointed at the Red Tribe Werewolf like an accusation.

"Mostly to keep an eye on you, Stockholm." Flint smiled as only rats can smile.

Ignatious Stockholm didn't care much for Flint's mannerisms, which always seemed to indicate that he was laughing at you.

"You seemed to have the situation under control, in any case," Flint returned his attention to his nails. "I just came along to keep an eye on your temper."

Stockholm harrumphed loudly. He stalked past Flint with a sort of dangerous, militant swagger that had become second nature to the burly Red Tribe.

"Come on, Flint," he said over his shoulder, stopping just a few yards shy of the street.

Stockholm knelt and grabbed hold of a sewer access grate in the alley—one of the many forgotten ones that nobody seemed to notice, even when they stepped right over them. The only people who felt the grate to be of any importance tended to come from the tavern Flint had been leaning against. Most of those individuals found it made an ideal puking spot. "We've got to get back to the Guild hall and make ready for the meeting. William's coming back this evening, and I'd rather the place wasn't in total chaos."

Flint shrugged his shoulders, pocketed his knife, and followed the massive Werewolf down the access ladder, and into the sewers.

* * * *

Anna had just placed their plates on the kitchen table when Harold, opened the front door with a loud grunt and heave on the heavy wood.

"Sweetie!" She ran into the living room and launched herself at him.

Harold caught her mid-air, spinning her as best he could for a moment before setting her down and giving her a deep kiss.

"Your timing, as always, is excellent dear! I just got dinner on the table," she said.

Harold looked into the kitchen, where she had set their dishes and lit two candles, dimming down the rest of the lighting in the kitchen. The scene held a romantic quality, one that reminded Harold of his wife's obligations.

"You've got another big conference, don't you?" He looked into his wife's eyes.

Anna's smile dropped off a little, but she simply nodded and led her husband into the kitchen by the hand.

"I understand, dear. Being a Councilor's advisor has a lot of responsibility attached to it." Harold beamed at his lovely wife. Some folks tended to describe her as handsome, a term that Harold usually assumed should only be reserved for men. But sometimes, just sometimes, she reminded him of her brother, William Deus. So perhaps handsome would be a proper term.

Husband and wife took seats across from one another at the small kitchen table, Harold waiting to push in his wife's chair before taking off his overcoat and seating himself. He sighed heavily, having had a rough end of business earlier, and having to practically drag their donkey, Mr. Pibble, through the streets. The ornery animal had been a present from the Merchants' Guild of Desanadron when Harold had joined their ranks the year before, and he couldn't have been happier at first. Using Mr. Pibble to haul the cart from the Deus residence to the marketplace and back had made things much easier the first few days he owned the beast. After a month, Harold had managed to put some weight on from the meals his wife cooked for him, because he wasn't burning everything off by dragging the cart himself. However, as animals often do, Mr. Pibble soon developed an attitude. Some days Harold had to drag both beast and cart. Today had been one such day.

"So, how did we do today, hon?" Anna asked before taking her first bite.

Harold stopped his fork halfway to his mouth, trying to think of a graceful way to tell her he'd been accosted and almost robbed. She worried about him terribly sometimes, he knew, and he didn't like to see Anna upset. He loved the natural smile in her eyes, the way her laughter gave his whole body a weightless feeling. He didn't want to tell her, but he supposed that, as usual, she'd find out eventually. She'd talk to her Councilor, and he would in turn talk to the city guards. She'd find out, and she'd be furious with him for not telling her.

"Well, dear, we did okay most of the day." He pulled out his little notebook and read over the figures one more time. "Total profit of eleven gold pieces."

Anna smiled widely as she chewed her food.

"That's great. That's half the month's rent and one left over. But you do realize you used the qualifier, 'most', don't you?" She gave Harold a sly gaze, and he knew his tongue had, once again, trapped him.

Anna's own thoughts drifted back on their four happy years of marriage, and the long, dangerous trips that Harold had to make on occasion to Traithrock in the north. He traveled to the Dwarven city in the mountains once every few months for materials to make his jewelry, always coming away with a great deal. She would love to tell him to stop making his trips there, for the road to Traithrock wound through some very dangerous territory, and some day even her own precautions wouldn't protect him. Anna always provided protection for Harold's journeys, though he didn't know. Still, she couldn't tell him to stop.

Her own line of work took her out of town for weeks at a time, and in two instances since their marriage, months. But every time she returned, it was to a loving husband who accepted the circumstances, regardless of what they might be. Her thoughts doubled back to the present moment, and she waited patiently for Harold to explain what 'most' meant, with regard to his day.

"Well, I was doing my calculations, checking the numbers before I closed up for the day…" he delayed the story with mouthfuls of food.

A cheap tactic, Anna thought, but one he'd try until death or divorce did them part.

"I sort of, well, noticed these two fellows—a little Human and a big Jaft. The, ah, Human, well, he tried to pocket one of the bracelets. The six gold ones," he said, knowing that Anna kept a good track of his inventory. "Well, I told him he'd have to pay for it, and his Jaft friend sort of disagreed, heh heh." He tried to smile bravely at Anna.

"I see." She chewed her food meaningfully. "So we're out six gold?"

"Oh, no, not at all dear." Harold exploded into details about the Werewolf who had terrorized the Human thief into fleeing. He recounted the fight between the Jaft and the Werewolf, though he carefully left out the bit where he had been hoisted and dropped by the blue-fleshed humanoid.

Anna raised her eyebrows and held them there for a moment, and finally smiled her approval. *Yes*, she thought, *the boys are good at keeping an eye on you, Harold.*

"And that's about it." He concluded his story and his meal. "Had to fight with Mr. Pibble all the way home, the obnoxious little oaf," he grumbled, taking his plate to the kitchen sink. "How're things here?"

Anna put her fork down, hating herself intensely for the continuous lie she had to spoon-feed her husband in a moment.

"I have a conference tonight, Harold," she said. "The Councilor is most likely going out of town for a few weeks afterward, and he wants me along with the caravan. I'm sorry." She hung her head in disgust.

Harold smiled warmly at her, however, and the sight of his kindly, gaunt face made her want to break down and cry, tell him everything there was to tell. But she couldn't, and she knew it.

16

"Don't be sorry, dear." He walked behind her and rubbed her shoulders. *Gods, he's good at this*, she thought.

"Your job is very demanding, sweetheart. I'm frankly surprised you've had as much time off lately as you have! No evening sessions for weeks, no trips, no conferences for almost a month. It's been great having you home every night." He kissed the top of her head, ruffling her long hair slightly. "Just promise me you'll do the best you can to come home in a good mood."

Anna put her left hand over her husband's right, and almost broke into tears once again. Gods, she hated leaving him.

A familiar, comfortable silence settled over the household then, with Harold going into the den to read one of the used novels he bought from the bookstore every week, and Anna heading to their bedroom to pack. She looked back into the den just once before heading to their room, a single streak of dampness running down her cheek. *Stay with it, girl*, she told herself. *This is the life you chose!*

In their room, Anna knelt down beside their bed and pulled her custom-made suitcase out from beneath. A Gnome Tinker friend of hers had built it especially for her, and she rejoiced in having it. She popped the lock and opened a hidden compartment, which in truth made up almost the entire space of the luggage. She checked the contents therein, making certain she had everything she needed.

Length of rope, check, she thought. *Throwing knives, lock picks*, check.

She heard then the faint creaking of the floorboards in the hallway, and swiftly snapped the compartment shut, her spare dresses and feminine products now the only visible items.

A few seconds later, she let Harold pounce and wrap his arms around her. *He's getting too thin*, she thought as she held his arms in place around her. *I hope he isn't getting sick.*

"I love you, dear." Harold rested his head on her shoulder.

"I love you too, Harold. I should only be gone a couple of weeks." Her words sounded hollow and deceitful to her ears.

"Is that all?" He stood and pulling her up with him.

They faced one another, wrapped lovingly in each other's arms. He was smiling warmly, though she saw the hint of chagrin in his eyes.

"You've been gone much longer than that before. Before we even got married, when we were just living together, do you remember? You were sent out of town for three months! I thought you'd been killed! No thanks to your brother," he grumbled.

"Now don't start in with that again, dear." Anna chided him. "William is simply misunderstood."

"He's a bloody thief, Anna! One of the worst in the west."

Though they often disagreed about her brother William, they never let it get between them. Neither would let go of the other. "I suppose he is family, though. You going to take him more clothes?"

"I may not get a chance to see him," she replied. Her lies always went unchecked by Harold. He believed her without question. Then again, she thought with a wry smile, most people did. That went with the territory of her profession. "I'll write you from the road." She stuffed some men's clothes into her bag.

Harold rolled his eyes, knowing full well who they were for. Anna may try to say they'd be for the Councilor, but he knew they were for William, in case Anna did get a chance to see her brother.

"You'll be okay on the road?"

"Of course, dear. The Deus family is a very strong bunch." She flexed her right arm as best she could. "That's why you took our name, remember?" She closed the suitcase then and stood up, hoisting it with her. She walked over and gave her husband a long, deep kiss. "I love you Harold."

"Love you too, dear. I'll be waiting," he said.

Together they walked to the front door of their home. She departed without saying another word, both of them understanding that any more good-byes would just make things more difficult.

Harold Deus watched his wife's back for a long moment before he shut the door, and retired to the den. His books would keep him company until her return.

* * * *

A dark-clad figure darted from alley to alley, keeping to the shadows and away from the known guard patrols. He ducked and dodged around the drunken homeless and their piles of discarded belongings, never staying in any one place long enough for anyone to fix a keen eye on his face. The bandana over his forehead and hair whipped back and forth a bit as he ran, jumping over a refuse bin and kicking off of the wall of a residence to avoid landing on a sleeping dog in the alley.

Stockholm wouldn't appreciate him landing on a dog, he thought.

A brace of knives rested easily in a belt around the man's waist, commonplace for members of the Hoods. His Guild waited patiently for his arrival, he knew, but he liked to hustle just a little so as not to wear on Flint's patience. The Wererat was the figure's right-hand man, though he lacked the patience of his immediate subordinate, Ignatious Stockholm.

Thoughts of the two men's clashing styles of leadership propelled the slim, agile man on. He'd hate to think of what might happen if he never came back to keep order over the Guild. The two of them might kill each other. *No*, he amended, *Stockholm would slaughter Flint outright*. No contest involved there.

Around a bend in the alley lay the sewer grate that he would drop down through to make his way to the Hoods' headquarters.

"Time to play the game," he whispered, throwing the grate open and dropping down in without bothering with the ladder or checking to see if anyone stood in the way. He landed in a crouch, water splashing near him as Stockholm stutter stepped backwards.

"Ye Gods, boss man! Watch where you stick that landing."

"Cram it, Stocky." The lithe Human figure he stood up straight and marched forward.

Stockholm fell into step beside him, a torch in his right hand.

"Give me the run-down."

As they approached the first turn in a series of tunnels, Flint fell silently into step on the Human's other side.

"Well, it's been fairly quiet the last five nights. It'd still be nice if our Guild Headmaster put in an appearance more than he does. Hint, hint, William."

William Deus made a face at his third-in-command as he rumbled on, and Flint clamped one hairy hand over his snout to keep from laughing.

Stockholm curled his lip disapprovingly for a moment before continuing. "Standard operations, essentially. However, our outside advisor friend is here to see you. He claims it's urgent."

William Deus knew, from both Stockholm's tone and the way he described the friend that the werewolf referred to Lee Toren.

"Lee Toren," William said aloud, his slightly high-pitched voice rebounding off of the tunnel walls and back at him. William Deus had first worked with the reputed Gnome Pickpocket and self-advertised 'gentleman' five years before, when he had been selected as the Hoods' new Prime by the former Guild Headmaster, Remy Torago. Lee Toren had been contracted on for an expedition to a set of recently uncovered ruins in the northeast, a little beyond the Port of Arcade. The city of Palen at that time sent a group of mages to investigate strange fluctuations of magical energy in the area of the ruins, and they unearthed the entrance to an ancient, underground city. News of the ruins spread quickly throughout Tamalaria.

Most notably, the word circulated around to thieves' guilds like wildfire. Who knew what treasures lay in wait down there? Remy couldn't resist sending a team to investigate, and Lee had a reputation across the continent as both a great Pickpocket, and an excellent tomb raider. Remy hired him to lead a group of five of his finest agents into the ruins and filch whatever they could.

William had taken an immediate liking to the quirky Gnome. He proved to be good for a laugh, and competent in his fields. William, Flint, and a handful of others had they plundered the ruins swiftly and profitably. Of course, they hadn't counted on the mages of Palen posting guards, and a few scuffles had left one man dead and William wounded. The only one among the company who had any first aid knowledge was Flint, and he had learned more about William at that time than any other.

"Yes, Lee Toren, the little trouble maker," Stockholm grumbled. "William, I know you like him, and I agree that he's an amusing little fellow. But he's bad news."

The trio continued on towards their main lair in relative silence, the squeaking of the occasional rodent filling the air and the splash of sewage into the main ducts filling the air with both sound and scent.

Just before they arrived at the door that would lead to the primary meeting hall, Flint inserted himself between William Deus and Stockholm, taking his boss by the arm.

Stockholm raised a curious eyebrow at the Hoods' Prime, who smiled winningly at him.

"Just need to have a word with the boss in private fer a tick, heh heh," he said, hauling William around the corner of an access tunnel.

"Go on ahead without us, Ignatious," William called out.

A moment later they heard the huge iron door open to admit the Hoods' *Chief*, Stockholm's position.

19

"All right, Flint. What's this about," William whispered, his face scant inches away from the Wererat's snout in the cramped access tunnel.

Flint looked around, making certain with his eyes and ears that they were in fact alone.

"Still wearing that cheap musk cologne?" he asked his Headmaster. "In case you haven't thought about that, let me make something plain. The big red woofy-dog we know and love is going to numb up to the silver dust you put in it. I'm not allergic to silver, Werewolves are, but he's going to numb to it eventually. And when he does, he'll know." Flint made another check of the tunnels.

"Oh come off it, Flint," William said. "Him finding out's a long way off yet." Without another word, William headed for the large iron door that would let him into the Guild.

Flint darted around in front of him, smiling his knowing smile.

"Long way off, eh? Not if he sees that strap, sir."

William looked at his shoulder in dismay, and tucked the blue strap of cloth back under his shirt.

"How d'you forget taking that off before doing the wraps?"

"Look, it's out of sight now, okay?" William said. "It was a minor slip, Flint. I've just gotten back into the routine back home, and at home, without the bra, they sag. It's not easy, you know. You try cross-dressing for a living, rat."

"All right, all right, I'm sorry." Flint waved his hands to keep her quiet. "Let's just get in there before Stockholm comes looking for us. Okay Anna?"

Chapter Two
Guild Business

Annabelle Deus, in her role as William Deus, renowned Rogue, stepped through the open doorway and into the meeting hall of the Hoods.

Her and Flint's arrival started a volley of hails and cheers. Several men, and a couple of female agents, shouted above the din, "Oy, William!"

She met and greeted many of them on her way up to the elevated platform at the opposite end of the hall, where she always gave her speeches and handed out members' assignments.

Stockholm stood ready at his post on the platform as Anna and Flint tried to part the sea of members and agents.

"Clear the way!" Stockholm's booming command silenced almost the entire crowd, and Pickpockets, Rogues and Strong Arm Thugs made way for their leader and her second, the Guild Prime.

Anna hopped easily up onto the stage.

Flint took one large step up, and the three stood for a moment of silence before the Guild. On Anna's right, Flint held the post of Prime. On her left, Ignatious Stockholm held the post of Chief. Together, they led and governed this crowd of thieves from day to day, making certain that some semblance of order held.

Anna smiled broadly at nearly two hundred men and women, holding her hands up for their total attention. Their side conversations slowed, and ultimately stopped as she felt a swelling of pride in her bosom. True, theirs may not be a noble profession, but at least the Hoods retained a code of honorable conduct. Nobody got hurt, they didn't shake down merchants for 'protection' money, and they didn't take from those who had nothing. On rare occasions, these rules were broken, usually by new members of the Guild. That led to disciplinary action, and the Guild Chief's primary function was to enforce the Hoods' code of conduct. Stockholm believed in harsh, firm punishment, so most members kept their noses clean.

"All right, ladies and gents, let's do this quick and get to business," she began, speaking loudly and directing her voice at the back of the room, where her voice would echo back and around to everyone present. "I've got a lot of tasks to assign, paperwork to go through, and oral reports to listen to tonight. First order, of course, is the recitation of the Code of the Hoods. Mr. Stockholm! If you would please do the honors?"

The massive Red Tribe Werewolf took the center stage, clearing his throat audibly. As he opened his mouth to speak, somebody in the audience whispered to his neighbor, and both chuckled just loudly enough to be heard. Stockholm closed his mouth and glared meaningfully in the jokers' direction. A moment of tension passed as he pulled his lips back just a small bit.

The front row of agents tried to push back away from the stage at that snarl, and Anna thought on the nickname many of them used behind Stockholm's back: 'The Red Menace'. She supposed more members feared him than respected him, but Ignatious Stockholm gave good reasons to be afraid of him. She also knew of his kinder nature, the true persona he hid beneath his gruff, battle-worn and tested exterior. She believed she knew a great deal more about him than even he knew, and she intended to keep it that way.

21

Once more he cleared his throat, and brought his left hand to his forehead in a salute. Every agent in the hall, Flint and Anna included, followed suit.

"These rules I shall vow ne'er to breach," he began, "as a member of the Hoods! Firstly, I shall never take that which is necessary for survival from those who do not deserve theft! Secondly, I shall never steal from a Hoods brother or sister, for reasons other than jest or official Guild tests of advancement! Thirdly, I shall never cause harm when it can be avoided."

He continued reciting the rules of the Guild alone. This, Anna had discovered, proved much more efficient than trying to have two hundred men and women repeat every word.

"Fourth, I shall never follow orders blindly. I shall question judgments handed forth that do not seem sound. Fifth, I shall honor and obey the Guild Headmaster," he said.

Anna nodded, raising her salute hand skyward for a moment.

"The Guild Prime," Stockholm said, and Flint raised his hand.

"And the Guild Chief," he said, raising his own hand. "Lastly, I shall do nothing to bring shame, or the authorities down on the Guild!"

The assembled Guild members brought their hands down and stomped their right feet once.

Stockholm stepped back, and took his position on Anna's left hand side.

Before Flint stepped forward, the Red Tribe had one final statement to make. "Ignatious Stockholm, Guild Chief!"

Flint remained planted to his spot, but raised his head a couple of inches. "Flint Ananham, Guild Prime!" Anna then stepped forward into the center of the stage.

"William Deus, Guild Headmaster to the Hoods!"

Cheers rose up from the crowd, the agents taking heart in once again seeing their leader after a month-long absence. She had popped in from time to time over the weeks, but only infrequently, to take reports from her Prime and Chief. She hadn't addressed the entire Guild for too long, and they had become dispirited by William Deus's long absence. Now, the agents all exhibited a sense of energy.

She stepped back and faced her two best men. "Gentlemen, I'll be in my office. Flint, I'll see you first for your reports, then you Stocky."

The Red Tribe rolled his eyes and murmured something under his breath.

Anna spun on her heel and stalked off through a second smaller, wooden door to the right of the stage.

"Cheer up, mate," Flint clapped Stockholm lightly on the back. "He gets to all of us. It's what makes him great."

"You know I don't like that nickname." He narrowed his eyes as he once again spotted the two agents who fancied themselves comedians. They had spoken out of turn. He would have none of that. "Go on, Flint. I've got a couple of smart-asses to flay."

* * * *

Annabelle Deus made her solitary walk to her office with a certain bounce in her step, one she hadn't possessed for nearly a month. She opened the door to her office, which appeared to be an ungodly mess. In truth, however, it remained just as she had left it. What appeared to others as wholly and completely destroyed made total sense to her. She walked easily around the desk to a small wardrobe in the back left corner, and started to take off her tunic top. Before she had it half off, a knock sounded at the door. She hastily pulled the shirt down and called out, "Enter!"

The tip of a brown snout poked through the door, a toothy smile plastered to the owner's face. Flint slipped into her office and locked the door behind him, doing the chain latch as well. He sauntered up to the chair across from Anna, who took off her tunic shirt and rummaged through her wardrobe for her shears.

"So, tell me about the last few days. Only the big stuff." She took hold of the shears and cut the straps of her bra.

"Your husband was accosted by a couple of goons at the close of business. I suppose he already told you about that."

He nearly guffawed with laughter when he saw the trouble Anna was having trying to reach behind her and cut the straps in the back. He got up from the guest seat and came around the desk, taking the shears from her and cutting away the straps just above the tape wraps that held down her breasts. "He came to no harm, and he lost no profits," he said, returning to his seat and pulling out one of his daggers, cleaning under his nails again. "As for the harm, well, let's just say one of the fools stuck around and got quite a bit from ol' Stocky."

"Yes." Anna pulled on her shirt once more. "I imagine he taught the goon quite a lesson." She drew a leather vest from the wardrobe, one she commissioned from a local Alchemist, Jonah Staples.

The young Alchemist constructed the vest with the use of a Focus Site, enhancing its durability through his powers of science.

She did up the zipper, and smiled with satisfaction. It creaked and bent like real leather, but she knew from experimentation that the vest protected her better than iron plate armor. "Stocky mentioned that Lee is here?"

"Yeah, he is ol' boss." Flint did not look up from his distraction. "I doubt it's anything too important, regardless of how he chooses to state the situation. It never is. Although—" he grinned. "—he did get us that job a few months back in the Manor District. That paid off well."

"Ha ha! Yes it did." Ann finally took a seat and put her feet up on her desk. "Isn't that one of Lord Falco's rings, in fact?" She pointed to Flint's right hand.

He looked at the solid gold ring and chuckled.

"In any event, he can wait until I get the rest of your and Stocky's reports. So, what else do you have for me?"

Flint rattled off a few menial reports, promising Anna that he'd have the treasury report ready and on her desk in a couple of days.

She thanked him for the information and discretion, and instructed the friendly Wererat to send in Stockholm on his way out.

Flint opened the door after undoing the locks, and, as expected, found the hulking Red Tribe leaning against the wall outside of her office.

"He'll see you now, Chief," he said.

Stockholm glared at him, a hint of pent-up aggression in his fiery, crimson eyes.

Flint hoofed it away from the Red Tribe Werewolf as quickly as his legs could carry him, and Ignatious Stockholm ducked through the doorway and into William Deus's office.

As soon as Anna saw his lumbering form squeeze through the door, she brought her feet down off of her desk. She didn't have to—after all, she was the Headmaster of the Hoods, not he. But Stockholm conveyed a heavy aura of power and authority, and always had. As far back as Anna could recall, he always filled the position of Chief. Perhaps, she thought, part of her reaction was still instilled by his once being her superior.

Stockholm stood a couple of feet behind the guest seat and saluted smartly. "Sir, Guild Chief Ignatious Stockholm present," he announced, taking a deep sniff of the air.

She laughed to herself and relaxed, remembering their positions.

"Sit down, Stocky. And don't worry, I had Norman construct that chair with you in mind."

Norman Adwar, one of many Gnomes in the Hoods' ranks, held the honor of being the Guild's only scientist, a Tinker without equal in the city.

Stockholm eyeballed the chair with heavy suspicion. The last chair collapsed under his great weight, and he didn't trust Norman's engineering in the slightest. He'd seen better in his long years. Still, he shrugged his shoulders and sat easily in the chair.

It held, much to his surprise. He took another sniff of the air.

"Sir, I know I've hammered this in as hard as I can, but I still think someone makes your cologne with traces of silver in it," he said, wrinkling his snout.

"We've had this discussion many times, Stocky. I like this scent," she said, lying through her teeth. When applying the musk cologne, her eyes always watered, and always would.

"One more thing before we get started, sir," Stockholm shifted in his seat uncomfortably. "Could you please refrain from calling me that?" His voice was like an overcast sky. "It's humiliating."

"It's endearing, mister Stockholm." She leaned forward and planted her elbows on the piles of paperwork that comprised her desktop. "At least, it's always been meant to be. Now, on to business, Stocky." She twisted the nickname like a knife in a wound.

Stockholm growled and made a fist, but he dutifully rattled off a slew of oral reports and statistics, handing her matching documentation all the while. When he handed her the last piece of paper, she spun in her chair and opened the top drawer of a filing cabinet clearly marked 'Stockholm's reports'. The top drawer she normally kept nearly empty, as it was reserved for those reports she hadn't read yet. Now, however, she had nearly and inch and a half of papers to stuff in there. She sighed wearily—Stockholm made a great Chief, but sometimes, he was all too thorough. If he ever left the Hoods, he'd make some police captain very happy.

"That's everything, sir," he rumbled, getting up to leave.

Before he got to the door, Anna remembered a standard question.

"Wait, Stocky. Any disciplinary problems?"

The Red Tribe turned around and gave her one of his trademark grins, the kind that turned lesser men's intestines to gelatin.

"Three of them, sir. The Saurenson boys tried to break into Styge's room without permission. When we found them, they were about four clicks south of the city. They thought they were being chased by a pack of Dreadnaughts, sir."

Ah, Styge, Anna thought.

"The Saurensons. They're the triplets that joined near the end of last month, aren't they?"

Stockholm nodded, mercifully dropping his smile.

"So they don't know the old man's an Illusionist?"

"No sir. They're near the end of their time in punishment, so I'll send Styge to inform them. A little scare should do them some good. Especially from, as they call him, an 'evil miser of a Necromancer', sir."

Anna smiled despite herself.

"See to it, Chief," she said. "When you find him, by the way, send in Lee Toren. I'll read your reports while I'm waiting for him, so take your time. And Stockholm?"

Once again, the Red Tribe turned to face his Headmaster.

"Get some rest. I can see the bags under your eyes." *Even canines get bags*, she thought, and his fairly drooped. However, he never slept much, so the shapes under his eyes could just be permanent markings now. *I'd rather err on the side of caution*, she thought.

He nodded his acquiescence, even though she knew that was a load.

"I'll go and fetch the little pest first, sir," Stockholm called over his shoulder as he squeezed out of the doorway. He closed the door softly behind him, and once again, Annabelle Deus was left alone in her office.

"Business as usual," she muttered to herself, taking out one of the Chief's reports.

* * * *

Flint leaned easily against the wall of the Guild's taproom, a small, private lounge that the Guild had for its drinking agents. Not all of the Guild's members drank, but most did, and heavily when they saw an opportunity. The Wererat was no exception. He seldom actually sat down, keeping his drink on a nearby table, a hand-rolled cigarette in his hand, smoke pluming up out of his snout. A single smoke ring hovered up past his face and he looked down into the face of Lee Toren.

Lee stood nearly four feet in height, large for a member of his Race. But he also maintained a decent girth, much more appropriate for the men of his peoples. He blew another ring after taking a drag of his own cigarette, and smiled widely up at Flint.

"Hey there, little man," Flint said. "Long time, no see," he said.

"Oi, 'ow's it goin' me mousy lad?" Lee took a sip of his drink, and set the mug down next to Flint's.

Before the Wererat could clout him one, the Gnome Pickpocket waved his hands defensively. Flint hated being called a mouse. "Sorry, sorry, I know I shouldn't 'ave said it. Just couldn't resist, ya know? Anyhow, when's Will gonna see me?"

"Oh, I imagine he'll send Stocky after you shortly." Flint took another pull of his drink. "How's things been for you? Seen or heard from Amon lately?"

"No." Lee held a drag of his smoke for a long moment, then puffed out four little rings, each smaller than the last. "Ran into his nephew not long back, though. Gave him a little help as was needed at the toim."

Tiberious Amon, Flint thought. Thirty or so years had gone by since Flint and Lee had helped the crippled Khan get to a safe location in the southern lands. "Why you ask?"

"Oh, just making conversation. Figured I may as well, seeing as you're about to be hauled out of here." Flint caught Stockholm's scent from down the hall. The taproom had no door to maintain an environment of privacy, because nobody thought it necessary to lock up a taproom in a hidden sewer-based compound. People tended to get loud when they drank anyway, and every drunkard likes to have an audience, Anna reasoned. However, she also had plans to install a vault door and implement the taproom as a last resort refuge.

"Hauled out? By whom, exactly?" Lee grinned smugly. His harsh laughter echoed through the room until he saw a streak of crimson fur approaching down the hallway, towards the taproom.

"Oh Gods," he whispered, almost to himself. Stockholm had never much cared for Lee, and the Gnome Pickpocket knew it. Everybody knew it, because Stockholm never held back his opinions of people. Lee had essentially been branded ever since he'd barged into the Chief's private chambers one evening. *Without knocking*, Lee amended mentally, because that had been the biggest problem. That alone had created a chasm of a rift between he and the Red Tribe, a rift nobody liked to talk about.

Stockholm fairly exploded into the room, but Lee got lucky for a moment. Stockholm's attention turned immediately to one of the female agents at the bar, and instead of laying right in to the Gnome, he stalked up to the woman.

The taproom fell deathly quiet, like a funeral parlor.

Stockholm barged up to the bar, and snatched the girl's hand up in his own huge paw. "What the hells do you think you're doing," he growled at the stunned young Human woman.

"I was just having a glass of wine," she blurted, tears welling behind her eyes.

For the first time, Lee noticed a slight bulge in the front of the woman's shirt. "It's nothing," she almost whispered.

"It's not nothing, Sara," Stockholm growled, pulling her off of her stool as gently as he could without losing his grip on her wrist. "You are not allowed drink, remember? Get to the infirmary right now, young lady. We'll discuss appropriate punishment later!"

He growled menacingly, turning to face the current server. "As for *you*..."

The Wererat tending the taproom bar shrank back as far as he could against the racks of booze.

"You and I shall have a little man-to-man in a few minutes. I have something else to tend to first." He left the Wererat to sweat and seriously consider his immediate future.

Lee thought with a grimace, *he doesn't have one*!

Stockholm approached him slowly, easily. He tried to keep his temper in check, because for once, Lee wasn't the one doing something stupid, or unwelcome.

"Lee Toren," Stockholm rumbled, towering over the Gnome at an impressive seven and a half feet in height. "William wishes to see you. Now," he said, letting the word hang there for a moment, daring the Pickpocket to make any kind of wisecrack.

Discretion, Lee recalled someone saying, is the better part of valor. "Yes, of course." He put his smoke out in the available ashtray near his drink. "I'll just pop on over there. Good seeing you, Flint," he said, heading for the hallway.

Flint watched him go for a minute before he turned back to the Chief. "You know, you terrify him."

"Comes with the job." Stockholm snatched the cigarette out of Flint's mouth and stubbing it hastily in the ashtray.

Flint raised an eyebrow at his red-furred cohort.

"It's a disgusting habit," Stockholm said without looking at Flint. "Now, sir, if you'll excuse me, I have a bit of discipline to administer. If you don't mind?"

Flint shook his head slightly, and Stockholm threw him a salute. "Prime," he said.

Flint returned the salute half-heartedly. *Best to humor the woof-dog*, he thought.

"Chief," he said, and watched as Stockholm leaped over the bar from a running start, landing heavily on the Wererat barkeep.

* * * *

Away from Stockholm, Lee's attention turned to the news he had for William Deus. Excited, he burst into his office without knocking, flying into the seat across from the Hoods' Headmaster, watching the thief's eyes widen with surprise as Lee landed in the chair.

"Oi, Will! How's things?"

Anna looked at the Gnome, noticing the vague signs of age that had marked his bushy beard since last she'd seen him.

A Gnome's beard grows naturally white, and only darkens when they get to their upper years. Spots of brown and black peppered Lee's scraggly facial hair now, present when they had not been a few years before. Smile lines formed on his once flush face, the yellowish hue of his skin slightly lighter along the lines.

"Just fine, Lee, just fine." She set aside the report she had been working over from Stockholm, surprised to find that he had started making charts of the pregnant female agents, connecting them to the prospective fathers where and when he could. No Guild rules restricted such relationships, and it appeared, from the nature of the reports, that the Chief was trying to make certain none of the fathers tried to shirk their responsibilities. When a father was confirmed, Stockholm filed the necessary forms and made requests for her to approve of a transfer of Guild wages. Fathers had a portion of their monthly cut taken out and given to the expecting mothers. She'd already signed off on twelve of these forms.

"Will, have I got big news fer you." Lee broke Anna's drifting train of thought. "You're never gonna' believe this!"

"You're right," she said bluntly. "I probably won't." She knew Lee had a penchant for exaggeration.

"I've got this informant, roit? Human fellah, name of Townshend," Lee began.

Anna found herself paying attention immediately. Lee may not be very honest, but his informants always got paid well for their services, and never withheld anything from the Gnome Pickpocket. Not when the pay was as good as it was.

Lee continued by telling Anna, or rather William as he thought her to be, about Townshend's allegiance to a Paladin by the name of Reynaldi. Townshend had related the events of the Paladin's escapade into the ruins of a guild outpost of some sort, and his discovery of the fabled Glove of Shadows.

This discovery sent Anna reeling. *The Glove of Shadows.* The mere name blazed a familiar tingle in her thieving fingertips. *Oh, what an artifact!* The Glove allowed anybody to take whatever they wanted, and somehow nobody knew anything had happened when the Glove was used. The Glove stood as all thieves' Holy Grail, an object so profoundly useful, in the right hands, that whoever might have it could honestly proclaim themselves the best thief in all the lands. With it, she would be the undisputed king of thieves. And it now sat in the hands of a Paladin.

"He told me that Reynaldi intends to find a way to destroy it, Will! We can't let that happen!"

"No—no we can't." Anna's mind raced to formulate a plan. With the glove in their hands, the petty wars between guilds could be ended. "Lee, did anybody else hear this informant of yours?"

"Well, yeah." Lee looked away from Anna, his cheeks flushed with embarrassment. "I was in a tavern in Vershak, south of 'ere, when he rushed in to tell me. One of me mates was sharin' a friendly drink wif me, and he's sort of in our field of expertise, Will. 'E took the information, er, elsewhere in the city."

A twinge of fear streaked up Anna's spine.

"Oh no." She sighed deeply. "He didn't, did he? Please tell me he didn't."

"He did, Will. He's gonna sell off the info to the Midnight Suns."

Anna ground her teeth and sat back in her chair, mulling over anew her hastily formed plans. *The Midnight Suns*, she thought. *Those bastards'll take his information and kill him.* The Midnight Suns resided chiefly in Desanadron—the Hoods' rival thieves guild. Their organization consisted mostly of Ninjas, Strong Arm Thugs and mercenaries of several other Classes. They employed the most brutal tactics of theft, resorting to armed mugging and outright murder to attain coinage for the Sons. Their Headmaster, a Black Draconus by the name of Thaddeus Fly, came directly from the Obura Clan of Ninjas in the southeast of Tamalaria. Anna had had a few scraps with the dangerous martial artist, coming away with many more wounds than she ever inflicted.

The Midnight Suns also resorted to a time-honored Ninja tradition for the bulk of their business—assassination. They killed the target without fail, sure, but they often left everyone else in the immediate vicinity a corpse as well. Anna despised their methods and their ways, but she knew they were capable and highly skilled at what they did.

"So, they're going to know about the Glove, too. Well…" she put her chin on her palm. "That's just great. Fly will no doubt get ready to set out after our good Mr. Reynaldi as soon as he finds out. Thank you, Lee. Send Flint in when you find him, but don't be taking off." Pulling open one of the lower drawers of her desk, she heavily thumped down four small sacks on her desk, and looked from the sacks to Lee.

The Gnome's eyes had glossed over with greed.

"Advance payment for your help, my friend. You'll be coming along with us."

Chapter Three
The Other Side of the Fence

Crash! Another *tetsujin*, or metal training dummy, crashed to the concrete floor of the basement in pieces. A large group of the lifeless puppets stood scattered around the dusty, cavernous chamber, a single Black Draconus in the middle of their faceless numbers.

Without flinching at the impacts, the dragon-kin kicked and wheeled at the dummies, lashing out with ferocious blows from his hands and feet. A single drop of sweat ran down his scale-covered forehead as he came to a halt, the remainder of the *tetsujin* destroyed.

Thaddeus Fly barely discerned the sound of another Ninja's footfalls, an agent he knew well. His second in command, a gray-clad Human sans mask, stood in the wide stairwell opening, sneering mockingly at his Headmaster. The Human tossed him a towel, which he caught with ease.

"Thank you, Markus." Fly wiped his brow. "What have you to report, Mr. Trent?"

The Ninja, Markus Trent, gave a brief bow before stepping onto the basement floor proper.

"An informant bears news for you, Headmaster Fly." A sly smile played over Trent's lips, revealing teeth yellowed by coffee and cheap cigarettes.

Fly flinched inwardly at the sight of Trent's teeth. *A true Ninja should take better care of himself,* the Draconus thought.

"He won't reveal his information to anyone but you, he says. I tried to tell him that as your first officer he could relate the facts to me, but he refuses to yield." Trent's lips turned downward with the last few words.

Fly had a good idea what that meant—it meant that Trent had grilled the man as hard as he could without using force.

Markus Trent held the position of first officer in the Midnight Suns, an unofficial title, as most in the Guild were. Only Thaddeus Fly held claim of an official position in the Midnight Suns, as its founder and leader. But Fly relied on Trent to act as his second in command, retaining their respective ranks from their days together with the Obura Ninja clan. Fly reasoned with people, and slowly added members to their little band of thieves in the beginning, while Trent used other, less subtle methods. While the Headmaster of the Midnight Suns did not precisely care for the disturbed Human's methods, he turned a blind eye to them as often as possible.

"I assume you tried to, ah, persuade him he could talk to you." Fly smiled wickedly back at Trent. True, he turned a blind eye to the man's compulsions, but not to the scheming, plotting look the man always had in his eyes. Markus Trent had a Vision, Fly knew, and the Draconus played only a minor part in that Vision. He was cast as the first of many victims.

"I simply explained my position to him." Trent lied poorly. He thought about Fly's policy against outright torture of a civilian, and his stomach churned. *Five minutes in my chambers, with my darlings,* he thought vehemently. Just five minutes, and the Gnome would beg to give the information to him. But no. So long as Fly stood in the way, his darlings would have to content themselves to the few meager offerings Trent brought them.

He would bring Fly to them one day, he thought viciously. A handful of plans had been foiled over the years, leaving some of Trent's loyal subjects dead and buried. But he would find an opportunity eventually, and he would lay Fly low. He had to, in exchange for what had been done to him because of the Black Draconus's actions long ago.

"I'm sure you did." Fly noncommittally removed his gloves. Hard, scaled hands fumed, clouds of heat coming from them in tufts. "Have Akimaru send him to my quarters when I'm ready, Trent."

Markus Trent bowed once more before departing from the basement dojo, stalking up the stairs toward his room.

Trent mentally fumed, despising the way Fly treated him like a lapdog. "Who's he, anyway," he growled at one point during his walk down the corridors of the multi-storied building that housed the Midnight Suns.

A few agents turned their heads to watch his lithe form slip from hallway to hallway, chamber to chamber, not so much as giving them a second's thought.

Finally, ascending to the second floor, Trent slowed his pace. He stood in a narrow hallway, the wallpaper dank and musty, forgotten in the midst of so many agents busy with more important matters. Trent moved almost woodenly to the third doorway on the left side of the hall, stepping into an open alcove where only one agent sat.

The agent wore a simple, body-covering Ninja uniform, all white from the face-concealing mask, to the short *tabi* boots covering the smallish feet.

"Akimaru," Trent said, and the Ninja looked up from his book, his vibrant, purple eyes meeting Trent's own.

Markus experienced much the same feeling at that moment that everyone got around the quiet, white-clad Ninja—it felt as though he was looking through you, not at you, and his eyes changed color often, between purple and gray.

"Yes, master Trent." Akimaru's quiet, whisper-like voice directed itself straight into Trent's head.

Another queer observation most agents made about Akimaru, Trent noted. The man's voice sounded like an echo in the listener's ears, as though the words appeared in the mind without passing through the open air.

Akimaru sometimes put off even a sadist like Trent, but this feeling always passed. Akimaru was always, if nothing else, helpful and obedient.

"There is a Gnome informant here to speak with the Headmaster," Trent reported flatly. "See to it that he goes to his personal chambers when the Headmaster is ready for him."

Akimaru stood and bowed respectfully, and Trent exited the reading room, heading for his own personal quarters.

Up two more flights of stairs he ascended, his thoughts turning to his waiting darlings. The gray Ninja turned the knob to his room and entered in a rush, immediately closing the door behind him. He turned with a reverential expression plastered to his face to the wall directly opposite the door.

Flames of passion burned deep in the pit of Markus Trent's soul, passion no amount of water or dirt could extinguish. He took slow, measured steps towards the set of tools hanging on the wall, his hands tingling as he removed his gray cloth gloves. He took one of the devices down off of the wall, and hit a button, activating a twisting, serrated knife blade. The baleful smile returned to his lips. "Don't worry, baby," he said to the device. "You and I, we'll get to play with ol' scaleface soon. You, and me, and all of our friends." He spread his arms to take in the entire wall of torture devices. "Oh, we'll have a grand old time!"

* * * *

Three floors below the warped conversation in Markus Trent's chambers, Thaddeus Fly sat with his legs folded, wearing his official traveling and combat gear. His own chambers had been torn apart and remade from scratch, modeled after the Obura clan's dojo. Simple, freshly scrubbed wooden floors shimmered with a recent coating of wood polish. He sat on one side of a knee-height table, laden with teacups, saucers, and a teapot with a floral design on one side, and a twisting dragon on the other.

A slat-style door stood opposite him, open to admit entrance to anyone the doorman saw fit to allow in. The doorman, at that time, was Akimaru.

Fly sipped his tea, and gave the white-clad Ninja a small hand gesture.

Akimaru bowed swiftly, and waved his own hand at a person standing on the other side of the paper wall of Fly's room.

A small Gnome, decked in forest travel gear, puttered forward and into the chamber, smiling nervously at Thaddeus Fly. He remained just inside the doorway, until Fly gestured him forward.

The Gnome, his naturally yellowish skin made more so by the candles used to light the room, laughed a little as he shuffled slowly up to the table. "Um, where's the chairs?"

Fly smiled gently at him and shook his head.

"We don't use them in my quarters." Fly poured the Gnome a cup of tea. "Please, be seated or kneel."

The Gnome informant knelt, taking the offered cup in his hands. He blew on the hot drink, and took a short sip.

"Hm. That's quite nice." The Gnome squinted his eyes at the liquid. "What is it?"

"It's called ginseng, Mister..." Fly let the space hang for a moment.

The Gnome blinked his eyes rapidly, and then realized he was being asked his name.

"Oh, Brandon, sir. It's Brandon," the informant lied.

"It's a traditional tea for Obura clan Ninjas, Brandon," Fly said with that fake, gentle smile once again. "Myself and about one quarter of my men are Obura clan Ninjas. Most people think of us as thieves." He took another sip of his tea, measuring the confused look Brandon wore.

"Um, I thought you were thieves, myself. No offense meant, sir."

"Oh, none taken Mr. Brandon, I assure you." Fly waved the statement off with a lazy hand. "It's a common misunderstanding. Obura Ninjas are more focused on combat—ranged and melee—than stealth. A few of our number get good at the stealth, but we aren't your typical Ninjas. We don't traipse around in the shadows, taking money and lives whenever the urge hits us. We're more disciplined than that." Fly noticed the way the Gnome's eyes kept darting from his face back down to his teacup. *Nervous*, he thought. *And it's not just Akimaru or me he's nervous about. He's got something big to tell me, and he's afraid he's made a mistake in bringing it to me.*

"So, how do you's make money, then? I mean, this is a guild, roit?" Brandon took the last of his tea into his mouth.

Without thinking, Fly responded almost immediately. If he had hesitated a moment, or if the Gnome had swallowed faster, nothing bad would have happened. But Fly responded punctually.

"Mostly through assassination contracts," he said

Brandon choked, spewing tea all over the table, himself, and Fly's face.

The Gnome thought for sure he was a dead man, but he watched Fly calmly wipe his face with a napkin, not even showing a brief sign of irritation. Unfortunately for the Gnome, he was no mind reader. Had he been, he might have bolted at that moment on the off chance he'd get past the white-clad doorman and out of the building.

Disgusting, low-class, foul little buffoon, Fly's inner voice howled through the landscape of his mind. A vision of his claws tearing through the Gnome's throat played in his mind's eye. But he stayed his hands, and checked his temper with an effort. "Ask me no questions, Mr. Brandon, and I shall tell you no lies. Now," he said, wiping the last of the spewed tea off of his dragon-like face. "You have some information for me, I believe?"

"Oh, roit, roit," Brandon blurted, remembering himself. "Well, it's big news, see? You 'eard of the Glove of Shadows?"

Fly nodded, pouring Brandon tea in a fresh teacup.

The Gnome gladly accepted it, draining most of the warm contents right away. "S'real good stuff, chief. Anyways, this Elven Paladin, real holier-than-thou sort, he found it in an old ruins a couple of days ago. He's going to lock it up and try to sort out how to destroy it once and for all, Oh, that would truly and surely be a dark day for all thieves, mister Fly." He set down the cup and wiped his sweating hands on his wool pants.

"How reliable is your information, Brandon? How can I be certain of the Glove's existence, and its discovery?" Fly raised one thick, hairless eyebrow. *The Glove of Shadows,* he thought. *A marvelous artifact.* If it truly had fallen into the hands of a Paladin, however, it wouldn't be put to proper use, what a pity. But if he could confirm that it actually existed, and had been taken away from its prior location, he would immediately formulate a plan to take it for his own.

"That's the great part, gov," Brandon said excitedly. "This Paladin, Rey-something-or-other, it's 'is job to go 'round and seal away dark artifacts and ghosts and such for the Order of Oun. An' one of his chaps, a member of his crew, told me about it. He'd been there for the discovery."

Fly leaned back a little, mulling. He hadn't detected deceit in the informant's voice, but he sensed that something was being withheld, some crucial fact.

"A couple of days ago," Brandon continued, "he popped in on me and one of my other occasional co-workers at a tavern in Vershak, to the south. Told us all about it!"

Fly's cup had been halfway to his lips, and he set it carefully, slowly, back to the table.

"Your, 'other', co-worker? Where, pray tell, is he?" Fly's smile was gone, his tone businesslike.

"Oh, he says he don't work wif you blokes, onna count of 'im one time robbing this place blind."

Fly silently fumed. Only one thief had ever managed to break into the Suns base of operations and get away wholly undetected until the next day, when the guild's vault had been discovered—empty. *Lee Toren.* Of course, he would run right to William Deus and his blasted Hoods. Toren took to that weird little ragamuffin outfit and their charming con-man leader. *No matter*, he thought. *I'll burn that bridge once I've crossed it.*

"Very well. We thank you for your valuable service, Mister Brandon. Your payment…" Fly indicated Akimaru, whom Brandon hadn't heard or seen leave, or come back with the small trunk in his hands.

The white-clad Ninja came into the room proper, and set the trunk down next to Brandon, stepping back and bowing deeply to Fly.

"Wow! You're too kind." The Gnome opened the trunk, and removed several sparkling jewels from the container. His eyes glossed with the drunken rapture that a barfly has when he managed to land a date for the night. "I'll be sure to do business with you again!" The Gnome stood, performed a horrible parody of the Obura bow, and stuffed the jewels in his pockets as he darted out of the room, away from Thaddeus Fly and the silent Akimaru.

Fly finished his tea and wiped his lips daintily. He clapped his hands once, and Akimaru immediately set to clearing the small table as Fly stood up. "A nice touch with the teacup, sensei," Akimaru said.

Unlike Trent and the majority of the agents in the Midnight Suns, Akimaru's strange method of speech didn't jar Fly in the least. Nor did his piercing gaze. Fly smiled smugly and looked at Akimaru, standing at the small washing sink, cleaning the dishes meticulously. Fly waited for him to dry the teacup that Brandon had used, and Akimaru dutifully held it out for him to take.

"Shall I see to the return of the jewels?"

"Please do, Akimaru." Fly opened an overhead cupboard and pulling out a small glass jar. He set the jar on the counter, and opened the top gently, revealing a thin, white paste inside. The Black Draconus opened a drawer, withdrew a small brush, and carefully started applying a coat of the paste to the inside of the cup.

Within seconds of the brush's passing, the paste dried over, and looked to be a part of the cup itself. "Remember though, my pupil, that this stuff takes an hour or so to run its course, so there's no rush. Wait for the time, and then get the jewels." Fly closed the jar of poisonous paste, and set it back in the cupboard. When he turned to dismiss Akimaru, he found the white-clad Ninja missing, the dishes already done and sitting in a rack.

Chapter Four
Assemble the Team

Anna leaned back in her chair, hands webbed behind her head as she stretched her legs out on her desk. Flint sat across from her, his eyes wide and his mouth agape. "The Glove of Shadows. Boss, we gotta have it! Say the word and I'll round up a team."

"No, you won't," Anna said, interrupting the Wererat. "*I* will. I'm leading this one personally, but no worries, old friend. You'll be coming along with me, too. Now," she brought her feet down off of the desk and leaned forward. "Who's got the most seniority and rank under ol' Stocky? Hopefully someone with similar qualities?"

Flint took a few minutes to think her question through, finally arriving at an answer.

"Borshev," he said slowly, not entirely certain where Anna was going with this question, or of the name's pronunciation. "Our only Minotaur on the Enforcement Squad. He'll be good to bring along with us for sure, boss."

"I'm not bringing him along, Flint," she said, standing up and moving to her travel bag in the corner of the office. "He'll be in charge while we're on the road. We're taking Stockholm with us, along with Norman and Styge."

Flint shot up from his seat, his heart racing and his mouth moving before he could think. "We *can't* bring Stockholm! That would leave no senior member here to see to the operations." He pounded one large, furry hand down on her desk to gain her full attention.

Anna looked up from her bag, and saw Flint's finger pointed toward her office door. "Those men and women out there are skilled, loyal, and energetic, sure. But without you, me, or especially Stockholm here to keep an eye on them, they're a whole lot of trained monkeys! They need us to keep them in line. One of us has got to stay behind." He paced back and forth in front of her, running a hand through his hair.

"Do you think Fly is going to bring anything less than his best?"

Flint stopped in his tracks.

She had told Flint every last detail of her conversation with Lee, and the Wererat had flinched when she mentioned that another informant had gone to the Midnight Suns. He knew that Thaddeus Fly would go after the Glove for his own purposes and indeed, the Black Draconus Ninja would travel with only the most elite of his guild's members.

"I expect Borshev, Hollister and Coats in here, pronto. They're out counterparts on a lesser level. They'll be charged with keeping things in order while we're gone, because as you said," she set her face set, her tone stern. "Our men are loyal. They'll listen when I tell them those three are to be in charge."

Flint thought back on the last time Anna and Stockholm both left the Hoods' home of operations, and he shuddered. Utter chaos didn't seem, upon retrospect, an adequate term to describe it. It had been ruination, and had almost destroyed the guild. As soon as the Hoods' troublemakers discovered that 'William' Deus and Ignatious Stockholm no longer stood in their midst, anarchy ensued. Flint stalked the streets of Desanadron that first night, bringing as many rogue agents into line as he could. He found merchants being hustled, elderly Humans being robbed at knifepoint, and guild members pounded each other in the back alleys in order to put to an end long-time grudges.

All of these activities spat in the face of the Hoods' rules and traditions and Flint had done the best he could to punish the offenders. Punishment, in his case, had consisted of mounting and punching most of the little tits until they apologized. Some found themselves expelled from the guild altogether. But in the end, dozens, perhaps scores of offenses against the rules went unpunished, either because Flint couldn't possibly witness them all, or he didn't have enough proof to punish the offenders.

When Anna and Stockholm had returned, the list of injured in the infirmary had doubled, and for perhaps the first time since Anna had become Headmaster, Flint said nothing when she greeted him, simply handing her a pile of disturbance and disciplinary forms. All in all, his time without Anna and Stockholm present had been a disaster. Stockholm had been left alone and in charge many times before, but on his watch, nobody dared break the rules. Flint just couldn't handle the guild agents as well as the Red Tribe Werewolf.

"Boss," he said, still trying to reason with the obstinate woman. "The three of us haven't been on the road together for years. There's no real telling how well we'll work together." He paced back and forth in front of her desk.

He'd started fiddling with his claws, a sign that he was nervous, Anna knew. He really didn't want the three of them to go. "Norm, he's smart, clever, very good with mecha, but I hardly think he's a good choice for a field agent. And Styge?" He turned and faced Anna, his hands on his hips and his head cocked to the side. "That geezer could kick at any given moment."

"You'd be surprised how good Styge is in the field, my fine, whiskered friend." Anna leaned back in her chair once again. "He's got some ancient Illusionist spells and abilities at his disposal, and he mastered them in a much shorter time than most. Helps to be Human, sometimes," she added, almost under her breath. "One of the spells lets him bring any illusion or artwork image to life for a short period of time."

Flint scratched his furry chin. "So that's why he's always doodling in that pad of his." He shook his head and threw his hands up in defeat, leaning back against the wall next to her office door and drawing out his nail-cleaning dagger. "Fine, we'll do it your way, for now. But why Norm? Lee's plenty capable, and I know he's coming with us. Why the need for two Gnomes?"

Anna had stood, and began packing extra clothes and first aid equipment into her suitcase for the long trip ahead. They only had a vague idea, from Lee's information, where they would be heading. They would have to collect further information on the road, and nobody could be certain where Archibald Reynaldi would be taking the Glove of Shadows. Her company could wind up on the road for weeks, even months.

"Because, Norman gives us an extra dimension over Fly and his goons." Anna closed her luggage for the last time. "Norm knows how to use, create, and manipulate mecha better than most self-proclaimed experts in the realm. He's been as far east as the Port of Arcade, and as far west as here, Desanadron. He's yet to find an equal. The Midnight Suns don't use mecha. They prefer the old ways, the ways of the Obura Ninja clan for the most part. They adhere to the sort of ethos that existed well before the Rise of Mecha."

"And for good reason, my fair lady." Flint dug at a particularly difficult to reach bit of dirt under one of his claws.

Anna shot Flint a baleful eye for calling her a lady while he stood so close to her unlocked door. It may have been soundproofed, but anyone at all could waltz in, at any time. Questions would be asked, and she'd have to answer them by shoving a knife into Flint's eye.

"Mecha and technology nearly brought the world to an end, Anna. That's historical fact, and proves, at least to me," he pointed at himself with his dagger. "That mecha shouldn't be toyed with. You can't convince me it'll come to any good." He waggled the knife tip at Anna before going back to claw cleaning duty.

Flint knew what he was talking about, though not from personal experience. Almost nine hundred years had passed since the Fall of Mecha, enough time that only the long-living Elves, who almost never died of age before two thousand years, could be trusted to accurately depict what they had seen in that time. However, Stockholm's people, the Red Tribe of the Werewolf Race, were an exceptionally long-living people as well. Stockholm said that he himself had only been a pup when the last days of the Fourth Era, also known as the Time of Mecha, had fallen upon the world. But he had known much of that time, and on the few occasions that Flint could get him to talk about it, the Wererat listened intently, taking in every detail.

His opinion of mecha and technology had been formed mostly out of the information he'd gleaned from those tales, in addition to his own rodent Race's distrust of machines. *Still,* he thought begrudgingly, *if anyone can handle the stuff, it's Norman Adwar.* "So, what do you want me to do when I've nipped out of here, sir?" Flint gave the 'sir' a small edge.

"I want you to get Borshev, Hollister and Coates in here. While I have my conference with them, go assemble the others. We'll be leaving as soon as possible, so put a hustle on it."

Before she could turn to dismiss him, having gone into a desk drawer to check for her finest flask of booze to take along with on the trip, she looked up and found her office door slightly ajar. Flint had already set about his duties.

* * * *

Stockholm sat a sturdy oak desk in his private chambers, several tall, metal filing cabinets behind and to his side. He took a moment to view his private sanctuary. It really was an enormous room, and contained shelving units all along the walls, each packed to the brim with map scrolls, books and trophies. Racks of weapons rested against the back wall, pressed between two bookcases. An open-faced fireplace stood in the opposite wall, heat gently circulating from the flaming logs therein. No bed could be seen anywhere, however, and he smiled to himself as he looked at the large, cushioned dog bed in front of the fireplace.

The Red Tribe Werewolf stood and walked over to a coat rack and taking down the sleeveless chain shirt he wore under his open fronted vest. He donned the shirt, putting his vest on over it and returning to his desk to read a set of reports. *Guild Chief,* he thought. Ignatious Stockholm hadn't moved up or down the ladder of authority in the Hoods for many, many years. He had been present when the Guild was formed, and had been assigned the post the moment it had been named by the Hoods' first Headmaster, Tomur Rekendo. Now, nearly sixty years later, he still held the post. William Deus didn't know that, however, thanks to his careful manipulation of his own personnel file.

The entire city above him, mighty Desanadron, had been little more than a withered settlement when he had first arrived, over eight hundred years ago. His previous hometown had been crushed in the Fall of Mecha, the great fifteen-year war that had nearly destroyed all of Tamalaria's inhabitants. A grand metropolis had developed from the colony he had arrived in, and now he sat in an office, underground, a forgotten cornerstone to the city's success.

A moment later, Flint, who had decided to talk to the Red Tribe first since he'd probably have the same initial reaction as the Wererat himself, casually tossed the door open and sauntered in, closing the door behind him. With his back to the room, Flint didn't see the Werewolf move, and thus jumped almost out of his skin when a huge, double-headed axe buried itself in the wall next to his head.

"Hwaagh!" Flint stumbled backward into the room, next to the desk from which Stockholm hadn't even risen. The Wererat looked, flabbergasted, at Stockholm, the huge right arm still cocked forward from the throw. "What the bloody blue fuck was the axe for?"

Stockholm stalked to the door, removing the axe with an easy jerk on the handle.

"You didn't knock," Stockholm said flatly. He carried the axe back to his desk and set it under the leg cubby. "Anyway, what is it you want, sir?"

Stockholm retook his seat and sat with his hands clenched together, his elbows propped on his desktop, patient and formal.

His use of the word 'sir' held no sarcasm, Flint noticed. Stockholm only withheld his sarcasm when he was impatient. He sincerely worried about his prospects for leaving the room unharmed.

"No need to be formal, Stocky. No need to be so uptight." Flint seated himself across from Stockholm.

"You may be my superior, Flint, but you do not get to call me by that nickname. Now, what is the purpose of your visit?"

"Pack a bag, Ignatious. You, me, Norm and Styge are going with Will and Lee Toren on a road trip."

Stockholm remained silent for a moment, bursting into derisive laughter. When Flint didn't say 'just kidding,' he shook his head and waved a hand, dismissing Flint's statement as nonsense.

"Impossible," the Red Tribesman said. "You or I must remain here to ensure the proper operation of the Guild. And I mean no offense when I say I am better suited to that particular task, sir."

Flint nodded, trying to think of how best to proceed.

"I would normally agree whole-heartedly with you, big guy, but boss man says Borshev, Hollister and Coates will be left in our stead. She'll be talking to them soon."

"Hmm." Stockholm shot up from his seat, moving swiftly to one of the many file cabinets in the enormous chamber. He shuffled around in the cabinet's upper drawer for a moment, coming back to his desk with three folders. He sat down heavily, and opened the records he'd selected, reviewing the three men's files in his head and partially aloud. "Borshev I know well enough. He's a Minotaur Knight, one of our Enforcers. A good lad, all in all. Hollister, one of our only Sidalis. A good Pickpocket."

"He's the fellow looks like a turtle in clothing, right," Flint asked.

Stockholm nodded.

"Coates worries me, though." Stockholm tapped the third man's file. "Human, a Rogue like William. But he's ambitious, a little too much so. He may try to con Borshev into giving him too much authority. May even get away with it."

Flint smiled wickedly as he stood up from his seat.

"When Will's done with them, you wants I should send Coates in to you?"

Stockholm returned the serpentine smile and cracked his knuckles, closing the file folders.

"Yes, you do just that," he said. "I'll have a few words with him. Very, STRONG, words."

Flint left the Red Tribe's chambers, feeling a little sorry for Coates.

* * * *

Elsewhere in the large, underground labyrinth that was the home of the Hoods, in another private chamber, an older Human gentleman lay snoring on a rickety cot. The floor of the chamber seemed to serve as a sort of flop ground for the old man's clothes and garbage. A number of art supplies, and a large painting easel with a work in progress on it, dominated the center of the chamber.

Flint opened the door slowly, having heard the old man's snoring from the hallway. He poked his snout into the room, looking around at the piles of garbage and heaps of clothes. *Ah*, he thought, *reminds me of home.*

He stealthily entered the chamber, creeping around the piles of garbage and art supplies. He made his way silently over to the cot, looking down at Styge as the Human slept on his cot.

The old man's mouth hung open, revealing a set of rotted and blackened gums, most of the teeth missing. His cropped goatee was snow white, and his head was host to a similarly bleach-colored Mohawk. His robes, slightly disheveled and dirtied, rested over his limp form, the purple cloth hemmed with gold string and embroidered with arcane symbols.

Flint knelt next to the cot and gripped the side, smiling all the while.

With a sudden jerk, Flint shook the cot hard.

Styge woke up screaming, clutching his chest tightly.

Flint fell backward into a pile of clothes, laughing hysterically as Styge panted, his legs swung over the side of the cot. Finally, after he wiped away a tear, Flint sat up from his laughing fit. The last chuckle escaped his mouth along with a loud "Ow!" The impact of Styge's cane with the top of his skull made almost no sound, but Flint had felt it well enough. "What in the Hells is wrong with you old man? That bloody hurt!" Flint groaned and rubbed his head as he stood up.

"That's the whole point, youngster." The sixty-three year old Illusionist lit his ever-present pipe. "Wake an old man in the middle of a sweet dream like mine, you're bound to get smacked."

"It was the one about the hooker in the red lace again, wasn't it?" Flint asked.

39

Styge said nothing in reply, blowing a cloud of smoke in a heavy plume. "And don't call me youngster, Styge. I'm two hundred and seventeen years old. I've seen lots more than you of the world."

"Maybe so." Styge shrugged his shoulders and moving over to the three-legged stool before his painting easel. He planted himself slowly on the padded seat, and took another puff of his pipe. "But Humans don't live so long, you know. The Gods, therefore, give us wisdom and knowledge much quicker than the other Races, boy. Now tell me why you decided to ambush a defenseless old man in his sleep."

Flint briefly outlined the mission he would be joining with Anna and himself.

At first, Styge said nothing, puffing along until the tobacco in his pipe was burned out. Then finally, he turned on his stool and looked Flint squarely in the eyes.

"All right, Flint. I'll go along with you young 'uns. I'll need a little bit to get ready, though." He was already collecting sketchpads and art supplies.

Flint gave him a thumb's up, and left the old Illusionist to his task.

* * * *

Norman Adwar, Gnome and proud Engineer (not Tinker, as most assumed him to be), kept himself sequestered away in a work lab far removed from the rest of the private chambers of the Hoods. The repetitive hammering, welding, and the occasional explosion issuing from his previous lab had drawn down a long list of complaints, and Stockholm had been kind enough to move him to a quieter, more stable room. Currently, the last bits of his current project occupied Norm's attention as he slid the remaining bolts into place, securing them with tools he'd had specially made by a Dwarven blacksmith up in the city proper.

Flint made sure to open the door to Norm's lab and living space slowly, but loudly and obviously. Norman scared easily, and when he scared at work, things tended to go 'ka-boom'.

Norm turned around, and Flint found himself looking at a miniature golem, it seemed.

With the welding mask on, Norman looked more like one of the artificial creatures than a Gnome. A moment later, he cut off the torch, set it on the bench, and lifted the hinged mask. His sweat streaked, yellowish face smiled at Flint, revealing a full set of fake teeth. Norm had lost his own over the years, blowing apart pieces of his mouth when one of his smaller wrenches just couldn't do the job his mouth could to turn a nut.

"Ey there, Mr. Flint. Dandy you comin' along just now." Norm took off his gloves and hopped off of his stool. "I've just last night finished a very useful device for the Guild, sir. It's over 'ere." He moved into the back corner of his lab.

Flint took a couple of experimental steps into the room, careful to step around the heaps of failed experiments and the cases housing properly operating machines. He also tried to note the tables housing ancient mecha artifacts, including a weapon labeled 'rail-gun' on a plaque at the front of the table. The bulk of the metal weapon gleamed dully in the fluorescent lights Norm had installed in the ceiling, giving it a deathly appearance. Flint imagined, from the bolt plates along its bottom, that the weapon had been mounted to a mecha vehicle of some sort. A large one.

"This'll really wow you sir," Norm said with pride.

Flint sauntered over to Norm, pulling his gaze away from the rail-gun and looking now at a tall, cabinet-shaped object under a tarp.

"Sir, I give you, my gift to the Guild!" Norm grabbed a section of the tarp, and ripped it down off of the device.

For a moment, Flint simply stared at the strange contraption, moving closer to get a better look.

"Um, what exactly does it, ah, do?" The Wererat experimentally tapped the front of the device with a long, extracted claw. *No explosions*, he thought, *very good by my book.*

"Ere, let me show you." Norman pulled over a rolling cart with various assorted coins on its surface. He took the upper tray and poured the coins into the open chute on the front. All of the coins rattled inside, clinking and pinging off of one another. After some more grinding noises, a slip of paper shot out of a slot in the front. Norm took it out, and held it up to Flint's approving snout. "See here? The machine takes and counts all forms of currency coins, and a prints out the totals here," he said, pointing to the bottom of the paper slip. "I calls it, 'Norm's currency counter'! What'cha' think?"

Flint felt thoroughly impressed. Many of Norm's purportedly useful trinkets for the Guild had only been useful for those few who knew what to do with mecha, or how to operate them to some degree. This rolling cabinet would come in quite handy, and it hadn't blown up or injured anyone.

"I think it needs a new title, but otherwise, it seems very sound, Norman. I'd like it moved as soon as possible to the treasury."

Norman saluted and hustled away to his bench.

"It'll make the treasury reports a lot easier to put together."

Norm wasn't paying attention, however. He was busy scribbling a note on a piece of parchment, and he quickly inserted the slip into a tube, sending along a pipeline he'd installed in his room. The pipeline extended to every chamber in the Guild's sewer base, and stood as an effective way of communicating to other Guild members, so long as they took an interest in the system. Outside of the Gnome members and the two Kobolds who stood in their ranks, few did.

"There, message sent," Norm said.

"Still won't be much good for appraisals, though," Flint said.

Norm shrugged his shoulders. "I can only work with what I've got. Anyway, what brings you round, sir? I know it's big if you're here for more n' a couple of minutes."

Flint smiled wickedly, and filled Norm in on the mission ahead of them, including the overall objective of obtaining the Glove of Shadows for the Hoods.

"Cor," Norman said at last. "Guess I should get packing, yeah?"

* * * *

Across the city of Desanadron, in the multi-floored complex belonging to the Midnight Suns, Akimaru returned to Thaddeus Fly's chambers, setting the jewels in their box.

"Sensei, what would you like me to do now," the white clad Ninja asked as he bowed deeply to the Black Draconus.

Fly returned the bow briefly, and smiled at his exceptional student.

"We shall pursue ownership of the Glove of Shadows, my pupil." He sipped of his fresh cup of oolong tea as he walked around the room. "Inform Mr. Trent, the good Miss McNealy, and Rage that they'll be coming with you and I on a mission of utmost importance. But inform only Mr. Trent of the target of our quest," Fly added, pointing to Akimaru to make sure the youth understood.

Akimaru remained silent, motionless. A barely perceivable head nod acknowledged his sensei's wishes.

"Very good. Have them meet me here as soon as possible. We'll speak at length when all are assembled. Gather them in the order I have stated, and return with Rage at the finish. Dismissed," he said, bowing to Akimaru.

Watching the enigmatic youth's back get smaller and smaller as he headed for the stairwell down the hallway, Fly wondered once again, as he had many times, why Akimaru never made a move against him. Akimaru seemed to respect him, seek his approval. While Fly had taught him many fighting skills, Akimaru hardly needed his tutoring. Fly had no evidence, but over the years he had developed the sensation that Akimaru could kill him whenever he chose. Yet somehow, for some reason beyond Fly's comprehension, the white-clad Ninja sought his approval.

Letting the idea go, Fly sat on the floor of his personal chambers, and thought over the mission ahead.

Markus Trent skillfully drew a razor-thin scalpel through the bird's abdomen, using a pair of pliers to push the tiny ribcage open in the most excruciating fashion possible. A weak, warbling cry escaped the swiftly dying animal as Trent felt a draft blow across his back from the door of his room being thrown open almost violently. He spun on his heels, facing away from his 'work table', as he called it, and found himself staring at Akimaru.

With so much of his face hidden by the white mask, Akimaru could often be hard to read, but Trent saw there in the young Ninja's eyes something he had never seen before—outright disgust.

"Don't you ever knock?" Trent spat at Akimaru, then turned his back on the white-clad youth. He found the bird on the table had died of shock and blood loss. *Oh well*, he thought, *not as satisfying as the real thing.*

"Master Fly wishes you to meet him in his chambers, Mr. Trent. We are going on a mission. The informant who arrived earlier relayed to master Fly that the Glove of Shadows has been recovered by a Paladin, and it is the sensei's wish that we claim the Glove for ourselves."

Trent, a sudden gleam in his eyes, gazed over his shoulder at Akimaru. "The Glove of Shadows? Truly?"

Akimaru nodded, saying nothing.

"That's big." Trent mulled the possibilities. "How many of us will be going with Headmaster Fly?"

"Four, plus sensei makes five in all. Myself, you, sensei Fly, Miss McNealy, and Rage. Go directly now to Headmaster Fly." Akimaru shut the door hard behind him as he left Trent's quarters.

The Glove of Shadows

Trent looked from where Akimaru had been standing to the bird on his worktable. Had such a trivial creature's torture and death angered the young Ninja, he wondered. Or did he just not like the idea of being on the road with Trent and his precious sensei, where only he and Fly's own skills stood between Trent and leadership of the Guild? Trent smiled from ear to ear like a sewer rodent, already scheming.

* * * *

Lain McNealy kept her personal chambers on the ground floor, and Fly allowed her free reign to do to the room what she wished, for which she'd been eternally thankful. Her skin resembled paper in color and shade, with the overall appearance of a starving waif of a woman. Her jet-black hair, lank and dirty looking, hung halfway down her back and spilled over her shoulders in the front and back. Her own personal choice in clothes ran to the gothic, which was, of course, very fitting. Lain, alone among the Midnight Suns, studied the magic of Necromancy. She had many years ago earned the title of Sorceress Supreme. The title of Sorcerer Supreme or Sorceress Supreme could only be bestowed by the Council of Power, an assembly of educated mages seated in Palen. One Sorcerer or Sorceress was awarded this title for each of the schools of magic, and in Necromancy, none could claim the sort of power or skill Lain had over the reanimated dead.

Five years before, Thaddeus Fly had recognized the useful applications he could set her to, and had extended an invitation for her to join the organization.

Bored, with little else to do and nowhere to call home, she had accepted. As soon as she moved into the room, she'd asked Fly if he could arrange for her floor to be torn up to reveal the hard packed earth beneath.

He'd immediately dispatched four of the Suns' largest bruisers to take care of the task. There, over the course of the next five years, she had placed her greatest accomplishments, committing them to the dirt until she felt she needed them again.

Only one of her wonderful Lordly Zombies had remained active and in service. She had eventually released him from his fealty to her, though he never strayed too far from the Guild's building. She smiled to herself as she knelt before the small stone altar she'd had brought into her room the year before that moment.

Lain felt someone's presence at her open doorway, though whoever it was remained outside, waiting patiently, silently.

Her eyes remained closed, her hands clasped before her as she made a final prayer to Necrata, the Dark Goddess of Necromancy. After her final prayer, she remained kneeling for a minute, then blew out the candles on the altar and stood. Her long, tattered black dress swished the bare dirt as she turned to find Akimaru standing in her doorway, his hands behind his back. He bowed deeply to her when she looked him in the eyes.

"Miss McNealy," he said quietly, politely.

"Akimaru-san." She returned the bow in kind. "I'd like to thank you for not interrupting my prayers. I was lost in deep thought, thinking about my title and my time here with the Suns. Please, enter." She gave him a black-lipstick smile.

Akimaru slipped forward, barely moving his feet it seemed as he approached the Human Necromancer. He stopped a few feet from Lain, and turned towards the altar, giving it a small bow as well.

"You honor me greatly, Akimaru," she said. "You know there's no need for that, though."

"Respect in all things, miss McNealy," Akimaru said flatly, his voice low and even. "Headmaster Fly requests your presence in his chambers. You shall be accompanying us on an expedition." He looked away from Lain's eyes, once more at the altar. "Please be expedient."

He bowed once more, and took his leave of her.

The Necromancer woman stood where she had the entire time Akimaru had been in the room, and she realized, now that he was gone, that his presence had numbed her legs. Much like everyone else in the Midnight Suns, she gave pause for a moment, to consider what she really knew about the white-clad Ninja.

* * * *

Orcs had little business in thieves' guilds. In the general opinion of most of the civilized and enlightened members of Tamalaria's societies, Orcs stood as one of the Greenskin Races that could only ever be used as muscle and manual labor. Rage fit that bill squarely, but in the Midnight Suns favor.

Standing at six and a half foot, weighing three hundred plus pounds, the green-fleshed bruiser presently twisted his hips slightly to the left, hauling on a handle attached to a pulley, attached to weights. The Orc Berserker was working out—an activity that generally occupied up to fourteen hours of his day. His muscles bulged, and the sleeveless shirt he wore stretched with his efforts. He decided he'd have to go another size up when he went to market later, pulling in the opposite direction of his previous strain.

Thick tattoos, mostly uncolored, lined his upper arms and lower legs. Each depicted one of his most difficult opponents, most with a huge 'X' over their portrait. Of the seven figures depicted, only one was female, and one hadn't yet been crossed over yet. The man whose portrait hadn't been crossed over yet was Rage's father. Sometimes, the Orc worried that he would die without getting the chance to mark his father's face with the black 'X'.

Rage let go of the handles in his hands, and let the weights crash down unfettered as he felt the presence of someone entering the weight room. The Orc grabbed his sweat towel, and hastily wiped his face and dabbed under his arms before draping the towel over his shoulder. Heavy steps sending small vibrations through the concrete floor, he moved through rows of exercise equipment, passing out of the weight room and into the cardiovascular portion of the gym. Twenty yards away, approaching easily with his hands behind his back, was Akimaru.

"Hey, Aki," Rage breathed with relief. "Good ta see ya, pal." Rage bowed awkwardly to the white-clad Ninja. Rage had always liked Akimaru, because unlike many of the Suns, Akimaru didn't pick on him for being dim, didn't antagonize him for his way of life, and never tried to pick a fight with him. Akimaru, like Lain McNealy, seemed genuinely interested in him. *Unlike the rest of the assholes in this place*, he added to himself.

"As it is also a pleasure to see you again, Rage." Akimaru returned Rage's attempt at a bow. "Headmaster Fly would like you to join him in his private chambers for a meeting. You will be coming with us on an expedition, honorable Berserker." Akimaru led Rage out of the Midnight Suns' gym. When they passed out of the doors, several other Suns walked in after them, not wanting to be around when Rage used the gym for himself.

"Really? We's goin' on a trip?" Rage smiled hugely at the Ninja, who appeared positively miniature in comparison to the hulking Orc.

"Indeed, Rage. Miss McNealy will also be joining us."

At this, Rage smiled and laughed, and clapped Akimaru on the back. The white-clad Ninja, powerful though he was, nearly found himself splattered on the floor from the blow. He could have easily avoided the clap, but knew doing so might make Rage feel badly. He didn't want to upset the Orc Berserker unnecessarily.

"Dat's great! Anybody else comin'?"

Akimaru hesitated for a moment, and then informed Rage of their other companion.

"Markus Trent." Rage's right hand twitched and curled into a tight fist. He hated Trent, because the miserable little Human was always riding his ass about his mistakes, and mostly about being brick stupid. Rage wasn't a genius, and he knew it. But sometimes Trent's lashing remarks really hurt him, inside, where he couldn't put a bandage, as the Orc had once told Lain in confidence.

Aside from the comments, Trent moved too quickly for Rage to pose a threat to him, though Trent could do little to harm the Orc. Together with Akimaru and Lain, however, Rage imagined their expedition would be okay. He might even get to brutalize something on the way, and that suited him just fine.

* * * *

Fly stood at the back of his private chambers, directly opposite the sliding door to the hallway. Trent had arrived swiftly, but the two hadn't exchanged any words. Lain had arrived some twenty minutes later, smiling to herself and, to Fly's perception of such things, to the room in general. Fifteen more minutes passed before the Orc, Rage, finally entered. And now, right behind him, came Akimaru, bowing to Fly.

"Sensei, all are present and accounted for," Akimaru said.

"Very good." Fly looked around the room. He motioned for Akimaru to shut the door, and once he had done so, Fly grinned at them. "I have summoned you all here, as you now know, because we are going on a little treasure hunt. I have allowed Mr. Trent and Akimaru to be made aware of the object we seek. However, since you two aren't officially ranking members of the Guild," Fly said, indicating Lain and Rage. "I cannot at this time divulge to you said information. You need only know that you're coming with us."

As Fly said this last, Trent made a face at the Black Draconus.

"You mean to bring along these two," he asked, incredulous. "You really mean to? I thought that perhaps your little puppet had developed a sense of humor." He pointed at Akimaru.

"She is just a creepy little necrophiliac," he said, wheeling on Lain with his teeth bared. "And he's a bumbling simpleton, who'll draw way too much attention to us on the road."

"The term is Necromancer, Trent." Fly came to Lain's defense, since she had turned red in the face and appeared on the verge of striking his first officer. "She's a Necromancer, and a Sorceress Supreme. You would do well to remember her title, and show her some respect, first officer." He punctuated

Trent's title with sharp, staccato pronunciation. "As for Rage, Markus, I believe you know that William Deus is going to go after the target as well?"

The Human Ninja, in his gray uniform, scowled a little less severely and nodded.

"Then you know it's possible that he'll be bringing along that huge red brute of his. Ignatious Stockholm is nobody to sneeze at, Trent."

"Maybe not, but I don't think we need Rage to deal with him," Markus Trent shot back, making it clear to the room as a whole that this moment would stand as another testament, later on, that he more than Fly deserved to lead the Suns. He turned a little at the hips to look the huge Orc in the eyes. "He may be Stockholm's physical equal in terms of brute force, but the Red Tribe knows a hell of a lot more about fighting and tactics than our bumbling green buffoon here."

Rage's left eye twitched, and his blood boiled in his veins. He felt the urge rise in him to lunge across the room and pummel Markus Trent until he turned into little more than a bleeding pile of broken bones and torn muscles. But he couldn't, not while the Headmaster remained in the room. *Besides*, he thought, quashing the urge with practiced concentration, *if I did that, I'd just be an animal.*

"You forget yourself, Trent." Lain interrupted a minute-long silence that had settled in the room. The only sound that had made itself audible in that interim had been the gnashing of Thaddeus Fly's dagger-like teeth as he mulled over Trent's outbursts. "You insult Rage all the time, but do not forget that he has aided some of our agents many times. Often, when cornered by city guards much more adept at fighting than those agents, Rage kept them alive and safe. Don't forget that you yourself once used his help to evade capture by the police. Who wound up in lockup for three months for that?"

The unanswered question lingered for a time much shorter than the previous silence, as Fly seemed to want to press on with matters of business. He cleared his throat to gain the room's attention. "We shall take the remainder of this day and much of tomorrow to prepare. I had originally wanted to set out sooner, but we should make absolutely certain we are fully prepared for this journey. No half-ass measures, understood?"

Fly scanned each agent's eyes with his own slit-like, reptilian eyes. In each of them he could see, even feel the potential. Even Markus Trent, if he could overcome his darker impulses, could be made into a fine Ninja master.

In Akimaru, he knew mastery of the Ninja ways would be honed. But only if the boy allowed someone to connect with him. 'There is enigmatic, and there is cryptic', Fly's master had once said to him. 'Make yourself enigmatic to your enemies, and to a lesser degree to your allies. But never become cryptic, for to do so will lock you away even from the world's spirits'. Fly grinned to himself at the memory, his eyes locking now on Lain McNealy. *There, oh, goodness*, he thought. *There's power in that woman, potential she has yet to tap.* Frightening, considering what she was already capable of.

He knew, as many had whispered in the halls he passed through daily, that she did not belong with the Midnight Suns. Some day, he would have to dismiss her with the best of wishes, because she would be beyond them all, way out of their league. Best not to let her waste her time, he thought sourly. I'll test her on this journey, see if she's ready yet. If not, I'll give her time.

The Glove of Shadows

Onward, to Rage's barrel chest and trunk-like arms. Here, Thaddeus Fly had found something close to a paternal instinct, because the Orc, while brutal and capable in close quarters combat, was almost child-like in intellect. Fly resisted the strong urge, natural to his people, to guard the Orc from harm, letting him learn from life's harshest lessons. Through those lessons, Rage had become an accomplished warrior. True, he sometimes needed a little monitoring while he walked around the city of Desanadron, but lately, he'd been in control of his explosive temper. *Thanks no doubt*, Fly thought, *to his training with Lain.* The Necromancer woman had taught him meditative thinking techniques over the course of the last few months. Her success with him had been most impressive.

After closing the meeting by dismissing them all, Thaddeus Fly turned his thoughts towards not the journey ahead of them, the quest for the Glove, but to William Deus. How would he deal with the Rogue and his Hoods if they met on the road? Mulling the possibilities, the Black Draconus performed the movements of a kata, and formulated strategies.

Chapter Five
Preparation

Anna's head reeled after her meeting with the three agents who would temporarily take over leadership of the guild. Coates, the Human Rogue, had an air about him much like her own—cunning, conniving. But Borshev had made it clear that he would not let her down, and had even made a few threatening comments about what would happen to anyone who tried to usurp and abuse his temporary position. He'd been very graphic, she thought, smiling as Coates had turned greenish in the face.

After dismissing them, she had been further comforted by the sight of Stocky taking Coates by the shoulder and leading him away from her office toward his own. Gods only knew what sort of violent promises would be made there, but she knew that unlike the Minotaur, Stockholm would keep those promises. Nobody in the Guild, or in their rivals' Guild, wanted to suffer such a punishment as that.

She leaned back in her chair, taking it all in. The legendary Glove of Shadows. "I'd love to have that on my mantle," she whispered aloud to the four walls. Sometimes, these walls stood as her best friends. They would stand there and listen, and wouldn't talk back. They couldn't judge her, couldn't hold anything against her. Sometimes, she felt, a wall alone could say it was innocent. Unless it collapsed on someone, she thought with a measure of chagrin. She'd seen it happen before; damaged buildings whose large, ominous brick sidings had teetered and tottered just enough to fall flat on someone, crushing them flat. There really wasn't anything for it. Who blames a wall for anything, except for prisoners who feel they're too thick or sturdy?

Restless, now that nobody occupied the other chair of her office, Anna stood and stalked around the desk. Flint should be close to finishing his task, and soon the small chamber would be packed as Flint, Stockholm, Styge and Norman each made their way to be briefed on the mission.

The first knock came after only two circuits around her desk, and when Anna opened the door, she found the Wererat standing there, smiling faintly.

"You've told them all," she asked.

"Yes'm boss," he replied, bowing his head dramatically. "As I'm sure you may have suspected, Stocky thinks the whole idea's mad to the core. Says you should just leave 'im behind. I can't say's I wholly disagree with him, boss." He closed the door behind him as he stepped in, the claws on his feet scraping the stones of the floor harshly. "It's a little crazy to expect Borshev, Hollister and Coates to do the exact same job as us."

"They aren't exactly amateurs, Flint," she said in the three men's defense. She retook her seat behind the large desk, as another knock sounded, much heavier and with the quality of wood hitting wood.

She motioned her hand at the door, and Flint opened it, admitting Styge, the old Illusionist. He smiled wanly at Anna, one hand on his back, one on his walking staff.

"Maybe not," the Wererat said, continuing his original argument without a word to Styge. "But they're not exactly all-pro either. Sort of semi-pro, really."

"They'll handle it," Anna said, putting the hint of masculinity into her voice once more. "Styge, it's good to see you up and well," she said to the elderly Human Illusionist.

He graced her with a smile that sent wrinkles over his leathery face.

"Likewise, young man," he said.

Anna paused for a moment, wondering if perhaps, since he was an Illusionist after all, the old man saw through her disguise. She had to admit to herself that it wasn't much of a disguise. No fancy makeup or artificial parts to enhance it. If he saw through her, though, he never let on, and she decided that that was well enough.

"You'll have to remind our Prime here how to properly wake up his elders," he grumbled, looking up at the grinning Wererat.

Back leaned against the wall, Flint had once again taken to cleaning his claws with a small dagger.

Another knock at the door, light and rapid, announced Norman's arrival, and before he could close the door, Stockholm ducked down and squeezed into the chamber.

Hail, hail, the gang's all here, Anna thought. "Close the door would you Stocky?"

As the Red Tribe Werewolf closed the door, she faced the four of them, now on her feet. "All right everyone, let's get down to business. We've got the evening and tomorrow morning to prepare. However, I don't want to set out any later than mid-afternoon on the morrow, as Fly and his compatriots won't wait long themselves. With any luck, we'll get out of the city ahead of them, take a good lead."

"Where are we even going to go first," asked Flint.

"Lee Toren will lead the way for the first leg of the trip." She crossed her arms over her chest and stood as aloof as she could. "He's already making preparations, so he can get a good night's sleep tonight. After he's taken us to our first checkpoint, we'll have to utilize our information networks. This includes, of course, talking to everyone we can with similar professions as ours." She looked at the group to gauge their reactions. "I understand that won't be easy for you, Styge, or you, Stocky, but you're going to have to socialize. Only enough to get us moving again," she added, and saw Stockholm sigh heavily.

Styge didn't seem at all affected by her plan. Old and crotchety though he was, the Illusionist made himself available for conversation and company easily enough. But when he came in contact with other Illusionists, he became fiercely competitive, and refused to speak to anyone until he proved he was the superior practitioner.

"Perhaps if Styge and Stockholm conversed with folks more along the lines of your and my trades, Will, they'd make better progress," Flint suggested.

"Fine, whatever," she rasped. "So long as everyone tries to learn what they can. Lee said the first village we're heading to would be one of the stops on Reynaldi and his company's path back home. Someone local will likely know where to direct us after that."

"Hmm," Stockholm rumbled.

All eyes turned and looked at the timeless bruiser.

"You know." He moved to a map on Anna's left hand wall, pointing at Desanadron. He traced his finger north, and then a little east. "There's lots of little villages about three days north of the city on foot. Does Lee know exactly which one to lead us to?"

Anna nodded.

"Then so did Lee's companion. The one who offered the information to the Midnight Suns. We'll have to get one hell of a big jump on their crew if we want to get to the village and make out of there before running into Fly and his men, sir."

Anna looked at the map, and cursed under her breath. Once again, Stockholm's growling, bass voice had spoken the truth. If they wanted to avoid a confrontation with Thaddeus Fly and whomever the Black Draconus Ninja brought with him, they needed an alternate route to the village. But since only Lee knew where they would head, they'd have to wait to confer with him. The Gnome Pickpocket gathered himself for the journey even now, elsewhere in the Hoods' underground lair.

"What do you suggest we do about that Stocky," she asked. For once, he smiled genuinely at her use of his pet name.

"I suggest we stay the course," he said, surprising her and Flint both. They stared at him, eyes wild and incredulous.

"What," he said, spreading his arms wide. "I haven't had a good fight in a while, and it would behoove us to get a fight with them out of the way as quickly as possible. We can slow them down with injuries, maybe make certain that they stay the hell out of our way for the rest of the trip." He shrugged his huge, furry shoulders. "Just, you know, tossing the idea out there."

"Well, I for one disagree," piped in Norman, adjusting his taped together glasses. "I say we just take an indirect route to the village Lee wants us to go to." The Gnome Engineer regurgitated the words that had only been thoughts in Anna's head. "I think it would be most efficient if we avoided confrontations on the whole, particularly with such an unsavory bunch as our rivals." He looked around at the taller members of the group, his eyes beseeching them to be reasonable, to listen for once to the intellectual of the room. However, the aye's already had the vote locked—Stockholm's course of action would be followed, come what may of it.

"Sorry Norm, but you're outnumbered on this point, four to one," Anna said. "Very good. Now, everyone's to meet here at noon tomorrow, regardless of how much prep work you have left. We'll decide at that meeting how much longer before departure, but trust me, I'm not going to waste time. Get some prep done this evening, and early tomorrow morning. We should be able to leave in the middle of the afternoon, as I said before. Everyone," she said, standing straight behind her desk. "You are dismissed."

They all gave brief nods of the head before exiting the room, one by one, leaving her alone with her friends once more, the walls.

* * * *

Lain McNealy sat in her private chambers, all six of her black candles burning in a loose circle around her.

Her eyes closed, her hands resting limply on her knees, the waifish Necromancer focused her inner sight on the place she returned to when she needed to center herself.

Slowly, steadily, the image of a chamber set in a tomb settled around her mind's eye. Her body remained still and cold, in the building that housed the Midnight Suns. Her spirit, however, now hovered lightly several miles away from Desanadron, deep in the earth itself.

Surrounded by a host of bodies, each waiting for its turn as one of her servants, Lain spotted one peculiarly garbed body, and floated over next to it for a closer inspection. The clothes appeared rather foreign to her, articles from an era long before any she'd been familiar with. Strange too, she thought, were the weapons the bones held fast to and the ones strapped to him.

Never mind that, she thought after a moment's hesitation. The body piqued her interest, and so she summoned the magic necessary to force the earthen floor around the body to absorb it and its possessions whole, that they might be transported to wherever she stood when she opted to call it forth in her service.

When Lain opened her eyes and felt once again the soothing warmth of the burning candles, she realized someone stood in the doorway, waiting for her return to the here and now. When she looked, she made out the outline of the Guild Headmaster, leaning against the doorframe. "Headmaster Fly, do come in," she droned, her body drained by the use of her magic.

The Black Draconus bowed his head to honor her, and stepped into the chamber. He didn't bother to close the door behind him—where Thaddeus Fly ventured, few dared to eavesdrop.

"What brings you by," she asked.

"Listen to me, and listen well, Ms. McNealy," he whispered, glaring powerfully into her eyes. "I know not how long this trip of ours is going to take, but rest assured, at some point Markus Trent shall attempt another maneuver against me. I'm not going to ask you to take sides, Ms. McNealy. That would be," his eyes roved as he sought the proper term. "Presumptuous of me."

"How so, Headmaster," she replied, her own voice low now on purpose, to match his tone.

"I would be presuming that you gave a damn about which of us came out of the conflict the victor. Your loyalties are to the realm of the undead, Lain. Your eventual destiny does not lie here, with this Guild. So it is folly to choose a side, you see?"

But she didn't see, didn't understand what exactly Fly was driving at.

"Sir, you have me at a loss," she admitted.

Fly leaned away, taking a seat on the dirt floor. He stretched his arms out behind him and to either side, lounging.

"Ms. McNealy, to make it simpler," he said, his words light and quiet, but his eyes full of fire, "if a struggle occurs between he and I, quietly remain at a distance. Neither of us can then say afterwards that you had anything to gain or lose from your choice of alliance. I'd rather not have someone with your potential go by the wayside because of an internal power struggle in the Guild."

Without leaving her the opportunity to say anything more, or ask any of the questions she had now forming in her mind, Thaddeus Fly left her chambers.

For an hour after his departure, she wracked her brain, trying to think of why he'd never been so candid with her before.

* * * *

The Black Draconus stalked down the west wing hallway up on the top floor of the ten-story building, the shadows pooled together in large sections. The word 'murky' came to his mind as Thaddeus Fly moved softly, silently down the hall, making his way to the only new door in the corridor.

Second from the end, on the right, he thought, turning now and facing the chamber. He didn't like what he was about to do, but he could think of few agents in the Guild more capable of maintaining order in his absence. Akimaru or Trent would have made ideal and sensible choices, but as they would be accompanying him on his jaunt out of the city, only this man would do.

Fly took a moment and breathed deeply, steeling himself for this encounter. He raised his gloved right hand, and half a moment before he knocked, he heard from the other side of the door a muted, gruff male voice call out to him. "Door's open."

Fly sighed, and slowly opened the door, keeping back to avoid any traps the man inside the room had set in the entryway.

"Mr. Striker," Fly said in greeting.

Striker stood at about two inches shy of six feet, with a wiry frame that belied his actual physical strength. The man stood partially hunched over, a putter in his hands as he lined up a small ball with a plastic cup across the room, near a seldom-used fireplace. His open black vest hung loosely over a simply white tee shirt, the sleeves ripped off, leaving tattered threads hanging off of his shoulders. A pair of blue pants, made of a material recently created by Human tailors called 'denim', was cinched around his hips with a long leather belt. His shaggy blond hair was covered with a dark blue bandana, perpetually tied to his head. He didn't look away from the ball, and tapped it with the putter before he looked up at Fly.

The ball rolled easily into the cup as he leaned on the putter with one hand, the other on his hip.

"What brings you here, Headmaster?"

Striker's voice reminded Fly of coarse sandpaper being rubbed against metal. The very sound of it made his legs tremble.

"Mr. Striker, you may not be aware, but I'll be taking several members of the Guild on a mission out of the city," Fly began, still remaining outside of the room.

Striker moved over to a dresser standing in the corner, next to a simple cot, and flipped a switch.

Fly heard several clicking sounds in the doorframe. He stepped through, unharmed. "Nobody of significant rank will be here to keep an eye on things. I think you may be aware of what I'm going to be asking of you."

Striker said nothing, rubbing the short, coarse whiskers of his cheek stubble. He smiled at Fly as he went still, revealing a set of steel teeth.

"You need me to take the post of temporary acting Headmaster," Striker said. He set the putter on his cot and shrugged his shoulders indifferently. "Sure, why not? Any idea how long you'll be gone?"

"Not at this juncture." Fly's hand itched to reach for a weapon, if not to use immediately, then just to keep between himself and Striker. But Fly wasn't prone to rash actions, and such a sign of discomfort would damage his already tenuous relationship with this man. "We depart tomorrow. Upon our leaving, you will be in charge here, and will have to maintain operations. I know you're up to the task, Mr. Striker."

Striker smiled again, wider. Gleaming, dagger-like in appearance, his teeth reflected the torchlight in his room perfectly.

"Very much so, Headmaster. Of course, I'm sure I have no choice in the matter," Striker took another step toward the taller, reptilian Ninja. "I still have that debt to repay, after all."

"I wasn't about to bring that up, Mr. Striker," Fly said honestly. "However, since you mention it, yes, you do. And it's still a long time coming to be repaid." He let a hint of superiority slip into his voice. "Until it is, we own you Mr. Striker. Don't forget that." He jabbed a gloved claw into Striker's chest.

"Oh, I won't, Headmaster," Striker replied in a low growl. "I won't. Best of luck on your mission."

The door was shut with a loud echo through the corridor, and Thaddeus Fly once more counted himself lucky that the creature called Striker was good to his oaths. Because if he wasn't, Fly knew, Striker would have left a long time ago.

And he would have left the Guild's building a sepulcher.

* * * *

Among other things, Ignatious Stockholm didn't tolerate stupidity. He had before him a young agent of the Hoods who fit the bill of 'stupidest of the day' perfectly.

Since taking a seat across from the Red Tribe Werewolf, Timothy Dent hadn't said a word. This course of action alone kept him from being officially labeled.

"I want you to tell me what, precisely, you thought you were going to accomplish by this foolishness," Stockholm rumbled patiently. He leaned forward, his fingers knotted together with his elbows on his desk.

William Deus had advised him to get some sleep, but the Guild Chief had too much work to clear up before they departed the next day. He wasn't about to leave it behind for Hollister or Coates. Neither would be able to handle the task. "The silence is your cue to speak," he rasped.

"Oh, um," Dent stammered, trying to maintain his composure. Dent was a Sidalis, or mutant, whose appearance was mostly Human, with the exception of webbed fingers and feet that resembled flippers. His mutant power was his ability to teleport short distances, one hundred or so yards at a time. He'd thought about using this ability several times since being summoned to Stockholm's office, but knew that it would prove fruitless. The big red menace would find and corner him eventually, and he knew Dent's weakness—paper. Whenever Dent came in physical contact with paper of any kind, his powers ceased to function, and his breathing became erratic. Stockholm would use that to his advantage if he had to give chase, and Dent didn't want to piss the man off, ever.

"I'm waiting," Stockholm said, his voice low and even.

"Well, sir, that is, um," Dent started. "I didn't see any harm in it. I just thought, you know, a little extra pocket change would be good to have around for once." He gave his most winning smile.

Stockholm shook his head slowly, unlaced his fingers, and reached into the top left drawer of his desk. He pulled out a manila folder, slapping it down on the desk. He tapped it with one long, crimson finger.

"What's that, sir?"

"It's your personnel file, Dent," Stockholm said. He opened the folder to the first of many, many pages. "Says here we recruited you right out of Southhouse penitentiary four years ago, when you managed to escape after discovering your Sidalis power. You were eager to join, your recruiter noted," Stockholm had already read through the entire file, memorizing it before calling Dent in for this little chat. "He said you knew you could use your abilities to do good work for us. Now," Stockholm flipped past the statistics sheet. Beneath the first sheet lay a stack of pink sheets—disciplinary reports. "What we have here, is a failure to communicate." Stockholm grinned wickedly. "You know the rules, Dent. All proceeds procured from any target are to be reported to the treasury and dropped off for distribution on Fridays. Yet, here, we have nineteen incidents of failure to report and drop off all earnings, six conflict reports, and two instances of unsupported extortion." Stockholm raised his voice, feeding anger into his tone with each set of reports. "Pardon my language, agent Dent, but what the fuck is your damage?"

"Now Mr. Stockholm, you know I didn't start those fights." Dent leaned back in his chair as Stockholm edged himself over the desk on his huge arms. "I'm not like that. I wouldn't hurt a fly, sir."

"Except," Stockholm said, thrusting the six conflict reports toward Dent, "there were at least four witnesses in each of these incidents! You're already skating on thin ice here, agent Dent. And then you pull this shit again," Stockholm spun on his heels, taking another pink sheet off of his pin-up board. Flint had submitted the report, so the big Red Tribe had no question of its authenticity. A thief Flint may be, he thought, but he never lied about this sort of thing. "You robbed the house of a police Sergeant," Stockholm shouted, waving the report in front of Dent.

"I didn't know," Dent lied, flustered and afraid.

"Bullshit! Every watchman, every constable or police officer in the city, has a shield hung over their door! Did you forget that?"

He hadn't, but Dent had been seriously hoping that the robbery would be blamed on the Midnight Suns. However, he'd been seen exiting the house by Flint himself, who had immediately gone back to the Guild and reported his suspicions. When their contact in the tenth precinct had reported the theft to another agent, the young woman had gone to Flint, who confirmed the report and posted it in Stockholm's office.

"Um, no sir," Dent said. Best to be honest now, he thought. "It's just that, well, I don't make a whole lot here, sir. I don't think it's fair."

"Nobody asked you if you thought it was fair," Stockholm bellowed, swooping around his big oak desk and standing only a foot or so away from Dent, who remained glued to his seat. "You received information regarding our payment practices before you took the oath, didn't you? Answer the question."

"Yes sir!"

"And you agreed to follow the oath once you'd recited it, right? Answer the question."

"Yes sir!"

"Then what was this about?" Stockholm voice went soft, his movements and words deadly slow and purposeful. He stood now behind Dent, his enormous, clawed hands resting easily on the Sidalis' shoulders. "Was it the officer who pinched you in the first place, sent you to prison? Did he somehow wrong you in some other way? We're not big on revenge here, but we do understand it, in a way," Stockholm said, tightening his hands slightly.

"It was just greed on my part, sir." Dent burst into tears. He buried his face in his webbed hands. "I wanted some extra scratch to buy a new crossbow, sir. Mine's all worn and doesn't aim right. I thought I'd get some extra money on my own and buy a new one, sir. I'm sorry, sir!"

As Dent cried, he became aware of the air around him buzzing with movement, and then a sense of calm. When his tears slowed, he looked up and saw that Stockholm was seated behind his desk again, his feet up on its surface. A small pouch rested next to his bare feet. "Sir?"

"I'm putting this in your folder," the Red Tribe said tiredly. "We'll mark it down as an unauthorized operation report. But seriously, one more big one like this," he said, waving the folder as he put it back in his desk. "And you're ass is out in the street. Now, take that, and go," he growled.

Dent reached for the pouch, opened it, marveled at the gold pieces inside, and sped out of the office. Despite his seething anger, the Red Tribe Chief smiled a little before checking his timepiece. Eight o'clock, evening. And he still had eight more meetings to go before he'd go to bed.

"Gonna be a long night," he said to the four walls.

* * * *

Flint roamed the eighth residential district of Desanadron, his bare feet telling him he was near the border of the ninth district, the soil road about to turn into cobblestone. He turned down Folly Street in order to stay in the eighth district. When he came to the next intersection, he'd be near his favorite dive bar, The Pint Palace.

Once upon a time, the eighth district was a place where the city's prominent members of government resided. However, thirty years ago, when the city had come under attack by Richard Vandross and his minions, the district had been left in shambles. Minimal effort was put into reconstruction, and now the poor and shady residents of the city's populace made it their home.

The Pint Palace had benefited the most from the reconstruction, because it turned out that those of low income did a lot heavier drinking than the well-off, a fact the tavern's owner had come to revel in. His profits had skyrocketed in the years immediately after the attack, and now he had a steady flow of customers. As a Dwarf, he had many years yet to enjoy the profit.

Flint opened the saloon-style doors stepped inside, and was immediately engulfed in pipe and cigarette smoke. His snout wrinkled, though only a little, as he popped a smoke in his mouth and lit it with a match. The usual crowd of ne'er do wells sat around the tavern, seated at the bar or in small groups at the tables—*all of which could use a serious washing*, Flint thought.

No other lycanthropes here, he noted from the doorway. A moment later, he made his way up to the bar, where a rotund, cherry-cheeked Human by the name of Rudy was tending bar.

"The usual, Rudy," he said as he exhaled a plume of smoke.

Flint took a seat in the only empty stool at the bar, wedged between a Human who looked as though he'd fallen asleep with his head on the bar on his left, and a stone-faced Lizardman on his right. Flint subtly scanned the Lizardman, and he saw that the gray robed reptile had a spiked mace on his left hip, and an amulet wrapped around his left wrist.

A Battle Priest, Flint thought.

Rudy set a bottle of beer down in front of him, and Flint produced a silver coin, laying in Rudy's palm.

"Much obliged." The bartender moved to another customer further down the bar.

Flint turned on his stool to look around the tavern. *Mostly Humans and Jafts*, he noted, the stench of the blue skinned humanoids masked by the heavy odors of cheap booze and smoke.

The Wererat stubbed out his smoke in an ashtray, and quickly downed his drink. He thanked Rudy for the beer, and made his way out. *No good marks here tonight*. He'd only come in to see if he could pick some pockets. Unfortunately, he already knew all of the patrons, and knew he'd be taking what little rent money they didn't squander on drink.

Once outside, Flint stared up at the gibbous moon. *Around nine o' clock*, he thought.

"May as well get some shut eye," he said to no one in particular, moving back toward the sewer grate he routinely used for getting in and out of the Guild. He turned the corner of Folly Street, and bumped into someone, taking a guarded step back as he looked down to find a white clad man standing there, unmoved by the contact. Flint knew the man he was looking at, and wasn't sure how exactly to react.

"Good evening, Mr. Flint." Akimaru bowed slightly to the Wererat.

"Uh, yeah." He checked to make sure his money pouches were still in place and his weapons strapped to his side. *All clear*, he thought. "Good evening, Akimaru."

Awkward silence filled the air, and Flint looked around to make sure nobody else was on the streets. But it was late in the evening, and most folks in the eighth district were either in bed, or out and about in other parts of the city. "What brings you out of your cocoon?" the Wererat asked, lighting up another cigarette.

Akimaru shrugged his shoulders vaguely. "Just enjoying the quiet of the outdoors." The Ninja's soft tone betrayed nothing to Flint's sensitive ears. "And you?"

"Oh, me? Just getting a drink, trying to be social," Flint lied. Well, half-truthed, he thought with a grin. "Look, ah, sorry about, you know, running into you."

"Oh, no problem, Mr. Flint. My apologies to you." Akimaru bowed again.

Did the air just get colder out here? Flint wondered.

Without another word, the two agents parted company, each heading back for their respective Guild. Flint had been spurred on by Akimaru's appearance. He would tell Anna right away, and advise her that their group should leave at high noon the next day. If Akimaru was still around, then so was Fly. And that meant they could get the jump on the Midnight Suns.

The Glove of Shadows

When Akimaru got back to his Guild, he said nothing to anybody.

* * * *

Anna slept fitfully, her wraps making her uncomfortable, until around three in the morning, when she locked her office door and stripped half naked, sleeping much more soundly now that she could breath. However, some hours later, when a knock came at her door, she immediately pulled the blanket up over her bare upper body and called out to ask who it was.

"It's me, Flint," she heard the Wererat call through the door.

"Oh, all right. Come in, but shut the door behind you." She looked over at her timepiece. It was only five in the morning. What could be so important?

Flint picked the lock in record time, entered, and locked the door behind him. He turned to Anna, who had set the blanket down and was doing up her wraps.

"Sorry, boss lady, but I had to tell you as soon as I thought it'd be safe to wake you up." Flint stared at her.

"Eyes," she said.

"What?"

"My eyes," she said. "They're up here." She directed his attention away from her still exposed upper breasts.

He laughed harshly, turning around until she gave him the okay to turn around again. She was now fully dressed, and in William Deus mode. "Now, what is it?"

"I ran into Akimaru last night." He watched as the shock registered in her face. "After I left the Pint Palace. Bumped right into him out on the street, boss."

"Did he attack you?" She inspected him for signs of a struggle.

"No, Anna, he didn't. And I didn't attack him. It was weird, but I didn't sense any hostility from him." Flint didn't mention the aura of deathly chill that had radiated from the white clad Ninja.

"Hmm," she mused. "Still, that changes things. If he's still around, then so is Fly. We can get a good jump on them if we hurry up and finish preparations. Get the others up." She spun into motion. "Get packed, and get ready. We're going to head out a little after noon."

No need to suggest it now, Flint thought with a smile.

"Lee's already awake, I'm sure. Find him, and tell him to meet us all on the north end of the city. We'll head for that village of his just as soon as we meet up. Let him know he's got to get all of his provisions before we meet up with him. I'm not going to stand around and wait on the fat little prick to buy food after we meet up!"

She was on fire now. Thaddeus Fly would surely bring Akimaru along on the quest to track down and steal the Glove of Shadows. Or, she feared, though she wouldn't say it aloud to Flint, the Black Draconus had already left the city, and had left the Guild in the care of the enigmatic Akimaru. She sincerely hoped for the former rather than the latter, but she couldn't be certain. If Fly took Akimaru and Markus Trent, since he'd never leave Trent behind to try to usurp his position again, then who would be left in charge in his absence?

"Striker," she said aloud to herself. Anna didn't know much about the man she only ever heard referred to as Striker or Mr. Striker, but over the course of the last three years, it had become apparent to her that her Chief, Stocky, knew something about the man. He had advised Anna, or rather William Deus, as he knew her, to stay far away from the man. He told her he'd handle the man if it ever came down to it, and she'd left it at that. But though Striker may be deadly, what kind of leader will he be in Fly's absence?

She already knew, because once before, two years ago, Fly had taken Akimaru and Trent to a mixed Ninja clan meeting in the southeast. Striker had been left in charge, and operations had continued as normal for the Midnight Suns. However, several agents mysteriously disappeared, never to be seen or heard from again. She had the distinct impression that Striker had done them in for disciplinary reasons. Fly wasn't so harsh, and Striker seemed the type. Would Borshev be able to handle anything Striker threw at him? she wondered.

Anna exited her office, locking it behind her.

In the hallway outside her office, she heard several Hoods agents engaged in early morning conversation, coffee mugs in hand as they saluted her when she passed.

"Oi, Will," she heard behind her.

She turned on her heel and found Lee Toren gasping hugely in front of her. "What's this Flint tells me about leavin' at noon? Are you blinkin' mad?"

Anna shook her head and set her stance.

"No, I'm not mad, and I'm not joking. We leave at noon, Lee. You'd best go get your provisions now." She knew how long it took the Gnome Pickpocket to shop for food. He was as bad with that as she was with shopping with her husband for shoes. She never bought a lot—she just liked making one concession to the stereotype of her gender. That, and it drove Harold crazy.

Lee harumphed. "Foin, foin, I'll go get me foodstuffs then. I'll wait at the north gates, loik you asked. But really, wot's the rush?"

"Just trust me on this, Lee."

Through the chambers and halls of the underground base she stalked, making her way for Stockholm's quarters. She knew he wouldn't have gotten much sleep, and hated herself for interrupting the little rest the big crimson Werewolf would be enjoying. But she had little choice, and wasn't about to leave the task to anyone else. She stood in front of his chamber door for a long moment, greeting the agents who passed by casually, finally opening the door and slipping inside.

Stockholm lay in front of the fireplace. A huge, red furred wolf, he was curled comfortably in front of the burning fire, his tail twitching now and again of its own accord.

She saw huge, dark bags under his eyes, and his brow was furrowed as if in anger or dismay. Anna started toward him, then noticed a small, framed portrait lying on the floor in front of his snout. Creeping forward as slowly and stealthily as she could, Anna made her way up next to the slumbering giant, plucking the picture up off of the floor.

It was a painted portrait of a young Tanner Werewolf, his slender arm wrapped around what appeared to be Stockholm's waist.

Old war buddy, she wondered. Distant cousin? She wasn't sure, and she looked down at Stocky, making certain he hadn't woken up and caught her snooping. Setting the portrait back down in its original spot, Anna made her way back over to the door, faced the Werewolf, and cleared her throat loudly, purposefully.

His eyes fluttered open, and his long, lupine tongue lolled out as he got up on all fours and stretched. Stockholm looked up at her, and she watched as his body underwent the swift change from animus to bestial state. Oddly enough, she'd never seen his humanoid form.

Perhaps he didn't have one, she thought. Some lycanthropes didn't, just as some didn't have an animus state. While rare, it often denoted the fact that the particular lycanthrope was highly powerful in one of his or her other states. Anna knew exactly which state Stocky was most efficient in.

"Headmaster." He rubbed his baggy eyes.

He looked down, snatched up the portrait, and stuffed it in one of the pockets of the vest that had materialized on his upper body.

Anna wondered where a lycanthrope's belongings went when they underwent their changes. *No matter,* she thought. *Bigger things to worry about.*

"Stocky, I know you probably haven't had much sleep, but we've got to get ready. We're heading out at noon."

His eyes snapped open.

"I understand, sir. I'll make my final preparations right away." Stockholm darted over to his weapons and took his chain shirt off of its hook. "Where are we going to rendezvous?"

"The in-house tavern," she replied. Just before she left, she felt obligated to say something more. "By the way, Ignatious." She used his first name in a rare display of concern. She looked into his hardened expression, looking for the little hint of vulnerability she usually found in people's eyes, the lines of their face. She caught a glimmer of it, fading fast as he became more awake and alert.

"If there's ever anything you need to talk to me about, you know where to find me," she said.

He gave her a reassuring grin, and nodded. Anna moved out of his chamber.

When she got to the in-house tavern, she found Norman Adwar and Styge seated at a small wooden table, steaming mugs of coffee set before them.

Styge looks well rested at least, she thought. But Norm looked like a total wreck, his hair disheveled, his hands still covered in grease and soot from the previous night's work. He had a notebook in front of his bleary eyes, and was furiously jotting down notes and calculations.

"Good morning, gentlemen." She took a seat between them.

"Mmf, gn mrnerhrm," Norm muttered, which she mentally translated.

"Top of the day to you, sir," Styge offered. The old Illusionist already had his rucksack next to him, packed and ready as he blew on his coffee and took a good swig of the brackish fluid. "All is in readiness with me, William. I'll be ready to go just as soon as the others are."

"Well, it could be a few hours." She s gestured to another agent to bring her a cup of coffee.

It was produced in record time, everyone around her high-strung. Apparently, there was a lot of tension amid the Hoods agents over her departure, and the fact that their Prime and Chief would be gone as well wasn't sitting well with many of them.

"Um, Will," Norm said. "Is it okay if I bring the autocart?"

Ah, the autocart. The autocart was one of Norman's most successful and useful contraptions, modeled on an ancient mecha device called an 'automobile'. The mecha was a cart of metal mounted on a system of chains, pulleys, and four large, rubber tires. The whole big thing moved automatically once it was started, and it could be steered by a device mounted in front of a small leather chair called a 'steering wheel'. The problem was, Gnome engineering had become notoriously unstable, with a reputation for making things that went 'boom'. Gnomes made things that weren't meant to be weapons, yet still these things often exploded. Imagine opening your Gnome crafted refrigerator, and having the motor in the back explode out at you, a flaming heap of metal death.

"You can bring it, but you're responsible for maintaining it on the road. The second it becomes a liability, we're leaving it behind."

Despite her warning, the Gnome Engineer smiled broadly from ear to ear.

"What about you old man," she said. "Any questions?"

"Just the one obvious question, Will." The Illusionist kept his eyes shut for a moment. A moment later, after he turned out a bit of flatulence, he smiled and sighed with relief. "Why're you bringing me along?"

"You know, Flint asked me the same thing." She accepted a cup of coffee from a middle-aged Half-Elf agent. "You've got field experience, and you can offer us some good insight along the road. Plus, you bring your particular talents to the table in our favor. You know the Suns are going to be after the Glove of Shadows too." She watched as the old man's eyes turned hard.

"I'm well aware of that, young man," Styge said. "I just wish you'd make things a little clearer for me. Like, what's my primary duty? Where are we going after Lee Toren takes us to the village to the north? And what are we going to do with the Glove once we have it, William?"

Well, she thought. At least I have an answer to those first two questions. She hadn't, in fact, given much thought to what she would do with the Glove once she got it.

"Fair enough." She squared her seat off to face Styge. "First, your initial duty is going to be to cover our tracks after we head out. If we try to cover them with conventional methods, Fly and his men will find us out quick enough and give chase. As to that second question, we'll have to snoop around in the village for details about Reynaldi and his company before we can make another move. And lastly, I don't presently know what the hell I'm going to do with the Glove once we've got it. If we get it," she amended, knowing full well that defeat was a possibility. Thaddeus Fly and his Midnight Suns weren't going to be her only opponents in this mission. Anna knew full well she couldn't saunter up to a Paladin like Reynaldi and simply ask for the Glove. Especially since he intended to destroy the artifact.

"Well, at least we'll keep it away from Fly, right?" Only the left half of Norman's face seemed to have taken the full effects of the coffee thus far, leaving his smile slightly marred.

"True, me boy, true. But is that reason enough to take something like that into our Guild?" Styge sipped his coffee.

Damn him, Anna thought. *That's a good point.* If that stood as the only reason for taking the Glove, then perhaps it made better sense to let the Paladin destroy it. But the potential uses for such a marvelous item seemed endless to

Anna's mind, the mind of a true thief. Imagine being able to take anything you wanted, off of anybody, and they were left with no idea they'd been mugged. Such an object couldn't be ignored. But what exactly would she steal, and from who? The Glove wasn't entirely necessary for most things she wanted. She could take them any time she wanted. So what exactly would she use it for?

"We'll find a good use for it another time, Styge. The point right now is to get our hands on it first. Once we've brought it back here, we'll talk about how to use it. Until such time, let's just get our thinking straight. Any other devices you want to bring along Norm?"

"Just the usual stuff." The Gnome finished his drink. "My pistol, incendiary devices, scanning and scouting equipment."

Anna gave a brief nod, and stood, her coffee unfinished.

"Where you headed off to, boss?" Anna smiled down at him, showing her teeth for a flash of a second.

"Last minute business to take care of," she said. "Wait here for the others. Flint should show up soon, he'll be better for conversation than me right now." With that, Anna left the Guild's private tavern and headed for the one room she liked the least of all the public chambers in the Guild—the records room.

* * * *

Thaddeus Fly woke up an hour or so after Anna Deus had parted company with Styge and Norman. The first thought to shoot through his head was *finish up*.

He had almost completed his own preparations for their departure later in the evening, but had one more personal matter to attend to. He swung his bare legs over the side of his bed, rubbing his temple with one hand. The thick, jet-black scales on his hand felt cold to the touch, yet he knew he had sweat up a storm in his sleep. He always did.

Standing and stretching, Fly took a good long look at himself in his full-length mirror. He thought about the similarities between his Race and the Race of Lizardmen. While similar, the two species were different under close observation. For starters, Lizardmen only came in vibrant green, yellowish green, or brownish green. Draconus, on the other hand, came in as many varieties as there were Dragons in the sky. Secondly, Lizardmen had tough, leathery flesh, lightly scaled all over. Draconus bodies were covered with scales.

These, of course, stood as the most obvious differences. Fly opened his mouth and belched a short streak of lightning from his throat. Another key difference, especially in combat, was that Lizardmen didn't have breath weapons like the dragon kin. Fly seldom used his, preferring to use the Ninja combat arts. And then, finally, there came the subtlest of all of the differences, one that Fly reminded himself of every day.

Lizardmen lived in packs and tribes. Draconus, however, had little or no sense of family. Once hatched from the egg, a Draconus grew to the size of an average Human adult in a manner of weeks, feeding off of kinetic energy around them. Once grown, the Draconus relied on conventional means of digestion, seeking out food by either hunting or collecting. It had always been the one thing he envied his lesser cousin Race. Despite being a Ninja, Fly never acclimated to the being a loner.

The Midnight Suns' Headmaster got dressed, attaching his weapons belt and double-checking his rucksack, ensuring that he had everything he would need once they set out later in the day. Silence hung heavily in the air of his private chamber.

How long had it been? he thought. *How long since I really felt like a part of something?* Sure, he had the Guild, but he was the Headmaster, and was treated as such. He seldom got invited out when he ordered a Guild-wide break. Only Akimaru ever kept him decent company.

As soon as he thought about the white clad Ninja, there came a knock at his chamber door. "It's open," he called.

Instead of Akimaru standing in the hall, he found himself looking at Markus Trent.

"Please, step inside," he grumbled at his second-in-command.

Trent smirked at him and took a couple of steps inside, clearing his throat dramatically.

"Fly, I thought I might try to convince you this morning, since you've had a good night's sleep, to replace Rage and miss McNealy with more experienced agents." Trent's voice held a hint of mockery. "Two particular gents come to mind."

Fly refused to look at Trent, much less give him the satisfaction of asking who he had in mind.

"We will not discuss this matter, Markus." He turned and faced off with the Human.

Impudent, smug little prick, he thought. *I know exactly why you've thought of two other agents for this mission.* "I have made my decision, and I'll not have you questioning my judgment on the topic. Now," he stepped toward Trent. "Do you have anything else to say?"

"As a matter of fact, yes, I do." Trent's hands itched to wrap themselves around the Draconus' throat and squeeze the life out of him. *Ah, my lovelies,* he mentally called to his torture tools up in his chamber. *How I long to use you against this tyrant.* "If you insist on bringing them, I humbly request you leave me behind and replace me in the party. I'll be able to take care of things here."

"Absolutely not." Fly pressed his face a mere two inches from the shorter Human's. "The last time I did that, you'll recall, I came back and found myself set upon by a number of my own agents. My men, turned to your agenda."

"Ah ah ah, you don't have any proof of that." Trent waved his finger in the 'no no' gesture.

"If I did, you'd have been disemboweled already." Fly pressed his size advantage, getting even closer to Trent. "But I know it was you behind their attack, you worm. I had to slay fifteen of my own men that day, thanks to your scheming and conniving." He sparked a bit of lightning in his mouth as he spoke. *Finally,* he thought at the flicker of fear in the smaller Ninja's eyes. "I'll not risk another attempted insurrection, and I'll not let you bring your traitors with our company. You'll just have to try something a little more clever, Markus." He put one hand on the man's chest and shoved him back out into the hallway. "Try, try again," he muttered as he slid his door shut.

He heard Trent's receding footsteps, hard and full of anger. *Thwarted again, he'll be thinking.* Once again, Fly felt the need for a family or closer friends. With Markus Trent constantly trying to undo him, a few friends would be nice.

* * * *

Flint never thought much about food supplies. Hunting for wild game gave him not only a thrill, it gave him something to do on the otherwise uneventful trips he took away from Desanadron. He traveled the unmarked Shadow Roads, the paths and routes long before established by the longest surviving thief Guilds throughout the realm of Tamalaria. Few adventurers took the footpaths through the hills, fields and woodlands, as they would certainly be set upon by crafty road agents the moment they stumbled on the paths.

However, for such an open-ended mission, he knew Anna wouldn't have Lee lead them down the Shadow Roads. As such, he might find himself competing with other travelers for game, so a quick purchase of a new quiver of bolts for his crossbow was in order. After a quick stop over at a weapons shop, the Wererat Guild Prime sauntered over to a small diner and sat by himself by a window.

He checked his wrist timepiece. "Nine-thirty," he muttered to himself. "Time for a meal and a cuppa. Miss," he said, hailing an Elven waitress.

Ten minutes later, his meal set in front of him along with his fifth cup of coffee, Flint drew an old map of the continent out of one of his pouches, laying it flat on the table.

"Wotcha' lookin' at friend," someone asked at around his chest level.

He looked over and saw Lee Toren's smiling mug, coffee in hand.

"Mind if I have a seat?"

The Wererat took a sip of his drink and motioned his rodent snout at the opposite side of the booth.

Lee hopped up into the booth, and stood on the seat, leaning over the map. "So, takin' a quick look over the land?"

"Sort of." Flint spoke around a mouthful of breakfast. "I'm trying to think ahead of William, figure the route he's going to want to go. Where, exactly, is this village you're taking us too?" Lee looked at the map, and used a small pen to mark the spot.

"Village of Prek," Lee said flatly. "You gonna eat that toast?"

Flint handed the Gnome a slice, which he quickly covered with jam and devoured.

"S'a small village along the Toag River. Fisherman for the most part, but they also grow tobacco in the fields. Premium grade smokes made there." He pulled a cigarette from his nearly empty pack and took a long first drag, exhaling out of the corner of his mouth and right into the face of a passing customer. "Somefin' on yer mind there mouse man?"

Flint ate his food slowly, ignoring Lee Toren for a moment.

"Shows here that there's an Order of Oun fort not far from Prek. But this map is a little outdated," Flint finally said. "Reynaldi would head there to report in if it's still in service. If it isn't, he may move on towards Fort Flag, more directly east of Desanadron. But either way, we'll have to head to Prek first to find out, won't we?"

Lee gave him a short nod, chewing Flint's other piece of toast.

Flint realized he hadn't seen the Pickpocket nick it off of his plate. Lee really was very good at his job. "You know, you could order your own food."

"What, and pay for it? Thanks no, I already did my good deed fer the day and paid full price fer me travel rations. Total rip-off they was, too." Lee sounded genuinely offended.

"I'll just bet." Flint shoveled the last bits of his meal into his snout. "Look. Just don't lead us into anything unhealthy for us. You have a bad habit of drawing unwanted attention from some very powerful people." The Wererat pushed his empty plate away.

The waitress dropped off his bill, which he paid with a smile on his face as he exited the diner. "Remember that time when you went and took Councilor Chamlin's heirloom sword? Tried dropping down a sewer grate?"

Lee thought back on that particular job. Taking the sword had been a ruse —the real target had been a gold inlaid bracer, an artifact kept in the Councilor's possession for years. Lee hadn't discovered its function until after he'd pawned the item.

"Yeah, I remember. Didn't the cops wind up findin' a coupla' your boys wiv it?"

"Yes, they did. And we've never heard back from those two. I've always suspected that Chamlin had them unduly punished." Flint voiced his opinion on the topic for the first time. He'd never trusted a few of the city Councilors. They were bigger thieves than anyone in the Hoods, and they abused their positions to be so. "To a very, very small degree, I blame you for that," the Wererat mused aloud.

Lee blinked up at him, grateful that Flint was a fairly forgiving person when it came to business accidents.

"Stockholm, however, holds you almost entirely responsible."

"No big surprise there," Lee commented. The two thieves walked down the road as the street market stalls started setting up for the day's business. "'E'd blame me fer anyfin' he could fink of. 'Ere now, I'm gonna head up to the north gates." Lee checked his wrist timepiece briefly, then said, "I'll see you in a couple of hours, mate."

Flint nodded, not looking down at Lee. His eyes roved over the assembling crowds of citizens as the city truly awoke with a surge of people going to their jobs, children heading for the school houses if they attended, and other Hoods agents popping in and out of the crowds, earning their keep.

Flint loved the city of Desanadron deeply, and felt certain he was as patriotic as the next fellow. Sure, he stole for a living, but he bore no grudge against the citizenry. In fact, he loved the smiling, jovial inhabitants of the city-state's main territory. Without them, he'd have no career. Can't pick a pocket or rob a home with no residents, now can you? However, he was soon going to have to leave her, his fair lady, his beloved home for so many years. And he wasn't sure he'd make it back to her in one piece.

Sighing deeply, Flint made for the Guild once again. Anna wanted everybody to meet up in the drink hall, or in-house tavern as she called it, and he didn't want to disappoint.

Chapter Six
On the Road Again

When Flint walked into the drinking hall, he found that he was the last to arrive for the pre-departure meeting. Styge, Norm and Anna sat around a circular oak serving table. Stockholm stood a couple of paces behind the Guild Headmaster, his arms hung loosely at his sides, his weapons already strapped to his belt and his broad back.

Flint noticed that the Red Tribe Werewolf had donned his usual sleeveless chain mail shirt, and his open-fronted vest. Stocky knew the company would be on the road for a while.

Anna looked up as Flint approached, and gave him a small smile. "Well, now that we're all here, let's discuss last minute details." She looked around at the others. "Anybody know where exactly we're heading yet?"

"The fishing village of Prek," Flint replied immediately.

All eyes turned on him, and he gave them a wry smile. "Had breakfast with Lee this morning. He brought me up to date."

"Prek, eh?" Anna said. "Can't say as I've ever been there. You gents ever been?" Norm shook his head, as did Styge, but Stocky, ever the wanderer back in the day, nodded.

"Any thoughts, big guy?"

"Last time I was there, Will, the place was little more than a big fish market." Stockholm cleared his throat. "Of course, that was about ten, eleven years ago. I'm sure it has grown in size and population since then."

Anna thought it over.

"Okay, so that's where Lee said he talked with his contact in Reynaldi's company. Where might they go from there?"

Flint pulled out his old map of the continent, pointing to the marking Lee had made of Prek.

"My guess would've been the Order of Oun outpost northeast of Prek," he said, pointing to the position of the old fort. "But Lee and I aren't sure it's even still in service. They could just as easily have gone east of us to Fort Flag." The Wererat rolled the map up and tucked it away.

"We'll have to check in Prek with the locals, find out which way they headed after leaving the village. It shouldn't be too hard." Anna stood. "It's eleven, so we'd better start for the north gates. Norm, you got the autocart up topside yet?"

"Yeah, I had some of the boys take it up on the lift into the old stables," Norman said. "You know, the place just next to the forth residential district?"

Anna nodded. "Good, that's on the way. Everybody, get your gear and meet me at the stables. Let's move out people!" Anna Deus darted out of the in-house tavern, leaving the remaining four members of the company standing or sitting at the table.

"He's fast," Styge said as he hauled up his own bag. He struggled with it a moment before Stockholm lifted it easily out of his hands, letting it hang off of his right shoulder. The Werewolf's own bag was already secured on his broad back, but Styge's belongings weighed nothing to him. "Thanks Stockholm."

"Here then, mind carrying my things?" Flint jokingly offered his bag to the colossal Werewolf.

Stockholm sneered at him, harrumphing loudly.

"You're young and able-bodied." Stockholm moved out of the hall with Styge next to him. "You carry your own load, rat," he called over his shoulder.

Flint looked at Norm, who shrugged his shoulders.

"It was worth a shot, mate," the Gnome offered with a smile.

* * * *

Anna kept to the side streets and alleys, even though it was a clear and sunny day, leaving little in the way of stealthy cover. Though she knew her chances of remaining completely unseen were slim, she didn't want to be seen by a Midnight Suns agent, particularly with a large traveling bag strapped to her. Word would travel swiftly to Thaddeus Fly, and he would ditch all of his preparations to pursue of Anna and her group. She didn't want the Black Draconus to know she was gone until long after she made that a fact.

She got to the fourth residential district, in the northern part of the city, without incident. She ducked inside of the old, dilapidated stables, scanning the interior as best she could with her sun-affected vision.

In one of the broken stalls, the autocart gleamed in the sunlight that poured through a hole in the old thatch roof.

The thing could easily be mistaken for some sort of monster in the dark of night, she thought, taking in the sharp angles and spiked points that characterized the machine.

Not long after she sat down with her back to a wall, Stockholm and Styge showed up, the Werewolf carrying both of their bags. He set Styge's pack down gently near Anna, taking off his own bag next and leaning against a support beam across from the Guild Headmaster. He crossed his arms over his barrel chest and leaned back, shutting his eyes for a moment and breathing a deep sigh.

"So, Norman and Flint still haven't shown up yet," he asked.

Anna checked her timepiece—twenty after eleven. They still had plenty of time. "Let's hope they didn't get sidetracked again," he said, opening his eyes.

Gods, Anna thought, *he looks so tired. This trip may give him a chance to get some sleep when we camp.*

"What's up," he asked, seeing the look she was giving him.

"How've you been sleeping, big guy?" Her tone lilted up a little with genuine concern, and she was afraid for a moment that she sounded too feminine. Her appearance as a young man helped her convince most people that her high voice was an affect of her age. William Deus was only supposed to be in his early twenties, after all. However, when she showed too much emotion, she lost control of the masculine hint she infused her voice with.

Stockholm raised an eyebrow at her, but no more than usual.

"Not well, William, to tell you the truth." He sighed again, then rubbed the bridge of his snout, between his eyes. His head, while lupine, had a very expressive face, much unlike many of his kinsmen.

He looks beat, she thought. "I was up until midnight taking care of disciplinary issues," he said. "Then I had some final reports to finish. The usual business, boss." His smile came off as a grimace—a rather frightening one, considering the number of teeth in that mouth.

"Perhaps you need a good break from the usual business, big fellow," she said, taking a small bag of cookies out of one of her hip pouches. "I worry about you sometimes, you know." She thought she saw him blush a little, but with his thick, crimson fur, it was hard to tell.

The three of them waited another six minutes, and then Flint showed up with Norm in tow.

Anna finished another cookie and stuffed the pouch away again. She got to her feet, brushed the crumbs off, and looked at the company. "Well, let's get going. Norm, get the autocart rolling."

The Gnome Engineer smiled broadly. He took his bag to the back of the cart, putting it in the cargo area. Styge brought his own bag over, and Norm turned and deposited it next to his. He climbed up into the pilot seat, and the old Illusionist hopped into the back with the luggage.

"Riding in style." The old man smiled wildly.

Stockholm approached the front of the machine, which Norman had brought to rumbling life.

"You sure this thing is stable?" The big red Werewolf leaned down to get a close look at the autocart.

"Course I'm sure." Norm beamed with pride. "I put this baby together from the ground up. Modeled it after the old 'automobiles' of the Fourth Age. I've tested it in the field a couple of times, rode it around the city," Norm said, flipping a couple of metal switches. The rumbling suddenly became very low and quiet, barely discernable. "S'a silent mode, see? I got it working last week."

"Have you tested it in this 'silent' mode, Norman?" Stockholm peered into the Gnome's eyes. *Great,* he thought. *Of course he hasn't, but he's going to lie to me and say he has anyway.*

"Of course I have." Norm's eyes told Stockholm his suspicions were well held. "I'm a scientist, man. I never leave anything untested."

A tad defensive, aren't we, Stockholm thought. He slung his rucksack and headed toward the exit to the stables.

"Stocky's got the right idea, folks. Let's get moving." Anna moved out behind the Chief.

Flint followed, and Norman and Styge, riding the autocart, brought up the rear.

They were maybe ten minutes away from the northern gates. Anna felt certain that if nobody had noticed them by this point, they were in the clear.

She didn't see Akimaru watching them from atop the nearby church bell tower.

* * * *

Thaddeus Fly checked his clock. Eleven-thirty. "I should take a nap," he whispered to the empty room. He had once again come to the basement training room, and *tetsujin* lay in ruins around him. His arms and legs throbbed from the exercise, but it felt good to release some of his aggression. Fly tested his breath weapon on a handful of them, and had been satisfied when the six metal dummies he struck with his lightning exploded.

He wiped his scaled forehead with a towel, and headed to the showers.

Fifteen minutes later, he found Akimaru standing amid the broken dummies, his hands behind his back, his legs slightly apart.

He has something to report, Fly realized. "Akimaru, what is it?"

"Sensei, I just spotted William Deus and four of his men heading for the northern gates." The air temperature dropped a few degrees around the Black Draconus, and his heart skipped a beat.

He's already heading out? Damn him and his Hoods!

"Get everyone assembled at the fifth residential district library." Fly strapped on his weapons and tossing his towel to the floor. "No more delays, no excuses. I'm not going to fall behind William Deus this early in the game. Go!"

Akimaru bowed, and darted away, gone so fast Fly barely saw him move.

Fury spurred the Draconus on. As he stomped up through the halls of the Guild building, he snarled at every agent who stood in his way. The path cleared up quickly.

In his private chambers, Fly strapped on his rucksack, and took a final moment to make a prayer. As soon as he was finished, he left the Midnight Suns' building, walking out into the light of day.

His building sat smack in the middle of the tenth business district, and the trip to the library in the fifth residential district would take him a good seven or eight minutes jogging. He started off, his legs moving him swiftly and deftly through the crowded streets, past street vendors and visiting adventurers. The handful of people who recognized him were quick to stay away from him, and even the city guards didn't attempt to impede his progress.

Turn here, run down there, duck, jump, dodge.

He cleared the distance between the Guild and the library in six minutes flat, standing now outside of the library without so much as breaking a sweat. He checked his pocket watch.

Nearly noon, he thought, impatient to be off north after William Deus and his group. He couldn't be sure that Akimaru would find all of the members of his traveling group in the Guild building, and that could cause further delays. But he didn't think the problem would lie with Lain McNealy or Rage—they seldom left the building. It would be Markus Trent who would cause problems.

"Damn you Trent," he grumbled aloud.

The doors of the library opened, and a young Human almost fell right on top of him.

Fly took a quick step to his left, helping the youth up off of his face. "You've got to be more careful." He looked down at the stack of books the young Human had been carrying that caused him to fall.

The Human hadn't been able to see around the stack, most likely, and thus hadn't noticed that near the bottom of the steps leading up in to the library, one of the steps was shorter than the others.

"Sorry about that," the young man said.

Fly piled books back onto his stack.

"I just get a little wrapped up in my thoughts."

Fly recognized the bumbling Human—Jonah Staples, a local Alchemist with a store in the eleventh business district. His wife, an Elven girl, ran the shop most of the time these days, but apparently this was temporary. The books

Jonah had appeared to be borrowing were theoretical research journals. Perhaps he was doing research for a new service?

"It's understandable young Mr. Staples," Fly said.

The Alchemist smiled. "So, you're familiar with my work?"

"A little." Fly set the last book on top of the stack. Fourteen in all. "I'm not exactly what you call scientifically minded, Mr. Staples. I don't trust to science." He decided to be honest with the young Alchemist.

"That's too bad," Jonah said. "I'm working on a theory for the basis of the ancient Focus Sites."

At that point, Fly found himself in foreign territory.

"I believe that the actual source of the power of science and magic—" he stopped when Thaddeus Fly put his hand up to silence him.

"Sorry."

"No need to apologize, Mr. Staples," Fly said, grinding his teeth. "Just leave me be."

Jonah Staples darted away as quickly as he could while maintaining his stack.

At around ten after noon, Lain McNealy showed up. One of her creatures, a skeleton draped in purple robes, carried her bags.

"My, aren't we being lazy," he shot at her.

Her face fell from a dim smile to a blank glare.

He sighed lightly, and let himself deflate. "Look, I'm sorry," he said, waving her over towards him. "I'm just a little irritated. We're already falling behind Deus and his men, and there's been no word from Akimaru."

"Well, Rage is a few minutes behind me." Lain tried out her gentle smile once more on the Black Draconus. "Akimaru just got a hold of us. I don't know where exactly Trent is, but he left the Guild earlier this morning. I saw him ducking out with one of the tracking agents."

Fly thought long and hard about this little tidbit. He thanked Lain for the update, and checked his timepiece once more. Fifteen after noon. Nothing much that he could do about it, except wait for Trent. What would the troublesome little usurper be doing with one the Midnight Suns trackers? Unless...

He let the thought go unexplored, deciding instead to rip Trent a new one for being difficult to find.

Rage lumbered in as they took a seat on the steps, the undead skeleton servant standing a few feet off to the side of Lain. The city guards that passed gave the group suspicious looks, but since they weren't doing anything illegal, they let the company be.

"Hey boss, hey Lain," the Orc said in his rumbling bass voice. He scanned the area for a moment, his huge, rock-like head rolling back and forth. "Where's Aki? Or Trent?"

"Akimaru is likely trying to find our truant Mr. Trent." Fly rested his head on his hand. "For now, we've got no choice but to sit and wait for them. Akimaru would not make us wait. He is highly reliable and diligent in his duties."

"Yeah, dat's fer sure." Rage hopped a squat on the dirt road in front of Lain and Fly. "Oh, Miss McNealy, it's like dis, right?" He reached into one of the pockets on his huge black trench coat, the only article of clothing he wore on his upper body. He routinely wore shin-length leathers on his legs, custom-made by one of the more talented female agents at the Guild. The Illeck woman had been kind, he thought, and she'd only charged him twelve gold coins for the service. Lain had told him he'd been ripped off, but Rage didn't know much about money. He could only count to ten, a matter Lain was trying to help him with.

He produced from one of the pockets a small notebook, and handed it to her. In large, childish writing, Rage had produced a single word-'CAT'.

Lain smiled at him gently. "That's very good, Rage. And it's correct."

Fly nearly rolled his eyes at the display. Still, he envied them both, because they seemed to keep each other going much better than others in the Suns. Once again, his status as a lone wolf loomed over him.

"You's okay, boss?" The Orc took the notebook and pocketed it.

"I'm fine. Just getting impatient. Lain," he said, catching her attention. "Do me a favor? Go over to that cafe and bring me a coffee."

The Necromancer hustled off, her skeletal servant left behind.

He checked his timepiece again. Half past noon, he saw. Too far behind now to ambush Deus and his company, Fly settled in to wait for Trent and Akimaru. He had ways of catching up to the Hoods, and as he rubbed one of the pockets inside of his uniform, he smiled. There are ways.

* * * *

"It's about toim you lot showed up," Lee Toren complained. William Deus and his group arrived four minutes late, which normally wouldn't have been much. However, Lee had become anxious, suspicious that someone would already be on their tails.

"Ease up Lee," Anna said. "We're leaving, now."

Lee Toren took up the lead, marching out through the northern gates, between two Minotaur constables. Lee and Anna strode side by side, with Flint walking alongside Norm and Styge in the autocart, and Stockholm taking the defensive position of a rearguard.

The muscular but agile Red Tribesman turned and gave the guards a slight nod, which they returned in kind. The Hoods' Chief had taken some time the previous evening to have a short conversation with these two gentlemen. He had warned them that a handful of dangerous slavers were after him and his friends for setting a Gnome captive of theirs free. The look the two guards gave Norman said it all when Stockholm nodded to them—they thought the Engineer had been the captive.

Stockholm couldn't be certain that Thaddeus Fly and his group would come past the northern gates. If the Suns avoided the north gate, they'd have to go around the outskirts of the city, where smaller groups of bandits and toughs would be waiting for them, looking to settle old scores with the larger Guild. Either way, they had more time than Lee thought they did.

Flint looked east and west, enjoying the scenery. Verdant fields to the west, farmland to the east, crops sewn and reaped for the consumption of Desanadron's residents. How much capital, he wondered, went into running a city? More than he'd ever see in his lifetime, and maybe that much just to keep the place running for a day. Desanadron's population, according to the latest census conducted by the police, numbered 850,000 strong, and rising every year. Nearly ten percent of the continent's populace lived in or around the metropolis of Desanadron. The only other city the Wererat could think of that supported nearly the same number of people was Ja-Wen in the far east. That city's population was somewhere near a quarter that of Desanadron—around 200,000.

Tamalaria stretched vastly to the east and west, with small villages and hamlets accounting for most of the civilized societies.

Flint glanced ahead at Anna, who was looking back over her shoulder past him. She graced him with a brief smile, then faced forward again, locked in conversation with Lee Toren.

The Wererat admired the brave little Pickpocket—his meandering travels taking him far and wide into every corner of the lands. The Gnome took little with him in the way of weaponry or equipment. He relied largely on his wits and his fleet feet, conning here and evading there, constantly on the run from one body of authority or another. His skills in the field were remarkable. Add to that the fact that the Gnome never seemed to age, and Lee Toren stood as a truly wonderful man.

Norman Adwar listened to the quiet thrum of the autocart beneath him.

Styge kept asking his questions about how the "damned contraption" worked, but Norm only knew a little about the actual power supply system. He'd discovered a battery cell system of some sort, and had simply attached it to the mechanical cart. Before he'd equipped it with the battery, the cart had used a kinetic energy collection pump, which involved him, or someone of similar size and stature, using a set of pedals to pump energy into a kinetic energy battery his friend Jonah Staples had designed. This energy, Jonah had told him, could only be safely stored for a few days before it needed to be hooked up to a device and used.

For long trips, Norman's calculations showed that the kinetic energy battery wasn't practical. When it ran low, he'd have to manually pedal the cart in addition to using the storage pedals to gather up energy. He just couldn't do it, and he didn't have the materials to modify the seat and pedals to fit someone larger, like Flint, or even William Deus. In short, he'd had to go with the untested battery because he thought it would hold out longer. He certainly meant no offense to young Staples.

Anna, whom only Flint among them knew to be other than William, walked along with Lee Toren, keeping up small talk about his recent travels. "So you say that was about five months ago," she asked.

"Yep," Lee said, exhaling smoke. He took another long drag off of his cigarette. "Never expected to run into 'im on such short notice. Portenda's the sort to usually contact you a few days in advance. You ever met the man?"

"Can't say as I have." Anna felt glad of the fact. She'd heard of the strange Simpa Bounty Hunter, and if his reputation held even half true, she never wanted to be on the wrong end of a contract of his. Even she might not get away from him. "Anything else interesting about him?"

"Well, now that you mention it, somefin' does stroik me as a bit odd abou' 'im." Lee scratched his white, wiry beard for a moment before looking up at Anna again. "Aside from the usual stuff. Seems 'e owns properties in three or four cities, apartment buildings. He's a bit of a landlord."

Anna raised an eyebrow at the Gnome Pickpocket.

"I know, I know, seems a bit wronky vat a Bounty Hunter would supplement 'is income wif rental properties, dodn't it?"

"I should say so, yes." Anna once more looked out at the vast plains. The Upper Plains baked in the early afternoon sun, dehydrating everything in sight. The members of the company constantly took drinks from the water skins, and Anna hadn't seen another traveler or animal on either side of their route for a half an hour. She checked her timepiece. "Well, it's one o' clock. How long until we reach Prek?"

Lee rolled his eyes a little, thinking. "Jus' abou' two more hours."

Good. Anna wiped sweat from her brow where her bandana didn't cover it. *Too much more of this heat, and I'll be a husk.*

The company continued in relative silence without incident.

Another twenty minutes passed, and they reached slightly cooler flatlands, trees smattered here and there across the landscape.

Flint sped his pace for a minute, to approach Anna and ask for the company to take a couple of minutes' break.

It's moments like this, he would think later, that cause events to occur. The little, almost imperceptible moments when something is done out of the established norm. Had he continued at the pace he'd already set, he felt, nothing would have happened. But he didn't, and so something did.

As he got a few feet in front of Norm's autocart, the machine give a loud cough.

Norm's eyes filled with panic.

As Flint took a split second to start his feet moving away from the group, the autocart bucked under Norm's hands, and spun toward the Wererat, now moving at full tilt.

Oh gods, the Wererat thought, *I'm going to be crushed.*

Only seconds had passed, and already the rest of the company had fallen into confusion. Anna stopped dead in her tracks and watched helplessly as her Guild Prime and good friend fled from the rumbling, menacing machine.

The steering wheel had come off in Norman's hands, and he was flailing and screaming, trying to undo the straps that secured him to the seat.

Styge, Anna saw, had bailed almost right away. He was rolling over in the grass, trying to bring himself to a complete stop before he struck his old head on something too solid.

Where's Stocky? Anna's mind raced as the world moved in slow motion around her. In times of panic, her perception slowed to a near crawl, allowing her to take in the most minute details around her.

As she swiveled her eyes toward Flint's fleeing form, she saw a blur of crimson motion seeming to impose into the space between Flint and the machine.

As reality around her came back into full motion, she watched Stockholm bend low, letting the autocart's front bumper flow over his outstretched right hand. As soon as it was over his lower arm, he clamped onto a block of metal, hauling straight up toward the sky.

The entire front end of the autocart lifted into the air, and Norman stopped tearing at his restraints, suddenly positive that getting out now could prove more hazardous for his health.

As Stockholm hauled up with his right hand, he shifted his body weight, throwing his left arm underneath the carriage of the autocart. With one more heave, the Red Tribe Werewolf lifted the churning, sputtering machine over his head—an impossible display of brute power.

Anna watched the muscles in Stocky's arms and shoulders quake. She'd never seen such strength from a creature of mortal flesh and blood.

An instant later, the Red Tribesman lifted the machine up half an inch more, sliding out from under it.

As it hung in midair, he grabbed the back end, and slammed it into the ground. Parts flew off and got crushed under the force of the blow. The wheels stopped. The only noise issuing from the autocart was Norm's low sobbing.

Flint, a few yards away up in the tree he'd marked as his safe retreat from rolling death, breathed a heavy sigh of relief. He'd been almost certain that the autocart was going to crush him, but of course, good ol' Stocky had taken care of things in his usually rough manner. Close to a ton of moving machinery, and the Red Tribe Werewolf hadn't even blinked at lifting it.

Anna rushed over to Norm's side, undoing the buckles and lifting him out of his seat like an injured child. He groaned again as she carried him away from the smoldering, smoking machine, setting him down on the soft grass.

"Norm? Talk to me Norm." She pulled a water skin from her hip and pouring some of its contents on his face.

The Gnome Engineer sputtered and splashed, waving his hands back and forth.

"I'm okay, I'm okay Will." His eyes shot wide open as he looked at his damaged machine. The Werewolf loomed over it, pulling the bags from the back. "Crikey. I could've killed someone," he whispered, horrified that Flint had only escaped by a few feet.

"Yeah, namely me." The Wererat hopped out of the tree, landing nimbly next to Stockholm, who was finished retrieving the belongings and was now pushing the cart over onto its side. "Where's the old man?"

Styge, still lying on the ground, raised his hand from his side. He appeared to be stretching out for a nap, but Flint saw his other hand held his side.

"Styge, are you hurt?" Anna called over to the old Illusionist.

"Mostly my pride, youngster," he called back, trying to sit up.

Flint helped him to his feet gently, handling the old man as if he might break like a vase.

Styge brushed his robes off, and gave him a crooked smile. "Now that was exciting!"

Flint patted him on the back as they walked over to Anna and Norman, who had one of his notebooks in front of his eyes.

He looked over, and watched as Stockholm ripped the battery unit out of the autocart, casing and all.

Mental note, he thought. Never make that man excessively mad at you.

The Red Tribesman stalked over to the group, and dropped the battery unit unceremoniously at Norman's feet. "What's this?"

"That's a power supply unit." Norm tried to keep his voice from cracking as he craned his neck almost entirely vertically to look into Stockholm's scowling countenance.

"Who engineered it, Norman?"

"Um, not really sure. I found it in the field, down in some old ruins to the northwest."

"What happened to Jonah Staples' battery system? The last time I saw this thing in service, you had his kinetic energy unit hooked up to it."

Norm blinked, surprised at Stockholm's knowledge. Without mecha knowledge nobody should be able to tell the difference between the two systems, and Werewolves, regardless of tribe, tended to distrust technology.

"It, ah, wouldn't have been up to the long trek." Norm looked down at the ruined battery unit. "Of course, neither apparently was this thing."

Stockholm crossed his arms over his chest and shook his head slightly. "This came from a vehicle in the Age of Mecha, Norman. The vehicle was called a Mass Transit Train." Stockholm bent and picked up the power unit. He scrutinized the blacked harness casing, searching its surface carefully. "Says right here it shouldn't be used for anything less than two metric tons."

He lowered the unit for Norman to see. The Gnome, however, couldn't understand the writing on the side of the unit. He marveled at Stockholm's knowledge of pre-Fall civilization. Then again, hadn't the Red Tribesman lived during that time?

"Um, I couldn't read that." He looked up at Stockholm. "I suppose I should've field tested the autocart first, huh?"

Stockholm hurled the battery unit into the distance.

"Look, big guy, Flint, Will, I'm really sorry about this," Norman said.

Anna shrugged her shoulders.

"Everyone's okay, and we've only lost a few minutes on this fiasco." Anna turned toward the north. Lee had already departed, setting the pace for the rest of the trip. "Styge, get back on covering our tracks. Norman, try to keep up. I trust the rest of your gadgetry is in order?"

"Oh, quite sir," he said, brightening. "Right as rain it is."

"Good. For now, get in the middle of the pack." She moved forward to rejoin Lee Toren. "Let's move it people!"

Anna Deus's company moved north once again, minus the heap of mecha left smoking near the oak tree.

Stockholm once more carried Styge's belongings, leaving Norman to carry his own as punishment for his carelessness.

Thankfully, Norm thought, Flint didn't yell at him, or seem to carry a grudge over the incident.

The Wererat himself couldn't help thinking that the world would be better off if mecha had never been rediscovered.

* * * *

Fly's timepiece struck one o'clock when Markus Trent finally showed up, Akimaru walking slightly behind and to his left.

The Black Draconus was on his feet the moment he spied Trent. "Where the mighty hell have you been, Trent? We've lost precious time waiting on you!"

74

The Human Ninja gave a mocking low bow, smiling toothily at his Headmaster.

"My sincerest apologies, Headmaster." He looked up from his bow. "I was conducting some last-minute business before we departed from the city."

Trent stood to full height, looking at the others of the group. "Everyone's here, so shall we be going?"

Great, Fly thought, not even out of the city, and he's already vying for control of the party. I may have to put him in his place sooner than I'd hoped.

"That we shall. Take point, Markus," Fly said.

He waited for Akimaru to walk alongside him, then leaned close to the white clad Ninja as Markus took a good twenty-yard lead on his group. "What news, Akimaru?"

"I am not certain, sensei." Akimaru didn't take his eyes from Trent's back. "He was conversing with a female tracking agent, Miss Noriko Shibata. Whether their discussion was personal, or Guild business, I could not tell. I could not risk getting close enough to hear them."

Fly heard the suspicion in his favored agent's voice. Akimaru didn't appear to trust Trent either, a fact that Fly savored as Trent approached the northern gates.

Bringing up the rear, Lain McNealy worked with the Orc Berserker on his grammar. "Remember, dear," she said, sounding more like a schoolmarm than a Necromancer. "'I' is followed by 'am' when talking about oneself. So the sentence is, 'I am going to the market'. Now, try again," she said, looking ahead at Thaddeus Fly and Akimaru.

"I, am going, to the market." Rage focused as hard as he could on the structure of his sentence. "Dat way, right?"

"Correct, deary. Now, let's work on your pronunciation. It's, 'that way', not 'dat way', all right?"

Rage shook his head, rubbing his temples as he thought over her lessons.

"Don't know why she bothers," Markus Trent muttered to no one in particular. "Like trying to teach a rock," he said with an absurd grin.

As Trent walked through the archway of the northern city gates, two lumbering Minotaur policemen stepped out in front of him, axes held at the ready.

"What ho, gentlemen," he said smoothly as Fly and the rest of the company halted behind Trent.

The Minotaurs looked at one another, and gave each other a brief nod.

"We have some questions for you people," the one on the left said as Trent placed his hands behind his back.

Fly could see that he was letting a knife slip from his sleeve down into the palm of his hand. *He's good*, Fly thought. *Still knows standard Obura Clan procedure.*

"Certainly, constable," Trent said amiably. "Ask away."

Another knife dropped into his other hand, and he gripped the tips of the weapons tightly between thumbs and forefingers.

One of the burly officers cleared his throat to begin.

"We've had some disturbing reports about slavers in the area. You folks wouldn't happen to know anything about that, would you?"

Wait a minute. Fly took a good look at the guards. They had left deep impressions in the dirt of their posts. They'd been on duty a fairly long while, and should have been relieved by now. Why would they still be standing here?

Then he had it—Deus! The Rogue had obviously given these bozos a bogus story about slavers, and given the guards his company's general description. He scanned the white clad Ninja. Then again, he thought, Aki does tend to stand out like a sore thumb, when he wants to be seen. His attention returned to Trent, as he began to speak once again.

"Slavers? Well, I can't say as I'm surprised, gents," the Human Ninja said casually. "Desanadron is a big city, and it would be easy for such fiends to hide out inside of her walls."

As the guards looked at one another briefly, Trent looked back at his Headmaster, the question in his eyes. Fly nodded, averting his eyes afterward.

As the two guards turned their heads to face Trent again, the Human Ninja let his throwing knives fly, each finding their mark in a guard's right eye, buried all the way to the hilts.

The bodies hadn't even dropped before Thaddeus Fly and his party was through the gates and out of the city.

They ran for a clean mile before slowing to a walk, catching their breath. Akimaru and Rage weren't even winded. Fly panted only from sheer rage and indignity at the setup he'd so carelessly walked into. Trent and Lain had started to breath a little heavily. Her skeletal servant appeared to be falling apart, and she took her rucksack from it before banishing it back to the soil, which opened up and swallowed the creature in seconds. Fly shuddered; the sight of her power still chilled him to the bones. "Damn him," he growled under his breath.

"Who, sensei?" Akimaru asked.

"William Deus, who else? The little rat bastard knew we'd be following them out of the city, and he took some pains to ensure we were slowed down." Fly looked at the assembled company, and wondered for the first time if his choice of operatives had been poorly made. Three Ninjas, a Berserker and a Necromancer. All in all, they weren't a very diverse group, he realized with a bit of chagrin. Still, his decisions had been made. Let someone else question them. "Come on. We'll head north, hopefully pick up their trail. Markus, take the point again."

Once more they moved ahead, Markus Trent in the front, followed by Fly and Akimaru, with Lain McNealy and Rage bringing up the rear.

They walked for perhaps half an hour before Fly noticed that there were no tracks on the road ahead of them. Surely if Deus and his men had come this way, they would have left some sign of their passage.

"Trent, turn direction. Let's head a little east, see if we can find their trail."

The group followed his directions, moving directly east for another twenty minutes, before Trent came to a stop. "What is it, Trent?"

While normally hateful and distrusting of his Headmaster, once out in the field, Markus Trent was an efficient, if not entirely obedient, agent. He scanned the ground around him, shaking his head. "It's the ground, Fly," he said, not looking up from the grasslands around and beneath him. "It feels different. It feels right."

"And on our original path?" Fly asked.

Trent shook his head vaguely, trying to think of the right words.

"The ground back west felt, disturbed. It was as though someone had taken a horse-drawn cart through the fields. Here, the soil is traveled as well, but I can clearly see it."

Fly looked back in the direction they had come. *Another hour wasted, by the gods*, he fumed.

"Very well. Reverse direction. We're heading back to where Mr. Trent says the soil was 'disturbed'. When we get back in that area, keep a sharp eye out for anything suspicious. Let's move people."

Twenty minutes later, they were standing right back in the path they'd been taking before.

Fly scanned the area with his eyes and ears, but couldn't see whatever had been making itself obvious to Trent. "What are we looking for exactly, Markus?"

"I'm not sure," the Human Ninja said.

Lain had gotten down on all fours, and was running her hand along the ground.

Trent looked over at Fly, and suddenly shouted, "Stop! Stay right where you are Fly!" The Black Draconus tensed for battle, certain that Trent had chosen this moment to strike. But it was so soon, and besides, Fly thought as Trent approached, he hasn't drawn any weapons.

Trent stood next to Fly, then crouched, placing his hand through the ground.

Through it, Fly thought, bewildered.

Trent's hand disappeared without effort beneath the soil.

"What the devil," Fly whispered.

Lain crawled over and placed her own hand next to Trent's.

"What trickery is this?" Lain let a small amount of her magic flow into the illusion, dissipating it as she did so.

For miles north of them along the path, Fly saw the illusion fade, revealing a deep set of tire tracks, and several sets of foot tracks.

"An illusion," Lain said as she stood. "A minor trick, performed either by someone with very little actual power, or a crafty Illusionist. If the spell were more potent, it would have been obvious to me from the get-go."

"And me," Akimaru said.

Was that a trace of irritation I heard, Fly wondered. Nothing escaped Akimaru's piercing gaze, but apparently, something had, this time.

"The old man, Styge." Trent shook. "I can't believe he's still alive."

Thaddeus Fly was surprised, too. Styge was, after all, Human. Age should have claimed him by now.

"Well, at least we've undone his little trick," Trent said, grinning at the Midnight Suns' Headmaster.

"True. Let us hope that doing so hasn't set off any more nasty little surprises."

Fly's company continued on, trailing after William Deus and his Hoods.

Chapter Seven
First Blood

"Lady luck, why do you hate me," Anna whispered as Stockholm tended to Styge. The old Illusionist had survived the crash of the autocart with a few cuts and scrapes. But here, maybe a little less than an hour later, he had tripped over a rock and apparently sprained his ankle.

The big Chief wrapped Styge's foot in medical bandaging he'd brought along, just in case such an emergency arose. While he and Flint could regenerate, the other three weren't quite so lucky.

Add to this aggravation the fact that Norman had wandered off down to a nearby stream to refill his canteen, and she found herself looking at a serious delay in the schedule. The sun was going down, and her timepiece showed her it was a little after two o'clock in the afternoon.

"Stockholm, are you almost done there," she spat a little testily.

Her Chief shot her a poisonous look, and she flinched at the sight of it.

"We'll be ready soon. I don't want to rush this, he is old after all, and just a little more fragile than yourself, William." Stockholm helped the old Illusionist up, and let him climb on his back, carrying him piggyback. "I'll have to carry him for a while. The salve I administered will heal the sprain, but it needs a few hours to work. Meantime, I think everyone should take a minute to get themselves something to eat."

Anna took out a few pieces of dried cheese, eating slowly, watching for Norman's return. *He should be back by now,* she thought.

"Flint, go fetch Norm," she said around a mouthful of food. "We need to get going again soon. Lee says we'll make the village of Prek in *another* two hours," she said, looking over at the Pickpocket. "I thought you said this village was only a few hours away."

"Well, yeah, it is." Lee tried not to look her in the eyes. "By horse," he added in a whisper.

"What?" Anna dropped her small piece of cheese and grabbed Lee by the front of his tan tunic as Flint nipped off to find the other Gnome of the company. "You never said that before." She shook him back and forth.

Lee threw his hands up, his eyes filled with panic.

"Sorry, sorry! I would've said somefing before, but you seemed to be so pleased wiv our progress. Will, you're gonna break my neck." She stopped shaking the Pickpocket, dumped him to the ground, and approached Stockholm and Styge.

"Sorry Chief, looks like you'll be carrying Styge for the whole trip at this rate," she said. He gave her a questioning look, to which she replied, "Lee just told me he made his trip by horse."

Stocky grumbled low in his throat.

"I've told you time and again not to trust anything he says, William," he growled. "But you never listen to me. Still, it could be worse." He set Styge down gently. "As long as we've got the extra travel time tacked on, we may as well have a proper meal." He pulled his cookware out of his rucksack.

Anna was surprised once again. Nobody else had thought to bring cooking gear, and as far as she knew, she was the only one who could cook a decent meal. *Perhaps there's even more to ol' Stocky than I thought,* she mused.

"What's going on?" Flint came up behind Anna, Norman held aloft by the back of his shirt. He set the Engineer down, and looked curiously at Stockholm as he struck up a fire.

"Lee miscalculated," Anna said, sparing Lee from another interrogation. "He forgot that when he made the trip to the city from Prek, he was riding a horse. No big deal, Flint," she said, glad that at least the Wererat didn't seem perturbed by the delay in the schedule. "We're going to have a meal, and then head out again. Norman, you get your canteen filled?"

The Engineer nodded with a wry smile, and sat down with his notepad of calculations.

The company settled in for a decent meal, unaware that they wouldn't get to finish it.

* * * *

One-thirty, Fly thought, looking again at his timepiece. The wreckage near a sturdy oak gave him a little heart, as it meant that Deus and his company would have been delayed. Smoke still billowed from the machine, and Trent used the small flames to fry a squirrel he'd hit with a shuriken.

Lain concentrated her energy nearby, calling up a strangely clad warrior from an era long since past. The zombie had a mecha weapon clutched tightly in its rotting arms. Fly didn't like the look either the creature, or its strange weapon, but he knew that Lain would make the most of it.

"How long since they passed through here, Akimaru," Fly asked as he tore his gaze away from Lain's undead servant.

The white clad Ninja was crouched low, peering intensely at the tracks.

"Perhaps a little less than a half of an hour," he said. "At least, since they left. The incident appears to have taken them twenty minutes or so to deal with. The damage done to that machine," he said, pointing to the autocart. "Someone of immense physical strength did that, and quite easily if I'm any judge."

Fly looked over at the ruined mecha. *Ignatious Stockholm. William Deus's little trump card*, he thought. *Well, maybe not so little.* "Shall I investigate further?"

"No, that'll be all." Fly turned from Akimaru and approached Lain and Rage. "Thoughts?"

"Just a few." Lain didn't look away from her new servant. "They're making good time, but this was one hell of a delay for them. We're still about five hours from Prek, on foot. If they have another delay, stop for food or something, we'll catch up to them."

"Yeah, but we gots to leave now," Rage added.

"Indeed." Fly said. "Everybody, let's go! Trent, on point!"

The Human Ninja did as he was told without complaint, much to Fly's satisfaction. *He's getting into his groove*, Fly thought with a grin. *Good.*

Thaddeus Fly and his group moved north, following the tracks left behind by William Deus and his Hoods.

"Smoke," Akimaru said after another twenty minutes. Fly looked up from his thoughts, seeing the small plumes of smoke hanging in the air a little more than fifteen minutes away.

"Excellent," he said. "Everyone, double time! Eight minutes." The company got into a jogging stride.

When he called them to a halt, they were just out of earshot of Deus and his company. Fly couldn't clearly see them, but knew they were only a few minutes away.

He didn't want to risk being spotted or smelled by the Red Tribe Werewolf or the Wererat, so he kept the company at the foot of a hill that would lead them to Deus and his men.

"Everybody, gather in," he said softly.

When everyone was huddled around him, he looked them each in the eyes. "All right, here's how we're going to play this. Lain, take your servant and Rage right at them, harry them for a few minutes. Trent, Akimaru and I will head east and then north, bypass them," he said, drawing a small slip of paper out of his belt. "This is a locator sutra, Lain," he said, handing her the small paper. "When the three of you have harassed them long enough, use this sutra. It'll bring you all back to me," he said.

"It won't work on him," she said, indicating the silent zombie. She had left the creature over where she'd summoned it.

The zombie groaned, a low, dry rumble from deep in the decayed and rotted stomach.

"Then again, none of them are meant to be permanent. How does it work?" She took the small scroll.

"It's magic in a way," Fly said. "Ninjas, Monks, and Samurai can imbue small scrolls with Chi magic, to be used whenever they're needed. I never learned a lot of them, but the sutra of returning has come in handy for me a number of times."

Lain graced him a small smile as she tucked the sutra into the front of her dress. "Remember, only engage them for a few minutes, while we make our way around their party. You have to injure at least one of them, a little," Fly said, looking seriously at Rage. "Sorry big guy, but I'm not sending you to try to kill any of them. There'll be plenty of time for that later."

Fly led Akimaru and Trent east about a mile, then turned north and stopped. He turned back in Lain, Rage and the undead creature's direction, taking another sutra from his pocket. He threw it into the air, where it turned into a sparkling flare.

The signal was given, and Lain led the way toward William Deus and his group.

Fly smiled despite this early run-in. He would be in the lead after this, and he relished the idea of setting a trap for Deus and his men as the Rogue had done to him.

"Do you know what the best thing is about payback, gentlemen?" he asked the other two Ninjas. He looked each in the eyes for but a moment before striding off north once again. "It's one of the only things you can savor without paying a tab."

* * * *

Stockholm sniffed hard at the air, wrinkling his snout as he finished making the grilled cheese sandwiches.

"Something wrong, big fellah?" Flint asked. "Burn the bread did ya?"

"We're not going to get to finish our meal." The big man stood and cracked his knuckles.

Anna looked up from her simple stew. In the distance three small figures quickly became larger.

"Who is it?" She gained her feet and drew throwing knives.

One of the figures towered over the other two, all green and menacing. At least she knew who that was, though the knowledge was not exactly comforting. Rage, the Orc Berserker whom Thaddeus Fly kept around as a countermeasure to Anna's larger agents. The other two figures were still too far away, too small for her to make them out.

"Lain McNealy and one of her servants," Flint said, pulling out three huge hunting knives from his brace of daggers. They were almost the size of short swords, perfectly balanced for the Wererat's short to medium range throwing attacks. "I can't make out what the thing is carrying, but it looks like a weapon."

Anna's company, their lunches forgotten and their travel equipment gathered into a central pile, prepared themselves for battle. Lee made tracks, leaving a cloud of white smoke behind him as he tore off into the hills as fast as his stout legs would carry him.

"Fucking coward," Stockholm shouted after the retreating Pickpocket.

Styge retreated a short distance behind the group, sitting cross-legged on the ground. He pulled out a pipe, tapped some tobacco into it from his hip pouch, and started smoking it casually, like nothing at all was wrong.

Norman, rummaging through his tool bag, finally drew out a small power tool that buzzed and whirred. He pulled out a circular, serrated disk, and mounted it to the end of the gadget, giving the deadly blade another spin.

"Nobody take the first move." Anna crouched in a fighting stance. "Let them come at us. When we turn them aside, we'll have something to hold over Fly's head."

Rage closed to within fifty yards, and drew his left hand back, grabbing a small throwing hammer and whipping it in Stockholm's direction.

Despite the blinding speed with which it flew, its accuracy left something to be desired. The bulky Red Tribe Werewolf reached out to his left, and plucked the weapon from the air.

Flint hurled his hunting knives at the approaching Orc, only to watch them sink a few centimeters into his blocking forearms and be ignored. Anna's smaller weapons didn't even penetrate Rage's thick green skin. Instead, they bounced harmlessly to the ground.

"Stockholm," she shouted.

The big Red Tribesman started forward—but a short beam of energy lanced into his huge chest, blasting him several yards back.

Anna's shocked gaze found the undead creature standing in a shooter's stance, the end of his mecha weapon smoking.

"Thrice-damned Necromancer," she growled, spotting Lain McNealy a few yards behind the zombie.

Flint, who had just witnessed the biggest bruiser he knew being thrown back like a rag doll, darted toward Rage, closing the thirty-yard gap as the Orc slowed his own pace. Hunting knife in hand, he lunged at Rage, screaming bloody murder.

The Berserker deflected him handily by punching him right in the face, his longer arms reaching farther than Flint could with his hunting knife.

Teeth flew from the Wererat's snout as he twisted and fell bleeding to the grass, his vision blurred with pain.

For a moment, Rage's mind blared to finish the job. However, he had orders, and his orders were to harass, not kill. Besides, he thought, poor little guy looks like he's in a lot of pain.

This, of course, was a huge understatement. Though Rage didn't know it, as he stepped over the fallen Wererat, he'd broken part of Flint's faceplate.

"Stocky, get up." Anna crouched next to the Red Tribesman.

He'd gotten himself into a half-seated position, his fur and flesh singed slightly. Thankfully, she saw, his chain shirt had absorbed the majority of the blast, but it wouldn't survive another hit. On top of that, she realized, nobody else in the company was wearing armor. She turned and watched Rage come slowly toward her. Flint screamed on the ground behind the Orc, and her heart dropped.

A blur of crimson shot forward from her side. Stockholm took advantage of Rage's slowed movements. He launched a roundhouse kick to Rage's head, sending the Berserker reeling to the left, clutching his head.

Stockholm brought his hands up, bouncing slightly on the balls of his feet. "Come on then, green one."

Rage punched at him, and Stockholm shifted his weight, grappling the arm and thrusting his own hips into the Orc as he hauled.

Rage, heavy even for a member of his Race, flew through the air as easily as one of Anna's knives, landing hard on the ground a few yards away.

"Fire," Lain shouted at her undead minion.

Another pulse of energy erupted from the end of the mecha weapon, scorching the ground next to Anna as she tucked her head into her chest and rolled away. How in the Seven Hells was she being bested by two of Fly's agents and a shuffling zombie?

Styge, she saw, hadn't moved from his position on the hill, smoking away at his pipe. She couldn't be sure, but she thought he would be the most obvious choice of targets for the mecha weapon blasts. Was McNealy holding it back?

Before Anna could find out if that were the case, she was happily surprised by the return of Lee Toren. The Gnome Pickpocket stealthily ran to the zombie's side, reaching up and plucking the mecha weapon from its hands as he stuck his tongue out at an infuriated Lain.

The Necromancer woman hadn't even seen him, or heard him coming. In fact, she hadn't she seen him abandon William Deus and his men? Apparently, Deus's company had a few tricks up their sleeves.

Still sprinting full out, Lee sped past Norman, who had taken cover behind the party's belongings. He dropped the weapon into the Engineer's hands, and smiled like a devil at him.

"What's this?" Norm looked down at the heavy metal weapon.

"Wot's it look loik, mate?" The Pickpocket set a boot on Norm's shoulder and pushed. Lee replaced Norm in the cover spot, and motioned toward the ongoing battle with his head. "S'a weapon! You'll be able to take out that dead thing at least."

Norman looked down at the bulky metal weapon, figuring out its operation relatively quickly.

"Nice and easy, at least." The Engineer crouched low and ducked out of hiding. He opened his eyes wide, taking in the scene in front of him. Flint was just now getting up off of the ground, his lips and snout fur covered in blood, spitting teeth. He looked groggy, and swayed drunkenly from side to side. Stockholm had Rage in check, the two of them trading blows, Stockholm landing the majority of the strikes.

The Chief can handle himself, Norm thought. As for the undead creature, it was reaching for another mecha weapon at its hip, one Norman recognized immediately. It was called a hand cannon, due to the enormous punch it packed, and could easily kill someone.

Stockholm wondered how even Rage could largely ignore his blows. The Orc Berserker hadn't gone into Berserker Fury, a point that Stockholm took some small comfort in. However, without that lack of control, the Orc managed to block and dodge some of his attacks, frustrating the Chief.

Rage's own attacks, however, were powerful, though Stockholm wouldn't give him the satisfaction of seeing it. He only took a few hits, but the Orc made them count.

Behind him, Stockholm heard another discharge from the zombie's mecha weapon, and once more he prayed he didn't get hit. When the sound passed, shock registered in Rage's eyes. He used the hesitation to land a vicious uppercut on the Orc's jaw.

Rage stumbled backward, falling flat on his back after a few stuttered steps.

The Chief turned, and saw a triumphant smile on Norman Adwar's face. The Engineer had the mecha weapon, and had blasted the head of the zombie clean off of its shoulders. The ancient body slumped to the ground, truly done in.

"Rage! We're out of here," Lain shouted as she avoided getting shot herself. The Necromancer sprinted past Stockholm, weaving to the side as he grabbed at her, and laid a hand on the Orc.

A moment later, she drew out a piece of paper, and the two Midnight Suns disappeared in a flash.

First blood has been drawn, Anna thought as her Hoods gathered in around her. *And from the look of us, we were the ones drawn from.*

* * * *

Half an hour later, Flint and Stockholm had regenerated their wounds.

Anna led the way again with Lee Toren next to her.

Nobody said much of anything, choosing to remain quiet and alert as they made their way north again, at a much slower pace than before.

The hours wiled away, and as the sun disappeared beneath the horizon, they realized that they would have to camp out for a few hours at least before making their way to Prek.

Stockholm cooked the meal again, while Styge and Flint laid out everyone's sleeping bags.

Anna, lost deep in her own thoughts, looked over at Norman, who had taken apart the mecha weapon he'd received earlier.

He was inspecting the device intently, trying to see if it was marked with a date of creation. *Of course it isn't*, he thought bitterly. *I could only be so lucky.*

How far behind Fly are we now? Anna wondered. *Two hours, three?* It didn't matter, she decided. If he got himself and his men around Anna's group, as she suspected he had, they could already be in the village of Prek. However, if Reynaldi and his posse holed up in an Order of Oun fort, it wouldn't matter what kind of a lead Fly got on them. The Black Draconus was a Ninja, as were two of his companions. Lain McNealy probably couldn't come within five miles of a Paladin or Knight without her presence and nature being felt.

Anna smiled to herself a little. Her own troop wouldn't have any trouble getting into a fort, so long as Lee made himself scarce. After all, *he* was a well-known criminal across Tamalaria, especially among the Paladin forts. Only one ranking member of the Order, Byron Aixler, had ever pardoned the Gnome. Even then, the Paladin had only done so to recruit Lee for his own purposes.

"How's the jaw holding up now, Flint," she asked the Wererat as he took a seat next to her on a fallen tree they had gathered near to set camp.

"Just fine, boss." He shook his head dismally. "Never expected to get hit so hard, you know."

Anna looked into the Wererat's eyes, and saw there that he was reliving the blow. "I can't remember the last time someone that strong just, you know, out and wailed me one."

"You should have known better, lunging in like that." Stockholm didn't move his eyes from the meal. He started serving portions into bowls and handing them around to the members of the company. "You may be quick, Flint, but you weren't a match for Rage head-on."

"I didn't exactly have the element of surprise or any sort of urban sprawl to use to my advantage," the Wererat said testily. "I'm not some freakish, moody bruiser like you are, my red friend," he spat.

Now he had Stockholm's attention, as the Werewolf was done handing out the food except for his own. Flint had his bowl in hand, but kept his left hand empty, available for action.

"Boys, there's no need to squabble," Lee Toren said around a mouthful of food. "Each of us brings somefin' different to the table. Styge," he said.

The old Illusionist looked up from his bowl, which already sat half-empty in his hands.

"You're good at what you do, and what you do is distraction, misdirection and deception of the senses." Lee looked over to Norman, who had reassembled the mecha weapon before starting his meal. "Norm, you've got a knack fer technology, me bucko. Big advantage over Fly and 'is lot. Flint," he continued, though the Wererat was still glaring at Stockholm. "You've got some quick wits in that head of yours, and you're very personable. You can get without much effort what a bloke loik meself 'as to bust his arse for. Stockholm, well, you're pretty obvious, ain't yeh." Lee chuckled but he saw that the big red menace wasn't amused. Instead, the Red Tribe Werewolf simply lowered his eyes and started eating. "And then, of course, there's William, who keeps us all wrapped togever and on the same page."

"Well said, Lee," Styge said between mouthfuls. "William, are we camping for the night?"

"Just for a few hours," Anna handed her emptied bowl to Flint, who set it aside to be washed when everyone was finished. "I'll keep watch with another volunteer."

Stockholm raised one paw halfway to the air, and they all finished their meals and headed to their sleeping bags. Styge rolled up Anna's and Stockholm's before nipping off for some sleep himself, leaving only the Red Tribe Werewolf and the woman they all called William Deus to keep watch.

Fifteen minutes into the watch, Anna still felt unsettled by the tension between her Guild Prime and Chief. She would normally have kept an eye to the north and west of the camp, while Ignatious kept an eye on the south and east. Instead, she sauntered over to the stoic Werewolf.

His arms were crossed over his chest, and he scowled off to the east as she approached. Before she could open her mouth to speak, he whispered to her, "I'm sorry about before, Will. I should not have been so foul with Flint."

His back was still to her, and for a moment, she thought she might leave it at that. But no, she thought, there's something else there, something weighing on his mind. He never opens up to anybody, and that's got to change.

"It's all right, Ignatious." She put a hand on his elbow to catch his attention.

He turned only his eyes toward her—a disquieting look. When a man stands a good foot and a half over you, and has the head and some torso elements of a huge, red timber wolf, you only see one big eye swivel down at you. She felt him looking not at her, but into her, searching out the secret she held.

"To tell you the truth, he frustrates me sometimes too. Now come on," she said, giving him a friendly punch in the arm. "Tell me what's on your mind."

At first, he remained silent, glaring down at her with that one visible eye.

Her nerves stood on end. Something primal, far down in the core of her body, told her to run as far and as fast away from this beast as she could. Yet her feet remained planted, unmoving.

Finally, he let out a huge sigh, and half turned to face her better, his hands still folded over his battered chain shirt. "There's a lot on my mind, sir. Like how you crept into my room yesterday morning and tried to set my picture back without my noticing."

Anna's heart jumped up into her throat—he'd been asleep. She had been absolutely certain that he'd been dead to the world asleep when she picked up the portrait. Didn't he ever just lie there and rest?

He waved one hand to dismiss her worries. "Don't worry about that, Will. Everyone gets curious now and again—can't help themselves."

"Anything else, big guy? And I'm really sorry about that." She patted him on the shoulder. *Quite a reach to do that*, she thought.

"Some other things." He started to walk the perimeter of their camp. "This trip, for instance. I haven't wandered outside of the city in years, and I'm afraid I might not want to go back right away when we're done. I like the wilds." His deep, rumbling voice carried easily on the night air.

She followed a few paces behind him as he walked along, checking the surroundings every minute or so. They appeared to be in the clear, but in the plains, forests and hills of Tamalaria, one didn't take chances. Monsters and hostile highwaymen roamed everywhere, leaving no one unmolested.

"Plus Lee," she offered.

He grunted. "Yeah, plus him. Do you know why I dislike him so much?"

She shook her head, because she honestly didn't. She had suspicions, but nothing confirmed.

"Because he knows something about me that none of the rest of you do, and he shouldn't," Stockholm said. "He knows a secret I've been keeping from all of you, and it's not something small."

"Is he blackmailing you with it?" She was truly worried for both Stockholm and Lee, for different reasons.

Stocky shook his head and let his chin drop toward his chest for a minute.

"No, though I'm surprised he hasn't. And he never reminds me that he knows, but he couldn't possibly have forgotten what he saw," he growled.

"If it makes you feel any better, I've got a few secrets of my own." Anna felt the wraps pressed down over her breasts. Her whole existence as William Deus was a cover-up, and she knew if her cover were blown, she'd be pretty steamed too.

Stockholm nodded, suddenly wheeling on her, leaning down close, the tip of his snout almost touching her nose.

"I know," he said, but there was no hostility in his eyes, or his tone. "And I know that whatever your secret is, you think you've got good reason to keep it from me. But Will, I get the distinct impression that Flint knows your secret, and that eats at me. I'm your Chief, William—have been the Guild Chief for over twenty years. I've never sought promotion, because I'm not a real thief. I'm a fighter, a brute, William. A bruiser, as Flint puts it so liberally."

Anna could have been mistaken, but she thought she heard a pang of guilt, or sadness, in his voice.

"A fighter, yes," she offered. "A bruiser, maybe. But not a brute." She stood directly next to him. "And certainly I know how intelligent you are. You're very well read. Even though some of that's because of your age, which I don't know precisely, a lot of it is your own willingness to learn. Stocky," she said, looking up into his deep, crimson cast eyes.

She feared asking him the question, but all this talk about secrets was starting to make her feel guilty as sin that she had only shared her own with Flint. Stockholm was loyal, efficient, trustworthy, even if he was a tad enigmatic. She decided that she would tell him her secret. That she was really Annabelle Deus. "Stocky, what is it that Lee saw? What do you guard so closely?"

And so he told her.

Chapter Eight
The Village, the Forts, and Madmen

Thaddeus Fly felt the sutra's magical connection pull, and he stopped in his tracks as the sun began its decent toward the horizon.

Lain McNealy and Rage fell out of the air itself a few yards away, the large Orc bowling him over as he tumbled through. Lain herself was literally hurled by the force of the magic's expenditure through the air.

Luckily, before she could smash her face open on a sitting stone nearby, Akimaru caught her deftly, standing her upright and brushing her off.

She was impressed by his speed and hidden strength, and with his manners as well. He didn't let his hands stray where they shouldn't.

"Thank you very much, Akimaru. Any reason you didn't catch Rage?"

"He is many times my size, Miss McNealy. I would have been flattened."

She giggled a girlish laugh, and thanked him again.

"Well, it's good to see you're uninjured," Fly said.

Rage shook his head.

"Something wrong, big man?"

"I'm feelin' pretty bruised up, boss." The Orc Berserker held his ribs on his left side, and Fly noticed a nice lump on his forehead. "The doggy-man gave me what for, boss."

Fly nodded, saying yes, he could see that.

The group moved on, into the setting night. After another three hours' walking, they arrived at the outskirts of the village of Prek.

Fly stopped the company, telling Markus Trent to scout ahead, see how many, if any, sentries were posted throughout the small fishing village. When he returned, Trent grinned ear to ear.

"Nobody, Headmaster. It looks like the townsfolk pretty much guard themselves. Not that there's much to guard," he said with mild disdain. "It's a fishing port, little more. Only place open right now's a tavern, not much to look at." He pointed at Rage. "Not sure he'd even fit in the doorway. Residents look to be mostly Human and Jaft."

"Jafts are good fishermen, natural sailors," Fly commented, not really thinking about what he was saying. "Okay, we'll all head in, check the place out, see what we can learn. If you get anything pertinent, report it to me right away. Rage, you'll have to stand outside." He said that apologetically, but Rage didn't seem to mind.

The Midnight Suns moved into the village like a pack of serpents, moving quickly and stealthily into the village center, following Trent to the tavern. Rage posted himself like a bouncer at the doors, and Fly, followed by Trent, Akimaru and Lain, walked inside.

The four agents split up, Fly and Trent taking seats at opposite ends of the bar itself, Akimaru and Lain taking seats at two separate tables. The Guild Headmaster discreetly picked over the gathered customers with his reptilian eyes. Trent had given him a good review of the residents—almost all of them were either Humans and Jafts. The bartender was a portly Human fellow, who looked like he was a few years away from a massive coronary, Fly thought. The man to his immediate left stank not only of the flesh of the Jaft Race, but also of fish. The woman to his right, a Human, looked to be in her middle years, and he immediately typed her as a barfly.

The great thing about barflies, he thought with a smug grin, is that they usually know a little about everything that's going on in their particular haunt. He ordered himself a sake, and when the barkeep gave him a queer look, he sighed heavily and instead ordered mead.

The woman gave him a tipsy smile. "Not exactly from around here, are you, honey?"

Gods, Fly thought, her breath reeks!

"Not exactly." He let a little of his old south-central plains accent slip into his voice. "Just passing through, looking for some friends of mine."

The barkeep brought his mead, and he held him for a moment with a raised finger. "One more of what she's having."

The barkeep nodded.

The woman graced him with a smile, and he knew he could get any information she might have by getting her drinks. He sincerely hoped that was all he'd need to do for her. Anything else, and he'd have to cut her throat.

"Much obliged, sir," she said in as sultry a voice as she could muster in her alcohol-induced stupor. "So, these friends of yours, what do they look like," she asked, taking her drink and draining half of its contents in one go.

"Paladins and Knights, mostly. May have passed through not too long ago." He looked away from her eyes. They'd screamed at him when he looked into them, the hunger, the need bare for anyone to see.

"Well, I don't know about that, but there was a big fellah come through about a week back." She rolled her eyes toward the ceiling as she thought back. "He stopped in here, asked for a scotch. One drink and he was gone." She was clearly confused at such behavior. "Big guy, looked like a Simpa, but he had black stripes on his arms, like a, what's they called?"

"A Khan." Fly realized that he'd purchased her a drink for nothing. She clearly hadn't seen Reynaldi and his men. He shouldn't be surprised; after all, what would a Paladin do in a dive bar like this? They only frequented nice, clean establishments. And scotch hardly seemed a Paladin's drink of choice. Yet, he knew to whom she referred. "The man's name wouldn't have been Portenda, would it?"

"Yeah, that was him." She gave a wide smile. "You looking for him? I hear he's a Bounty Hunter."

"He's possibly the best, but no, we're not looking for him." Fly said nothing more, paying for his drink and hers and heading outside. He needed to clear his head. He usually had more patience than this, but he knew that William Deus and his Hoods would only be a few hours behind him. Even if the Hoods stopped to rest, Lain and Rage were exhausted. One of Deus's small throwing knives had landed her a glancing blow on the thigh, bleeding her pretty good before Lain noticed it. And Rage was stiff with bruises, having been struck several hard blows by the Red Tribe Werewolf.

The Midnight Suns themselves would have to stop for a rest before the sun came up. And that may very well put Deus ahead of him.

"Sometin' on yer mind, boss," Rage asked from the other side of the tavern's doorway.

Fly could smell the odor of cheap beer and cheaper patrons wafting out into the calm night air.

"Indeed," the Black Draconus Ninja muttered, half to himself. "I am finding that there are a few flaws in our present travel strategy. If we take too long here, we'll be caught up with. I refuse to deal with the Hoods again so soon. What we need," he said, thinking long and hard. "What we need is a lead, and then a route that Deus won't take. We need a ruse, something to slow him down," he said.

"Sensei," Akimaru said as he stepped out into the night air. "I have learned something of value."

Lain and Trent came out only a minute later.

"Go ahead," Fly said.

The group huddled like a sports team, keeping close together.

"One of the customers recalls seeing the Elven Paladin. The customer was once a Knight on duty at Fort Flag," Akimaru said. "He informed me that the other fort, the one closer to Prek, is still in service. However, he also informed me that Reynaldi is an Elf while the nearer fort to Prek consists mostly of Dwarves, Werewolves and Cuyotai."

"Dwarven Paladins?" Lain asked incredulously. "That'd be strange to see."

"No, Dwarves do not make themselves Paladins," Fly explained. "They'd be Knights or Soldiers in service to the Order. So, Reynaldi would most likely go to Fort Flag. But we don't have to let Deus know that," he said with a smile. "Akimaru, go back in there and bring us that gentleman directly." The Midnight Suns' Headmaster positively cooed. "We need to have a few words with him."

* * * *

"Oh, wow," Anna said.

Stockholm's confession hadn't been as earth shattering as she had assumed it was going to be, and in truth, she couldn't say as she thought it mattered much. But apparently, it mattered a great deal to Ignatious Stockholm. His secret hadn't had anything to do with his age, which she still didn't know. It hadn't been a grisly family secret or curse. The secret hadn't even explained any of his other sometimes strange or mysterious behavior. He wasn't some heir to any kind of throne.

Ignatious Stockholm was homosexual.

Lee Toren, Stocky explained, had never meant any harm by walking into his private chambers in the underground base of the Hoods. But he had caught him at an awfully awkward moment, conjoined as he had been with his partner.

"And that's about the half and whole of it," Stockholm said.

A trivial matter, Anna thought, yet this big guy acts like it's the most important secret he's ever kept. Time to trump that, she thought with a light chuckle.

"Stocky?"

"Yes," he said, and found himself staring wide-eyed at his Headmaster. As he'd been telling her about Lee's interruption, she'd undone the uppermost wraps around her breasts. As soon as he'd said 'yes', she popped the upper buttons of her tunic undershirt, revealing herself and her secret to him.

"Oh, mighty hell," he whispered.

She did up the wraps again, and smiled wider than she had all day. It felt good to let somebody else know, especially someone as close to her as Stockholm had been over the years.

"You're Anna," he said—not a question, but a flat statement.

As William Deus, she had told her many agents over the years that she had a sister in the city—a sister by the name of Annabelle. She'd also ordered her 'brother-in-law' be protected, and so he had been.

Stockholm had to suppress a laugh. "No wonder Harold's so miserable when you're down with us!"

"No need to remind me." She looked back toward the rest of her company. "Until now, it was just Flint who knew. He found out when he treated my wounds, back when we were plundering those ruins about seven or eight years back," she said. "Only reason the Guild was left to me when Remy died," she whispered. Stockholm placed a huge, hairy hand on her shoulder, ever so gently.

"That's not true, Will. I mean, Anna." He gave her a gentle squeeze. "You were left in charge because you were the Prime, and because nobody else keeps things in order as well as you do. Nobody else in the Guild thinks with the sort of strategy you do." The Red Tribesman looked over at the rest of the company then, nodding sagely to himself. "There's something else I'll bet you don't know about me," he said.

"What's that," she asked.

"I'm one of the only Red Tribe Werewolves in Tamalaria who doesn't know a lick of traditional magic," he said with a smile. "My peoples are renowned for their prowess as mage-warriors. There's only a few of us who don't know something about elemental magic. Me, I'm one of those few."

"Doesn't seem to slow you down any." She headed over to the rest of the company. "Come on, big guy. Let's get these slackers up and moving. We've lost enough time on Thaddeus Fly, and I don't intend to lose any more."

The rest of the company was awakened, and they got themselves moving north again. Lee took the front once again, this time with Stockholm.

Anna hung back in the middle of the pack along with Flint, and she walked next to him easily, smiling as she walked under the moon's guiding light. Flint looked groggily over at her at one point, raising an eyebrow as he lit a cigarette. He offered her one, and for the first time in many months, she accepted, lighting it with a match she lit off of her belt buckle.

"What's got you so perky, boss?" the Wererat asked quietly.

She leaned over and tiptoed as close as she could toward his ear.

"I told old Stocky my secret."

Flint stared ahead, and a moment later, choked and sputtered on the smoke he was holding in.

"May I ask why?" He took another pull on his smoke after one final, ragged cough.

"I had to, Flint." She realized that their entire conversation was being held in whispers and hushed tones. "He trusts me so implicitly, and it just seemed wrong to keep it from him any longer. Besides, he's not going to out me on it."

"What makes you so sure? I mean, I trust the big red menace as much as the next guy, but come on." Flint tossed the spent butt into the near distance and lit another cigarette.

The Glove of Shadows

Mighty Groma, Anna thought, *he's on the road to being a chain-smoker.*

"Let's just say, I know something you don't, now."

Flint smiled back at her and let the matter drop.

* * * *

"So you understand what you must say to them, then?" Thaddeus Fly asked.

The former Knight in service to Fort Flag smiled nervously, trying not to let the fog in his head tip him forward. He nodded only slightly—too much head movement would send his throat down on the *kunei* Akimaru held just a few inches away.

"You should speak your answers for now, my man," the Black Draconus said.

"Yes, I understand. Reynaldi serves out of what is now Fort Branick. That's my story, and I'm sticking to it," the former Knight said.

"Very good little man," said Markus Trent. Fly would have let Trent hold the blade, except that the Human Ninja's own tendencies would cause the weapon to get too close to his throat.

"Headmaster, we should probably be away now. Deus and his group may be approaching very soon."

Fly nodded, and Akimaru vanished his weapon once more. No straps or sheaths could be seen over the white uniform clothes, and not for the first time, both Fly and Trent found themselves trying to see exactly how Akimaru made the weapon disappear. Neither came away any better informed.

Thaddeus Fly led the group away, east and south, their march now taking them towards Fort Flag. It would be a three-day trip on foot, but he was thankful for the edge the misdirection would give him over Deus and the Hoods. *However,* he thought, *what happens when we get to Fort Flag? How are we going to get the information we need? And what are the odds that Reynaldi hadn't even stopped at the Order of Oun Fort?* He had yet to discover which of the many Order Forts across the continent served as the Elven Paladin's home base, and without that knowledge, they would be forced to try and pick up information as they could.

Instead of dwelling on their lack of knowledge, he thought instead on how to approach the problem of Fort Flag. No chance that Trent, Akimaru or himself could even get inside. Their clothes and equipment spoke volumes about what they were. Sneaking into a Fort would result in immediate imprisonment. Lain McNealy would also be known for what she was on sight. No Paladin would mistake her for a pilgrim—that much was certain.

But what about Rage? he asked himself. Sure, the big Orc Berserker wasn't precisely articulate, or clever for that matter, but he followed orders to a T. With the right coaching, compliments of Ms. McNealy, he'd say anything. Dim as he was, he'd believe anything they told him, so no Knight could detect a lie from him. Because, in essence, he wouldn't be lying. "Rage, Lain, if I could have a word with the two of you as we walk." He smiled like a demon.

* * * *

Midnight arrived, as Anna and her company reached Prek.

The village, they all saw, was small, and the inhabitants didn't seem to be out and about.

Flint looked in all directions for constables, until he finally realized there wouldn't be any in a village of this size. His nostrils flared, however, at the scent of Jaft residences, his lycanthrope nostrils exceptionally sensitive to their natural stench.

Stockholm, he saw, had a hand clamped over the end of his snout, and the big guy's eyes were watering.

"Not always an advantage to have a more sensitive snout than mine, eh," he chided the Red Tribesman.

Stocky shot him a warning glance, and he laughed.

Anna scanned the streets, her ears picking up on loud and boisterous conversation, the kind every small town had this time of night. She led the company over a couple of streets, and found the source—the town's watering hole.

"Okay, who's going in?" She looked around the gathered company.

Lee and Norman had already ducked inside for a drink, and Anna rolled her eyes. Even though the Gnome Race was a collection of thinkers, they drank nearly as heavily as their mountainous cousins, the Dwarves.

"Styge, you going to partake?"

The old Illusionist frowned and shook his head.

"Flint, Stocky?"

Flint nodded and headed inside.

"Keep an eye on things out here," she told Stockholm.

The Red Tribe Werewolf nodded, and stood outside the tavern with his back to the wall.

As his Headmaster ducked inside, he smelled something familiar on the wall —the scent of Orc flesh.

Rage, he thought with a deep growl that startled Styge, who had taken up a spot next to him, sitting on the street with a sketchpad in hand.

"Be at ease, elder," Stockholm said to the Illusionist. "I growl not at you."

"They've already been here, you know," the white haired Human said without looking away from his pad and pencil.

Stockholm nodded, and concentrated on his senses, focusing on the smell of the air, the ground, the tavern itself. Though the stench of Jaft flesh nauseated him, he had to search with his nostrils for what his eyes couldn't tell him.

He didn't have the heightened hearing of Flint, because that was a talent latent in Wererats. His kind had their snouts to rely on, and he tried to take advantage of that now, coming up finally with the scents of the Black Draconus, the Human Markus Trent, and the scent of death. *That would be Lain McNealy.*

There was a curious addition to these smells, he noticed. One of the lingering scents reminded him of the smell the air took on just before a lightning storm, the smell of burnt ozone and spent power. *Whose scent is that?*

Inside, Anna strode up to the bar and took one of the two empty seats available, ordering a gin and tonic.

The barkeep, a rosy-cheeked fellow with a big, fake smile, handed it to her, along with a scotch.

"From the Gnome gentleman at the other end of the bar," the barkeep said.

She looked around the barkeep at Lee Toren, who raised his glass to her.

She could see that his free hand had found the money pouch of the patron next to him, and he was already stuffing it down the front of his pants. *Always working, that one*, she thought.

She nursed her drink and listened in to the nearby conversation, until finally Flint showed up next to her, seemingly out of nowhere. "I think I've got something boss." The Wererat took a drag of his cigarette, and led Anna over to a corner booth where a single middle-aged Human sat, his breath and clothes already heavily scented with cheap house whiskey.

"Mr. Johnson, this is my employer, William Deus," Flint said by way of introduction.

Anna sat and shook the man's offered hand.

"Will," Flint said. "Mr. Johnson and I were talking about Paladins, and he remembered something. Would you care to repeat it for Mr. Deus?"

"Sure," the middle-aged man said. "I used to be a Knight, served out of Fort Branick. T'other day, an Elven Paladin, name of Reynaldi, passed through here, recognized me, and gave me an invitation to come back to the Order. I turned him down, of course," he said, taking another sip of his whiskey.

"Why so, Mr. Johnson?" she asked.

The man looked up, and she saw there a deep, anguished soul.

"Because the Order isn't what it used to be, Mr. Deus," he said, his tongue heavy and his speech starting to slur ever so slightly. "And I'm no longer fit to call myself a Knight. Most days, I spend my daylight hours working on the river. At night, I come here to forget everything. Drink enough, and you'll forget why you started drinking."

He looked out of the small window set next to his booth. Anna and Flint gave each other a glance then, in the awkward silence. "Anyway, I told your employee here that Reynaldi served mostly out of Fort Branick, when he's in the region," he said, making certain to play to the script that the Black Draconus and his goons had given him.

"Thank you very much, Mr. Johnson. We happen to need to catch him up, and you've been very helpful in that regard."

When she stood, the former Knight had an instantaneous moral crisis, and he clamped a heavy hand onto her wrist.

She looked him in the eyes, and knew he had something more to say, something to get off of his chest. She also noticed, out of the corner of her eye, that Flint had a hunting knife held against his leg, ready to strike the drunkard.

She stayed him by putting her free right hand over the Wererat's. "Something else, Mr. Johnson?"

"Yeah," he said. "Fort Branick has a lot of records on the higher-ups, personnel files and whatnot," he said, staring at her. His eyes cleared a little of the alcohol-induced fog, and she saw the man behind those eyes clearly for a moment. He had seen something, an event awful enough to make him abandon the path of the Knight. An event to make him take to drink, to help him forget. However, something of the Knight he'd been lingered, and she saw it there, just faintly, beneath the surface. "You may find more information about Reynaldi there, vital information," he said, letting go of her hand at last.

"Thank you again." She moved away from the booth and stalked over to Norman and Lee, who had already gotten themselves tipsy.

She grabbed Norman by the back of his tunic and hauled him up, setting him down roughly on the wooden floor. "Come on," she said, as Flint duplicated the maneuver on Lee. "We're leaving, right now."

The four of them made their way outside where they found Styge packing his tools away.

Stockholm was down on all fours, sniffing intently at the ground.

"Gentleman, make ready. We're going to start for Fort Branick, due east of here," she said.

"That's not where Fly and his troop went," Stockholm objected. "Their scents lead away to the south and east, to Fort Flag." He looked at Anna, who shook her head and started east, out of town.

"That doesn't matter, Stocky. Let the Midnight Suns flail and twitch in the wind. Reynaldi may have gone that way, but that won't be where the Paladin is heading. We'll find out where he's going, and then head there ourselves, because Mr. Johnson back there just told us everything we need to know."

She intended to go to Fort Branick and look through Reynaldi's records, find where his home was.

Instead of following the Paladin, they would head straight for his destination. *We may even be able to throw him a welcome home party*, she thought with a grin and a chuckle.

The company walked in relative silence, moving out of the village, across the river via one of the many large, stone bridges crafted by the mountain-dwelling Dwarves some hundreds of years ago. The plains and wooded areas this far north tended to be dangerous, and Anna chose, for once, to stick to the main trading routes that travelers kept to when traveling the lands. She didn't want to encounter the more hostile denizens of the night right now. They were going to have trouble enough when they got to Fort Branick.

By Lee's estimation, which Anna couldn't be certain she should trust, they had a day and a half's travel ahead of them at a moderate pace. If they hauled ass, he'd said earlier in the night, they could make it in less than a full day. However, it had been a good long time since Anna had been outside of Desanadron's walls, and walking out in the countryside felt good. The city, while it contained all of the life and business she could handle, just felt oppressive.

When she retired, she thought, she'd like to get a nice little place out in the middle of the plains or forests, settle in with Harold and be nice and cozy, away from the hustle and bustle of the big city.

At around four in the morning, she called the company to a halt after Norman complained for the umpteenth time about his feet hurting him.

"Your feet hurt because you spoil yourself with your trinkets, young man," Styge offered as they sat huddled around one another for warmth. No fire would be lit, Stockholm had said, at least not in the region they had passed into. Despite an Order of Oun Fort nearby, he had explained that the sparsely wooded area they were passing through was inhabited by madmen, Goblins, and Troke, the fiercest of the known sentient Races in Tamalaria. Made of a strange material, the Troke were a Race of shape-shifters, able to take on the appearance of any living or non-living thing they touched. But most Troke were still wild, primal beings that hunted small territories, claiming them as their own.

"They don't go down easy," Stockholm had said to the group as they settled in for the brief respite. "And it's even harder to keep them down." And so, they had abstained from lighting a fire, and Flint kept his cigarette cupped in his hands, to hide its glow. Norman agreed not to tinker with any of his equipment, because at a moment's notice, the company may have to move out if threatened. Nothing came at them when they got their things together and headed out again.

Anna wondered how long their luck could hold out. Travel in Tamalaria was uncertain at best, and even if one took the main roads. The dark of night brought creatures that had to be slain to be dealt with.

Yet they made it through to the morning hours, the sun coming up to warm them as its light wound its way through the woods and flatlands. The way had been largely easy to travel, but Anna saw now, as the sun illuminated their path, that easy travel was about to disappear. Huge stumps of trees long since cut pocked the ground, as did the corpses of animals, and some of men and women less fortunate than she.

She thought back on something Remy had once told her as she looked at the first of the crow-pecked bodies. 'The worst monsters in the world are the ones that don't go back into hiding when the sunlight strikes them.' *How very, very true*, she thought.

Flint, now up front with Stockholm, looked around the expanse of cleared woodland, listening to the surrounding area as his crimson companion sniffed the air deeply.

The rest of the company came up behind the two lycanthropes, now relying on their keen senses to scout around them for danger.

Flint knew that Stockholm would probably smell any danger before he heard it, but he still wanted to be helpful. Stockholm moved off a little to the south, leaving the company a good forty yards away. He stood there, sniffing the air, when Flint heard the first indication of trouble to the north of them. He turned his head sharply, keeping his left ear directly open in that direction, concentrating.

He couldn't make out the words, but he knew the sound of the language well enough. What were *they* doing this far north?

He turned back to face Anna squarely, and saw Styge muttering under his breath and making small and forceful hand gestures that made the sleeves of his robes billow and swish.

"What is it?" Anna's face twisted with worry.

"From the sound of it, it's Illeck. Dark Elves," he whispered. "I'm not familiar enough with the language to understand it, but I recognize it."

He turned to look for Stockholm, and his heart dropped when he didn't find the Red Tribe Werewolf standing where he had been only shortly before. "Where's Stockholm?"

"I saw him duck back into the wood line," Lee said.

Styge finished his incantations and the air fairly shimmered around the company.

"Nobody make a move, and try not to make a sound," he rasped at the company.

Flint understood what the old Illusionist was up to. He'd made them appear as natural formations in the environment, so that they would not be seen or heard by anyone outside of the company, or the spell's range of affect.

A surprised cry went up to the north, and four Illeck emerged from the underbrush, their eyes wide with disbelief. Their query had just, well, disappeared.

"Spread out, and find them," a voice shouted. Its owner stepped into Flint and Anna's view.

The man was garbed in strange, long purple robes, and on his head rested a sort of crown tinged with rust. Without doubt, the man's Race was Half-Elf. From the ashen cast of his skin, the Elven half was clearly Illeck.

Anna couldn't see his face, but his movements seemed jerky, random.

When he sauntered over to a corpse being claimed by a murder of crows, he shooed them away, and starting himself picking pieces of dead flesh from the body.

Well, she thought dismally, *we've found the first of the madmen.*

One of the scouting Illeck crept to within ten yards of the company. He stood there, staring right at them, yet not at them. He seemed to be focused on a spot some hundred or so yards behind the company, and Anna breathed a small sigh of relief as he turned and stalked away.

The Illeck didn't appear to be armed with anything more than some short swords, but she was sure that one or two of the marauding madmen would know some magic. Elven folk were naturally attuned to magic, after all. Insane or not, they'd know how to use a few choice spells.

After nearly a half an hour, while they stood about helplessly, tensely, the Illeck scouts all returned to their crowned leader, shaking their heads sadly.

Words were exchanged in the harsh, guttural language of the Dark Elves, and four of the five scouts turned on the fifth man, running him through from all sides.

As he lay bleeding on the woodland floor, their leader reached down, grabbing for the scout's face. Anna felt her throat fill with bile at the sound of the scout's screams as the mad Half-Elf plucked his eye out and bit into it. She held down the urge to vomit.

Norman, it turned out, wasn't so strong.

* * * *

Stockholm, it has already been noted, was much traveled across the continent of Tamalaria. He'd been across the Southern Blue and visited the continent of Tallowmere, returning with a head brimming with information, which he quickly recorded in a thick set of blank tomes he purchased in Desanadron. His trip had taken him away from the Hoods for a year and a half. Nobody currently in the Guild's employ knew about the tomes.

In that strange land, he'd learned to appreciate different religions, and so upon his return to Tamalaria, had devoted himself to re-learning the ways of the many official religions, cults, and sects of the lands. In Tallowmere, one's religion was one's life. The Red Tribe warrior had found this odd, but he didn't hold it against the peoples of Tamalaria—or that of Tallowmere. One's way of life should never be questioned too thoroughly, he'd thought. Best to live and let live. Perhaps, if he'd kept that in mind long ago, he wouldn't even be here.

In his studies of the cults that formed in the Third Age of Tamalaria, as recorded in the histories and cultural texts from the era, he had come across a particularly fascinating order. By outsiders, they were known as the Madmen of Maragshet. Study in Desanadron's largest library had revealed to Stockholm that the members of the order referred to themselves as The Blessed Children of Maragshet.

One of the only gods in Tamalaria's history to survive the constant shifts in philosophies and ideologies, Maragshet was recorded as a god of madness and chaos. The Red Tribesman had known about that all too well, even before reading the information in Tamalaria. Curiously, nobody in Tallowmere knew of the mad god.

Stockholm had gone far to the east, near Palen, where a well-known church had been erected by followers in the Fourth Age. The church had become a compound about fifteen miles due west of the city. The compound, at the top of a hill, was surrounded by marshland, difficult to traverse in the best of conditions. But traverse it he had, arriving at the gates of a very sturdy facility. He had been met by a wizened Human, who had told him that the Great Maragshet had told him of the Red Tribe warrior's coming.

"Your god gives you good foresight," Stockholm had said evenly to the elderly Human. The man cackled like a hyena, then performed three cartwheels back through the gate. He bade Stockholm follow him inside, which the Werewolf did.

Inside, he was given free access to the compound. Inside, he had observed many forms of madness, taking hold of every occupant therein. He had stayed for ten hours before he asked the elder to pardon him, he really must be going. As he'd left, the elder had pushed an ancient, leather-bound book on him.

Upon returning to the Guild, Stockholm had devoted two whole weeks to the study of the book. It had been penned in the blood of many creatures. Judging from the book's contents, this had been the journal of a man whose name had been Maragshet. The journal had started in the early years of the Second Age, and followed the man's journeys for several years, telling of the strange things he felt compelled to do.

Apparently, Stockholm had thought, sitting in front of the fireplace in his chambers beneath the city, the journal had fallen into someone's hands. Someone very impressionable, he thought. Maragshet's life and ways had been interpreted as holy writ, and now he was a god. Or at least, that would be how most interpreted what he read. He himself knew better.

Seeing the inside of the compound, Stockholm had seen many men wearing rusted, battered crowns. Through his research, he had learned that the Blessed Children of Maragshet organized themselves in small families, and the leader of such groups wore crowns to identify themselves.

When he'd seen the man with the crown from atop a tree some fifty yards away, he'd gone in search of the family's home—where they would keep a small altar in honor of their god.

He had found it only been ten minutes into Anna and the company's wait. The family home was a ramshackle building, made mostly of hardened mud and thatch. Inside, he found the altar.

It was a strange thing, in the shape of a two-headed turtle and a red herring, as were all of the cult's altars. This one had been made out of small pieces of kitchen utensils, and Stockholm knelt down before it. What he was preparing to do, he had only done twice in all of his long, long life, but everyone would be the better for it. He closed his eyes, concentrated, and called out to Maragshet.

The response was almost immediate.

He was baffled that any god would respond so quickly to his calling. As twice before when he'd performed this task, he found himself standing in a misty chamber with the god.

Maragshet appeared as a homely man, all rough scar tissue about the face and shoulders. His left arm hung all the way to the floor, hairy and muscular like a gorilla, while his right arm was of normal Human length. He was wrapped in a suit of bird feathers affixed to some sort of animal pelt, and he smelled of the fecal matter he'd used to paint arcane symbols on his forehead and the backs of his hands. On his head, he wore the hollowed skull of an ox.

"What brings you here, to me, outsider," the mad god asked, his eyes locking onto Stockholm's.

The Werewolf fumbled for the right words for a moment, baffled by the appearance of the mad god. After the initial hesitation, he knew exactly what he had to say.

"Great and mighty Maragshet, father of the Blessed Children, I come before thee truly as a mortal and an outsider." Stockholm bowed deeply. "I pray you forgive me. However, I must ask that you allow myself and my friends safe passage from your Children, lest we be forced to take up arms against them."

Maragshet rubbed his chin, apparently letting the Red Tribesman's words sink in and take hold.

"Many have taken up arms against my Children in the past, crimson wolf-man," the old, mad god said slowly. "My Children remain faithful, however rough the road gets."

"This is true," Stockholm said, folding his arms over his barrel chest. "In the Fourth Age, the last era before the Fall of Mecha, your followers were hunted down and slaughtered wholesale by the Order of Sergia. They formed in the Elven Kingdom, and saw your Children as a blight upon the lands. Thus, they sought to exterminate them. However," he said, really grabbing the mad god's attention now. "You told your Children to go into hiding, to worship you in smaller ways, in subtle ways. You told them to go happily into the asylums and madhouses, that they may be free to worship without restraint." Stockholm quoted one of the lecturers he had listened to in the compound outside of Palen so many years ago.

The mad god stared in wide-eyed shock at the Red Tribe Werewolf. Then, he smiled the smile of the truly benevolent and kind. "I wasn't always crazy, you know," he said in a soft, warming voice. He tilted his head to one side. "One day, I woke up, and there were these ideas in my head. Strange ideas, you understand? And I couldn't get the ideas to go away, until I did what they were suggesting. But, you have no time for this. I shall grant you and yours safe passage, and in return, you shall do something for me, crimson one."

Stockholm stood rigid, proud, and nodded his consent.

"On the fifteenth day of this upcoming month, you shall take a fish, and you shall beat it first upon a house of brick, and then upon a house of wood.

Then, you shall eat the fish, whole. Yes, that's it," the mad god said, his eyes spinning in opposite directions. Stockholm bowed low once more.

"It shall be done, Maragshet," he said, and stood from the altar back in the mortal realm. Without another word, he left the shack, heading back for his allies.

* * * *

As Norman Adwar thunderously lost his lunch, Styge's illusion failed.

The group found themselves exposed, and the Illeck all turned and stared at them, mad glee in their eyes.

Their crowned leader directed his gaze skyward. His lips were moving, but Anna couldn't make out what he was saying.

From the woods behind the mad Illeck, Stockholm strode like a man tempered of steel, his pace even, his eyes and jaw set in his face.

Before he came over to Anna and the rest of the company, he stood before the crowned Half-Elf, and whispered something into the man's ear.

There was a loud, harsh laugh from the man, and he barked an order to the others. They all shuffled away, seemingly no longer interested in them.

"What in all the Hells was that about," Flint screamed as Stockholm faced them, crossing his arms over his chest, his favorite posture. "We might have had to kill them, you know!"

Anna led the group over to the Red Tribesman, her eyes searching for any signs of injury on the big man. Where had he been?

"You might have, but you didn't." Stockholm slouched, suddenly very weary. "Now if you don't mind, I need a nap."

His body thumped the ground as he hit the dirt.

Anna had Flint tear the Chief's chain shirt off, and they searched his upper body for wounds, while Norman and Lee opened his eyes and checked for a reaction.

Nothing but the soft rise and fall of his chest indicated that he was still with them. Still, they found no injuries, and Anna decided that they would have to make do with that.

Several hours later, Stockholm awoke, and found that only Anna had remained awake to keep watch over the company.

Instead of growling that somebody else should have been awake to protect the company, he looked around the small clearing, and saw the Blessed Children of Maragshet standing about, keeping watch in all directions.

Anna roused the company was roused, and they left, continuing east between two of the Illeck, who gave them waist-level bows. Anna looked at her Chief, and once again wondered how many more secrets he had up his sleeves.

* * * *

The remainder of the company's trip to Fort Branick passed without incident, a point that warmed Anna's heart, but delivered them unexpectedly quickly to the area surrounding the Order of Oun Fort. The woodlands ended about a mile away from the Fort, which sat in a small valley depression, skirted on the north by a stream.

They had a clear approach from the west, but before they had covered a quarter of the distance, Norman spotted guards with the use of his binoculars.

They were patrolling the area, he said, and looked to be comprised of four man teams.

Norm withdrew a small gadget from one of the back compartments of his belt. He inserted the device into his ear, and attached a long piece of wire to it. From deep inside of his rucksack, the Gnome Engineer withdrew a circular dish device. He plugged the free end of his wire into the base of the device, and flipped a switch.

"No offense meant, Mr. Flint," he said with a lopsided grin. "But I think this baby will pick out their conversation at a better range than your ears alone."

Flint gave him a begrudging nod of approval.

Anna was about to ask Norm what the device was when he held up a hand to silence them all.

The rest of the company crouched low or lay on their backs up on the incline west of the Fort. The sun descended toward early evening, and Anna decided that playing things safe for now was the best approach. She was thankful she'd brought Norm along, since his technology gave them another much needed edge.

Norman adjusted a small dial on the base of the device, and listened intently through the static and the sounds of the natural world that his eavesdropping device picked up, trying to filter through the stuff he didn't need to hear. Finally, he had a snippet of conversation, and he carefully adjusted the dial down further. "No, I think we're stuck on patrol for another couple of hours," a gruff, Dwarven voice said through the static. "It's all right. I figure they'll give us something to do tomorrow, lads. No worries."

"That's what you said yesterday." The second voice was low and cumbersome, as though normal speech didn't come natural to its owner. Norm thought he could pick out the accent of a Jaft, though he couldn't be certain.

He picked up his binoculars, and confirmed his suspicion. Three men slowly made their rounds around the Fort, a Dwarf, a Jaft, and a tan-furred Werewolf. Norman set the binoculars down and listened in again.

"I don't know about you two," said the Werewolf. The voice was husky, but definitely female. "But I'm getting a little tired of my duty here. I was promised a post at Fort Peril in the east."

Peril, Norm thought. *That's up north of the Port of Arcade.*

"Oi, we were promised lots o' things, missy," the Dwarf said. "Especially better wages than we's makin' roit now. Just hang in there, we'll get what we were after soon enough. You think I wanted to come 'ere?"

The Jaft joined his slight chuckle, Norm noted.

"Nobody wants to come here," said the Jaft. "It's just one of the first places they stick you. Dat's what my cousin told me, couple of years back. There's worse places than this, believe it or not."

A loud harrumph of disbelief came through the earpiece, probably from the Tanner Werewolf.

"You don't believe me? There's this one Fort, really small place down in the south central plains, what's it called?"

"Oh, roit," replied the Dwarf. "Fort Waves. That was one of the first Order of Oun Forts, set up way back in the Third Age. Place is a total dump, but they still keep twenty or thirty guys hangin' about. You know, fer appearances and the loik."

"Why bother," asked the Werewolf, and Norm realized that the feed was getting quieter as the trio moved away from their position. He would have to adjust his instruments to keep up with them or let them go and try for another spot in or around the Fort to listen to.

Something about the three guards rubbed him a certain way, however. He had noticed the lack of enthusiasm, and the sarcasm from the Dwarf. He'd also noticed that none of the three sentries seemed concerned with the goings-on around the Fort itself.

"Anything," Flint asked, his rodent snout right up next to Norm's unoccupied ear.

Norm just shook his head. "Nothing useful at any rate." The Engineer pulled the device out of his ear and packed the whole assemblage away. He kept his voice down, in case the next patrol had better hearing than the previous one. "But if I had to guess from the flow of their conversation, and their tones of voice, nothing much is going on around here."

"There'd be some sort of hubbub if a big-shot like Reynaldi had come through," Flint sulked. "We've been had."

Lee Toren didn't show any signs of aggravation, but he seldom did, and was being paid by the day. The Wererat watched him pull out a small notepad and add up another day's expenses to the tab. Suddenly, he wanted to plunge the knife into the smug little Pickpocket. "How can you be so calm about this, Lee?"

"Look at your boss," was his only reply, and so Flint did.

Anna was already deep in conversation with Styge and a smile split her face almost from ear to ear. Flint felt relieved and confused. "Way I figure it, he's got something in mind."

"He always does," Flint said.

Anna thanked the Illusionist, and gathered the party together in a huddle. "What's the plan, Will?"

"Styge used Norm's binoculars while he was using that, well, no offense Norm, gizmo thing-a-majigger," Anna said.

Norm didn't seem offended at all, and Flint and Stockholm both sniggered at her choice of words.

"He saw that the most recent patrol included a Jaft, a Dwarf and a Tanner Werewolf. He's presented me with some options, though what he suggests is a tad dangerous."

"A tad." The old man coughed wretchedly. He took a moment to get his breath back, feeling the bite in his lungs from the serpent of illness he was certain would claim his life some day soon. "More dangerous than a tad young man. If my spells go poof, you'll be locked up pretty permanently. And it'll be three agents gone, just like that."

"So we need volunteers." Anna pretended to ignore the old man's warning. "Stocky, you'll have to be one. We're going to take that patrol's place inside the Fort, with a little help from Styge, and you'll be playing the Tanner. Shouldn't be hard."

"Except the Werewolf's a woman," Norm interjected.

Styge spat his pipe out from laughing so hard, and Lee had to put a cloth sack over his head to keep them all from being spotted by the currently passing patrol. They would surely have heard the old fool's laughter had Lee been a second or two slower to act.

When Styge stopped shaking, he removed the bag.

"Not a problem," said Stockholm. "Just change the color of my fur, blunt my snout a bit, and give me tits instead of pectorals. Shouldn't be hard to pull off, should it old timer?"

Styge managed to keep a straight face. "I'll have to reduce your visible height about half a foot, too. No worries there, Chief, I've done lots harder before. Now, who's going to be the Dwarf?"

"I'll do it," Lee said, to Flint's surprise. "Got to earn my pay, after all."

"Very good. Lastly, who's going to be the Jaft? It's not going to be easy to pull off, because I'm not very good with smells," Styge admitted. "Whoever goes as the Jaft will have to be quite adept at it."

"I'll do it," Flint said after a long silence. "Can't risk letting the boss man go in, and I can get myself out of any pinch. Any idea how long we'll have once we get inside?"

"Two or three hours at the outside," Norman said. "And you'll have to be very careful not to, ah, bump into yourselves outside the Fort," the Engineer added.

Styge prepared his spell, weaving his magic into his hands, and finally, carving through the air around the three volunteers to make them look, sound, and smell like the patrol that Norman had listened to. Styge had each of them speak, and Norm gave them pointers to help make the Illusionist spell take stronger hold.

After a few minutes' adjusting, they had their roles down.

Flint pulled a small, corked vial from a hip pouch, and poured the liquid inside over his, apparently blue and bald head. Styge and Norman both wrinkled their noses, and when the aroma hit Anna she nearly gagged. She saw that Stocky had clamped the end of his snout. "What is that stench," she asked.

"Sewage, from back home," Flint said with a wide grin. "I keeps a bit with me whenever I go topside, in case the police sick the dogs on me. Really messes with their heads."

Flint, Lee and Stockholm waited until the patrol went past, and then Norman gave them the go ahead signal. They were gone in an instant, and before the sun had set, they were inside the Fort.

* * * *

Thaddeus Fly's company had a full day's travel ahead of them before they got to Fort Flag.

Under Lain's guidance, Fly had arranged for Rage to approach the Fort, claiming to be recently abandoned by his tribe, and looking to make a new home and life for himself under a solid, trustworthy organization. The Order ate shit like that up, he'd said.

Rage had professed confusion, because his tribe hadn't abandoned him. Thankfully, Lain had managed to convince him that it was just what he had to tell the nice men at the Fort.

Markus Trent, Fly noted, had been in a bit of a funk since leaving Prek. The company hadn't encountered any hostiles on the road, and without anybody to do bodily harm to, the Human Ninja was starting to come undone.

Fly decided he'd better have a talk with him.

Walking at the front, as usual, Trent didn't try to hide his building sourness when Fly came up alongside him, leaving Akimaru at the rearguard position. "What do you want, Fly?"

"I want to know if you're going to do something stupid that we'll all regret when we get to Fort Flag," the Black Draconus retorted. "I know you want to do something a little more, active, but for now, we have to play things close to the vest. Remember, until we have to, we're not going to kill anyone."

"That's my problem," Trent grumbled. "Seems like there's nobody else on the roads these last few days, and according to your plan, we're going to be avoiding the Hoods. I don't like it, Fly," Trent said. "You don't hesitate like this when we're in the city."

"I know the city, Trent. That's why I operate well there." The grass underfoot had gone from soft and springy to brown, dried, and a little coarse. The region had been torn apart during the War of Vandross thirty years before, when the marauding armies of Richard Vandross had swept across the area from Fort Flag to Desanadron, waging war on both the outpost and the city. Life had a hard time clinging to the land here, and it awed Fly to think that anyone had attained the sort of power that the one-eyed warlock had. Then again, that very power had proved to be his downfall.

Too much ambition, Fly's sensei had said, leads to too much vulnerability. Keep your goals in sight, and your dreams as well. But never let either get bigger than yourself.

Fly decided that Trent was a lost cause, for now, and he'd have an easier time dealing with the moody, deranged Ninja when he found something to pierce with his daggers. The Black Draconus fell back into step with Akimaru, who gave him a slight bow. "Anything to report to me, Akimaru? Thoughts, or opinions?"

The white clad Ninja remained silent for a long while, and Fly thought that perhaps he simply hadn't heard the question. But in time, Akimaru answered.

"Sensei, when first I spied Markus Trent conversing with one of the tracker agents, I believed he meant to have us followed. Now, however, I am not so certain." His words came slowly, as if from another time and place entirely. "Also, when next we stop for rest, I must meditate. There is something I must see to."

Fly agreed to the meditation, but further inquiry about what was on Akimaru's mind resulted in silence.

* * * *

The trio returned around daylight, full of smiles. Stockholm handed Anna a thick brown folder, and she scanned the papers until she found what she needed. Archibald Reynaldi, Second Class Elite Paladin in the Order of Oun and ranked as a Free Commander, made his home in the richest district of Ja-Wen. The issue of Ja-Wen being clear across the continent didn't even get brought up as Anna gathered the company together, and informed them that they were heading back to Desanadron.

After perhaps a half an hour, Flint dropped back to join her, and asked why they were heading home.

"Simple, my mousy friend," she said. "We need long range transportation. There are a few people who can provide that for us, but one young Alchemist in particular. Lee knows him fairly well, as does Norman. We're going to Ja-Wen, and it's going to take us no time at all to get there, with young Mr. Staples' help."

The Glove of Shadows

Interlude

Corporal Trogum had joined the Order of Oun in order to secure himself a steady paycheck. As a Dwarf, he'd have the option of a pension plan after fifty years of service. Not bad, when he considered the unstable economic situation of his homeland in the southeast. He hadn't worried about seeing exotic locales, or serving the god Oun, or any of the other nonsense that hooked so many of the Order's young members. He just wanted to keep his head down, do his time, and pray that another war didn't spring up during his time in service.

Keeping his head down meant staying out of trouble, so he wasn't sure why he'd been called down to Commander Jorlof's office.

The Snow Tribe Werewolf, whose fur was whiter than paper, had a reputation as a fair and hospitable man, a Knight whose passion and faith in Oun put many Paladins to shame. But equally well known were his harsh ways of punishing those who broke the rules, and one was only called down to his office directly if they broke the rules. Trogum felt certain he hadn't broken any rules, so why was he here?

When at last he was admitted to the office, Commander Jorlof, one of the shortest Werewolves in Tamalaria, growled at him to sit.

The Commander ranted and raved about rules and regulations, proper protocols, the chain of command, and the chain of custody. He preached for nearly an hour the merits of keeping a tight ship, even if Fort Branick did seem a little dull to the younger recruits. Still, he concluded, it was no reason to pull the sort of prank that Trogum had.

When the Dwarf asked what prank he'd pulled, the Snow Tribe Werewolf had gone ballistic, throwing furniture around his office, clawing the desk immediately in front of the corporal, and foaming at the mouth. "What kind of prank? How dare you?" he'd fumed. "How dare you! But in the end, the Knight's ability to sense the truth ate its way through his tribe's natural tendency toward anger and violence. Trogum was in tears as he babbled.

"I swear, I don't know anything sir." He hid his proud, Dwarven face in his hands. Dwarves didn't cry, but few Dwarves encountered the fury of an enraged Snow Tribe Werewolf. Jorlof put an easy paw on the corporal's shoulder and apologized.

"Look, I'm sorry corporal. But the records keeper said you and the other two members of your patrol went down there, and signed out Lord Reynaldi's file without using your real names. I just thought you were being smart asses."

He produced the sign out sheet, and Trogum stared blankly at it.

"Um, sir? That's not my handwriting," he said. "And at the time the file was signed out, I can vouch for my whereabouts, as well as the others."

"Where were you," Jorlof asked, raising a bushy white eyebrow.

"We were still on patrol, sir. Um, sir? I think we've been robbed. Of a personnel file, sir."

And after Trogum left, Jorlof destroyed his office, his mind a blank fury at the slack incompetence that had permeated the Fort.

* * * *

The next day, further south and east, at Fort Flag, a big, lumbering Orc was allowed passage into the Fort's walls, where he was wrapped with fresh blankets and offered a hot meal. A priest of Oun offered him his prayers, and the Orc thanked him for his kindness—he was sure his tribe hadn't meant to be so mean, but sometimes they were like that. He sure didn't want any part of their war-like ways anymore, no sir.

The priest and the Knights and Paladins who met the big Orc smiled and nodded, each thinking to themselves, *well, he'll make a fine addition to the Fort.*

And he'd asked, very politely, if any of them had ever heard of a Paladin by the name of Reynaldi, and hey, wouldn't you know it, the big guy had just missed him by about three days. They gave him new clothes, fresh food, and a room to stay in, and by nightfall, nobody had any idea where the big Orc had gotten to. But there was an awfully big hole in one of the secret doors near the southern gates out of the Fort, and could somebody get down there to fix it?

The Glove of Shadows

Chapter Nine
Domestic and Non-Domestic Problems

Two days later, when Anna and her company returned to the northern gates of Desanadron, she knew instinctively there were problems. An intangible quality to the city stuck in her mind, and she knew that she'd have some business here, at home, to take care of.

That intuitive knowledge did nothing for her mood, and she brooded as she led her company down familiar streets and back alleys to a sewer grate. Once they were all down in the system of tunnels that would connect to their Guild hall, the idea struck as loudly as any thunderclap in her mind.

Upon entering the main meeting hall of the Guild, Stockholm took a good look around and wanted to scream. Agents were lazing about, thumbing through books at leisure, not having noticed who'd come back to the base.

Lee excused himself to use the nearest bathroom, and Norm asked for permission to head to his lab for a few last items. Anna granted him her approval, but warned him that they'd be in the city no longer than a day. She looked into Stockholm's face, and Flint's, and an unspoken message rang through all three minds—*it's time to clean house.*

Anna sauntered through the meeting hall, making certain to remain inconspicuous, while Flint nipped off toward the exercise rooms. Stockholm got himself right up behind Coates, who should have been in Stockholm's office, taking care of reports this early in the morning.

The Human Rogue was laying on one of the couches, a magazine over his face, and Stockholm had no trouble getting himself set low to the floor, grabbing the underside of the couch.

Anna watched as he let out a horrifying, primal roar and flipped the couch over, spilling Coates to the floor and sending the couch crashing against a far wall. Anna slipped out of the meeting hall, toward her office, as the interrogation began.

"Fargan ooshka magento," Stockholm raged in his Race's tongue. It was a well known phrase around the Hoods, one he reserved for the agents who really deserved to have their hides tanned, and it translated roughly to 'What the piss, boy?'

Coates stared in wide-eyed horror up at the red menace, soiling himself as he scrambled to get to his feet.

"Stockholm, Chief, sir," he stammered, finally realizing that he'd pissed his pants. "Um, you have the advantage of me, sir." He tried to smile and be smooth.

Stockholm hauled the con-man up by the front of his overcoat, his eyes aglow with fury and his lips pulling taut over his lupine teeth.

"Don't try any of your smooth talk bullshit with me, boy." He pressed his forehead against Coates' face, so they were eye to eye. "You're not taking reports, and there's an awful lot of agents emptying this hall right now, which means they aren't out there earning their keep. What's wrong with this picture, Coates?" Stockholm hurled the Rogue to the floor, bruising the man's back quickly.

Coates moaned and tried to squirm away, but Stockholm grabbed him by the ankle, and held him aloft.

"Please, sir. Please! I just, I didn't know there was so much to your job, and I know you do a lot above and beyond what's needed, and the stress just got to me sir, I needed to relax, sir."

Stockholm wouldn't hear these pathetic excuses.

"We weren't gone but a week, at the most, and this is what happens? You are sorely in need of a large amount of moti-fucking-vation, boy! What is the title you were entrusted with?"

"Guild Chief, sir," Coates squeaked, hoping to come away from this with his body intact.

"And what is the Chief's primary function?" Stockholm shouted. Ah, he thought as he bellowed, it's good to be home.

"To ensure the continuous training and operation of field agents, and record all progress and mission status, sir."

"That's right, that's right. Very good, Coates." Stockholm dropped the con-man roughly to the floor. The Red Tribe Werewolf looked around at the few stragglers who were watching in awe and terror. He spotted one of the Hoods' regular troublemakers, and decided to show just how angry he was with Coates, by being kind to the young Gnome thief. "Jerry, get this man a gold fucking star," he shouted, and the Gnome took to his feet almost as fast as Lee Toren.

Stockholm turned, and loomed over Coates like Death wrapped in crimson fur. "We're not going to be home for long, but let me make something plain." He growled, crouching down so that his face appeared upside down in front of Coates' eyes, then smiled hugely, revealing all of his teeth. "If we come back, and I find you've been dicking off at my post, I will not hesitate for a moment to bury you, boy. I will use my claws to rend you apart, and then I will take the biggest axe in my collection, and I will ass rape you with it until you bleed out. Do I make myself perfectly clear?"

His teeth were less than an inch from Coates' nose.

The con-man nodded, and passed out from the fear.

"Excellent. I'll hold you to that," Stockholm said to the limp, unconscious form.

Yessir, he thought, good to be home.

* * * *

As Anna approached her office, she heard Borshev's deep, rumbling voice as he hollered himself hoarse. Somebody had apparently gotten on his shit list, Anna thought, and she would like to see whom.

The rough concrete walls of the hallways felt good under her fingertips as she walked along, her hand out to her side. The city really was the place for her, she realized. Even her brief time out in the plains and woodlands had been uncomfortable, the grass and soil beneath her boots giving her a sense of being an outsider on foreign territory. She supposed, however, that if she ever really intended to move out into the wilds with Harold that she had better get used to the discomfort. The open sun on her face, she mused, had felt refreshing. Operating almost solely in the darkness of night wore on a person's psyche after a while.

The door of her office flung open, and the brawny Minotaur manhandled a Wererat out of the office, his hands on the agent's collar and the hem of his pants. With a single heave and grunt, he hurled the Wererat down the tunnel opposite Anna.

She recognized the Wererat when she got a moment's look at his profile—the agent typically served as barkeep. Borshev rubbed his hands together, ridding himself of whatever issue he'd just dealt with.

"Might I ask what that was all about?" she asked.

The Minotaur whirled around, and his face registered open shock.

"Headmaster! I, I was just," he stammered, and she waved him off good-naturedly. "I'm sorry, sir. Things haven't been going so well. I ordered Sean to shut down the barroom until further notice, sir."

Anna motioned him into her office, and he immediately seated himself in the guest chair.

Anna took her old, comfortable chair, and leaned back, putting her feet up on the desk. The few papers on its surface appeared to be in order, she noted, but she didn't see Coates' signature on any of them. *Hollister has apparently been doing his own job, and the Human's as well.*

"Any reason you decided to do that?" She pulled a cigar from her top desk drawer, clipped the end off, and lit it with a match from the same drawer, striking it off of her belt buckle.

Borshev shook his head miserably, his eyes alight with fire.

"Because, sir, nobody's taking their tasks seriously," he rumbled. "We've got agents lounging about, drinking themselves into oblivion. Coates hasn't sent me a single report since you left, William. He shrugs his duties off onto Hollister, or myself. If I don't help the mutant," he said, referring to the Sidalis, Hollister. "He's going to crack under all of the pressure."

"So what exactly has Coates been doing with himself at night?" She blew out a huge cloud of bluish smoke. The air was heavy with it now, and Borshev gave a small cough before replying.

"He's been going into town and hunting the red light districts." The Minotaur spat on the floor, making a face at the thought of it. "And when he returns, with less money on him than when he departed, I know what he's been up to. The biggest problem, as I see it, is that he hasn't run out of money." He put up a hand to stop Anna's obvious line of questioning. "I've already had an audit performed on the treasury. He isn't dipping in for extra."

Anna nodded, her unspoken concern waylaid.

"So, Borshev, what do you suggest be done about him? What would you like to happen? Don't forget, when we head out again tomorrow, you're in charge here. I have entrusted you with not only the acting title, and all of the responsibilities it entails, but all of the authority and privileges as well. Use them efficiently." She stubbed out her cigar and picking up a report. Hollister's fine handwriting was neat, well organized, and concise. She didn't immediately dismiss Borshev, and the big Minotaur was now up and pacing back and forth on the other side of the desk.

Hollister had put together a summary of the first night's missions, the earnings, and had assembled an entire page in the report on individual agents' observations. *The turtle-like mutant seemed to have a knack for this sort of thing. Perhaps,* she mused, *when we come back for good, I'll assign him to Stocky as an assistant. Might take some of the load off the old boy.*

"Borshev?"

"Yes sir," he said, coming to full attention.

"When you see Coates, inform him that he is relieved of his report duties for the interim," she said, setting the reports in a single pile and tucking them under her arm as she got up and slipped around the Minotaur. "And tell him that all of the labor duties on Hollister's list are to be placed on his own."

"Um, with all due respect, sir," Borshev said, rubbing the back of his head awkwardly. "One of those duties is stocking the weapons room, and Hollister is suitable to it because of his strength. It'd take Coates hours to get it done." His eyes widened with revelation as the Headmaster's tactics finally made themselves clear to him. "Oh, right. Riiiight." He gave the thumb's up. But when he turned to give the sign to his Headmaster, William Deus was already gone.

He took a seat where Anna had been a few moments before, and leaned back, putting his big feet up on the desk as she had. Before he got back to his business, he wondered for a moment if William would mind if he took a cigar.

* * * *

"Wot the bloody blue fuck do you mean 'no booze'," Lee Toren growled at Sean Mackey. The Wererat tended bar during the daylight hours, and robbed the taverns topside during the night, until he had enough money and booze in his Void Bag to stock them for another week or so. He had three Void Bags in the stockroom, filled with barrels and bottles of the finest ales and wines the city above had to offer, and he felt it was a shame he couldn't do anything with it. At the moment, so did Lee.

"I mean, I have orders not to serve any alcohol at this time, Mr. Toren. Sorry." The Wererat wiped down a glass with a clean rag.

Habits form quickly, he thought. In every world, in every reality across the vast expanse of 'WHAT IS', every bartender can be found cleaning out a mug or glass of some sort with a rag. It just happens, and no mortal person is really sure why. "But Borshev says if I serve even one beer, he's going to rip off my genitals and force feed them to me."

Lee made a face, and got down off of his stool.

"Just great," he grumbled to no one in particular. "I'm going to have ta go topside and pay fer a drink. Wot's this world coming to?"

Lee Toren didn't think of himself as a cheapskate. He thought of himself as a man who could find anything he wanted for free, or for a reasonable trade. Reasonable, of course, meaning that he would swindle people into giving him things simply for his time and effort. In his own mind, his time was more valuable than gold, so trading his time to someone should yield him something.

When he'd brought William Deus news of the Glove of Shadows, he'd felt almost obligated to tag along. Now, he was tallying up the days as they passed, and the efforts he'd had to put in to their overall objective. Sneaking into Fort Branick had been a tremendous risk for him, and that alone added another one hundred gold pieces to William's bill.

As he climbed an access ladder up to the streets of Desanadron, he readied himself to add the drinks he'd partake of to the bill. However, as he set the grate back into position and was about to take out his notepad to check the running total, he felt a disturbing and familiar presence behind him.

When he turned around, he saw a man he had hoped to never see again.

"Fancy meeting you here, Lee Toren," said the man with the glimmering steel teeth.

* * * *

Flint had never seen his office so organized and clean, and he just stood in his doorway, staring. "Um, sir," Hollister tried to gain his attention yet again, finally succeeding. "Is there a problem, sir?" The Sidalis's huge, limpid black eyes shimmered with concern.

"Oh, no, no problems." The Wererat lit a cigarette. He scanned the top of his desk. "Where's my ashtray?"

"Oh, I cleaned it out, sir. It's over there, sir." Hollister pointed to one of the many previously disused shelves along the walls. "I don't partake myself, sir, so I set it over there for safe-keeping."

Flint grinned gently, impressed by the mutant's attention to detail and his apparently sound mindset.

When Flint had first opened the door, Hollister had been writing a report, which he now continued to scratch out in his fine, neat cursive writing. Reports weren't exactly Flint's forte, and he realized that Hollister probably should have been given the temporary post of Chief, not Prime. Of course, that would have made Coates the Prime, and from what Stockholm had told him, that just couldn't be allowed to happen. Ever.

"Hollister?"

"Yes sir?" Hollister adjusted the giant shell on his back. He set his quill down for a moment, folding his hands in front of him.

"You know, Stockholm and I are impressed with the work you've been doing while we've been gone. The Headmaster too." He exhaled a cloud of smoke through his nostrils.

"Thank you, sir," Hollister said with a shy smile.

"When we leave, keep up the good work. You'll note that we've given your labor duties to Coates, and you'll be taking his report duties. If you don't mind," Flint added, because Anna had made it clear to him that if Hollister didn't want the extra paperwork, he shouldn't be forced to do it. But he was damned good at it, she'd said.

Thankfully, he saw the shy smile widen into a genuine grin of bemusement.

"I don't mind at all sir! Anything to help out," the Sidalis said. "Um, how long are you back for, sir?"

"Just a day's time." Flint found his Pockchi game board assembled neatly on another of the shelves. The two decks of playing cards, the dice, and all of the pieces had been placed into wooden containers, and were set on top of the board itself, ready to take down and play at any time. It had been a long time since he'd played Pockchi, and the last time he had, Stockholm had trounced him with a handful of crap cards and a trunk-load of strategy. Even with his loaded dice, the Guild Prime had been bested. He shook his head and smiled ruefully, taking the board down and packing the game into his travel bag. "Why do you ask?"

"Well, sir, I was wondering if you could grant me a couple of hours' leave," Hollister said. "I'd like to head down to the gym, to use the pool."

Ah, yes, Flint thought. Hollister had to spend a certain amount of time immersed in water every few days in order to retain his full mental capacity. While not the most dangerous man in the Hoods, the mutant could get wily and combative if his mind slipped.

"Granted," Flint said without hesitation. "Go on out now, so's you can get back to work."

The Sidalis thanked him, and slipped out of the office, away and up into the city above. Flint looked around his office, and silently wondered how long he could keep it nice and organized like this. "I give it a month," he whispered to himself, starting to catch up on recent events.

* * * *

Striker, Lee Toren thought with mute horror. He'd met the man once, and had cleaned out his pockets and pouches. The man had noticed only a few minutes later, and had chased the Pickpocket out of Desanadron and into the flatlands west, following his trail almost all the way to the coast.

There, Lee had taken a passenger ship to Rest Island, a small island ten miles off the western coast of the continent. Decades before, Elves had traveled to the land and settled in, setting up a vacation resort for the more affluent members of the Elven Kingdom. It was rumored to hold a fallback compound if the capital of Whitewood ever came under massive assault again, as it had thirty years before.

Now, in a shadowed alley of Desanadron, the Gnome Pickpocket was face to face with the relentless assassin once again.

His left hand slowly reached back for one of his long knives, but Striker lashed out with a well-aimed kick, hitting Lee just above the elbow and knocking him hard into the wall of an apartment building on one side of the alley.

"Now, now, now, let's not be stupid," Striker sneered.

Lee didn't remember the man being so tall, but he eclipsed the little sunlight that filtered into the alley. Lee took a tentative step backward, toward the street, holding his injured left arm. No break in the bones, he thought, but gods it hurt!

"I don't mean to hurt you, little man, not unless you force my hand, or foot," Striker said with a snicker. "I just want what's due to me." Striker halted his advance and held out one gnarled, stained hand.

Lee looked at the outstretched hand, taking in the dirt and grime, the absence of fingerprints on the tips of his bare digits. Striker wore black leather gloves, with the fingers cut off, in order to keep his ability to grip and grab people and things.

Well, all things considered, he thought, *I'm getting off easy here.* Lee undid the strings of two of his money pouches, and dropped them in Striker's hand. The man with the steel teeth counted the money silently as Lee set his feet to carry him away from further confrontation.

"It's all there, every gold piece accounted for, mate." Lee flexed his left hand. The feeling had returned, and his flesh felt like it was on fire.

"As fer the jewels, well, I've pawned them, so that's why there's a bit extra in that gold."

Striker smiled again, that wide, glinting smile that reminded Lee of Death himself.

"This'll do, for now, Gnome." Striker adjusted the bandana tied over his blond hair, and stood up straight. "Didn't think I'd see you again so soon. Thought you and your little friends had gone on a little journey."

"Just stopped in to use the bathroom," Lee said with a fair amount of sarcasm. "You know me—bladder like a walnut."

"I know," Striker said, taking a step away from Lee. "That's how I tracked you to the coast, little man. Good of you to repay your debts, I must say." Striker turned his back on Lee. "I'll see you again, sneak thief," he growled, and leaped clear from the alley floor to the roof of the apartment building, a good four stories up.

Lee's heart lurched, and he worried that he would indeed see the creature called Striker again. And the next time he did, he wouldn't owe the man anything like money.

He'd probably owe him blood, by the gallons.

* * * *

Far to the east, Thaddeus Fly and his Midnight Suns walked along the Snake River's southern banks, making their way further east. Trent had found signs of Reynaldi's passage, tracks that were perhaps already a week old. The company had made good time, only having to stop to rest after dispatching a band of Lizardman highwaymen who'd asked them to pay a toll to travel the road they were on.

Markus Trent seemed much the better for the bloodbath, Fly thought, and Rage had performed spectacularly. Fly, Akimaru and Lain had simply stood back and let the Human Ninja and the Orc Berserker trample all over the six robbers, moving like a streak of lightning and an unstoppable boulder through them.

Now, four hours after that incident, Fly wondered at the wisdom of his current course of action. They would follow Reynaldi's trail, hoping to catch him out in the plains, the woodlands, or some foothills. Anywhere other than another Fort or a major city would be fortunate for them, but he had the sinking suspicion that when they did catch the Paladin, he'd be behind stone walls and have a large number of friends with him, ready to fight.

Unbidden, a familiar voice, cutting through the rest of his mental clutter. *They're back in the city*, whispered Mr. Striker's cold, steely voice.

Fly had left him a communication sutra, in case there were troubles back home and he needed council. He hadn't expected to hear from the man, but now, here he was, days and days away from Desanadron, and Striker was contacting him.

Who's back in the city, he thought, focusing on the mental image of Striker.

Deus and his lot. I had the good fortune to run into Lee Toren, Striker called through the sutra scroll. *He was good enough to repay me for our previous encounter.* Fly heard the intended chuckle, though it didn't surface into Striker's mind.

Why would they be back? Did he tell you?

No. He was a smart-ass, of course. Said they'd stopped in to use the bathroom.

Fly had to suppress a little laugh at this. While he loathed Lee Toren, he had to admit that he was quick of wit.

What do you want me to do about them?

For now, nothing, Fly thought in response. Keep me apprised of the situation, though. If there's any major trouble, I can make my way back easily enough.

Understood, sir. And then, Fly found his mind cleared, the connection broken. He looked around at the others of his company, all of whom were staring at him like he had three heads. "What," he said.

"Nothing, Headmaster." Trent smirked. "It's just that you stopped walking and started sort of twitching about with your head, like an epileptic. Sir," he added, as an afterthought.

"I'm fine, Trent," Fly spat. "I left Striker a communication sutra. He was just reporting in."

"Anything we should know about?" Lain looked at him suspiciously, as she always did whenever someone had a talk with Mr. Striker. She'd met the man three times in her entire membership to the Midnight Suns, and she'd never told anyone about her meetings with him. Fly assumed the man had given her the willies, but she never said. She just seemed fascinated by Mr. Striker, and took every opportunity to learn more about the man.

"Nothing major," Fly lied. As lies went, it wasn't very convincing, but nobody argued the point and he soon had them moving once again. He marched behind Trent, side by side with Akimaru once again. The grass felt good underfoot, the soil slightly spongier here than it was further to the north or south. The ground soaked up a good deal of moisture from the wide Snake River, and here and there, wild berries dotted the bushes that grew along the river. Fly watched with detached disinterest as Akimaru picked a handful of the fruit, stashing the berries away in a leather pouch. He looked back over his shoulder, and saw Rage eating large fistfuls of them, their juices smeared over his cheeks and chin.

What a savage, he thought. *Then again, that's why we have him along, isn't it?*

"Sensei," Akimaru whispered in his ear.

"Hm?"

"Sensei, I sense trouble ahead, on this road. I know not exactly what kind, but I know it is something dangerous."

Fly nodded, and called Trent back, bringing the company to a halt. He looked off down the road they traveled, noting the way it bent around and out of sight around a nearby set of foothills that flanked them on the south.

"Trent, we need you to scout ahead." Fly pointed to where they lost sight of the tracks. "Akimaru senses danger. Head into the foothills and see what lies ahead of us. The rest of us will remain here and rest up. Report back as soon as you know what we're up against. We'll plan our next move from there."

Trent grunted disapprovingly, but moved off at a trot anyway, leaving Thaddeus Fly and the rest of the Suns behind.

The Human Ninja had reveled in the bloodshed only a few hours before, stabbing, slashing and tearing into the Lizardmen with deadly grace and precision. He had rejoiced in the slaughter, but now he found himself bored again. In a way, he hoped there really was danger ahead, perhaps a more worthy set of opponents. The reptile warriors had posed no threat, as he and Rage had been plenty to deal with them. He wondered, briefly as he made his way up a path on the hillside, how it made Fly feel to see other reptile men cut down. He hoped it made the Headmaster cringe, because once again, he was reminded of the deep, boiling urge in his blood to kill the Black Draconus.

Trent made his way over rock outcroppings as he rose in elevation, climbing easily up the hillside. When he came around a group of scattered bushes, he immediately crouched, his eyes falling on the threat that Akimaru had perceived. Below, perhaps one hundred yards around the turn in the path, a scene of carnage was laid out. The savaged bodies of six or seven people, half of them heavily armored Dwarves, the others Minotaurs, lay strewn about. Thanks to his angle and his keen eyesight, he saw that they had been mauled to death by the three black, lumbering forms that presently tore at their armor and weapons.

Trent searched his memory for the name of the beasts. Large, heavily muscled bodies, appearing much like a panther's, sat hunched forward, tearing with claws and teeth at the armor. Where their hindquarters split off were six slick and scaled tentacles. Down their broad, black furred backs, a set of spiny spikes stood on end. Seeing them, he remembered their names. Thresherbeasts, monsters that came from rivers and streams that feed on metal.

He watched with a blend of terror and fascination as the thresherbeasts tore into the armor, biting into it and purring loudly as they chewed it with ease. Just three of the creatures had murdered both Dwarves and Minotaurs, all of them heavily decked out for combat.

Trent made his way swiftly back to the company, and reported. The river did not bend with the road, continuing on east, and he wondered if Fly would suggest they take to the other side of the river and continue on. But Reynaldi's tracks led right through the thresherbeasts. Avoiding the monsters might take longer than simply dealing with them—if they could.

"How many of the beasts are there?" Fly asked.

Trent reminded him that there were three, and they appeared to be larger members of their freakish species.

"Hmm. Suggestions?"

Nobody said anything at first. When Rage opened his mouth to speak, Fly regretted ever having asked.

"We could just go and kill them," the Orc said flatly. This was met with a groan of disapproval from everybody else, and he hung his head. "Just sayin'," he grumbled.

"Markus," Lain said, her hand on her chin, thinking the situation over. "How freshly dead are the men? The Dwarves and Minotaurs?"

"No more than a half an hour, at the most."

Fly knew right away where her question was aimed, and he nodded his approval before she even asked.

"Do it," he said. "Trent, take Ms. McNealy up to the spot you spied them from. She'll handle things nicely for us. Akimaru, Rage, we're going to head forward, to the corner turn in the path, and wait in case any of the thresherbeasts attempt to escape back into the river. If they try, we'll finish them off."

Rage smiled and nodded an exaggerated yes, yes.

"Very good. Let's do it, people!" Fly felt excited, like he always did when he had a good plan of attack laid out before him. Lain would raise the bodies of the Dwarves and Minotaurs, and set them on the monsters from the river.

Supernatural or no, the creatures were flesh and blood. Being set upon by zombies would not be their idea of a good time. Hopefully, they wouldn't have eaten the weapons yet, and the undead servants would kill one or two of them, certainly injure them all enough that when they attempted to flee to the river, Akimaru, Rage and himself would be more than capable of finishing them off.

Besides, he thought. Thresherbeast teeth sold for a high price in the right markets. A little exercise and a healthy profit, and this day will go down as a good one.

* * * *

Lee Toren darted looks over his shoulder as he sat in the Flaming Tongue tavern, expecting with each glance to find Striker looming over him like the angel of death. But he never spotted him, and by the time he was on his fifth drink of the hour, his recollection of the encounter was blissfully foggy. "Oi, Harry," he called, gaining the barkeep's attention. "Another mead, if you please."

The pudgy barkeep handed him another bottle, and Lee took it, slipping down off of his barstool. He made his way staggeringly over to men's room, making use of the facilities before he had his last drink of the early afternoon.

He quickly quaffed his mead and made his way out to the streets of the city. Lee wondered how long this job would take, and if it would be worth it in the end. He'd receive a king's ransom in wages from the Hoods, but he could be out there, among the citizens of the city, cleaning people's pockets for them with a smile and a joke while they turned away from him. He could easily make the money doing what he did best, but for some reason, he felt compelled to help William Deus. He guessed something about the Rogue's sense of honor reminded him, abstractly, of Byron Aixler. The Paladin had given him many tasks over the years, and he'd performed his duties quickly and efficiently.

Perhaps, he mused drunkenly, he just needed a break from the randomness of his life, and Will's gang footed the bill nicely. "Yes, that's it exactly," he said aloud, belching mightily.

A few ladies across the street gave him disgusted glares before moving on.

Lee grunted at them in return, but they had already turned away, shuffling daintily down the street.

Something in the way the Human women carried themselves reminded him of William Deus, though he couldn't for the life of him tell why. He let the idea sizzle and disappear into the alcoholic haze of his mind, and soon enough, he was back in the Hoods' meeting hall, asleep on one of their couches.

Striker never showed himself while he was out, after that initial encounter.

Neither had the tracking agent, but that didn't stop her from seeing him.

Chapter Ten
I Remember

Teresa Evergreen enjoyed her work. As a tracking agent in the Midnight Suns, she kept her head low, her nose clean, and had avoided promotion and singling out by being as invisible inside the Guild as she was to the rest of the world. It was her gift and her power.

As an Illeck, it wasn't a natural ability, but it was an ancient magic she had focused on and studied for years. It let her slip, unnoticed, through some tough spots.

It wasn't just that she could make herself invisible to the naked eye. That wouldn't have been much use, as lycanthropes in the police forces could have just sniffed her out. No, she had studied the magic and learned how to erase every sensory trace of her presence. No scent, no visible trace, and she made no noise when she focused. Only one other member of the Guild knew this—her lover, Markus Trent.

He had sent for her just before he departed with the Headmaster. "Keep an eye on Lee Toren," he had asked her. "And if you get the chance, keep an eye on Striker, too. But the Gnome is your primary target."

"Why," she asked.

"Because, if he and the Hoods get to the Glove of Shadows before we do, he'll inevitably take it for himself. He's good, Teresa. I don't doubt he could spirit it away right from under William Deus's nose if he wanted, and if he does, you'll be there to take it from him."

"Do you want me to hurt him at all, love?" She had blinked at him in that puppy-dog way she used to lure him to her bed. This time, she noticed, it didn't faze him.

"No," he'd said. "Just keep watch." And that had been that, she thought. Now, she watched Striker make his way from rooftop to rooftop across the city, back toward the Guild.

Instead of following him, she kept up with Lee Toren for a while, following him to the Flaming Tongue, where he got himself stupidly drunk.

So stupidly, she mused, that he led her right to the Hoods' home base.

The Headmaster knew the Hoods dwelled in the sewers, but he did not know the exact location.

Now, Teresa Evergreen memorized the route, and watched with detached interest as the Gnome Pickpocket fell asleep on a couch in some sort of main meeting den. She made her way out of the room, down a side corridor lined with Hoods agents swapping notes and stories, to a single, empty chamber.

The room was huge, expansive in a way she could never hope her own assigned room to be. It was well organized as well, with racks of weapons on the far wall, sets of bookshelves lined with historical texts and a few fiction novels, popular back when she'd been a gel. Curiously, she saw no bed in the room, just a dog bed by a cold fireplace. When she saw the red fur matted to it, she knew whose room she was in, and her heart nearly exploded. She had to get out of there, immediately.

Ducking back out into the hall as fast as she could, she lost a little of her focus, and the door banged shut behind her loudly. The sound echoed down the hall, but happily, nobody seemed to notice. She made her way back to the den, and from there back to the surface of the city.

She remembered her only meeting with Ignatious Stockholm and the hot, flushed feeling she got when he had pressed her by the throat against a brick building. He had such power, such raw ability, and it drove her to the edge of lust. She had only escaped with her life because he'd been disgusted by her sexual requests and he'd dropped her to the ground roughly, stalking away.

She remembered his power, and wondered if he was around, since Lee Toren was back in town. But her sense of duty to Trent kicked the thought aside, and she made her way, unnoticed by anyone, back to her own Guildhall. Time to check on Mr. Striker, though she would never probably learn much about him.

* * * *

Flint read through the last of Hollister's reports while Anna sat across from him, in his office for once, reading through the first one he'd handed her. He remembered a time when this was how they'd sat, he in the seat of authority, and she on the other side of the desk, a mere peon. Just another agent, he thought. It seemed so long ago. How much longer would he remain with the Hoods? Another two, three years maybe? But he'd thought this exact same response three years before, and yet, here he sat, Prime of the Hoods.

How long would *she* stick around, for that matter? He couldn't be certain, but he recalled the confused, boyish look she'd given him back when she'd first joined the Guild. He'd mistaken her for a teenage boy, and this idea wouldn't change for several years yet. He thought back to that first introduction.

"Hail and well met, Prime Flint. My name is William Deus," she'd said.

"Hail and well met, agent Deus. I'm told this is your first actual day with us." *Too young*, he'd thought then. *Just a boy.* "Well, have you met our Chief yet?" Anna's smile had disappeared, but she'd nodded. "Don't be too troubled, everyone finds him terrifying when they first get here. You'll warm up to him soon enough, lad." He'd given Anna a light slap on the back, leading her down to the common agents' quarters. After he'd knocked on the door, he remembered, Gladys Rim had opened it, giving him a big middle finger when she did. Gladys was a female Wererat, and felt the post of Prime belonged to her more than her male counterpart. Flint had smiled coldly at her. "Gladys Rim, meet your new roommate, William Deus. I know, it's not fair, being roomed with a young man, but yours is the only room right now with a free bed, so tough shit."

With a shove, he'd propelled Anna into the dingy chamber.

He'd left her there, making his way to Stockholm's office to register William Deus as Rim's roommate. When he'd entered, Remy was sitting with the Werewolf, and he peered at Flint with those piercing, ocean colored eyes. "Flint, what is it?"

He remembered Remy fondly as he sat with the last of Hollister's reports in front of him. A man of integrity, Remy never kept more than his share of the hoard. He gave some of his earnings to other agents when they needed it, especially the ladies of the Guild who found themselves with child. However, in Remy's days as Headmaster, after a female agent gave birth, she was expected to remain above ground with her family. She would essentially be discharged until the child was at least two years of age. Most of the women didn't return. Gladys Rim had been a member of the minority.

"I'm just here to register Deus as Rim's roomy, boss man."

Stockholm shook his big, shaggy head. "What's the matter? Sure, he's a lad, but he's a young lad at best. Surely he isn't going to mind bunking with her?"

"Sorry, Flint," Remy said. "I've seen the Deus boy in action, and he doesn't belong with the common rabble. We're putting Chambers with Gladys, moving William to her room immediately. You'd better go fetch him."

Flint had done as he was asked, and Anna, confused and a little bewildered, had been shuffled along like a leaf on the wind. When Flint had unlocked Chambers' former abode, he'd growled at Anna.

"What's wrong, sir? Did I do something wrong," Anna asked, cringing away from the Wererat.

"Boss man's already taken a liking to you, boy," he'd snarled. "Takes a lot to impress the head honcho 'round here, lot more to impress me. Watch your step, William Deus." Flint had pressed the tip of one of his hunting knives against Anna's stomach, just enough to let her know it was there. She hadn't even seen him draw the weapon, and he'd seen fear in those big, feminine eyes. "I don't take with anyone who doesn't pay their dues."

Flint came hurtling back to the present when Anna wrapped him on the head with the finished report. "I said, next one, Flint." She laughed at him as he shook off his nostalgia. "What's got you all distracted?"

"Sorry, Anna," he said. "I was just remembering the first time I met you."

She gave him a brief smile.

"Suppose I should apologize for the whole threatening to kill you thing, eh?"

"Think nothing of it, my mousy friend." She opened Hollister's second report as Flint handed it to her.

"Do you remember what it was like, for you?" She looked up from the folder, and looked off into the upper corner of the room, thinking back.

"Oh yeah, I remember."

* * * *

"Who's been in here," Stockholm whispered to himself as he stepped across the threshold of his chamber. He could sense that the room had been disturbed, but he finally chalked it up to Coates having used his room in his absence. He changed shape, moving over to the dog bed and lying down for a brief nap. He fell almost immediately asleep, and he dreamed. He dreamed of times gone by, and nightmares conquered.

Ignatious Stockholm stood on the corner of Fifth Street and Broadsword Lane, in the city of Shengone. His deep blue officer's uniform fit snugly over his rippled muscles, the cloth creaking threateningly whenever he crossed his arms over his chest in his trademark posture. The badge over his left breast pocket glimmered in the noon sun, and he waited patiently for somebody to do something stupid. Automobiles sped past on the pavement, and the city's populace milled about, going about its daily routine, but nobody nearby seemed eager to try anything illegal. It looked like it was going to be another boring day on the beat.

Stockholm reached back over his shoulder, thwacked the edge of his war axe, and listened to its deep vibration. He checked his belt for the hundredth time, making certain they hadn't mixed up his custom built revolver for a standard issue, as they had many times before. *But no*, he thought with a satisfied smirk, *they got it right today.* The high caliber weapon rested easily on his hip, and he drew it out, popping the chamber open to make certain it was loaded. "Very good," he said aloud, before holstering the weapon again.

Somewhere in the back of his mind, Stockholm realized this was just a dream, another memory surfacing to play out like a badly written play before his mind's eye. Yet he could not seem to change anything he was doing. He knew the Fall of Mecha was coming, that it would come to its apex twelve years after this remembered day, but his younger self, the gruff and slightly arrogant Red Tribe officer, could no more stop the coming events than he could fly.

The speaker on his left shoulder buzzed with incoming static as the dispatcher spoke through the channel. "Attention all units, attention all units. Incoming report of an armed robbery of a weapons shop over on Sixth Street, suspect is armed with conventional and mecha weapons of an automatic fire system, copy."

Stockholm grabbed his handset, pressing the button to respond.

"This is Sergeant First Grade Stockholm, I copy. I'm on the corner of Fifth and Broadsword, I can be there in five minutes." He was already sprinting along the dusty sidewalk. He let go of the button, and listened to the static. He covered half the distance to the corner of Broadsword and Sixth before another officer replied.

"This is Patrolman Second Grade Hastings, I copy. I'm on my way for backup, Iggy."

Stockholm smiled, comforted that the competent and capable rookie was on his way. Timothy Hastings was a Tanner Cuyotai, an excellent marksman with both his crossbow and his rifle, which he took everywhere. Not so good in a melee situation, Stockholm thought, but that didn't matter much. He didn't foresee the situation deteriorating that far, especially if the suspect was armed with an automatic weapon.

The two canine officers almost ran into one another as he turned the corner of Broadsword and Sixth. "Whoa, big fellah," Hastings said as he took a step back. They smiled knowingly at one another, and Stockholm's heart accelerated just a little. He hadn't known how he felt about Tim at first, but a few nights spent at his apartment had told him. It had told him a lot about himself, truths he'd carry for the rest of his mortal life. "I think I passed the place on my way to get you, Iggy. You ready?" Stockholm drew his firearm, and nodded.

"I was born ready," he said, and Tim laughed.

"That's funny," Tim said as the two of them crept along the sidewalk, making their way for the squat weapons store. "You didn't have dinner ready when I got to your place yesterday."

"Now is hardly the time to talk about this." Stockholm got himself in front of Timothy, now only about twenty yards from the weapons shop. "Besides, I don't remember you complaining about dessert."

"Keep it up, big guy, and you're sleeping on the couch tonight."

Stockholm chuckled under his breath. He straightened and stood with his back pressed flat against the wall of the weapons shop, next to the door.

"I'm gonna go in first." Stockholm set his face, his tone deadly serious now. "Be ready if he gets past me." He kept his voice low.

Timothy Hastings nodded, and got his rifle ready, sprinting across the street and taking up a sniper point while he used hand signals to direct the few surrounding pedestrians back into their homes, stores and workplaces. The street cleared, and Stockholm set himself square to the door, blasting it inward with a solid front kick.

The scene inside caused him to hesitate just a moment longer than was safe. The storeowner, a morbidly obese Human with his wig askew, was dead on the other side of his counter, a single row of bullet holes marring his chest. His three customers sprawled around the main shop, torn apart by some bladed weapon. No suspect was anywhere in sight. The door leading into the back stockroom was ajar, and the Red Tribesman leaped over the counter, bursting into the back room with his weapon raised, shouting "Freeze!"

Once again, he was puzzled to find no perpetrator in the room.

He scanned the room slowly, ducking down and sweeping his weapon back and forth as he peered beneath the two benches in the room. Nothing, and no back door. However, a set of metal rungs led up to the roof.

"Oh, shit." His heart dropped into his stomach. He rushed back through the door enough to shout to Timothy in warning, but too late.

A single, booming report of gunfire, and Timothy's skull burst apart, showering the street with his blood and brain matter.

Lycanthrope fury took hold of the crimson warrior as he watched his lover die. The world blurred, and his vision suddenly flooded with the color of his fur, the color of blood. He recalled, vaguely, spinning about as his body stretched and expanded even further, his uniform shredding apart at the already stressed seams. He recalled feeling bullets riddle his arms and chest as he flew through the air—a frightened and maddened Human atop the weapons store, pumped round after round of ammunition into his body. But he was in thrall to the Huntress, the spirit that called forth to all lycanthropes when their anger and despair turned to bloodlust. He was in thrall to her as he caught a bullet aimed at his face, crushing it into powder. He was in thrall to her when he snatched the machine gun away and broke it in half over his knee.

He was in thrall to her when he ripped the bastard's arms off at the shoulders with casual ease, tossing them over the side of the roof as he pounced on the man, ripping his throat out. His dream faded, blurred, and reformed itself into the discharge office, where he was signing the last of the papers that declared him no longer fit for duty. He took his meager pension, shook the police chief's hand, stalked out of the central headquarters and into the streets. He felt an emptiness inside, one that could not be filled by getting another job, or moving to a new city.

He had learned, after killing the suspect, that Timothy's weapon had jammed when he tried to fire at the suspect. The Cuyotai sniper hadn't been fooled, and a witness reported that he had reacted in an instant to the flash of a gun barrel on the roof. But when he'd taken aim, his weapon hadn't responded. A mecha in his hands had failed to save him, while one in the hands of the perpetrator had sealed his fate. On that day, Stockholm resolved never to use a mecha weapon again.

When he awoke, after only an hour-long nap, he was surprised to find he was crying.

* * * *

Lain McNealy certainly had a talent, Trent thought, watching the zombies lay waste to two of the thresherbeasts. The monsters couldn't figure out why their meals had started moving, and when their claws did nothing more than slow them, they panicked. In an attempt to escape, two of them stumbled over one another, and were quickly slain by undead Minotaurs. The third escaped, only to be pelted with twenty shuriken thrown by Fly and Akimaru. Finally, Rage crushed its head with a mace.

Fly, having borrowed Trent's 'interrogation' pliers, removed the teeth, pocketing them swiftly.

Trent and Lain rejoined Fly, Akimaru and Rage, and together, they went on.

Lain let the corpses of the Dwarves and Minotaurs drop to the ground, dead again, for the final time.

As Trent wondered how Teresa was coming with her assignment, she suddenly contacted him, using the same method that Fly had used to contact Striker. *Markus, love, I think I have something interesting to tell you.*

What is it? He looked over at his Headmaster. He prayed to the various gods who would hear him that the Black Draconus wasn't aware of his contact.

I just got back to the Guildhall. I'm following Striker, but at first I didn't notice anything unusual, until now. Do you know what this guy eats?

Trent shuddered as he pictured it.

I'm well aware of his, dietary needs.

I'm sorry, but that's just disgusting. Anyway, he doesn't seem to be doing anything to worry yourself over. I'll get back to you when I can. Trent thanked her, and continued at the front of the company until the sun started to set. Fly called a halt to their progress and they struck camp. Trent kept his distance from the moody Draconus, who seemed lost in thought.

Fly cycled through his memories, thinking back on the last days he spent with the Obura Ninja Clan. He had roamed the wooden halls of their training grounds, shackled hand and foot, led by elite guards of the clan. He'd held his head high, unashamed of his choices. He had done what no other in the history of the clan could do—he had slain his instructor, one of the most talented Ninjas in all of Tamalaria.

After his graduation ceremony, Thaddeus Fly had felt empty, as though his whole training period had been for nothing. He had been granted the purple sash of his clan, to signify his elevation to the rank of agent, but the accomplishment felt hollow. As the Obura elders bowed to him, he bowed in return, and donned the sash. He had left the Hall of Ceremonies with it tied around his waist, and had left it on when returned to his private chambers.

A soft knock came at his door. One of the other graduates, Markus Trent, slid the door aside, and smiled in at him.

He really was my friend, then, Fly thought as he recalled the Human's smile. It had been genuine, then.

"Congratulations, Thaddeus," Trent said. "Head of our class! I thought it would have gone to Kenachi," he said, referring to one of the only Obura Clan Wererats in the compound.

Fly shook his head, slowly, methodically forming an idea in his head. He sat still on his bed as Trent entered the room and shut the door behind him. "Where's Aki?"

Akimaru had been assigned to share a room with Fly two weeks before, and the elders had declined to tell Fly why. They told him only that it was important that he keep an eye on Akimaru, because even they knew very little about the fifth year student. With two years left before his own graduation, Fly would have assumed that the white clad Ninja would have many questions for him. But no, the mysterious youth had said little or nothing in the time he'd been in Fly's company. Trent had made it plain that he didn't like him early on, but Fly had assured his friend that Akimaru was no threat.

Students of the Obura often killed one another, as a matter of course, and sometimes, for extra credit. The clan brooked no weakness, and rewarded students for weeding out the class numbers. "So, now that you're an agent, you think Akimaru will try anything? It'd be one hell of a feather in his cap," Trent said with a grin.

"No, he won't." Fly's voice remained flat, void of inflection, but only because his revelation was now upon him. He knew what he had to do to prove himself better than a mere agent and head of his class. He had the presence of mind to elaborate on his answer, however, before he addressed his friend with his revelation. "Akimaru just doesn't seem the type. I don't know why, but I don't think he'll try anything with me. Trent?"

"Yes, Thaddeus?" Trent was reading a small paperback novel, a privilege he enjoyed now that he was a graduate. He'd actually smuggled the book in a few months back, in readiness for his graduation. Fly saw he was already halfway through the story.

"I know what I'm going to do tonight."

Trent looked up from his book and grinned ruefully at the Black Draconus. "You'll get completely shitty on cheap booze and opium like the rest of us."

When Fly didn't laugh, his smile fell. "What are you thinking of doing?"

"Markus, if I did something, something that would get me kicked out of the clan, would you leave with me?" The question came out abruptly, unexpected. But Trent, Fly was glad to see, didn't hesitate.

"Without a doubt, and without a backward glance. You're really going to do something crazy, aren't you?"

Fly nodded, but said nothing more. He didn't want his friend to be interrogated after he completed his self-assigned task, and so he sat in silence, until Trent left a couple of hours later, off to go celebrate graduation in the nearby town.

Fly drifted into the town only long enough to purchase an expensive bottle of wine, and returned immediately to the wooden training compound. Down several hallways he stalked, the purple sash getting him respectful bows as he passed by both trainees and instructors, all of which he returned in kind. He made his way, without error, to his instructor's room. *Sensei Dolan*, he thought. *Tonight, I honor you with death.*

He wrapped lightly on the door, and his instructor, a lithe Red Draconus, slid the door open. Candles were lit on his small altar at the back of his room, opposite the door.

"Thaddeus Fly. Agent Fly, I should say," Dolan said with an impish grin. "I am pleased to see you. What can I do for you now?"

"You can share a drink with a humble former student, sensei." Fly bowed his head and held up the bottle of wine.

Dolan took it, seeming to measure its weight. He grunted, and stood aside, admitting his former student into the room.

Fly saw a wall scroll with several tribal paintings on it, each representing an ancestor. "Ancestor worship, sensei?"

Dolan nodded, and procured a pair of drinking bowls. He sat with his back to the altar, and handed the bowls up to Fly, who fumbled one and dropped it. It broke on the wooden floor, and Fly bent to pick up the pieces.

"It's okay, agent Fly," Dolan said.

"I apologize, sensei. However, I did bring my own bowls." He pulled a pair of smaller drinking bowls from a hip pouch. "I offer you one of my bowls, to replace the one I have broken."

Dolan accepted the bowl, and uncorked the bottle, sniffing its contents with an air of deep suspicion.

"Is there a problem, sensei?"

"It's nothing," the Red Draconus said, his voice deeper than the ocean and just as full of contained fury. "I was smelling for poisons."

Fly gave him a wide-eyed look and started to guffaw, but the older Dragon-kin put up a hand to stop him. "It is no offense to you. It is simply that students in the past have tried similar stunts."

"I've never heard of it," Fly said.

"That's because I saw through their deceptions and killed them where they sat," Dolan said evenly. He poured a measure of the wine into each bowl, and raised Fly's to him in toast. "In recognition of your graduation, Thaddeus Fly. May many moons pass you by without notice."

"And you." Fly drank deeply from Dolan's bowl. They both smacked reptilian lips after the first bowl, and set them down, staring each other in the eyes. After a few minutes, Dolan's eyes went wide, and Fly stood to his feet, slowly, menacingly. "I did not poison the wine, sensei Dolan. This I told you in truth. But I did apply poison to my drinking bowls," he said with a smile and flourish. In his left hand, he held the other of his drinking bowls.

"How, how did, you know, you'd only drop, one, of my, bowls," Dolan said through ragged breaths. His innards were on fire, and he was grappling with his throat to get the words out.

"I didn't. The paste I applied to the lining of the bowls has an anti-toxin, which must be taken prior to consumption. I took my pill an hour ago," he said, now drawing out a long knife. "How about you?" He cocked his head to one side, and watched as his former sensei gagged, puking up blood. "I applied a second coat to both bowls, to make certain it would act faster than normal. I couldn't have you catching on too quickly, you see." He walked around the side of the room behind Dolan.

"You, won't, get away, with, this," Dolan muttered. Fly was on the verge of manic laughter, feeling the triumph well up inside of his heart. The hole was filled, he thought. *I am a true Ninja, now.*

"I just have, sensei. Now, I shall honor you by granting you a swifter death than this." With one hideous jerk of his arm, he slashed the Red Draconus' throat, spilling his life on the floor.

Fly's memory blurred for a few minutes as he stared into the fire, pulling his eyes away to look over at Trent. They had been friends, once. Why had that changed?

His mind's eye fogged over, and he found himself once again in shackles, back in the Hall of Ceremonies. The elders had found him standing over Dolan's body, as they had gone to fetch him so they could do their own celebrating. Fly had been tackled and chained up immediately, but much to his own surprise, he hadn't been executed. Instead, they'd dragged him to the Hall of Ceremonies, where he stood smiling in silence.

Dolan's corpse was deposited a few minutes later, right on the floor between Fly and the elders, who were all knelt in deep thought across from him. "Do you know what you have done," asked one of the gray haired Human elders.

"I am aware," Fly replied. "I have assassinated an instructor. I have slain one of your lesser elders," he said. The elders nodded, and muttered amongst themselves.

"This has never happened. No student, not even an agent graduate, has ever slain an elder, much less their own sensei," another Human elder said, his voice almost awed. "How long have you been planning this?"

"Less than a day," Fly said, and there were more whispered mutterings from the elders as they crouched closer together, to better confer with one another.

"Don't get me wrong, I didn't hate him. I granted him an honorable death." Fly filled his voice with confidence.

The elders seemed to consider this, and they fell silent. The eldest among them, an Illeck who had been of the second generation of Obura, stood and spoke.

"Thaddeus Fly, you have us at a loss," he said. "You shall remain bound and guarded for three days, while this council decides what is to be done with you. Guards," he said, turning his back on the Black Draconus. "Take him to his quarters. Akimaru will be moved when he returns from the town."

The guards had manhandled him to his room, and tossed him inside without a word. He laughed at them as they slid his door shut, laughed like a madman who knew the world's best punch line.

The first twenty-four hours passed without a word. The guards refused to talk to him, and when Akimaru was let inside to collect his things, he said nothing. But Fly saw the awe and respect in his eyes. That look alone said all that needed to be said, as far as he'd been concerned. The second day brought him a visitor, Markus Trent. The guards had let him in, a little grudgingly, and he stood on the other side of the room, just staring at Fly.

"They're going to execute you, you know," he whispered to the Black Draconus. "What were you thinking? I thought you were going to pull a gag on someone, maybe a really bad practical joke, but this? This is madness!"

"If they let me go, will you still come with me," was Fly's only response to any of this. Trent stared at him blackly for a long time, saying nothing. Then he nodded, and asked the guards to let him out. The third day passed the same as the first, and before he knew it, he was being let out by the guards for a walk around the hallways. Eventually, they led him to the Hall of Ceremonies, where Markus Trent and Akimaru both stood, much to his surprise.

The eldest of the council alone stood, the other elders sitting with their hands on their knees.

"Undo his shackles," the elder said, and the guards complied immediately.

"Give him his weapons," he said.

The guards handed him his belongings.

"And now, Thaddeus Fly, come forward." Fly was a little confused, because as far as he knew, executions didn't go like this. Shouldn't he have been stabbed by now, his throat cut, or looped with a noose?

"Thaddeus Fly, the council of the Obura Clan has come to a conclusion regarding your punishment, and we have decided the following.

"Thaddeus Fly was never with us," the elder said, and Fly stared mutely as his file was set into a cooking pot, the papers smoldering inside the otherwise empty pot. Soon, he realized, they would start on fire. "No such student ever attended this compound. No such student has ever been a member of the Obura Ninja Clan," the Illeck elder said loudly, as if proclaiming this all in the name of the gods.

Fly stared at him, unable to speak. He was not being executed, he was being outcast! No, he thought, that would require that they acknowledge I've been here. Which, apparently, they no longer will.

"Sensei Dolan, the records shall show, was taken from us by a lowly, cowardly sneak thief," the elder announced, and Fly felt the words strike him like a slap in the face.

He touched his hand to his nose, expecting it to come away bloody.

"Let the records also show that, bereaved by their sensei's death, the students Markus Trent and Akimaru took their leave of us. Neither student reached graduation."

As the Illeck elder ripped Fly's purple sash off, the Black Draconus saw that a guard had cut Trent's from him as well. "Go now, you three, and stay gone. Stay well away from this compound, for if we ever see you again, we will kill you," the elder said.

"Trent," Fly said, back in the present.

The Human Ninja came over, passing by Lain, Rage, and Akimaru on his way to the Headmaster. He stood next to Fly, who reached up and grabbed him by the front of the uniform tunic, pulling him down toward him.

Trent was taken aback, not expecting such a sudden, harsh movement from the Midnight Suns' Headmaster.

"Yes, Headmaster?"

Fly said nothing, just holding him down so that their heads were level with one another as he stared into the fire.

"Was it the sash?" He let the question hang in the air, unexplained, unfinished, but he felt a sudden tension build in Trent. The Human shrugged his hand off, and started to walk away again.

"As I remember, that was just the start of it," Trent whispered back at him.

* * * *

The Glove of Shadows

In the late evening, Anna realized that she was going to have to sleep sometime in the stopover in Desanadron. But her mind raced and wheeled, and she darted from shadow to shadow, making her way to the Alchemy shop. It would still be open, but only for a couple of hours. She wanted to make arrangements with Jonah Staples ahead of time, so they wouldn't be springing a surprise on him. A surprised Alchemist was a dangerous Alchemist, after all, and she didn't want her company to wind up in the ocean. One wrong line in a Focus Site, and they could even wind up with each other's body parts. That'd be a rude awakening, wouldn't it?

She made it to the front entrance of the Staples and Staples Alchemy Store, opening the door and listening as the quaint little jingle sounded above her.

"Welcome to my store," said a young man's voice from an adjoining room. "I'll be out in a minute!"

Anna sauntered around, taking in the various assorted gadgets, powders, potions and scrolls. Pre-written Focus Sites accounted for a high amount of Jonah Staples' business, she knew. Of course, she knew this because she'd had Flint break in one night and look over his sales ledger.

She heard a female voice from the other room say something in a low tone, the words just beyond her ken. Anna had heard a lot of Elven folk use their natural tongue, but she just didn't have a knack for the language. Jonah Staples came out a minute later, and gave her a wave.

"Mr. Staples. Good to see you again."

"Yes indeed," he said, mopping sweat from his brow with a handkerchief.

I'm no lycanthrope, Anna thought as she smiled at him, but I know the smell of sex.

"What can I do for you?"

"Myself and some associates need to travel to Ja-Wen, and we need to do it tomorrow. Late morning, around noon," she said.

Jonah took out a pad of paper and started to jot down notes.

"How many in your company?"

Anna thought on this for a moment, because two of the members of her company were rather large, and two rather small. Styge wouldn't appreciate being moved through space-time so roughly either, so she had a few factors to take into account.

"Well, there's myself, a Red Tribe Werewolf, a Wererat, a pair of Gnomes, and an elderly Human," she said, careful not to give names.

"Hm. And I assume the old timer's not going to want to go too fast?"

Anna smiled at young Jonah and nodded.

"All right. Well, the total's going to come to about two hundred gold pieces," Jonah said.

Anna paid for the trip up front, with two white gold coins. She was about to take her leave of the shop, when Jonah cleared his throat.

"Um, are you going to need lodging when you get there?"

She hadn't considered that, mostly because she was used to having a place to stay at all times. She would camp when necessary, and didn't mind the idea of leaving the city's limits to do so, with the right equipment.

"You know, I think we may at that, Mr. Staples. Any suggestions?"

Jonah pulled a small business card from a vest pocket, and handed it to her.

"This is just an address," she said.

"I know. Around this time of day. First floor, room 107. That's where the super's office is. You'll see a bell somewhere around, just ring it to get his attention. And don't worry, sir," Jonah said as he headed back for the adjoining room. "He may look menacing, and he can be a real jerk, but otherwise, he's an okay guy."

The trip arranged, Anna headed back to the Guild, and lay on a cot she had hidden in the wall of her office. She was asleep before her head hit the pillow.

* * * *

She is six years old again, reading a paperback book intended for students in their Scholar years of school. The room around her is tiny, dingy, and the smell of the rotting wood that makes up the building itself permeates the air.

Better than mama's perfume, she thinks.

The sounds from the next room are blissfully muffled by the layers of pillows she's nailed to the wall over the last year. She is absurdly intelligent for a girl of her age, but then, she has to be. Her wits are her only means of survival.

"Mama," she whispers, the noises not completely blocked out. She can hear the bed knocking against the opposite wall. She is precocious at six, but still has no idea what her mother is doing on the other side of the pillows and wood. She won't know for a few years yet. At the time, she thinks her mother lets the strange men, whose names all are apparently John something, beat her up for money.

Little Anna Deus hops off of her bed, book still in hand. She dog-ears one page, closing the book to carry it more easily, and heads off down to the park.

The night sky is brilliantly aglow with the light of the moon and the stars. This light filters down from the heavens above, and illuminates the city in a way that makes her eyes want to drink in the scenery for as long as possible. The slow, steady procession of city guards, their boots thumping hollowly on the streets, brings to mind images of the creatures she is reading about. In her current series of books, the creatures are called Thumpa-Thumpa, and they feed on the greed of others around them.

But her vision clears a little of the magic instilled by her imagination, and she sees no Thumpa-Thumpa, only the tired, haggard faces of those officers unlucky enough to pull the night shift. One of the guards, an old Jaft, his flesh oozing the stench of his people, kneels down in her path as she makes her way toward the park. Anna has never trusted the big blue men, because when they got hurt, the hurt place just disappeared. She thinks they are a Race of strange wizards, and she thinks the smell that comes off of them in eye-watering waves is because they don't like to take baths.

"You're in my way," she says bluntly.

The old Jaft officer's face creases with a friendly smile, and he puts his hands up to show he means no harm.

"You have my apologies, young miss," he says. "But shouldn't you be at home, in your warm little bed? It's late, and late time brings out real weirdoes. You shouldn't be out so late without your papa or mama."

Again, he smiles, and the absence of malice in the smile puts little Anna at ease. Enough so that she feels she can tell him the truth. After all, mama always said she could trust nice policemen, the ones who didn't yell at little girls.

"I have no papa, and mama's working," she says, easy as you please.

The Jaft's smile turns a little sad, she sees. He nods, however, and stands up.

"Well then, you stick by me, for now, okay?"

She doesn't refuse the officer's request.

"Where are you headed?"

"To the park, to read with the moon and the shadows." It's a line she read in the last novel she ripped through, and she sees it works wonders.

The Jaft looks at her with mild curiosity. "Um, donaga," he says. It is one of the few words of his language she knows. It means 'little one'. "What is your name?"

"Anna," she says.

He takes her to the park, where she reads until the sun rises. He walks her home, and the whole while, they do not speak. At the foot of the stairs that lead up to her home, she almost passes out, but he catches her. She tells him she lives on the third floor with mama, and remembers no more.

She is ten years old, and after reading some textbooks borrowed from the library, she now knows why men named John pay mama for her time at night. It is winter, and the snows come hard and furious. The men come less, but mama makes enough to get them by. It is an early morning, and mama is making her favorite breakfast. Omelets made with three eggs, strips of bacon, and chilled orange juice. She has a question for mama, but she wants to wait until she has her food in her stomach. She knows enough to know it's going to upset mama.

The meal eaten, she pushes her plate aside. "Mama, are you a whore?"

There is the sound of a plate breaking on the kitchen floor, and then nothing. The wind outside howls, a maddened banshee thirsting for the chance to choke someone on their own frozen vomit. Stillness, absence of movement. The inside of Anna's home is stopped in time, unbending, unmoving. Perhaps, Anna thinks, if I take a single step back toward my room, I can avoid the horrible slap I'm about to get.

But the blow never comes. Instead, there are words, words she has never heard mama say to anyone, even when she is angry as hell.

"Get out of here," mama says. "Get out of here and don't you ever come near me again, Anna. If I see you," she says, turning to look at her daughter with tears pooling in her eyes. "I swear to every god there is that if I see you near this apartment again, I will throw you out of a window. Get your things." She moves into her own room.

Anna doesn't say a word. She doesn't cry, she doesn't sulk, and she doesn't beg her mother to reconsider. She could shout, *I'm only ten! Who throws their child out at ten years old?* But she knows there are Races whose children never even meet their parents, except maybe on accident. She moves like a spirit into her room, and packs a large duffel bag with some clothes, and a selection of her favorite books.

In particular, she takes the James Colt novels, stories about a great master thief who gets through life without paying a single copper piece for anything. She is wise enough in the ways of the world to know that her mother's way of making money can be lucrative. But James Colt's way is much more exciting, and in a way, she muses as she tucks her only weapon into the bag, cleaner.

129

Out in the stairwell, mama hands her a small pouch of gold and silver pieces. "Take this, and get gone, fatherless child. Go see what the world is really like! Go out and live in the world where a child can call her mother a whore!" There are tears, crystalline and perfect, dribbling down mama's cheeks. She doesn't really want her to go, Anna realizes. Well, the joke's on her now, isn't it?

"Good-bye mama," Anna says. Without a glance back, she's gone.

Out on the street, she hefts the second money pouch to weigh it. She'd taken it right off of mama's waist, and the older woman hadn't even noticed. "I have a papa, all right," the ten-year-old girl says. "His name's Jim Colt."

* * * *

It was said in Tamalaria that too much time in the company of a friend could make them your enemy. Could too much time in the company of an enemy make them your friend? Markus Trent didn't bother thinking it over.

The sun poked up a little over the horizon, almost seeming afraid to shed its light and warmth to the realm. The look on the Human Ninja's face could certainly do that, if nothing else. He hadn't been able to sleep, and so he'd kept a silent watch over the group with Akimaru, who patrolled the edge of the camp. His mind burned with Fly's question the previous evening. 'Was it the sash?'

Of course it had been the sash, but that had only been the beginning of his hatred for the Black Draconus. He had agreed to be exiled, to be outcast from the Obura. He had never agreed, however, to be so thoroughly wiped from record.

Markus Trent had spent his entire adolescence learning about the elusive Obura Clan Ninjas, and when he had proven himself worthy of their tutelage, he started toward his dream. Thaddeus Fly's impulsiveness resulted in the destruction of that dream, and since his assassination of sensei Dolan, there had been no more of that spark in the Black Draconus. Fly, over the course of the next twelve years, had become lax, talkative, indecisive. He had killed an elder to prove a point, to make certain everyone knew he was the best. And now, Markus thought, he's become one of those doddering fools. Akimaru and he had sacrificed their honor to join him, and thus far, Trent didn't feel he'd regained anything worth the price. For that matter, he wasn't sure Akimaru had either.

He studied the white clad Ninja from across the fire, wondering what made him tick. In the twelve and a half years he'd known and lived with him, Trent hadn't once seen Akimaru without his mask. He'd never seen Akimaru bleed either, a fact which, at that precise moment, made him hate Fly even more. He should have been friends with the white clad Ninja, but Akimaru always seemed to be in the thrall of the Black Draconus. As a result, Trent had to take refuge in the company of his tools and weapons. He'd never been let in on any of Akimaru's secrets. He wondered if Fly had, either.

Akimaru came around the camp's perimeter, approaching with an easy stride. Trent listened for the sound of the switch grass under his white boots, but heard nothing. No sound at all escaped from Akimaru, he thought.

A stiff breeze blew down from the north, rustling the fire in the center of the camp, ultimately snuffing it. Soon, Trent and Akimaru would have to rouse the others and get marching east again.

130

The Glove of Shadows

As Akimaru closed to within fifteen yards, Trent felt a cold chill race up his spine, a familiar effect of being in the white clad Ninja's proximity. He scanned Akimaru's face, his eyes locking onto the shorter Ninja's pupils. He could glean nothing from this look into the windows of Akimaru's soul. Perhaps, Trent mused, a pang of true fear resonating from his stomach, Akimaru had no soul.

"It is almost time to awaken the Headmaster and the others," Akimaru said, his tone calm, neutral. "Before we do, however, I must ask you something."

Trent raised an eyebrow at him, but rolled his left hand, asking Akimaru to continue.

"For what reasons do you despise sensei Fly, and scheme against him?"

The question didn't surprise Trent, though having Akimaru ask it made him highly uncomfortable. How best to answer? Certainly not with the response he gave to others in the Guild, which was simply to mind their own business. He couldn't brace or intimidate Akimaru any more than he could a tree, so perhaps a semi-truthful reply would be best.

"I have several reasons, Akimaru," Markus Trent whispered.

The sun now spilled light over the fields to the east, showing the way they would have to travel. Trent looked into the middle distance, and saw the signs of a nearby village. Farmlands cropped up about a mile and a half away, and would inevitably supply a village, town, or hamlet not far after that.

"The first among them being the loss of my sash. You had no sash," he said, turning his attention back to Akimaru, who had come within a foot of him. He hadn't heard any movement, hadn't felt any disturbance in the ground, yet here the white clad Ninja stood, within striking distance.

Could he fell Akimaru if necessary? Best not to think on that, he concluded.

"So you wouldn't know what that was like for me. Six years of my life disappeared in an afternoon, Akimaru. All so he could prove a point." He looked over at Thaddeus Fly, who was stirring from his rest as sunlight spread over his body. "Other reasons I shall tell you at other times, Akimaru. Our Headmaster awakens."

In his heart, Trent knew that Akimaru would hold him to his word, and come back for further explanation. But would he tell Akimaru the reason he most hated Fly? Would he divulge that information to someone he hardly trusted, or knew anymore? No, he decided, putting one foot in front of the other as the company struck out. He'd rather die first.

* * * *

"Anna," a voice called to her from outside of the fog of her dream memories. She felt a gentle hand upon her shoulder, shaking her.

She opened her eyes, and was nose to snout with Guild Prime Flint.

"Come on, boss lady. We've got to shake a leg."

"What time is it?" A dull throb, centered behind her left eye, beat a staccato rhythm against the alabaster walls of her skull.

"Nearly nine o'clock, Anna." Flint lit two cigarettes and offering her one.

She took it instinctively, dragging hard off of it and hacking explosively.

"Easy girly, easy! Don't need you getting sick on us too soon," he chided, helping her up off the cot.

She stuck the smoke in the corner of her mouth, and crouched down next to her travel bag, double-checking that she had everything they needed,

131

including the business card. Just an address, she thought, flipping it over and over in her nimble fingers.

"Is everyone else up and ready to leave," she asked.

"Oi, 'tis so boss. Old Stocky seems in a bit of a mood this mornin', and Styge isn't at all pleased with our chosen course of action. Swearing up and down that he doesn't trust this so-called science. Norm's spent half the morning trying to convince him it's as safe as any magic." Flint stubbed out his cigarette in an ashtray on Anna's desk.

She slung her rucksack on, and faced the Wererat squarely. Her own dreams had plagued her all night long, and she could see her face reflected in Flint's huge, starry eyes. She looked like hell.

"Flint, did I ever tell you about my childhood?"

The Hoods' Prime seemed nonplussed.

"Can't say as you 'ave. Why?"

"No reason," she lied, shaking her head. She exited her office, Flint right behind her. "Remind me some time to tell you about it. I think someone should know."

She had never told Harold about her early life, choosing instead to lie to him about her background. She couldn't stand the thought of seeing the hurt in his too-kind eyes and she wanted only to love him forever, not drag him down. She felt guilty about offering the tale to Flint and not her own husband, but she needed to unload on someone. Flint was the natural choice, though now, she may find council with Stockholm as well, since she had revealed herself to him.

The streets of Desanadron already swarmed with morning market shoppers, travelers, and all manner of grifters, plying their trade as best they could in the light of day. Her heart swelled with pride—this was her city, the bright metropolis of Desanadron. Through wars, decay, and the decline of civilization, she felt certain this city would stand tall and strong, as would she.

She let Flint guide her to an open porch fronting a small eatery down the street from Jonah Staples' shop. The rest of the company lounged at one of the tables, eating and drinking their breakfasts with casual ease. Anna saw that Stockholm's face was as dark and forbidding as Flint had suggested, so she opened up with a simple "Good morning, everyone," to the group.

Greetings were exchanged, and she took a seat between Flint and Stocky.

"William, I still don't like the idea," Styge complained around a cruller. "Not too keen on the idea of using mathematical mumbo-jumbo for anything." He looked down at his sketchbook, adding rough lines to a drawing of an enormous sword.

Anna could tell from the scale of the thing, that only Flint or Stockholm would be able to use a weapon of that size.

Her eyes found Stockholm's line of sight as she looked at him, and she followed it to Norman Adwar's hip. He had a mecha weapon strapped to his waist, something she knew was called a 'pistol'. Seething hatred for the object swam in Stockholm's vision. Anna would ask him about it later.

"Well, like it or not," said Norman, "it's the fastest method of transportation available to us."

"And let's not forget," chimed in Lee Toren, sipping his cuppa. "Just because Reynaldi's home is in Ja-Wen, that don't mean that's where we'll catch him up." The members of the company digested this statement in silence, and Anna ordered herself a meal.

When the time of their appointment approached, she led the way down to the Alchemy shop, small talk striking up behind her. When she entered, she saw that Jonah was handling a few customers, and his wife was checking a clipboard —probably for inventory, she thought.

"There you are." Jonah smiled to a Kobold, the small, rat-like face of the little humanoid beaming as the Kobold left the store.

"Hail and well met, Mr. Deus," Jonah said as her company piled inside. "We've been waiting for you. Please follow me." A large Focus Site had been inscribed on the floor of a side-chamber in charcoal, large enough that all of them could stand within the circle.

"Everyone just get in the middle there, and I'll get things started, okay?"

"Still don't trust this," Styge grumbled. He looked up at Flint with a dour cast on his face. "If I die because of this, I want you to burn my body and all my drawings."

The Wererat laughed heartily, as Jonah Staples muttered under his breath, clapping his hands together. Twice more he clapped his hands, and the air filled with the smell and taste of ozone, glittering sparks of energy leaping from Jonah's pressed hands. With a flourish, he slammed his hands down on the edge of the charcoal symbol, releasing the energy into the Focus Site.

It glimmered brightly for a second, and then the world around Anna and the company dissolved.

Weightlessness, she thought, *that's the word*. She felt as though she were floating in an ocean of empty air, her body hurtling through time and space faster than a man could blink.

When she tried to turn her head to look for the others, she found that she could not move at all. After a short period, a portal ripped open at her feet, her eyes forced there by the force streaming over her head.

With a scream of surprise or fear, or a mix of both, she flailed out, crashing atop Flint on a cobblestone street she had no familiarity with.

She landed heavily, and heard his pained "Hoomph!"

She rolled off, looking up at the rift in the air just in time to avoid being crushed by Stockholm. She scrambled out of the way, and felt the Red Tribe Werewolf's impact through the street. She watched with fascination as Lee Toren and Norman Adwar fell through, landing on top of Stocky and bounding away quickly. Stockholm stood up, brushed himself off, and without looking up, put his arms out. He caught Styge just as the old man came falling through, screaming his head off.

Stockholm deposited the aging Illusionist gently on his feet, and took in the surrounding city. He noted, the new buildings around him, for he had been at this particular intersection before.

The company had been deposited at the intersection of Mill Road and Sky Lane, in the fourth residential district. Stockholm had lived here for a short while a number of decades back, taking a break from his time in Desanadron. He'd lived in a nearby apartment complex, earning his keep as a handyman around town, as well as a bouncer for a couple of the rowdier taverns.

"Okay, anybody got any idea where we are," Anna asked.

"Fourth residential district," Stockholm and Lee said, in harmony.

Lee continued. "I have a sneakin' suspicion I know the landlord our friend Jonah was referring to, and I don't loik it a bit."

"It's decided then," Anna chided playfully. "We'll go meet him right away." She pulled out the business card as Lee grumbled unintelligibly in his native tongue. The building they wanted was only a few hundred feet away. She led the way, and within minutes, after passing by several street vendors, they arrived in front of an eight-story apartment building.

She tucked the card away, and entered the main lobby. The air inside had a bluish tinge of old cigarette smoke, the scent mixed with that of the old Jaft who sat on one long, red couch, himself puffing away like a man on a mission. Several Kobolds passed the company, two of them actually using Stockholm's legs as an archway to pass beneath. He looked at them incredulously, but let it go.

"Wait here." She went to the room that Jonah had mentioned and entered a small, grubby office, with several weeks worth of dust on every surface, including the waiting chairs. She blew motes of dust off of the bell, and rang it, once.

A gruff voice called out from somewhere behind a curtain on the other side of the desk. "I'll meet you in the lobby."

Anna returned to the lobby, where everyone except Stockholm had taken seats.

No surprise there, she thought.

A moment later, a door down the hall creaked open, carving a track in the floor as it scraped the wooden floorboards. From the doorway, a larger-than-life man lumbered out, a man so large she felt completely dwarfed not only by his size, but his stature and presence.

"Greetings," the stripe-armed Simpa said, his voice a deep, rolling thunder. "My name is Portenda. And you are?" The Bounty Hunter extended a hand toward Anna. His hand was big enough to palm her face if he had been inclined to do so. She took his hand, amazed at how gentle the grip and shake were.

"William Deus," she replied. "Jonah Staples recommended we come to you about getting a place to hole up for a few days." She tried to pull her hand away, but Portenda held her still for a moment as he probed her eyes with his own. His were a strange, ashen color, gray as thunderheads. She didn't care at all for the feeling. Finally, she wriggled her hand free of his, and rubbed her wrist.

"I got a couple of apartments available." Portenda's tone was curt and businesslike. "Especially seeing as Lee is with your group."

"You know him?" Stockholm looked at Lee, who grinned.

"Unfortunately, yes," Portenda muttered. "I'll put you in 214, up on the second floor. Rent is eight gold pieces flat for the week."

Anna produced the coinage, surprised at the low rate.

"Head on up, it's unlocked. Keys will be under the mat inside." Portenda pocketing the money and moved back into his office.

Anna instructed Flint, Lee, Norm and Styge to head upstairs and get settled in. As they moved out of sight, into the stairwell, she turned to look up at Stockholm. "What's your take on him?"

"Not a man to be trifled with," he whispered. "Thankfully, I didn't get any sense of ill will from him."

She nodded, and took in the lobby. The building appeared to be in the renovation process, but she doubted very much that it needed it too badly. There appeared to be enough residents, as a few more people made their way past her and the crimson Werewolf. "Anything else, or shall we head upstairs?"

"Not just yet," she said. "Do you still have any old contacts or friends in the city?"

"One or two." Stockholm cracked his neck with a loud pop.

"Good. Find them, and glean whatever information you can about Reynaldi. If he hasn't shown up yet, all the better. And Stockholm?"

"Yes," he asked, already heading for the door.

"Um…" she wasn't sure exactly what to say, or how to say it, but over the course of the last few days, she had come to appreciate him in a way she hadn't before. "Thanks, big guy. For always being there."

He smiled at her then, a beautiful, genuine smile that gave him a softer, younger appearance for a brief moment.

"I always will be, when the gods allow it." He opened the door and left the building.

She would remember that statement in later years, but that is a tale for another time.

Interlude

Archibald Reynaldi sat patiently in the stone council hall of Fort Stone, turning the Glove of Shadows over in his hands like a child's plaything. Strange, he thought, that such a simple, humble-looking object could be so coveted. Yet every thief in the lands of Tamalaria would be clamoring to get their hands on it, if they knew of its discovery.

"My lordship," a gravely voice intoned from the open hall doors.

Reynaldi looked up from the Glove, and saw one of the Fort's commanding officers, Major Horace Vents, standing as tall as he could in the doorway. The Dwarven Knight maintained order in the Fort, and was well-liked by his superiors and subordinates both, but Reynaldi felt nothing for him. In his opinion, the Order of Oun should not keep Knights or Soldiers that did not worship mighty Oun in their ranks. Vents made it clear that his god of choice was Goragatha, an old Dwarven god, worshipped highly among the mountainous Dwarf folk.

"What news, Major," Reynaldi asked, his face set in stone.

"Your lordship, one of your company members has come to make confession to you. He claims it is urgent, that he must have your forgiveness for a crime against the Order." The Dwarf's grin said he relished the words. "Shall we send him in?"

"We?" Reynaldi grit his teeth. His eyes fell to Major Vents' knuckles, which he saw had a raw, well-used cast. Flecks of blood stained the thick, dark flesh. "What have you done to my retainer?" Reynaldi surged to his feet and dashed around the long table.

Before he could reach the Dwarven Knight, one of his own Knights was dragged two Human Soldiers into the room and tossed to the floor. They'd beaten the man within an inch of his life.

"We have interrogated him, lordship." Vents dismissed the Soldiers with a wave of his hand.

They retreated from the council hall, stepping onto the stone abutment that connected the main Fort to the tower the council hall stood in.

"When he admitted betrayal of the Order, he fell squarely within my judicial jurisdiction. Commander Thompson has agreed to let you speak with him before he is tossed from the Fort and the Order." The Dwarf stepped back out through the door as the Elven Paladin crouched next to his injured retainer.

"Just give a knock when you're done with him, your lordship." The Dwarf's sarcasm dripped from the word 'lordship'.

Archibald Reynaldi used a minor healing spell on the young Knight, stopping the blood running from his puffed face in rivulets.

The young man was still on hands and knees when he looked sorrowfully up into Reynaldi's eyes.

"Speak, Townshend. Tell me what crime you have committed against our Order. I may be able to aid you, right the wrong you have done."

"You cannot," muttered the young Knight miserably. "I have sold information, Lord Reynaldi. To a pair of thieves! I told them about your discovery in the ruins." Townshend clutched at Reynaldi like a leper seeking a miraculous healing.

Reynaldi stood, roughly pushing the man away. *Damnation*, he thought, *someone is definitely going to be snooping around.*

"Who were the thieves?" He didn't look down at Townshend.

"I only know one by name." The Knight coughed up a gout of blood. "Lee Toren, a Gnome Pickpocket."

Reynaldi walked away from the young man and stood before a large, open window. He knew exactly who Lee Toren was. The Gnome had arrest warrants pending in several city-states, and a handful of the smaller kingdoms throughout Tamalaria. Of course, many of the warrants could be eliminated by paying legal fees. Reynaldi knew that Lee Toren's thefts went largely unreported. He could easily pay off the fees with earnings from other jobs, and he had done just that many times, according to records.

Reynaldi also knew that the Gnome had a number of outfits that he sometimes worked with. "Where did Toren go after he purchased information from you, Townshend?"

"Desanadron," was the immediate response.

Reynaldi tried to remember the organizations that operated from the metropolis in the west. There were two groups, he could think of, the Hoods and the Midnight Suns. Toren would likely sell the information to both thief Guilds. The Elven Paladin would have to contend with both groups and possibly Toren acting on his own to steal the glove after he'd sold the information. In all likelihood, they were already on the move, hunting him down.

He would make ready for them.

Chapter Eleven
Setup

Ten hours after the rest of the company had settled into the apartment, Ignatious Stockholm stepped through the door for the first time. He hadn't learned much from his only remaining contact in Ja-Wen, an aging Human mercenary who went by the name of Crash.

Crash only knew that the Elven Paladin, Reynaldi, had a home in the northern residential districts, and that he didn't often frequent it.

A brief stop over to the Department of Taxation and Collections yielded the precise address of Reynaldi's home, and when Stockholm sped to the property to check on it, he found a palatial estate, spread over at least ten acres of property on the very edge of the city's limits. Security officers patrolled the grounds back and forth.

Using the utmost stealth and silence, he'd gone around and knocked every one of them out before making his way in to the manor proper. Inside, Reynaldi had the home immaculately cleaned, and decorated with paintings and relics from another age. "Impressive," he'd whispered to the empty corridors.

Moving through the manor, he came upon several bedchambers, dining rooms, studies, and an otherwise empty room in which only stood a single chair with leather straps all over it. The Red Tribe warrior moved into this room, the smell of old, dried blood lingering lightly on the air. Had he not been possessed of such a keen nose, he never would have noticed the scent, but being a Werewolf had its advantages. A brief look around the room revealed nothing, but a second glance at the northern wall, opposite the door, showed Stockholm a single brick that appeared to jut slightly from the wall.

"Hello Mr. Obvious," he muttered, quickly pushing the brick in.

He heard a sharp click behind the wall, and panels slid aside in front of him, revealing a keen looking set of 'interrogation tools'.

Rust and caked blood covered them—they clearly had been unused for some years.

Stockholm took down a belt from its hook, a long leather affair with sharpened screws set throughout its length. He set his rucksack down in front of him, and stuffed the belt inside among his travel supplies. Always good to have negative evidence on hand.

He pushed the brick trigger again, and the panels slid closed. Exiting the room, Stockholm took a brief look up and down the hallway. The hardwood floors shone with fresh polish, the scent of the natural oils used on them only a day or two old. He looked back into the stone torture chamber, and cocked an eyebrow at it. The manor, for the most part, was crafted lovingly with hardwoods and basic Elven carpentry. Why then, he wondered, would the place have a stone-hewn chamber for interrogation?

Up to the second floor he crept, silent as the best of sneak thieves. His massive frame moved gently and easily, and he found the master bedroom across from the top of the steps leading up. He opened the door slowly, noting with discomfort the way the hinges squeaked and rattled. The chamber within was lavish, decorated with fine watercolor paintings and tapestries depicting the history of Tamalaria. He moved slowly to one wall, noting the certificates of award and medals hung with pride. None of this, however, interested him too deeply. He had come looking for clues, and found little outside of the strange room downstairs.

"Pay dirt," he whispered to himself when he spotted the filing cabinet set in the corner to his left, on the far side of the four-poster bed.

Pulling the top drawer open, he found a daunting amount of paperwork packed into the drawer—each file labeled in fine Elven handwriting. Thankfully, Reynaldi had written everything in his people's native script—one of many languages Stockholm had learned over the centuries of his life.

He walked his fingers along the tabs of the files, finally finding the file labeled *Real Estate*. He tugged the file out, opened the folder, and found a brief history of Reynaldi's property. The previous owner had been one Arthur Digbut, a Dwarven Soldier and a Captain in the Ja-Wen police department. He had installed the stone 'briefing room' on the first floor after purchasing the manor from the city.

"Well, no big surprise there," Stockholm muttered, moving on down the line.

The upper drawer revealed nothing else of interest to him. The lower drawer was much less packed with files, though there was still plenty of paperwork in there. One file, entitled *Assignments*, caught his eye. He pulled it out and opened it on his lap in front of him.

"Bingo."

Archibald Reynaldi kept his assignment papers—apparently as a matter of record keeping. His latest appointment had been to Fort Stone, four days' travel to the north of Ja-Wen on foot.

"We'll be seeing you soon, Mr. Reynaldi." He tucked the two folders into his bag and left the manor behind him.

Now he stood turned the files over to Flint and Anna as he dropped his bag to the floor next to the door.

"Cozy setup," he said, looking at the two recliners currently being used as beds by the two Gnomes of the company. The furniture all had a secondhand appearance, the scent of wood rot settled into the square card table dominating the center of the room. Flint and Styge sat at opposite sides of it, a deck of cards set between them. Anna handed one of the files to Flint, who set it down at the empty third seat. Stockholm seated himself opposite it, at the fourth chair.

"Cozy? Not exactly what I call cozy, pup." Styge stared at the pair of kings in his hand. "There's only the one bed in the back bedroom, and the couch in the study. Course, those two can sleep just about anywhere." He craned his head towards the slumbering Gnomes. He laid down his hand, and Flint set down a full house, raking the copper pieces over toward his side of the table.

"Enough of this." Flint packed the cards into a neat pile. "You should get some sleep old man. I'm gonna play a game of Pokchi with old red here." The Wererat pulled out the board and its other components.

Stockholm replaced Styge at the table, and the elderly Illusionist walked back to the bedroom. Stockholm smiled appreciatively as the Wererat set up the game, dealing the cards with a practiced whip of the wrist.

"Flint—the file," Anna said.

Flint looked over at the file, and the Wererat looked at her with tired eyes.

"Another time, boss," he said. "I'm just going to play this game, and nip off to bed."

Anna didn't blame him for being tired. It was late in the evening, and they all felt fatigued from using the Alchemical transportation.

She took the file from the card table, and moved off into the study to read through the contents within. The handwriting was in Elvish, a language she couldn't read, but Stockholm had spent a fair amount of his time out at the local library, translating the files into Common. She set herself gently down on the couch, the cushion squashing to the form of her buttocks and thighs.

Anna got up from the couch before she started reading the first file, the one on Reynaldi's home, and locked the study door against intrusion. She opened her vest, and the shirt underneath, draping them both over the back of the couch, and set to work unwrapping her breasts. Her chest hurt from spending so much time bundled up, and she needed to get some proper air.

The last of the wrapping fell away, and she sighed deeply, letting her breasts free. "Gods I needed this," she said to the room at large.

She opened the file on the manor, and skimmed the contents as Stockholm had inscribed them in his frustratingly neat script. *Nothing too interesting*, she thought, though Stockholm had included a description of the torture chamber that the file laughingly called an interview room. She completed reading the file, and then turned over to the other one. Within were Reynaldi's Fort assignments —missions he had undertaken in service to the Order, and his instruction records, naming the various decorated officers who had been instructed by the Elven Paladin when they had first joined the Order's ranks. The only name that caught her attention was Christopher Hayes, son of James, who was now a Cleric in the Order.

She flipped to the last page of translation, and read what she could find on Fort Stone.

One of the largest Forts in Tamalaria, it stood as the training grounds for every Knight in the Order. If Reynaldi holed up there, it would be nearly impossible for them to get at the Glove of Shadows. Of course, Stockholm and Flint could probably get in under false pretenses, and Anna's true talents would work wonders for her.

Anna's most useful tool in the Rogue line of work was her ability to forge documents. Put a pen or a quill in her hand and give her some parchment, and she could provide proof that you were the next king of Zombowan, if that were really a kingdom. Give her enough time and some blank leather bound books, and she could provide a history of said kingdom, placing some little village smack in the center of the territory. It was her gift, a talent she had honed while reading the exploits of James Colt, learning from his methods. She could easily provide Stockholm and Flint with paperwork that would declare them and herself as new trainees to the Order. But it would still be highly risky, and she wasn't sure she dared enter the belly of the beast.

Anna stretched out on the couch, trying to get herself comfortable. The place was too warm, that was the problem, she thought. She got up and sauntered over to the window, throwing it open. An unbidden memory danced across her mind's eye as a chilly breeze blew across her bare front. Her mother had stood this same way in front of her bedroom window, luring customers from the streets below with the silent promise of a close-up view of her ample chest. Anna shuffled back to the couch, and stretched out, letting the cool air fill the study. After a few minutes, she fell asleep.

* * * *

Flint struck up his third cigarette since they began their first game of Pokchi. He was down twenty points, but he still had a jack of spades in his hand, available for a counterstrike should Stockholm use a strike move again. He exhaled a plume of smoke, and looked at Stockholm's stoic countenance.

"So, Will told you his big secret, eh?" The Wererat saw the trace of a twitch in the big man's cheek, and he grinned despite his position in the game. *Oh how I love making you feel awkward you big lummox*, he thought.

"Indeed." The Red Tribesman moved a defensive piece on the board and laid down a five of hearts. He bolstered his defensive unit's strike power, preparing for an attack from Flint's side of the board.

Clever, the Wererat thought, his mind only half on the game. He was very tired, and wanted desperately to sleep, but he'd have to wait until either Styge or Anna left their respective resting places.

"It doesn't change anything, you know," Stockholm said, looking Flint in the eyes.

"Not for us, anyway." Flint positioned an offensive unit two spots from Stockholm's recently moved defenders. "Might make a big difference if any of the regulars found out, though."

Stockholm watched dispassionately as Flint laid down a two of clubs, using a ranged attack. His defenders survived, but only with a few life points left.

"It *shouldn't* matter." The big warrior darted a look at the slumbering gnomes. "William is William, and he's the Headmaster. His, secret, as it were, shouldn't even enter into considerations. Why would it?"

"There's a lot of the old boys back home as wouldn't care for it, you know." Flint cursed himself as Stockholm moved an attacker into range of his command unit. "They would revolt."

"Let them try." Stockholm's upper lip curled back slightly to reveal blade-like teeth. "I cherish my position in the Guild and am happy to serve for as long as I am wanted or needed. But let them try to bring harm on her head. There won't be a Guild if there's no living agents to populate it."

Flint inched away from the table, and watched as Stockholm brought the game to a close with a final strike, depleting Flint's command unit of life points and further expanding his points lead.

"Well, you win." Flint packed up the game.

Styge came out of the back bedroom, and Flint checked his timepiece. He'd been playing for four hours, and it was now two in the morning. "Well, good night Chief. I'm going to get myself some shut eye."

As he was about pass Stockholm, the Hoods' Chief lashed out and grasped him by the wrist, hard, drawing him so they were snout to snout.

Styge excused himself and moved off into the small kitchen of the apartment.

"What's wrong Ignatious?"

"You aren't going to tell anyone, are you?" Stockholm whispered, low and faint.

Flint's eyes widened at the murderous glare in those deep eyes, and he shook his head no.

"Good. If you do, I will not hesitate to crush you, Flint. You're a good ally, and one of my few friends. I'd hate to have to hurt you."

Rubbing his sore wrist, the Wererat made his way back to the single bed occupying the bedroom, and lay down. He was asleep in seconds.

* * * *

The trail led Thaddeus Fly and his company to a squat cottage near the eastern fringes of the Allenian Hills region. Trent had reported that the tracks led onward, but Fly wanted to check the place out before moving forward. Some trace of the Paladin's presence might give them a better idea what sort of man they would be attempting to steal from.

The cottage was a one-floor ranch-style affair, crafted almost entirely of wood. This came as no surprise to the Black Draconus, as Elves and Humans seemed to prefer wooden homes to those made of brick or stone.

Trent probed the doorframe at the front of building, searching for traps set to deter intruders. He shook his head, and Fly kicked the door open, admitting the company into a small living room.

Fly, Trent and Lain entered the abode, leaving Rage and Akimaru outside as sentries. Fly didn't want to be interrupted, and if they were seen inside the building, he didn't want witnesses. He ordered Rage to crush anyone who tried to enter without his permission.

He took in the living room, his eyes passing over the various bookcases, display cases, and coffee table adornments. The place had a lived-in feeling to it —a feeling confirmed when a voice cried out, from the hallway leading back to a bedroom, "Who the hell are you people?"

Fly stood bolt upright, staring down the hall at a gruff-looking Human, who Fly assessed immediately as a Soldier.

"Building code inspectors." Lain smiled warmly at the man, who was only clothed from the waist down. He wore tattered greaves over black tunic pants, and his heavy, armored boots thudded on the floorboards as he tentatively stepped toward them. "We were just passing through the area, making sure everyone's prepared for the oncoming storm," she lied.

"What storm?" The man stopped about halfway down the hall.

Fly and Trent exchanged quick shrugs out of eyesight, watching with interest as Lain dealt with the situation.

"I don't know much about it, but one of the local shamans came to our offices a little south of here the other day, said there was a big rainstorm coming," she said. "You can go outside and ask him, while we check the building structure and interior."

Fly watched, dumbfounded, as the Human walked to the front door, intent on speaking to the shaman. As soon as the man stepped outside, a huge green hand grabbed him by the head and twisted. There was sharp, sickening snap of his neck, and he fell back through the doorway.

"There, taken care of," Lain said with a curtsy to Fly and Trent.

The Human Ninja clapped his hands sarcastically.

"Very well done, yes, certainly less trouble than just letting me stab him in the face," he said.

"Less mess to clean up," Fly interjected, defending Lain's course of action.

She smiled bemusedly at Trent as he glowered at her, and the two of them then followed Fly through the rest of the cottage. The only thing of interest they found was a pair of bracers emblazoned with the symbol of Oun.

"Take them out to Akimaru. He may be able to glean something from them," Fly said.

Trent gave him a curious look, to which Fly said nothing.

Outside, Trent handed the bracers to the white clad Ninja, who grasped them tightly and closed his eyes. A stiff breeze blew across the company, accompanied by the howls of strange creatures far to the north.

Trent watched with measured interest as Akimaru's head bobbed a little from side to side.

Finally, the Ninja's eyes opened, and he handed the bracers back to Trent. "They weren't Reynaldi's," he said flatly. "They belonged to a member of his group—a Knight by the name of Salvo. He was not with Reynaldi when he took the Glove. He was waiting here for his lord's return. The man we just killed was his younger brother, a Soldier in training to become a Knight for the Order of Oun. His name was Roderick. The Knight, not the younger brother," Akimaru added.

"How do you know that?" Trent asked.

Akimaru simply held the bracers toward Trent.

The Human Ninja took them, and almost dropped them right away. They were as cold as ice. "Answer me Akimaru!"

"No," Fly ejaculated. "There's no need to explain anything, Akimaru. Trent, a word if you would." Fly grabbed Markus by the collar of his tunic and dragged him about twenty yards away. Trent smacked his hand away and wheeled on him, his eyes aglow with fury.

"How dare you treat me like a childling?" Markus Trent hollered right in Fly's face. "Why do you not force him to explain himself? Why do you know he can do the things he does, and what the fuck *is* he?"

Before he could fume further, Fly slapped him hard across the cheek, stunning him into silence.

"Know your place, Markus Trent! All things will be explained, in time." He faced away from Trent. "I owe you as much of an explanation as I can give you. I don't know all of the details myself, Trent." He turned back towards the Human Ninja. "I only know that I trust Akimaru implicitly. I couldn't even really tell you why I do."

Trent let his hatred of Thaddeus Fly sit on a back burner as he listened. "Then tell me just this one thing. What did he just do? Those bracers were cold enough to burn, Fly."

"Akimaru can sometimes hold an object, and look into the past of its owner. He can decipher certain images in his mind and tell us about what he sees. That's about the half and whole of it, Trent," Fly said. "I sometimes get insight from him when I've got no leads on a mission. We make use of it when we need to. You'll have to wait for more information, Trent. For now, let's get back to the others and get moving. It's already three in the morning, and I'm not going to sleep in that cottage. We'll move for a couple more hours and then make camp."

Fly's company headed out, still unaware that the Hoods were much closer to their destination than they. Neither did they know that they would soon be walking into a trap not of the Hoods' design.

* * * *

Anna is thirteen years old again, rummaging through the shelves of a sundry goods store after the owner has locked up and gone home.

She is looking for the blank parchment scrolls, and once she locates them, she begins working her newly mastered craft. She writes a brief letter, and then rolls the scroll over her leg a few times, holding it high over a lit match to artificially age the paper. She rolls the scroll up, and heads back out the store's back door.

Out in the alley, she tucks the scroll into a back pocket, and makes her way down the darkened pathways. She has lived alone in the streets for three years, scraping and rummaging here and there keep herself alive and relatively healthy. She has grifted and conned her way through life for three whole years. She has nicked people's goods, their money pouches, and their jewelry. She has struck up a good working relationship with several pawnshop owners, bringing them the property of the rich to sell to the middle class, for which they pay her barely a quarter of the worth of anything she shows them. Still, she gets by on her earnings.

She heads to a small cottage, rented only sporadically throughout the year. She sneaks in through the bedroom window as she has for the last two weeks, and she sleeps until noon the next day.

Upon waking, she finds three constables standing over her, their eyes filled with deep suspicion.

"What are you doing here, girl?" one officer, a sickly looking Elf, asks.

She reaches into her back pocket, and produces the scroll she made night before.

The Elven officer grasps it and opens it, reading over the fine print. "Well, my apologies," he says. "Everything seems to be in order."

She thinks she has pulled a good one on them. She is in for a huge surprise.

"Let me see that," an unfamiliar voice says behind the officers.

They part the way, and Anna sees the owner of the cottage, the landlord. She is in deep shit, but can do nothing about it. She stands her ground, however, because there's nothing else she can do.

The owner, a Wererat with coarse, black hair all over, smiles impishly. "You know, I can't believe I forgot about this girl. Her father paid me the rent, that's why she's here. He'll be along in a few days, right young miss?"

She looks into the Wererat's eyes, and sees a hidden laugh. She nods mutely, and watches the officers saunter off. As soon as they are out of earshot, the Wererat approaches her, putting one heavy hand on her shoulder.

"Why did you do that? You could have had them arrest me. This is your property, after all."

"Aye." He pats her on the shoulder. "And this..." he hands her the scroll. "This is one of the finest forgeries I've ever seen, girlie. Most girls aren't quite so talented with this line of work." He looks down at her, and ruffles her hair lightly. "How old are you, girl?"

"Thirteen, sir." She's suddenly very uncomfortable with the smile he gives her.

"Hmm," he says, rubbing his long lower jaw. "You're pretty scrawny, kid, but you're quite talented. I'll tell you what. You need this place as a lay around?"

She nods.

"All right, I'll make you a deal. You got any other talents related to this sort of thing?"

Again, she simply nods, and his smile broadens. "Don't just stand there mutely shaking your head, young one. Tell me what you can do."

Anna pulls a single piece of mythril, shaped like a coin. The landlord's eyes go wide, and he snatches it from between her fingers. "When did you take this?"

"When you had your hand on my shoulder." She fully expects to be struck, or hauled over his shoulder and taken to the police. Neither occurs, however. He smiles again, and tosses her the disk of metal.

"Do that again around town, and give me ten percent of everything you make in a week. You know how to figure numbers, girl?"

She nods.

"Then we have a deal. Now, we shake on it." He extends a hairy hand.

At first, she hesitates, and he draws the hand back a little. "Don't shake if you've any intentions of stiffing me, my dear. There's a such thing as honor among thieves."

"You're a thief?"

"How do you think I made the money to get into real estate? Now, shake my hand, or take yourself elsewhere, orphan."

She shakes his hand, and he leaves her standing there, in the cottage bedroom, alone. It is how she will spend the next two years—alone.

* * * *

Stockholm played blackjack with Styge at the card table for an hour after Flint headed to bed. The old miser finally got up, and headed over to one of the recliners. Stockholm checked the door of the apartment, and saw that it wasn't completely closed, and Lee Toren was not present.

The Red Tribe warrior racked his back, slumping off toward the study. He was about to curl up on the couch, but he remembered that Anna was in there. "Oh well," he mumbled aloud. "Guess it's the floor for me." He turned the knob, which didn't budge. She'd locked it, of course. But locked or not, he was going in.

Stockholm gripped the knob and turned it, hard, splintering the tumblers inside. He stepped inside, pushing the door shut behind him.

No candles lit the room, and Anna left the overhead light off. She had never been big on electrical lighting.

Stockholm took his weapons off, setting them down next to the door and walking around the couch. He glanced at Anna's sleeping form, and fairly yelped as he stumbled back, landing flat on his ass.

Anna grunted, and opened her eyes dreamily. "Hm? Oh, Stocky."

Stockholm suppressed a genuine laugh.

"What?"

"Um, let's just say I think it's cold in here," he said.

"I thought your fur kept you pretty well insulated," she said, her head still filled with memories.

"Oh, *I'm* fine," he said, pointing at her bare chest. "My guess of the room temperature is based on your glass cutters."

She looked down and stared at her hardened nipples, standing on end in the cold air of the room. She hurriedly wrapped herself up, and pulled on her undershirt.

"Asshole," she grumbled as he snickered. "I'm lying back down now. No dogs on the furniture, you know."

He morphed into the form of a wolf, padded a circle next to the couch, and lay down to sleep.

* * * *

Morning brought with it sunlight, and in the eastern provinces of Tamalaria, the first snowfall of the year. Anna and her company closed windows throughout the apartment, secured their cold weather garb, and each member went about their day's business.

At breakfast, Anna had announced that they would take this day to fully prepare for the trip to Fort Stone in the north.

At dawn the following day, they would depart from Ja-Wen and make their way to the Order of Oun outpost, and find Archibald Reynaldi, or someone who knew where the Elven Paladin was.

After their breakfast meeting, Anna and Flint headed to a church dedicated to the worship of Oun in the northwestern area of the city. A thin, cold coat of snow covered the streets and buildings of the city around them, keeping many of the residents inside for the day. The winters in the eastern provinces never threatened for long periods, and they were not harsh as they were in the north and in the west. Anna looked up into the gray thunderheads hovering in the sky, each holding the promise of frostbite.

"You know, back home, this sort of weather isn't due for another four months," Flint said to her, bringing her attention back to the streets. "Kind of frightening, in a way. Without the Alchemy boy back in Desanadron, we'd have been marching and jogging for a week straight, and we still might not have been here." He watched a pair of Wererats dart into an alley after eyeballing him for a long minute.

"Think about it this way, Flint," she said. "At least Fly and his band of merry men will be that much farther behind us."

"Maybe not," Flint said, attempting to strike a match to light his cigarette. A brief arctic gust snuffed it, and the next three, out.

"It's a sign from the gods," she joked.

"Yeah, and it's saying to get a Gnome lighter," Flint grumbled. He finally got one to keep a flame, and inhaled on his smoke. "You think they'll be offended if I don't put this out before going in?" he asked as they turned toward the front of the church.

Potted plants, resting on the steps leading up to the central double doors, whipped this way and that in the wind, the snow already covering most of their green shoots.

Anna bent down and grabbed two of the pots by their arched handles, hoisting them up.

"One good turn deserves another, Prime," she said, motioning her head meaningfully to the other two plants. Flint shrugged his shoulders, stuck the cigarette in one corner of his mouth, and hauled the plants up. The two Hoods ascended the steps swiftly, and Flint set one of the plants down long enough to open one of the double doors long enough to prop it open with his posterior.

"Remind me why we're visiting this church," he said.

"It's a church of Oun, and it's the closest city to Fort Stone, if you don't count a couple of villages and hamlets on the way." She stepped through the door, into a warm antechamber. She set the plants down on one of two benches facing each other on the left and right walls of the room, and Flint set his down opposite, stubbing out his cigarette in the dirt. "Reynaldi more than likely visits now and again to recruit parishioners into the Order. We can ask whatever priest lives here about him."

Flint grunted, uncomfortable with the whole idea. Still, he followed her when she opened the inner door to the church, stepping into a sweeping cathedral-style chamber.

The pews on either side of the room stretched from the center aisle almost to the eastern and western walls, dominating the chamber with their sturdy cherry wood construction. The scent of jasmine flowed through the air, incense sticks burning on plates set at the end of each set of seats.

Support pillars rose at even intervals throughout the chamber, solid concrete rounded and engraved with the various runes indicative of the followers of Oun. And down the aisle, carried by the acoustics of the building's structure, a single low murmur could be heard, a priest in prayer and contemplation.

Anna and Flint saw a single Half-Elf man, kneeling at the end of the aisle, his hands clasped in front of him.

Anna deciphered his Race from the point of his ears, and the long, silver hair on his head. She thumped her boots on the thick carpeting of the aisle, hoping the preacher would hear her approach before she and Flint were too close for his comfort. The Wererat tried to stomp, but as usual, his furry, bare feet simply touched the carpet without effect.

"I heard you at the door." The aging Half-Elf rose and turning to face them, a benign smile lighting his sylvan features. "Please, tell me how I might better help you, Mr., ah?"

Anna cleared her throat and graced the preacher with her most winning smile, flashing her pearly white, perfect teeth.

"Mr. Deus," she said, and bowed. "And my associate is Mr. Flint." She let Flint take his bow. "We're actually here to ask about a man you may well know from the north."

The preacher raised an eyebrow, and motioned for them to follow him to his office.

A plain white oak door was set in the wall behind and to the side of the lectern, at which the father gave sermons to the faithful.

The office they entered was quaint, with a lived-in feeling. Anna's suspicions were confirmed by the sight of a fold-up cot set in the far corner from the door, behind the preacher's desk. A humble elm desk made years before the father purchased it looked worn and faded.

"So, you are searching for a man," asked the preacher.

"Indeed. Myself and Mr. Flint have been looking for him for a while, as we have received word from a close friend of ours that he has located an artifact of some great interest to the magical community." Anna's choice of words held enough of the truth to be believable. In the father's eyes, though, she saw a natural distrust of anyone he didn't recognize from a congregation.

He must have been a real man of the community of Ja-Wen, she thought, a man with strong ties to the area. This could go either way.

"And this, artifact..." the preacher said, pulling a jug of water from the floor on his side of the desk, pouring a glass for himself. "What exactly is it? What does it do?"

"We aren't at liberty to divulge that, father," Flint interjected. "We've come to confirm or disconfirm its authenticity. There are certain mage councils that would pay a hefty donation to the church if we were able to secure the artifact for their study." The Wererat gave a leering smile, which the preacher returned in kind.

"Well, the church of Oun can always use donations and benefactors," the preacher said slowly, carefully. "Very well." He sipped of his water. "Who is it you're looking for, Mr. Deus?"

"Archibald Reynaldi," Anna replied.

The air around her turned suddenly very cold, and the father's smile faded swiftly.

"Lord Reynaldi is presently at Fort Stone, to the north of the city, past Sharase. The artifact he has in his possession is the Glove of Shadows," the preacher said with plain disgust. "It is an artifact coveted by thieves and brigands, Mr. Deus. I don't know why Lord Reynaldi would keep such a thing around, but I am confident he will destroy the accursed thing," the father said. "I am sorry, Mr. Deus, Mr. Flint, but I do not believe the council that sent you will be able to inspect the object." The father rose and extending a hand toward Anna and Flint.

Anna shook his hand. "Thank you for your time, father. I just have another question or two."

The preacher nodded, but said nothing further. He looked at Flint, who shook his hand and left the office, slamming the door behind him angrily.

Anna, confused, looked at the door, wondering what had gone unspoken between her Prime and this preacher.

"Father, may I ask what just happened here?"

"You have my sincerest apologies, Mr. Deus," the preacher said, seating himself and taking another sip of water. "I detest people of Mr. Flint's species." He smiled warmly at her, and she recognized the cold sensation she'd felt a minute before. Wererats, for the most part, were natural thieves, and seldom broke away from this stigma. Some became Soldiers, a few trained in the arts of magic, and a very rare handful even became Clerics of one religion or another. But on the whole, the world viewed them as highwaymen and thieves.

"You're a racist, in other words," she growled at the preacher, whose smile didn't fade in the least. "Pompous, altar licking prick." She shoved herself up from her chair. Before she stormed out of the room, she turned to face the preacher one last time, and she saw that his smile hadn't faded. "You know, it's people like you who cause real misery, father. You preach the word of Oun, and you listen to confessions and condemn people for not following your ways, but I know something about your precious religion that you seem to have forgotten."

"And I suppose you are going to tell me that, Mr. Deus?"

"I will. 'There is no man in the world who is not deserving of mighty Oun's grace'. For a Half-Elf, your studies don't seem so thorough."

"I suspect there are exceptions. I also suspect that a man with your reputation for skullduggery and theft is rather a poor example of a person who is in any position to speak on moral matters. I have heard of you, Mr. Deus. I frankly have to wonder what sort of terrible parentage you had as a child to become such a man as you are, and mighty Oun condemns such louts as easily as he does men who make their livings by pilfering from others."

She hocked an enormous wad of phlegm at the preacher.

It struck him squarely on the cheek, but he made no move to clean it. She left the office, slamming the door behind her almost as hard as Flint had.

Together, the Hoods' Headmaster and Prime left the church.

In his office, the preacher took a cloth rag from his desk and wiped away the spit on his face before he turned to the closet behind him, which creaked open slowly.

"Do you know who that was," the voice of the woman in the closet inquired.

"I do," the preacher replied. "Your description of him was almost perfect. And you say they're going to try to steal the Glove of Shadows from Lord Reynaldi?"

"Indeed," said the disembodied voice. Though the closet door closed, the preacher could still discern no visible owner of the voice. The priest only knew that he could faintly detect the woman's presence. "And William Deus is a convincing Rogue, father. Make certain that Reynaldi is warned against him."

"I will." The preacher pulled a blank piece of parchment his desk, and dipped his quill in an inkwell.

The window of his office opened, letting in a small gust of early winter wind and snow.

He closed the window and wrote his letter to Lord Archibald Reynaldi, then opened the closet again, drawing out his messenger pigeon.

He looked over the other letter on his desk, tucked carefully under his Oun Bible, and wondered again about the strange, invisible woman who had come to visit him.

The letter warned of the coming of a second group of thieves, led by a Black Draconus.

He also wondered why the two groups were traveling separately.

* * * *

Markus Trent smiled ear to ear as Teresa Evergreen reported that the deed had been done.

The Midnight Suns were still four days' travel from Fort Stone, and Thaddeus Fly seemed impatient to arrive and take the Glove of Shadows.

Early in the morning, Teresa had made contact, informing Trent that she had followed Toren to an Alchemy shop owned by one Jonah Staples. The Staples boy had used the power of Alchemy to send the Hoods and, unwittingly, Teresa, to Ja-Wen. If Trent advised Fly to change course toward the city, they would arrive in three days' time, and be able to confront Deus and his men.

Instead, Trent realized he could use his knowledge of the situation to his advantage. The Glove of Shadows would be best off in his own personal possession, after all, and if he could manage to get rid of Fly and the others as well, so much the better! *Teresa*, he thought, waiting for her to respond.

I'm listening, love.

Locate a church of Oun in Ja-Wen, and contact whoever's there. Write a letter warning him or her of our approach to Fort Stone, but leave me out of the descriptions. Warn them as well of William Deus and his cronies, Trent thought, concentrating as hard as he could to keep his message in his head. Thaddeus Fly would surely kill him on the spot if he knew of the betrayal the Human Ninja planned.

I understand, Markus. Anything else?

Yes. A smug grin formed on his lips. *When Fly and the others are arrested, get into the Fort and follow Reynaldi. He'll lead you to the Glove of Shadows. Take possession of it, and bring it to me.*

Where will you be, love?

I'll be in Ja-Wen, of course, he replied in his mind. Trent loped ahead to Fly, and asked that he be allowed to detach from the group, to make certain that the Paladin wasn't hiding out in the city.

"Go ahead, Markus," Fly said with a hint of suspicion. "You're not scared of the Order, are you?"

Trent badly wanted to wipe the shit-eating grin off Fly's scaled face.

"No, Headmaster. I just want to cover all of our bases."

That had been four hours before, at noon. Now, in mid-afternoon, Trent led the way still along a hilly path through the plains just south of the Allenians. He wouldn't part from their company for a few hours off, but he was anxious to put distance between himself and Fly. The Black Draconus had given him permission to part ways, but the longer he remained with the group, the more likely it seemed that Fly would send one of the others with him. Rage would stay with Fly, because the Orc couldn't find his way out of a paper bag. And if Lain were sent with him, Rage would sulk about it until Fly agreed to let him go as well. Which, of course, Trent thought with a hint of chagrin, left Akimaru.

The footpath down which he led the company all the way to marshland through which Fly intended to take the Midnight Suns. It could be bypassed with an extra day and a half of travel to the south.

Perhaps, Trent mused, *I should take this as an early jump off point.* He waited for the rest of the company to catch up.

When they did, Trent pointed south of the marshlands. "I may as well make my way around. I'll be closer to Ja-Wen in any event."

Fly nodded and pulled a sutra from his pack.

"Take this." He handed the small scroll to Markus Trent, still avoiding looking the other Ninja in the eyes. "Don't use it, just keep it on you. When we

150

meet up again, I'll give you more answers to your questions." Fly turned his head slowly, meeting Trent's blue eyes with his own yellow, reptilian eyes.

Trent saw a deep seeded sadness in Fly's eyes, but ignored it, looking instead for the madness that had made the Black Draconus kill his sensei.

Yet again, he did not find it. For twelve long years that spark had eluded his scrutiny. If he went through with his planned betrayal, he realized, he would never have another opportunity to search for it, and his questions would go unanswered forever.

Still, he'd let go of his questions to rule the Midnight Suns. "Very well, Headmaster. As soon as I find out anything, where shall I meet up with you?"

"There is a village." Fly signaled Akimaru to lead Lain and Rage toward the marsh ahead. "It is two days north of Ja-Wen, one day south of the Fort. We shall head there, and await your coming or messenger bird. If there are any snags in the city, let us know immediately." Fly patted Trent roughly on the shoulder and heading after the others.

Trent watched until they disappeared into the lank, dark woods of the marshland. He wiped his shoulder with a rag, as though a leper had touched him. He considered throwing away the sutra that Fly had given him, but instead, he held it up to the sunlight, trying to read the script.

It was written in a language he didn't know of, but he assumed it was the script of Fly's people, the Draconus.

He tucked it into one of his various inner pockets, and started south, skirting the marshland woods.

Being alone in the wilderness of Tamalaria was never a good idea, but he knew the region well enough. If he continued south five more days after reaching the southern fringe of the marshes, he could come upon a woodland that stretched all the way south to the shores of the continent. Within those woods was a small village, inhabited by Elves, Humans, and a few Dwarves.

That particular village was only a half hour's walk to the Obura Ninja Clan. He knew the region he now traveled through because he had often come to these plains and hills, including the marshland, when he was given time away from the clan. Few of creatures lived in the lands he would pass through could pose much of a threat to him. Still, it had been twelve years, and a lot could change in that time—for the better, or for the worse. Twelve years had also hardened him, made him more capable.

As the first of the wintry winds blew past him, he realized that winter would be fully upon the eastern provinces, and he and Fly both would be passing into snow and blustering winds in a couple of days' time. Shivering slightly, he wrapped his uniform tunic closer to his body, and set off.

* * * *

Lee Toren watched his timepiece patiently, waiting for one o'clock and tapping his feet on the dirt road.

"Tell me again why we're just standing around here." Norman Adwar sat on a bench off to one side of the street behind the Gnome Pickpocket.

"I'm standing around, you're loafing on yer arse." Lee looked again at the door of the tavern.

A large, rough hewn wooden placard hanging in front of the window announced that happy hour started at one o'clock, afternoon time, and Lee was freezing his balls off waiting for the appointed hour.

As soon as the small hand pointed to the twelve on his timepiece, he shivered and smiled, turning to Norm and signaling with a wave of his hand for the Engineer to follow him in.

The usual suspects sat cloistered in groups at black slate tables the barkeep probably described as 'comfortable'.

Lee looked at the squat Dwarf, standing on a stool behind the bar to better serve the alcoholics that frequented his particular watering hole. He put a flabby arm around Norm's shoulders, and pulled him close, whispering conspiratorially in his ear. "Happy hour means drinks is cheaper, mate. Cheaper drinks means looser lips on the customers, and looser lips means better information."

"Yeah, okay." Norman's high-pitched whine of a voice seriously grated on Lee's nerves. "But what are we trying to find out? I mean, Will and Flint went to a church, and Styge went with Stockholm to pick up supplies for the trip. So what are *we* trying to learn?"

"We're going to see if we can find out specific information about Fort Stone. Hard numbers and facts, mate." Lee shoved Norman easily away, and approached the bar. He hopped up onto one of the stools, graced the red-bearded bartender with a smile and nod, and asked for a whiskey on the rocks.

He plunked down the two copper pieces, happy hour pricing for the drink, then hopped down off of the stool. "Don't hang about, Norman," he admonished, taking a swig of his drink. "Get yerself a drink, lest you should stick out loik a sore thumb."

The Gnome Engineer felt awkward in the smoggy tavern. He didn't do much drinking, and gods only knew what they put in the booze there. He climbed onto the stool, ordered an ale, and was handed a drink in the grubbiest looking glass the barkeep could lay hands on—of that Norm was certain.

He clambered down off of the stool, muttering to himself, "Germs, germs, germs. Who knows if this stuff is safe to drink?"

Lee headed over to the smokiest corner of the bar, inviting himself to an empty chair at a table where several Jafts and a Cuyotai were playing a game of cards.

Lee looked at the table for a minute, turned his head back to check on Norm, and gave him a small 'bugger off' with a wave of his hand.

Norman stood in the middle of the tavern, scanning the customers with a wizened glare, until he spotted a gray furred Werewolf on the other side of the serving bar.

He approached the Werewolf slowly, pulling a small device from his belt.

In the center of the device was a small, black screen, with two buttons above and three switches below. Two long, thin prongs stood out of the top of the device, and he pointed them discreetly at the Werewolf, pressing one of the buttons above the screen.

The words 'Storm Tribe Werewolf' blinked on the screen for a moment before Norman pressed the other button above the screen.

The word 'Knight' flashed across, replacing the first readout.

He smiled to himself, pleased beyond reason at how well the invention worked, and stuffed it away in its compartment.

Norman walked purposefully up to the Werewolf, and gave him a small wave.

The Storm Tribe Werewolf looked down at him, his pure black eyes ringed with bags either from drink or from lack of sleep.

From the subtle smell of sweat, and the absence of a condensation ring on the table from his mug, Norm concluded that the man must have just come into the bar not long before Lee and himself. The Werewolf wore thick leathers over a chain mail shirt, and nothing over his chain mail pants. "Mind if I sit with you?" Norman asked, his voice quivering only a little.

"Of course, little man," replied the Werewolf in a tired voice. "It's always good to have company. So, where do you hail from, Gnome?"

"Desanadron, actually." Norm grunted as he tried to climb into the Human-scale chair while holding his drink.

The Werewolf grabbed his mug, set it on the table, and let Norm clamber up onto the chair, standing on it so his head poked over the edge of the table.

"You're a long way from home then, Gnome. What's your name?"

"Oh, Norman," He bowed his head slightly to the Storm Tribesman. "Norman Adwar. You?"

"Trebonius Neverfall." The Werewolf offered a gnarled, heavily scarred hand.

Norm shook it as best he could, leaning over the table, and stood back, taking a swig of his ale. As soon as it was in his mouth, an image of rank seaweed, fermented under a thousand suns, came to mind.

His gag reflex started to speak, but he swallowed the foul booze before it could shout, leaving it no recourse.

"And from the look on your face right now, Norman Adwar, I'd say you don't do a lot of recreational drinking." The Werewolf chuckled.

"Not really. Look, I'm not gonna try to be sneaky or underhanded like the gentleman I came in with," Norman said in a rush of words.

The Storm Tribe Werewolf leaned back in his chair, but remained casual and smiling.

"We're here for information."

"Naturally," replied the Werewolf Knight. "Ask your questions, and I'll answer them in kind."

"Thank you very much." Norm pulled a pad of paper from an inside breast pocket. He clicked open a pen, a simple contraption erected from springs and a small plastic tube filled with ink. The Werewolf stared at it much as he might stare at a bull with the head of a sheep.

"Um, what is that?"

"Oh, this?" Norman held up the pen. "It's called a pen. Lots of folks use them these days for writing things down. Much more reliable than a pencil, because whereas lead fades after enough time, ink is pretty permanent. So long as it doesn't get wet, that is," he added. "Now, Mr. Neverfall, have you ever been to Fort Stone?"

"A few times," said Neverfall. "My professional occupation sometimes takes me to the Order of Oun, as I'm a soldier of fortune."

"A mercenary? Aren't you a Knight?" Norm raised an eyebrow as he realized he'd made a mistake.

"By Class, yes. And by the way, Mr. Adwar," the Werewolf said after taking a swig of his own drink. "How did you know that?"

Norm held out the device he'd used to scan the Werewolf, trying to explain its functions.

Neverfall waved off his explanation, clearly lost on the subject. "No matter. Yes, I am a Knight, and no, members of the Knight Class don't typically let themselves become mercenaries. But I'm not much of an adventurer, and I need to make end's meet, Norman. I have a place here in Ja-Wen, nothing to write home about, but it's mine. The odd jobs I take pay my rent and buy me food and drink."

"When was the last time you were there?" Norm's pen scrawled furiously on the notepaper.

"Couple of weeks past, actually. The Port of Arcade sent a request for an exorcist from Fort Stone two months ago, and advised them to send along some muscle to keep the preacher safe. I was passing by the Fort, asked the guards at the gate if they needed any hired help, and they put me along with the group since they were heading out the next day. There were horses to carry us to Arcade, so the trip was quick, but when we got to Arcade, we discovered that the actual problem was in a recently uncovered set of ruins north of the city. I'd tell you all about it," the Werewolf said, shuddering slightly. "But I'd just as soon forget."

"Not to seem too forward, Mr. Neverfall, but I was wondering if you could just tell me what you saw inside the Fort."

Neverfall described the inside of the Fort to Norman, his details slightly vague, but conveying quite well what the Hoods could expect to see if they got through the front gates.

Norm wrote down everything he could, trying to keep pace, and soon had seven note pages full of information. "Thank you very much, Mr. Neverfall. May the gods bless you wherever you go."

"And you too, Norman Adwar," the Werewolf said.

Norm headed over toward Lee Toren, only to find that the Pickpocket was roaring drunk, and about to be tossed out into the snow on his head.

Norman apologized to the barkeep for his friend, paid for the eight drinks Lee had quaffed, and dragged Lee out into the blustering wind.

"Oi, wot's this," Lee complained, looking around. "Did they open the windows or somefin'?"

"No, we're outside, you drunken devil." Norm helped Lee back toward the apartment. "I got the information we needed, by the way."

"Did you now?" Lee questioned Norman no further when the Engineer shoved his notebook under his nose. "Oh, so you did. Well, tha's great, nerd boy, just foin work there."

He stumbled over a snow-covered rock. "Who the bloody hell puts a rock in the middle of the road loik that?"

"You were on the side of the road, Lee." Norm helped the bumbling Pickpocket into the apartment, propped him into one of the recliners, and started to review his notes. *At last*, he thought, *I'm making a real contribution to the group.*

* * * *

Styge poked at several of the bags Stockholm had tossed in the cart, listening to the horrible little squishing noise coming from within. "What *are* they, precisely?" He followed the Red Tribe Werewolf down another aisle in the food market.

"They're called k rations. They're a civilian knock-off of military MRI pouches," the lumbering lycanthrope rumbled.

The elderly Illusionist looked up at him, a look on his face meaning 'I still don't get it'.

Stockholm sighed. "You tear off the top of the bag, pour a little hot water inside, and shake the bag. Poof, instant meal, elderly one."

Styge nodded, and gave a little whistle.

"Figure we'll need to eat on the move a lot, big man?" Styge reached up to one shelf, pulling down a can of beans and throwing it, and three of its brothers, in the cart.

"Probably. I'm not sure why, but I've got a funny feeling that Fort Stone isn't going to be our last stop." Stockholm read the label of a package of cookies, then set them back on the shelf—only to have Styge drop them in over his shoulder, probably breaking the contents apart inside the cheap plastic wrapping.

He groaned, shaking his head. "Must you?"

"Hey, if you want to have those disgusting sounding rations around, you'll have to make a few concessions." The old man waggled his walking stick a little at the Red Tribe Werewolf.

They pushed the cart to the checkout counter where a burly Minotaur tallied up their purchases on a pad of paper with a pencil.

Stockholm paid for the supplies, and divided them into individual bags, so everyone got an even share. The cookies he placed in Styge's assigned bag, as well as the beans, though he knew Flint would want at least a can to himself.

The foodstuffs purchased, Stockholm and Styge returned to the apartment, giving Norman a queer look after seeing the sad state of Lee Toren.

The Engineer simply shrugged his shoulders and made a little 'drinky drinky' motion with his hand.

Stockholm deposited the groceries on the kitchen counter and table, and returned to the living room for a moment. "I'm going back out, Norman. I'm going to get a few more things I think will be useful for the group. Stay here and keep an eye on things."

"Before you go, ol' boss, I think you may want to see this." Norman hustled over, nearly skidding on the floor where Stockholm's wet footprints had soaked it. He handed his notebook up to Stockholm, who grinned as he rifled through the notes.

"Got the info from a very reliable source I think. Lee didn't get much of anything useful, I think. Spent most of his time just getting soused."

"Yes, I imagine he did." Stockholm read over the last couple of pages of notes. Norman had been meticulous, writing down every single detail that

Neverfall could provide. "This is excellent, Norman." The Chief handed the notebook back. "Make certain William sees this as soon as he gets in."

He patted the Gnome Engineer on the shoulder, nearly knocking him down, and exited the apartment again. He had personal business to attend to, and it would only take him an hour or so.

Ignatious Stockholm descended the stairwell, passing by the aging Jaft with his perpetual cigarette in the lobby, and stepped out into the gently falling snow. Another inch had accumulated on the streets and the rooftops, and he shivered with the cold. It wasn't a deep chill, he thought, but he didn't think anyone in the company was properly equipped for it.

He made his way along the city's winter landscape mostly by memory. Memory served him well, he thought. He arrived in front of a two-story clothiers shop, owned by a man he'd known for nearly three hundred years.

He straightened his chain mail undershirt, brushed off his open-fronted vest, and smiled charmingly. "Time to call down old favors," he whispered to the wintry air itself before entering.

* * * *

Anna used Flint as a windbreaker, letting him walk perhaps a foot and half in front of her, keeping his broad shoulders at her own head level by walking with a very slight crouch. Together, they trudged through the snowdrifts, passing by two teams of Dwarves in bright orange jumpsuits.

Each member of the five-dwarf teams slid a wide shovel along the street. In this manner, the cities of Ja-Wen, Poregbal, Ushinwa and Desanadron cleared their streets, the city footing the bill for the Dwarves' time. Sometimes Minotaurs were used, but Dwarves, being low to the ground, made the best snow throwers.

After a while, she and Flint rushed through the door of the apartment, eager to get themselves wrapped in blankets. Small packs of ice clung to Flint, and Anna shivered uncontrollably as she looked at the old couch that hadn't been in the apartment living room the night before.

She looked over at Styge, who gave her a wrinkled smile. "I drew it up when I got back. Go ahead, give it a try."

Anna approached the couch, and sat down easily on it. Surprisingly, it held her weight perfectly.

"I know, it's a bit of a waste of power, but I think we needed another place for someone to catch some rest."

"No no, this is perfect." She relaxed her cramped legs and stretched as Flint sat opposite her on the couch. "How long until it returns to the paper?"

"The standard twenty-four hours." Styge lay down another card. "I've got a couple of doozies in this sketchbook, but the couch just seemed practical."

Anna took a deep breath, found that she was starting to offend, and excused herself for the shower room. She stepped into the small bathing room, locked the door, and stripped naked, running the warm water into the tub.

Ah, Gnome plumbing, she thought. *Good stuff.*

She got the water to an acceptable temperature, and stepped into the stall, pulling the curtain shut and enjoying the stream of water.

She washed herself down, rinsed off, and stepped out of the stall, leaving the water running. She reached into her pack, which she'd brought along into the room, and grabbed up a fresh set of clothing. She got dressed, wrapped herself up again, and turned back to the stall. She left the water running, and stepped out into the living room. "All right old man," she said to Styge. "You're next. We all need a good shower," she said to the group.

The Illusionist made no complaints, stepping into the washroom and shutting the door behind him.

Anna sat at the table, and Flint joined her, pulling out his Pokchi game.

She played a while with him, losing the first game, forcing a draw for the second and finally winning the third game. She didn't play with much strategy, and no single game took more than twenty minutes, but by the time they were finished, Stockholm came into the apartment with several large bags in his hands, and one strapped to his back.

"Oh no, nobody get up to help me." He laced his voice with sarcasm as a dagger might be with poison.

The guilt trip took Flint by the throat, and he helped the Red Tribesman by taking a few of the bags from his hands and the one on his back.

"You can all thank me later."

Flint reached into one of the bags and pulled out a thick, black wool sweater, a dragon design embroidered on the left sleeve. He held it up, and saw that Stockholm had written the Wererat's name on a paper tag attached to the collar.

He immediately donned the warm sweater, pulling it over his head with a tug. "Oi, thanks a' plenty, Stocky. Is this all clothes?"

"No." Stockholm pulled a treated tent tarp from one of the larger bags. "We may have some trouble traveling now that the winter's come on quick, so I got us treated tents to sleep in outdoors."

Stockholm distributed plenty of winter clothes to the members of the Hoods company—each article of clothing accepted with thanks.

"Where did you get all this stuff?" Anna asked.

"From an old friend of mine." Stockholm winked at Anna.

Ah, she thought, an old 'friend'.

Lastly, Stockholm handed Anna a sealed bag, and gave her a quick nod. She returned the nod, and took herself into the study as the others busied themselves with trying on their new winter apparel.

She shut the door behind her and tried to lock it, but saw that the tumblers had been broken. *Stockholm, of course*, she thought. She opened the seal on the bag, and looked down with one eye pressed to the small breach in the seal.

Inside of the bag, she saw a shimmering, purple dress, a formal affair to be worn at society to-dos.

She smiled, a newfound sense of appreciation for the big Chief warming her heart. It was the sort of dress Harold liked to see her in.

The door creaked open behind her, and the big Red Tribesman grinned at her like an idiot.

"I'd hug you if it were appropriate," she said

He begged off on that for the time being.

"Something else on your mind, Chief?"

"Yes, actually." His face turned to stone seriousness. "You'll want to talk to Norman. He's got some interesting information for you."

She spoke with Adwar for a few minutes then, reading over his notes, taking in every detail and memorizing it as best she could.

Now she knew the layout of the inside of the Fort, all she needed to do now was prepare the papers that would get her, Stockholm and Flint in.

Styge and Norman could make their own way in, as they wouldn't raise any suspicions. Lee might even find a way in, if Styge could use a little magic to disguise the Pickpocket.

Anna gathered everyone into a huddle in the living room, and reviewed her plan of approach with them, getting a round of approving nods of the head and mutterings before she took herself off to the study to wait for dinner.

After everyone had eaten, it was time for some much needed sleep. They would have two, perhaps three days of hard marching through the snow and wind northward, and then they would have to brave the danger of being found out at Fort Flag. They needed to keep their minds fresh.

She didn't know it then, but a fresh mind wouldn't be helping the Hoods any.

The Glove of Shadows

Interlude

A messenger pigeon fluttered through the window of Archibald Reynaldi's tower study, a small, mottled gray creature that chirped loudly once it perched on the inner frame of the window.

The Elven Paladin looked up from his current fiction novel and pulled his reading glasses off, walking easily over to the animal. He stroked its head gently with a long pointer finger, and took the attached letter from its leg, thanking it for its service before he shooed it away.

He opened the parchment and found a second letter inside, both signed by father Raymondo Alvisi of Ja-Wen.

He read the letters quickly, and smiled broadly, his teeth flashing into the empty expanse of the tower study. *It appears*, he thought, *that they'll both be arriving at about the same time.* There might be a slight difference in the tactics both companies of thieves used to gain entrance to Fort Stone, but Reynaldi would let both groups in, wait until they were away from the gates and seal them inside. Ambush units could snare any of the Guild members that remained outside of the Fort, in the event of trouble. He'd gather a nice little collection of thieves—a collection he intended to let rot in the dungeons.

Chapter Twelve
Captured!

Travel through the marshes proved difficult for Thaddeus Fly and his company.

Upon entering them, Rage had stopped and sat on the muddy earthen floor to stare at a glowing mushroom. He'd been so wrapped up in it that Fly had needed to enlist the aid of both Akimaru and Lain to drag the big Orc away. Only fifteen minutes later, he'd repeated the process with a moaning strand of algae sticking up out of the muck.

Fly had shaken his head, and dutifully pried Rage from the sucking mud around his rear end.

The whole first day in the marshes was spent carefully maneuvering around the dangerous portions of the quagmire and muck. Having studied for a year in these very marshes, Lain McNealy proved most useful in this respect.

Necromancers from all over the continent, she told the Headmaster, spent at least a year in this marshland, known to magic users of her kind as 'The Murk'.

"How very appropriate," Fly spat.

The rest of the first day passed, thankfully, without incident. On the second day, the wintry air from the plains beyond the marsh started to permeate the region. By late afternoon, Lain had excused herself to duck behind a tree and changed into thick blue jeans and a hooded sweatshirt with a skull design on the front.

Akimaru and Rage seemed unfazed by the change in air temperature, and Fly himself didn't mind too much. But the temperature was the least of their worries.

At around noon, Fly heard the soft, muted sounds of other creatures approaching them from all sides, an ambush set for any unwary travelers of the region. Within minutes, Goblin marauders and their large, wild dogs streamed out of the dank woods and mud pits.

Rage stampeded into the Goblin forces coming at them head-on, while Akimaru defended the group from the rear, his short swords and sickle and chain flashing out in streaks, leaving a swath of bodies wherever he darted. Lain conjured up the fallen Goblins and dogs, setting the undead against their former comrades and sending fear racing up the Greenskins' spines like desert cobras.

Fly simply stood in the path, waiting for the marauders coming from the south, or right of the path.

As soon as a clumped mass of attackers came within range, Fly opened his mouth, discharging pure lightning force into their midst.

The front ranks of Goblins and dogs sparked and fried, dropping to the ground in burned husks of flesh while their allies stumbled and tried to retreat. But Thaddeus Fly hadn't released a discharge of his natural power in a long time, and he had a great deal of it available for use. He opened his jaw wide and released another long trident of electricity into the fleeing attackers, splitting them apart and rending them asunder.

Eyes and skulls burst apart as the power surged through their bodies, leaving broken Goblins and dogs in a dotted trail to the southern marsh.

The company brushed themselves off, and continued on through the marsh. Lain kept one of the undead dogs, letting it stray from the path now and again to bring her herbs and assorted plant roots.

That evening, it strayed too far off, and they found it half an hour later, permanently dead.

As night fell upon them the second time in the marshes, they made camp, starting a small fire to keep themselves warm. Rage and Akimaru lay down, though Fly had his doubts that the white clad Ninja actually slept.

Lain sat next to Fly in front of the fire, uncomfortably close for the Black Draconus' liking.

He tried to inch away, but each time he did, she scooted closer again.

"Would it kill you to try to share some body heat," she chided.

He looked at her, nonplussed. "I'm cold blooded, Lain, remember?"

"Oh." Now it was her turn to appear nonplussed. She stared into the fire, nodding her head back and forth, humming a soft, quick tune. Finally she spoke again. "So, you really don't think I'm cut out for this Guild business?"

Fly considered her question for a few minutes, and spat into the fire.

"It's nothing against you, Lain," he mumbled, keeping his voice low. Though Trent wasn't around, there were a few things he wanted to keep close to the vest. "It's just that, well, you're too good at what you do to waste your time with us. You're very good with Rage, though, I'll admit that."

Unbidden, Lain shot her left arm around Fly's right, stopping his breathing and his heart for a moment.

"What if I *want* to waste my time with you?"

He looked at her pale, lovely Human visage, scanning her eyes to see if she meant what he thought she did. *Yes, there it is, that little twinkle when she bats her eyes. Oh, gods, how did I miss something so obvious?*

"Well, um, Ms. McNealy, ah…" Thaddeus Fly, while a fully competent and capable Ninja, had not a clue how to approach a romantic situation. His hands felt suddenly clammy, his soft palm scales covered with a cold sweat.

She leaned close against him, her ample chest pressing against his arm.

Oh gods, oh gods, what do I DO? "I guess that would be your prerogative." He stood quickly and took a few steps away, then faced away from her, his body quivering and buckling under the sudden pressure he faced. He just wanted to steal an artifact—how did things get so suddenly complicated?

She put one hand on the small of his back, running a finger up his spine.

"Lain, it occurs to me that perhaps we should let this topic of conversation wait until we get back home."

Her hand stopped, and stiffened a little.

"Very well. Perhaps we can discuss the subject more, *privately*, back in Desanadron."

Fly waited for a good ten minutes, turning around finally and finding that she had fallen asleep with her head on his rucksack.

Another familiar voice whispered in his ear. "Most interesting, sensei."

Fly turned and thought he saw a mischievous glint in the barely visible purple eyes.

161

"Oh, shut it." Fly put one large hand on Akimaru's face and shoved him away lightly. "I didn't ask for this. Besides, I guess it isn't exactly taboo. Draconus have mated with Humans before, even married them. But don't get me wrong," he gave Akimaru a stern look. "This in no way means I've gotten soft. And nobody at home is to know about this, ah, incident. Understood?"

"Perfectly, sensei," Akimaru said.

The two Ninjas walked around the camp a few times, keeping a slow pace, hands clasped behind their backs. Finally, Akimaru broke the silence. "Sensei, what is your take on Markus Trent's departure from us?"

"I think he's a coward and a traitor, Akimaru," Fly looked off into the marshy woods, spying a single raven seated on a bent, crooked tree. The bird didn't seem natural to him, out of place in the marsh. "What about you?"

"I am not entirely certain, sensei. I do not trust him, but I do not think he will betray us regarding the Glove of Shadows. He contacted a tracking agent prior to our departure from Desanadron. Perhaps he has personal business he employed her for in Ja-Wen?"

Fly noted with interest the way Akimaru walked in the marsh with him. The mysterious Ninja's feet never once sunk into the mud or muck.

On the few occasions Akimaru stepped in front of Fly, the ground radiated with a deep chill where the white clad Ninja trod.

"Akimaru," Fly said, halting in his tracks.

"Yes, sensei?"

"I need to ask you to do something I've never asked of you." Fly's face took a stone cast.

Akimaru turned, letting his arms hang loosely at his side.

"Akimaru, would you remove your mask?"

The white clad Ninja reached up, and pulled his mask off.

Thaddeus Fly couldn't even find the breath to gasp.

* * * *

At dawn, Anna Deus and the Hoods she had brought with her to Ja-Wen departed from the city's northern gates, trudging through the snowy fields and frosted grasslands with as much haste as they could muster.

Stockholm and Flint marched at the front of the pack, clearing the way with their larger lycanthrope bodies.

Directly behind them came Anna and Styge, with Lee Toren and Norman Adwar trailing by a few yards, their hoods tied close about their heads.

Anna kept the forged training papers tucked in her wool overcoat, each paper folded and set into a protective plastic folder. The members of the company slogged on in silence for the entire first day of travel. Miserable, damp and cold, they bedded down the first night in an open field, their treated tents keeping out most of the cold and chill. Lee and Norm shared a tent, as did Flint and Styge.

Anna and Stockholm alone had tents to themselves, and as Anna bedded down for the night, she was again reminded how much she missed her husband. She wondered how Harold was getting on without her. She'd been gone almost two weeks now, and she sincerely hoped that despite the mess the Guild seemed to be in, he was being taken care of.

Morning brought a bright, warm sun that melted off a good deal of the snowfall from the previous day, making travel easier on the hills and plains. However, it made the way messy and difficult when they descended the slopes of the valley that led them past a village between Ja-Wen and Fort Stone.

Anna kept checking over her shoulder to make certain they hadn't lost Lee and Norm, and early in the afternoon, they had to double back and help Norm out of a deep sinkhole of snowy mud.

Flint reached down and grabbed the small Engineer by the back of his belt, his arm buried in the murk to his elbow. The Wererat Prime hauled, and with a loud sucking noise, Norman came free.

Covered in mud and shivering with the cold, Norm caused them a slight delay as they struck up a fire for an afternoon meal, and to heat him up. They ate their meal, each Hood pensive as they neared their final destination.

Nobody wanted to admit it, but they were risking arrest, despite the level of skill Anna applied to forging her documents.

The long hours of the day were further lengthened by a fresh downpour of snow.

"Gods I hate the winter," Flint complained as he and Stockholm once again took a lead on the rest of the company, slogging through the fresh drifts of white powder. "And you're starting to smell like wet dog, my friend."

"Better than drowned rat, Flint," Stockholm quipped in response.

Flint smiled despite his frozen feet. It was good to see that the red warrior still had a sense of humor in the face of such terrible traveling conditions. After sunset, they continued for a few hours in the darkness, until the lights inside of Fort Stone shone in the distance.

"All right everyone, listen up." Anna gathered the company into a huddle. "We're going to wait until first light tomorrow, and then we approach. Styge, Norm, Lee, you'll stay here in the tents. Keep an eye out for anything suspicious, and keep things secured here. Stockholm, Flint and I will approach without all of our belongings, so you'll have to make sure they're secured. Got it?"

"Oi, that we do Will." Lee spoke for the trio being left behind. "Say, am I still being paid fer this?"

"Of course you are." Anna rolled her eyes and setting up her tent. "All right everybody, tuck in for the night. We've got a long day ahead of us."

The Hoods arranged their tents and everybody got as comfortable as they could for the evening.

Perhaps five hours away, slightly south and west of them, Thaddeus Fly was waking Rage to take the watch for the rest of the night.

* * * *

Morning came, and Anna, Flint and Stockholm prepared themselves, leaving behind many of their belongings for the others to care for.

The three head members of the Hoods' thieves Guild approached the fort amidst the morning glare of sunlight off of the snow blanketing the lands.

"You're certain these scrolls are going to get us in," Flint asked for perhaps the fifth time since the trio had woken up.

"Positive," Anna replied. She looked up at Stockholm, who hadn't questioned her in the slightest.

He did seem preoccupied, however, and wouldn't speak, she thought, unless he had something important to report.

When they closed to within about one hundred yards, the lumbering Red Tribe Werewolf halted in his tracks. "Something wrong?"

"We've got to get in there now, if we're going to at all," Stockholm said under his breath. "I can smell Fly, Lain and Rage."

Anna whipped her head around, her eyes following the direction of Stocky's snout.

She could see nothing for a while, until finally, her eyes fell upon the fringe of a marshland, perhaps two hours away. She could just barely make out movement, and knew instinctively that the motion was that of the Midnight Suns.

"Let's move you two. Got your papers?"

Both Wererat and Werewolf held their forged documents aloft.

"Excellent. Remember, we're here for training, and in Stocky's case, it's just a formality. I used parts of your old police service records to pad your file, big guy," she said.

The trio steeled their nerves against the coming risk, and within minutes, stood before the huge, wrought iron gates of Fort Stone.

Four guards, Humans all, milled about anxiously, until one of the taller, more muscular guards stepped forward.

"Hail and well met, travelers." His voice carried well over the ten yards still between his men and the trio from Desanadron. "Call hail to us, and tell us of your business here."

"Hail and well met, good sirs of the Order of Oun," Anna called back. "We come bearing scripts of transference, that we may receive training and induction into your ranks." She pulled her phony papers out of her jacket and stepping easily up to the lead guard.

He perused the papers for a few minutes, closed the folder, smiled, and nodded, handing them back.

"Everything seems to be in order with you, son," the guard said. "Head over there next to the gate, and wait for me to give your companions the okay."

She smiled warmly at him, tucked the papers away, and shuffled quickly over between two of the other three guards. One had gone inside the Fort, she assumed, to inform the first training master he could find that fresh meat had arrived.

Flint went next, his papers examined with a degree more suspicion than Anna's.

She shook her head, saddened by the clear racism on display by these followers of Oun as it had been by the preacher in Ja-Wen. Still, Flint was let through, and he joined Anna. Stockholm cleared without so much as a hitch, and the gates started pulling into the walls of the keep on either side of them on large winches.

The mechanisms provided a solid defense for the keep, because even a battering ram would be without effect, since they opened and closed by sliding side to side, instead of in and out on hinges.

They passed through the gates into an open air courtyard, where a gruff Half-Elven Knight with four blue stripes on the cloth sleeve of his uniform started in on them right away, screaming at them to drop their belongings and weapons and form a single file line facing left.

They did as they were told without hesitation, playing the part of dutiful little trainees.

Flint glanced sideways at the sergeant, which was apparently a huge mistake. The Half-Elf stamped right up next to him, his nose brushing Flint's shoulder.

"Are you eye fuckin' me, boy?"

Flint was honestly nonplussed, and started to stammer for a reply.

"I *said* are you eye fuckin' me?"

"Ah, no, uh, sir," Flint said before the sergeant got going again.

"Good! Because let me tell you something, maggot! I don't enjoy being eye fucked by anybody who isn't of the female persuasion. Now *march*!"

He screamed at them up and down as they followed his marching directions around the courtyard, spit spraying everywhere as he bellowed.

"Very good, very good ladies," he shouted, causing Anna a moment's panic. *Military*, she thought, remember, he's *military. That's a standard thing to call a trainee.*

"Now, follow me you three, double time it!" The sergeant jogged ahead of them. With Stockholm in the lead, they followed him into the Fort proper.

He led them into the main entry chamber of the keep of the Fort itself, which stood in the dead center of the overall Fort, surrounded by the training fields and barracks of the trainees. The sergeant took them down several hallways, around a lofty library, and finally, down several flights of stairs to a basement of sorts before bringing them to a halt.

Anna twitched. There were no other trainees down here in the basement.

"Present, arms!"

Dozens of Elven, Human and Jaft guards sprang from hidden sentry posts throughout the basement, spears, long swords and axes at the ready.

The sergeant smiled wickedly at the three Hoods. "You sure do make a good trainee, Mr. William Deus."

That hadn't been the name she placed on her folder.

"Terrible shame," he continued, "we have to arrest you and toss you down in the dungeons. Officer in the room!"

Around the three Hoods, the guards saluted.

Stockholm, Flint and Anna all turned, and saw a tall, regal Elven Paladin, dressed in royal purple tunics and silver half plate armor.

Stockholm flinched away from the Elf, the presence of so much pure silver igniting his lycanthrope senses.

"Bravo, William Deus, bravo," the Elf said.

"Archibald Reynaldi, I presume." Anna's voice went low, full of subtle threats. *Duped*, she cried in her mind, *seen through*. "To what do we owe the esteemed honor of meeting you in person?"

Reynaldi snapped his fingers, and four more guards descended the steps. Two held Norman between them, the other two, Styge.

Lee, she was glad to see, was nowhere in sight.

"In the flesh, heathen Rogue," the Elven Paladin sneered. The tunics underneath his armor showed where the armor didn't link, while his great cloak, the same purple as the tunics, remained neatly tucked behind him. Jasmine cologne wafted from the Paladin's body.

Anna nearly gagged on the scent, as it reminded her of the racist preacher in Ja-Wen and his self-righteousness. Reynaldi even had the same smug smile of piety plastered to his lips.

"You know," the Paladin sneered, "for all of the great tales told about you, you're pretty naive. What made you think you could just barge in here under false pretenses?"

"I was operating on the general principle that all Paladins are self-toffing baboons, more interested in reading dusty old Bibles than paying attention to the world around them." Anna mirrored Reynaldi's smile.

The Elf eased forward, fairly floating up to Anna, and slapped her hard on the left cheek.

Fire sprang through the nerves in her face, forking up to her temples. *For such a slight man,* she thought, her vision blurring with unbidden tears, *he's damned strong.* She spat on his breastplate, and nearly did a double take at the sight of blood. He'd split her lower lip.

"How very gentlemanly of you." Reynaldi moved over to stand in front of Flint.

"Flint Ananham." Reynaldi used the Wererat's full name. The Elven Paladin snapped his fingers, and the two extra prisoners were shuffled next to Stockholm. A guard who had been in hiding came forward at the same time, handing Reynaldi a thick folder, which he opened and thumbed through for a moment.

"This is quite an extensive criminal record, Mr. Ananham," he said, looking up with his eyes alone at the Wererat. "What have we here? Extortion, armed robbery, highwayman activity, burglary, arson, general theft, priceless theft, and a few dozen counts of assault. Quite the career crook, aren't we?" He flapped the closed folder on the Wererat's head.

Though he fumed inside, the Wererat could do nothing to stop him.

"I don't think he likes that much," Styge muttered, holding his aching back. "And you need to have a word with your soldiers here, youngster," he said, louder, to Reynaldi. "They've no idea how to rightly treat an old man."

Reynaldi, wide-eyed and flushed with sudden anger, stamped over in front of the elderly Illusionist.

"What god do you worship, old Human?" the Paladin asked.

Styge cocked his head to the side in a mockery of Reynaldi's fashion, and scratched his gray-silver Mohawk. He smiled brightly at the Paladin, revealing rows of wrinkles and creases in his face, as well as a mostly empty mouth.

"Certainly not one that trucks with treating helpless old men like dung."

Reynaldi, already stretched to the edge of his patience with these brigands, drew his hand back to slap the old man a good one. Before he could move forward, a blur of crimson hair and muscle had him up in the air by his throat and wrist.

Ignatious Stockholm growled a fierce, primal roar into the Paladin's face, waves of sonic force blasting the Elf's ears, huge ivory fangs mere inches from his proud, equine nose.

"You shall lay no hand on one so frail and helpless." His muscles rippling under his chain shirt, his breath came in ragged gasps, and his body seeming to expand.

Anna, Flint, and Norman all recognized the symptoms—lycanthrope rage. Stockholm was on the verge of becoming a rampaging beast, incapable of mercy or slowing down in his bloodshed.

With a deep shudder, Stockholm reeled himself in, setting Reynaldi down.

The Elf stared in sheet-white terror at the Red Tribesman, rubbing his throat and wrist.

"I meant you no harm, Archibald Reynaldi," he said, his voice low and even now. He closed his eyes, and breathed deeply for a moment. "We are indeed now your prisoners, it would seem. You have us at a distinct disadvantage. However," he said, opening his eyes and staring into Reynaldi's blank face. "I hereby invoke the holy book of Oun's teachings, in particular, chapter seven, verse eight. 'So noble and merciful is our god, that we his children shall be so as well. In times of war, when enemies are taken alive into our midst, we shall grant them imprisonment without torture, for to do otherwise would be to prove ourselves less than beasts'. End quote."

Impressive, Anna thought. I wonder if he's ever served in the Order?

Reynaldi shook off his temporary shock, and brushed himself off vaguely. "Yes, well, mister, um…" he looked at his subordinates. "Does anyone here have his file?"

"Um, milord," one of the Jaft guards, a captain in rank, said awkwardly. "I don't think we have one on the big guy."

Reynaldi stared at the Jaft as he would a stupid dog.

"I'm serious, sir. When you gave us his description, we couldn't find anything, and we've got files on every major criminal in all of the cities across the continent."

Reynaldi took a tentative step toward the Red Tribe Werewolf, looking up into his now passive features.

"Your name," he said.

"What about it," Stockholm replied.

"Give us your name, Red Tribe. You know, the one your mother and father gave you at birth?" Arrogance had returned to the Paladin's tone.

Watch yourself, Anna thought. You'll find that huge hand back around your throat.

"The name my parents gave me is not easily pronounced by those of the humanoid species, Lord Reynaldi," Stockholm said. "My given name is Ignatious Stockholm, if it pleases you." He gave the Paladin a deferential bow, tucking one hand into his stomach.

Reynaldi beamed at the show of respect he was being given by a man who clearly could kill him without a second thought.

"You are well read and versed, as well as mannered, Ignatious Stockholm. It is a shame we must throw you in the prison below us. You would have made a fine Knight in our ranks," Reynaldi said.

"I beg your pardon, Lord Reynaldi, but I have already long since mastered the arts of a Knight," Stockholm said. "I have also mastered the paths of the Soldier, the Boxer, some of the arts of the Monk, and the Wrestler." Several of the surrounding guards to backed y away, weapons and strength of numbers forgotten in the face of such credentials. "But have no fear. I seem to have burned my arm a tad when I grabbed you." He showed the Elf where he had brushed against the silver armor, and burned his palm in so doing.

Reynaldi nodded, seemingly satisfied with Stockholm's assurances.

"Very well. Now, you shall all be taken to cells below. Captain," Reynaldi addressed the Jaft officer. "See to it that they are all separated. They'll share cells with our other arriving guests. Though I suppose you can throw the stragglers in a cell together." He turned his back on the company from Desanadron. "A Gnome and an old man shouldn't pose much of a threat. Away with them."

As the Hoods were marched along, down a wide set of concrete steps and into the prison beneath the Fort, Flint couldn't abstain from being a wise ass.

"You know, Stocky, if you're so well spoken, how come you didn't talk us *out of this mess?*"

As he shouted, one of the guards on his left side clouted him behind the ear with a leather sap, and he lurched forward, his head throbbing.

"Because he couldn't, Flint." Styge was now being handled much more kindly than before.

"Reynaldi needed only get our big friend in a grapple, and none of the rest of us could have survived an onslaught very long. Let's just relax and take in the sights." He gave Flint a meaningful wink.

Ah, right, the Wererat thought. *They don't know he's an Illusionist.*

The cells, when they finally came to them, were solid concrete rooms carved into the foundation of the Fort. All had solid redwood doors, sealing all noise that might come from within, or without.

As the first door was opened, Anna and the company got a good look at their future lodgings. The inside of the cell was clinically barren, except for a pair of hardwood beds set against opposite walls. The rooms themselves were large enough to house up to six or seven healthy-sized Jafts if need be, and would be more than suitable for two men apiece. Well, one man and one woman, Anna thought. Cobwebs clung to the upper corners of the cell, thick and mesmerizing in the detail put into the designs.

Some very imaginative spiders must live here, Anna thought.

Stockholm was thrust inside the first cell, and the guards shut the solid door as soon as his back cleared the doorway.

Anna heard no click, saw no keyhole on the door. She didn't see any form of security device on the door.

Flint leaned in as close as his guards would let him, and whispered in her ear, "Magic seal, boss."

She nodded, thankful that Flint's keen senses picked up on the method of incarceration.

The Wererat was deposited a little way down the hall in his own cell, but not without a struggle. When his guards shoved him in, he wheeled on them, claws flying. He managed to gouge the one Human's face, three long, wide slashes spraying blood everywhere, before the Jaft assigned to him struck him hard in the throat with a stiff-fingered jab.

Gasping and sputtering for air, the Wererat flailed back into his cell, landing hard on the floor. Before the Jaft closed the door, he wailed on Flint's legs for a solid minute as the Hoods' Prime writhed in pain. The Human used a spell to heal his wounds, but his face was now flushed with anger.

Styge and Norman Adwar were walked into their shared cell, leaving Anna with both her guards and Flint's.

The Human whose face had been slashed clubbed her in the legs with a sap, and she tumbled to the concrete floor, her forehead crashing against the gray surface.

She nearly blacked out before they dragged her into her cell, shutting the door hard as they exited.

She lay in a heap in the middle of the floor, on the verge of tears, when the door opened and another limp form was thrown on top of her. She tossed the body off of her with some considerable effort, and nearly screamed when she saw the unconscious form of Thaddeus Fly, sans weaponry.

They had all been captured.

* * * *

Two hours earlier, Thaddeus Fly had watched with contempt as Deus, Stockholm and Flint were ushered inside of Fort Stone without so much as a struggle. He lowered himself against the side of the hill leading away from the outpost, cursing under his breath.

"A problem, sensei?" Akimaru asked.

Fly rubbed his temples, attempting to ease the throb of frustration.

"I'll say there's a fucking problem," he growled. "The problem is Deus and his tricks. He and two of his best men just sauntered into that Fort just now, and here we are, twiddling our fingers trying to figure out how to get in. It's very frustrating," he grumbled.

"I could try the trick we used at Fort Flag again, sir," Rage offered.

Such a trusting simpleton, the Black Draconus thought.

"No, Rage, that's not going to work. And quite frankly, I'm running a little thin on the imagination front." Fly strained for an idea, when he realized that he could feel movement in the ground.

Someone was approaching, at speed, and en masse.

"Everybody, get ready! We've got company!"

Before he could so much as draw a weapon, a thin wooden arrow pierced his left leg, just above the kneecap.

He howled in pain, and went down clutching the wound.

Rage spun, and found himself staring at the points of seven spears. Berserker or no, brainless as an Orc was liable to get, he had a little thing referred to as common sense. He threw his hands up into the air and grinned at the Knights and Soldiers as nicely as he could.

Lain McNealy got halfway through a summoning spell before a rounded mace found its way into her stomach, doubling her over. She wretched, vomiting explosively on the snow-strewn hill, and passed out in her own waste.

Fly looked over at Akimaru, watching as the white clad Ninja struggled against several armed followers of Oun. His daggers danced and flashed about, until he fished out his sickle and chain, lashing out at his attackers lethally.

However, it seemed that even a creature such as Akimaru could be bested. One of the Jafts, a Soldier, let the sickle bite deep into his breastplate and the meat of his chest, pressing his damaged armor in around the chain attached to the weapon.

As Akimaru tried to pull his weapon back, the Jaft grabbed the chain and gave it a quick, hard pull.

Akimaru flew through the air, and as he closed the gap, the Jaft put out his burly left arm and delivered an earth-shattering clothesline to the white clad Ninja.

Akimaru spun through the air, end over end, and landed atop the snow in a crumpled heap. They were utterly defeated, Fly knew, and about to be imprisoned.

The Midnight Suns were placed on litters and carried to Fort Stone, where they were lashed to their boards and carried into the main keep. Down several flights of stairs they were escorted, Fly receiving healing from a Cleric after the arrow was removed from his leg. Rage, not having been injured, plodded along in a semi-stupor, his eyes locked on Lain.

She didn't appear well, and despite the Cleric's healing, she groaned and moaned as she lay prostrate on the stretcher.

They were carried down into a large, square chamber. Several dozen more guards stood at the ready, and the lashings were removed.

Fly and Akimaru stood, rubbing their respective sores, and Lain was awakened by a stiff slap to the face delivered by an elegantly dressed Elven Paladin.

Reynaldi, Fly thought.

"Greetings, Midnight Suns," the Elven Paladin said, smug and almighty once more. He didn't detect the same sort of threat present in this group as he had with Ignatious Stockholm, but the white clad Ninja disturbed him. The presence of magic screamed at him, from both the Necromancer woman, and Akimaru. "I shall only give you the briefest of welcomes, as I have pressing business to attend to elsewhere. You are going to be imprisoned here, in Fort Stone, for the full duration of your criminal sentences, as recorded by the Desanadron police department. Your records are long and, truthfully, rather impressive. As for the Necromancer, Ms. McNealy..." Reynaldi lifted her chin with two long, thin fingers. "She shall be executed in two days' time."

"For what?" Fly screamed.

Rage stepped next to the Human Necromancer, putting a huge green arm around her shoulders and pulling her tight against his side.

"For the undead raising of the Cleric, Anthony Repuldi, in Ja-Wen." Reynaldi opened a thick folder handed to him by a Jaft captain. "In accordance with the laws of our Order, any Necromancer known to raise a deceased Cleric of the Order is to be sentenced to death."

"And she was supposed to know who she was raising?" Fly took a step forward.

Two Minotaur officers caught his arms from behind and held him fast.

Lain, now fully conscious, held up a hand to stay the Headmaster.

"Actually, Thaddeus, I did know," she said, leaving Fly with no solid argument. "I did it in order to complete my training. It is customary for Necromancers to raise the body of a holy man when they feel ready, as they are the most difficult kind of corpse to reanimate. I not only raised him," she said proudly, puffing out her chest. "I raised him as a High Zombie."

Fly was impressed. It took a highly skilled Necromancer to raise any High Zombie, but the corpse of a holy man? That seemed to define her skills right there. However, if they only had two days to escape, they would have to work quickly to do so, or Lain wouldn't be leaving with them.

Suddenly, his imagination started working again. "Archibald Reynaldi, you will not execute her—not in two days." The lie took form in his mind. Only Ninjas could lie to Knights and get away with it, and it was a talent he kept regularly maintained. "She is with child."

Only Rage, among the Midnight Suns, even flinched. "Yer gonna be a mommy," he whispered to Lain with a wide smile.

She nodded mutely, playing along.

"Hmmm," Reynaldi mused, rubbing his chin. "That presents a problem. The child is without blame, and must be allowed the opportunity to live. It is only right, in accordance to our Order," he said. "Tell me, Thaddeus Fly, do you know who the father is?"

Fly smiled meaningfully, and a shiver raced down Reynaldi's body.

"Right, never mind that. Lain McNealy," Reynaldi addressed the Necromancer and the room in general. "As you are with child, you shall not be executed until the infant is born. You shall be allowed to name it, and spend one day with it. Then, you shall be put to death, and the child shall be raised properly by a member of the Order. Or at least until its father," he glared at Fly. "Comes to claim it. All present, hear well! Though a prisoner, Lain McNealy is not to be put to hardship! We shall not be blamed for the death of an unborn child." He turned and walked away.

"Very noble of you, Reynaldi. I'll remember that when I escape and come to slit your throat," Fly shouted at the retreating Paladin.

Reynaldi stopped, and snapped his fingers. The lights went out for a while for Thaddeus Fly, and the Midnight Suns were deposited in their cells.

They each found that they were rooming with some interesting acquaintances.

* * * *

When the lights came back on for the Black Draconus, he was looking up into the face of someone he'd been waging silent war with for years now.

"William Deus," he rasped. "Fancy meeting you here." He sat up, or at least attempted to, until Deus finally helped him into a seated position. He instinctively reached for a knife when she put her hands on him, but found nothing but empty belt.

"I'm not exactly thrilled with the present situation either, Fly, but we're probably going to have to work together to get out of it. Now, tell me how it happened."

Fly related the events of the ambush, and when she inquired, told her who else had been captured with him.

"What about Trent? Isn't he your right hand man?"

"I have the distinct feeling, Rogue, that he is the very reason you and I are here." Fly sulked for a minute, looking around the barren chamber for something to work with. He got groggily to his feet, and stumbled over to one of the walls.

He pressed a scaled hand to the sheer surface, probing for flaws. As expected, he found none initially. *Perhaps when I can think more clearly*, he mused.

"I don't think that's the answer," Anna said.

Fly glared at her, his eyes filled with a dim hatred.

"Look, we can stare daggers at each other until the end of time, Fly, but we need to really sit down and think this one through. Together, much as I loathe that idea."

Fly sat himself on one of the hardwood beds, his body trying to persuade him to lay back and take a nap. His mind, however, convinced the body, despite protestations, to stay awake and alert. If the door opened for even an instant, he vowed inwardly, he'd be on the guard and then out of this blasted keep.

"Well, since we're likely going to be here for a while," he said, his thoughts turning in a different direction for the moment. "Let's get something out of the way. Why are you after the Glove of Shadows?"

Anna thought on his question a while, opting to say nothing until she had formulated a satisfactory answer. In the end, however, it boiled down to only one reason.

"Honestly?"

"We may as well try to be, for the time being," Fly said with a shrug of his shoulders.

"Well, mostly, it's so you don't get a hold of it," she confessed. She wondered, with a start, how much confessing she'd have to do while imprisoned. The cell only had one toilet, and it wasn't walled off. She was starting to think her little secret was going to become one of the worst kept ones in history. "How about you?"

"Well, I should think that's obvious. To keep you from getting it."

They stared at each other in tense silence, until finally, Anna started giggling at the silliness of it all.

Fly joined in a minute later, laughing heartily. He hung his head a moment, and gave her an odd look. "Look, William, we've been at odds for a long time now."

"Six years."

"Yes, six years." He looked up at the ceiling, high over his head. A small slot in the wall where it joined the ceiling allowed light to filter into the cell. He wondered how dark the prison would get at night. "Six years of little jabs at one another. Six years of occasional skirmishes between our men."

"And women," Anna added. She'd have to let Fly in on her secret, but she wanted to figure out how to him keep mum about it.

"Yes, and women. Speaking of, we don't have too terribly long to enjoy each other's company. Reynaldi will eventually figure out that Lain isn't pregnant, and then they'll fry her good." He stretched his limbs. He had full cognitive faculty again, and gave the conversation only half of his attention now. The other half of his thoughts were occupied fully with figuring out a plan of escape.

"She creeps me out, you know," Anna said.

"Me too. She came on to me the other night," he said casually, snickering at the grimace Anna made. "She's meant for bigger, better things."

Listening to him talk, Anna realized that Thaddeus Fly wasn't really the big bastard she'd always thought him to be. Remy had had a long-standing feud with the Black Draconus, one that he had passed on to Anna when he had died. Perhaps, she thought, there was no need for the battle.

"Fly, listen," she said slowly. "Do you have any, you know, secrets? About yourself, I mean?"

Fly gave her a quizzical look, like a pet might its owner when being called for the first time. "Anything you want to get off your chest? I'll tell you one of mine in turn," she added.

Fly lay down on the hardwood bed, and thought back. He remembered for a while, and decided that yes, he may as well tell Deus. What were the chances, he reasoned, that he'd let anybody know? Nobody would believe him anyway!

"Sure, I've got a secret." He sat up. "It goes something like this. I was once possessed by a demon. This particular demon was called pride, and when it took me over, it did one bang-up job of it. Made me kill my sensei, which got me expunged from the records of the Obura Ninja Clan. When I was let go, I realized the mistake I'd made, and I've lived with it ever since.

"You see, I assumed that if I killed a sensei, an elder at that, they would make me a member of the council in his place. Of course, I was mistaken, as I have often been. They didn't reward me. They erased me from their records entirely, along with Trent and Akimaru. When I left the clan, I couldn't feel anything for a long time. I couldn't even get angry—not at them, not at myself, not at anything. I sort of operated on instinct for a while, until I got the idea of forming my own clan, my own pack. I came to Desanadron with Trent and Akimaru, and we started gathering agents."

"That was how long ago? Remy told me you guys didn't come around until about twelve years ago."

Fly nodded, confirming the old Hoods' Headmaster's statement.

"Well, is that it?" she asked, a little disappointed.

"That's about the half and whole of it." Fly lay back. "The real secret, though? My people are usually very isolationist, William. We don't play well with others. We don't have a family structure to speak of. And that's my secret, you see—I want a family structure in my life, and that's just taboo for my species."

Okay, Anna thought, *that's a little better.*

"What about you?" he asked.

Anna cleared her throat, and steeled her nerves for this part.

"Will you excuse me a minute, I have to use the toilet," she said.

"I won't look, if it makes you uncomfortable. Some guys are like that," Fly said.

"Oh no, go ahead and look." Anna dropped her pants. "That's sort of the whole point."

Fly sat up, and his eyes shot wide open.

Anna used the toilet, and stood up, pulling up her trousers. "You see? That's my secret, Fly, and you'll do well to keep it to yourself."

Fly simply stared mutely at her, and then howled with laughter. "What's so funny?"

"Oh my god," Fly said between bouts of laughter. "You mean to tell me that the mighty, brilliant leader of the Hoods, is a woman? I'm sorry, but that's just rich!" He guffawed harshly. "I've never heard of a Guild with a woman in charge."

"And that's precisely why I need to remain William Deus in public, and around my men," she said, crossing her arms over her chest. "Flint and Stockholm know, but that's it. Oh, and now you."

Fly didn't respond. He'd stopped laughing, and fallen asleep on his bed.

Anna decided to follow suit, and quickly fell asleep. For once, she trusted a Midnight Sun enough to let her guard down. Strange, she thought, drifting toward slumber, that it would be their leader.

* * * *

Stockholm considered himself a Werewolf of average size, though he was, in fact, slightly bigger than most. So when the door of his cell opened and Rage was pushed inside with him, he realized how much space the two of them took up.

"Um, hi." Rage tried to shuffle to one of the beds.

My, what stimulating conversation this is going to be, Stockholm thought.

"Um, sorry about, you know, before," the Berserker said, rubbing the back of his buzz cut awkwardly.

"Don't worry about it." Stockholm peered around the room with its dismal lighting, letting his nose do the observing after the initial impression his eyes gave him. He inhaled deep and hard, soaking up every trace scent available. Sweat, most of it fresh and coming off of Rage in waves, took up most of the initial nasal sweep. Underneath the sweat was the heavy odor of old blood, coppery and thick in the air.

Stockholm stepped next to the bed not occupied by the Orc, and lifted the mattress on its side. "Caked on," he whispered to himself.

A single razor blade rested on the underside of the mattress, glued to the bed by the blood it sat in. Someone hadn't apparently wanted to sit around and rot forever.

"You don't have suicidal tendencies, do you?" he asked the Orc, prying the razor off with his claws. He held it sideways, letting the little bit of light coming into the room glint off of it. He smiled wickedly at the Orc, who simply shrugged his shoulders, palms held up slightly.

"I don't know. I don't know what dose words mean, so I ain't sure hows ta answer dat."

Stockholm gnashed his teeth slowly, uncertain how long he'd be able to abstain from correcting the Orc Berserker's atrocious grammar.

"Very well, we'll let the matter drop for now." Stockholm once again probed the room with his nasal senses.

Nothing could entirely cut through the smell of the concrete and the blood, or the sweat, but he could faintly detect soil, perhaps ten feet behind the wall opposite the magically sealed door of the cell. "Rage, just how strong are you?"

"I dunno, pretty strong. I can break walls, and some suits of armor. It's sort of my um, you know, thing you do really good."

"Specialty."

A slow, dumb smile spread across Rage's face. "Dat's it! It's my specialty! So, you got a plan ta get out? I'll do what I can, though, Ms. McNealy usually helps me with these things. You know, the speaking and whatnot. She gives me little lessons, and gives me little gifts, for doing good, you know?"

Stockholm let his temper slip away into the void. Here was a hulking green beast of a man, capable of a great deal of damage, with the mind of an eager child.

"And she gives you orders?" Stockholm looked at the back wall.

Rage agreed with a nod, and Stockholm rubbed his long chin.

"Rage, I want you to stand up, and go over to that wall. Pull your right hand back, like you're going to punch the wall."

The Orc obeyed the Red Tribe Werewolf's directives without question.

Stockholm took one of the sheets from his bed and tied it around Rage's fist. The sheet looked like a death shroud and smelled of decay.

Once he had the sheet bound around enough to prevent lacerations to the Orc's knuckles, he said in a very low, commanding tone, "Now start punching that wall, and don't stop until I tell you to."

The rumbling began, and Stockholm smiled ear to ear.

* * * *

Flint's head throbbed, sending shock waves through the world around him. Everything quavered and quaked, and he smelled something like sulfur. A low humming noise filled the cell, a catchy little ditty he almost recognized. When he sat up, he found himself on a hard, ancient bed.

Seated opposite the Wererat, with his legs swinging over the side of his own cot, was the white clad Ninja, Akimaru.

Flint shivered with preternatural cold, unsure of how the temperature outside of the keep could creep all the way down here. When he looked up and saw the slot in the wall near the ceiling, he knew that the light filtering into the chamber wasn't from outside. Rather, he felt certain that each prison cell was somehow connected to a works chamber above them that would provide light, heating, and probably their food. None of the guards would be foolish enough, he knew, to actually open the door to the cell once its inhabitants had been secured within.

"Hey there, Akimaru," Flint said conversationally. He tried to get up, but found that his legs still weren't cooperating. He'd only felt the first few blows to his lower extremities before he passed out from a combination of pain and lack of oxygen. He didn't know how long he'd been laid out, but he knew suddenly that Akimaru had moved him from the floor to the bed.

"Um, just one quick question, Aki. You could have broken my neck when you got shoved in here."

"No, I couldn't have," the white clad Ninja quickly replied. "I'm not the type. I have not been ordered to kill you, or to harm you in any other way. Since our present set of circumstances seems dismal, we shall have to work together. Mr. Flint."

Flint marveled. In the nearly one dozen encounters he'd had with Akimaru, the white-clad Ninja hadn't used a quarter of the words he just had.

"Now, do you possess any hidden talents or powers I should know of, Mr. Flint?"

The Wererat shook his head, trying to moisten his lips.

Akimaru walked over to the solitary sink fixture next to the toilet, and turned the faucet on. He cupped his gloved hands and caught the water, bringing it to Flint's cracked lips.

"Thank you, Akimaru," Flint wheezed as he gulped at the water.

Before he could get a good second pull on it, Akimaru pulled his hands away, keeping them cupped.

"What gives?"

"Not too fast." The white clad Ninja brought the water back. "You will throw it back up."

Flint took a few more small sips, spaced out half a minute each. As he drained the last of the liquid, he felt his throat almost freeze over. *Why was the cell so cold?*

"Now, think hard, Wererat." Akimaru's voice was low, level, and calm, but it held a subtle suggestion of lethal, violent potential.

With every word Akimaru spoke, Flint also noticed, the prison cell seemed to get colder. "Any powers at all?" Akimaru asked.

At first, Flint could think of nothing, and he lay back on his bed to reflect on the question.

He tried to gauge the time that had passed, but as they had confiscated his timepiece, he had no idea whether they'd been locked up for minutes or hours.

Eventually, the small slot at the top of the wall, where it met the ceiling of the chamber, opened, and a medium sized tray laden with food lowered to the two agents from a thin rope.

As soon as Flint could reach up and pluck the tray down, he hauled on it, and the rope broke. Instead of letting the broken rope just drop into the cell, the remainder was pulled up the wall and back into the room beyond the grate.

Flint pocketed the small strand of rope, and started in on his share of the food.

Bits of cheese, bread, and two bowls of some sort of mountainous stew were on the tray, and as Flint devoured his stew greedily, he eyeballed the small wedges and blocks of fresh cheese. He glanced over at Akimaru, who was sitting in a meditative trance on his bed, his eyes shut, a soft, steady hum vibrating through the floor. The Ninja did not react when Flint snatched up all of the cheese, or when he gobbled half of it for himself, tucking the rest away for later consumption. Akimaru, it seemed, had voided his consciousness from the room.

Flint drifted into slumber, his body sore and in need of rest. He kept himself awake just long enough to see Akimaru open his eyes wide for a brief instant, his eyes a brilliant, arctic purple. The Wererat pulled a blanket over himself, and fell asleep. He dreamed of cheese, and the glorious hunt for it as a rodent.

When he awoke the next morning, he had a plan of escape.

Chapter Thirteen
Treachery

Styge painstakingly ran the piece of chalk Norman had given him along the wall, making certain not to leave out any details.

He took a step back, leaning this way and that to get a better perspective.

He finally grunted approvingly, and turned to the Gnome Engineer, who was fiddling with the heel of his right boot. "What the devil are you doing, Norman?"

The Gnome Engineer looked up, the heel of the boot secured between his yellowed, rotting teeth. "Ung nryn oo et ve eel ov 'is oob." Norm finally pulled one of the tacks free to reveal a hollow boot heel filled with miniature tools. "Trying to get the heel off this boot, Styge old chum." He picked through the available emergency tools. He didn't have much to work with here, but it would make a start. If the old Illusionist had as much power as everyone said he did, they could be out of the prison in a few days.

"Okay, the first one, go ahead," Norm pointed to Styge's first drawing on the wall.

The chalk drawing was a brilliant depiction of a kinetic environmental energy absorber, a device Norman had researched extensively. He had assembled one in his time, but it had been faulty, as he hadn't been careful with his calculations. He hoped he'd learned the lesson.

Styge mumbled in the tongue of the ancient practitioners of his art, the first Illusionists, who worked hand in hand with Summoners. The elderly Human e danced back and forth, waving his hands toward the first of his various drawings on the back cell wall. Sweat beaded on his forehead, and Norm heard faint hints of tribal drums beating in the air.

The light filtering in from the wall/ceiling slot flashed brilliantly, blinding the Gnome Engineer as he shielded his eyes a second too late.

"*Fooroo doogenshi ki,*" Styge hollered.

The air thickened, hardening almost to the degree of tree sap, and the tribal drums could now not be drowned out unless one of the greater gods decided to poke his or her head into the cell and shout above it.

Norm felt a trickle of blood from his nose, and as suddenly as the air had thickened, it became simple, stagnant air again. He kept his eyes shielded for a moment, though, and soon heard first a heavy, metallic thunk, and then a much more concerning whump of a person collapsing.

When he finally risked a glance from behind his forearm, he saw that Styge had fallen over on the cell floor, sweat plastering his gray-silver Mohawk against his head. A vague twitch in his right eye told Norm he was alive, just deeply asleep.

On the other side of the room, directly beneath where the drawing of it had been, was a perfectly real, perfectly solid kinetic environmental energy absorber. Norm's plan for escape might actually work.

"Never underestimate a Hood, gentlemen," he whispered towards the ceiling. "Never."

His miniature tools in hand, he set to work modifying and adjusting the device, then waited patiently for Styge to wake up.

Their morning meal was lowered on a platter attached to a thin rope, from the slot high in the wall.

He took both his share and Styge's off of the platter, setting Styge's food on his bed, and digging into his own. Four more drawings stood boldly on the wall, and Norman Adwar pondered his course of action. The Knights, Soldiers and Paladins hadn't bothered to check his boots, and they had merely collected Styge's sketchpads into a single burlap bag, which they had tossed in the evidence room in the first basement level. The randy old Illusionist had made due with a concrete wall and a piece of chalk once, but how taxing would it be to materialize four more illusions for permanent use?

If Norm were any judge of such things, it would come close to killing the old man.

Escaping, he realized, might exchange a long imprisonment for a quick death.

* * * *

The night had passed—or so Anna assumed from her perceived passage of time. She woke stiff in the legs, but feeling much better elsewhere. She had undone her wraps in the middle of the night, opting to wear her undershirt and outer tunic with a little slack. Not that she had much to hide, but if she suddenly burst out of the mostly barren cell into the hall, she didn't want anyone else finding out she was actually a woman.

She rubbed her neck and swung down off of the bed, landing on cat's feet on the concrete floor.

She averted her eyes, hearing the universal signal of urine splashing in the toilet to mean 'turn around'.

When Fly was finished, he flushed the toilet, and as soon as he did, both Ninja and Rogue looked at each other with eyes filled not with sleep, but with revelation.

"The pipes." Anna dashed over to the toilet.

The single porcelain unit was set into the wall with solid masonry, but if they needed to, they could simply break the toilet. However, this left the unsavory thought that if her ideas didn't pan out, they'd be minus one pot to piss in.

"How can we use them to our advantage?"

"I'm not sure—not yet anyway," Fly said. "We have a toilet and a sink, each with running water. Good old Gnomes and Dwarves. Don't get me wrong, indoor plumbing is perhaps one of the best innovations the Gnome Race ever gave our lands, but in some ways, it makes it easier to keep people prisoner."

Anna stayed still as the Black Draconus, scaled feet clacking on the flat, concrete floor, paced.

"The pipes are way too small to fit through," Anna said, mostly to herself. The light coming from the slot above them brightened for a moment, and she thought she could hear a deep, thundering rumble somewhere nearby. No, she corrected herself, I can't hear it, I can feel it. What's it coming from? She shook the sensation off, and returned her thoughts to the situation at hand. "Fly, you've got a breath weapon, yes?"

"Yes, I can spit forked lightning. What of it?"

She looked down at the toilet thoughtfully, then over at the sink.

"All right, what do you suppose would happen if you sent a discharge of your breath weapon through the pipes from the sink?"

The Black Draconus squinted, trying to imagine the end result.

"I believe it's something along the lines of, boom." He clenched his hands together and then pulled them apart with an exaggerated motion. "However, while passing through the marshlands to the west of here, I used my natural power a few times more than I should have. I need a couple of days to store up the energy if we want it to truly be effective."

"Not a problem, Fly." Anna pounded on the cell door, but as she suspected, nobody bothered to answer from the other side. "Something tells me that for once, time is on our side."

* * * *

Despite Rage's hand-wrapping, the Orc Berserker's knuckles were rubbed raw and cut in places. He'd stayed up for the entire night, only sleeping when Stockholm finally instructed him to stop.

The Red Tribe Werewolf was frankly astonished that nobody above them, up in the keep and Fort Stone itself, noticed what was going on. They should have been found out by now, and beaten into submission. Instead, Rage had worked throughout the night, punching and kicking and tearing his way through three feet of solid concrete.

The tunnel he'd burrowed would easily allow himself access, and Stockholm would only have to crouch a very little bit.

Once Rage broke free of the mortar and concrete, Stockholm would take over, and dig them out through the soil, a task much better suited to his lupine kind.

"Seven more feet, about," Stockholm whispered to himself as he tapped the back wall of Rage's work.

The high slot in the cell wall creaked open, and two trays were lowered down on individual ropes. He took them both, set them on his bed, and ignored them. As soon as he released the ropes, they shot back up through the slot, which dropped shut.

The Order of Oun certainly knows how to keep prisoners, he thought. *A toilet, a sink, two beds, and three meals a day, delivered in the same fashion as the light and heating.* Though tall, even Stockholm only stood around half of the height of the cell. Even if he could reach it, the slot up near the ceiling didn't appear wide or tall enough for much of anything to get through, save the meals and water skins.

At noon, he roused Rage, who set back to work on the concrete wall. Stockholm sat and ate his meal now that it had cooled to an acceptable level. *What do we do once we escape?* He had no intentions of abandoning the others, though he felt certain that Anna and Flint would both work out a solution. And as long as Rage was aiding him in his efforts, he felt obligated to ensure the safe escape of the Midnight Suns as well. His method of escape, however, wouldn't work for the others.

He had to get some rest, he decided. Honest rest—that would do the trick. He told Rage to slow his pace, and to stop after two more food deliveries from the slot above them.

Satisfied that the Orc had understood him, Stockholm shifted into a red wolf, padded in a circle on his bed, and lay down for some much needed deep sleep. At Rage's current pace, they might get free of the Fort in two or three more days. What they did then, they'd have to wait to decide.

* * * *

Divided into two-man teams, the groups from Desanadron worked together to get themselves free.

By dawn of the third day of their incarceration, Rage had cleared through to soft soil, stepping back to let Stockholm take the lead. Styge manifested three more of the drawings he'd made on the cell wall, and the Engineer seemed positive that they had what they needed to leave the prison. Thaddeus Fly prepared to release enough electrical power into the Fort's water supply to rupture the pipes and open a path for them to get to the maintenance tunnels. Flint had convinced Akimaru to take the evening's meal off of a platter and set the Wererat, in his animus form, under one platter for the return trip up through the slot. Everyone was preparing to move out.

Lain McNealy had been tossed into a cell by herself, a cell specifically designed to suppress Necromancer spells. A number of Clerics came in on the first day, each one smiling and rotund like a cherub, trying to get her to 'walk in the light of Oun'. These men she barely acknowledged, except to smile wickedly at them.

The preachers left her cell without their previous smiles, thoughts of good old-fashioned burnings at the stake playing in their heads.

Her cell was also different in that she had a comfortable bed, a separate bathroom attached through an oak door, and her meals were brought in by a guard. The Order supplied her with good, hearty meals—a fitting diet for a mother-to-be.

Reynaldi himself visited her late in the evening of the first day, offering her amnesty if she would permanently relinquish her powers. The Elven Paladin explained a ritual, known to the more educated Paladins inside of Fort Stone, which could do just that.

Lain refused him gently, thanking him for the kind offer.

"You still have many months to think about it," Reynaldi said.

Thick iron bars on the windows of her room kept her from simply hopping the short distance out to the area. This, she thought, was probably the most important difference between her own lodgings and that of her allies. While they had all been taken downstairs, she had been thrust into one of the cells in the basement only for an hour before Reynaldi had ordered her moved. *The bars,* she thought. *There has to be some way to escape, and these bars are key in that effort.*

Two days passed as she attempted to formulate a plan that didn't involve her magic, as it was suppressed. She leaned on the window frame, her hands dangling out between the bars. Below, she felt a slight thrum in the keep itself, a steady vibration in the floor. She couldn't be certain what was going on down in the basement, but she was convinced that one of her company members was causing the vibration.

The door of her chamber creaked open, and a broad shouldered Jaft in chain mail rolled in a cart with her afternoon meal on it. His heavy metal boots clanked on the concrete floor.

"Your lunch, Ms. McNealy." The guard stood stiffly by the cart. "We trust you have been kept comfortable, ma'am."

She simply smiled, and the Jaft left the room as swiftly as pride would let him.

Lain picked at her steaming meal disconsolately, wishing that she could help Fly half as much as he'd helped her.

Birds chirped outside of her window, and Lain took one of the buttered rolls, tearing it into several smaller pieces, and went over to the bars. She stretched one hand out, and dropped the bread piece to the ground.

One of the birds, a sparrow, hopped on it quickly, and twittered up towards her.

The lip of the windowsill on the outside of the keep was littered with flecks of stone that had chipped and flaked off of the structure over the years.

These few birds, she realized, hadn't left yet for warmer climates to the west, and they may very well freeze to death before they could get safely away. Her heart sank a little, Lain feeling pity for the tiny creatures. They really had no hope of survival unless someone in the Fort took them in. "Fat chance of that," she growled to the sparrow as it hopped up closer, passing between the bars and into the room. "They probably don't allow birds inside, the self-righteous bastards."

She ground her teeth, and felt a strange pulse in her hands, which were still hanging outside of the window.

She looked away from the bird, down at the ground outside of the window. A single line of black power burned from her left hand down to the grass, draining life force from the individual blades.

So, their cell is not so secure after all.

She smiled, and brought her hands back inside, gripping two of the bars by their bases, set into the stone of the window frame. Her hands vibrated, and she pulled them away from the iron bars. Nearly a quarter of the bars' circumference had deteriorated.

She had her own way out now.

* * * *

The day that the Hoods and Midnight Suns were incarcerated, Markus Trent made his way past a patrol of Ja-Wen city guards, striding boldly right past them since he had done nothing wrong. They gave him piercing glares, but said nothing as he passed into the western business district.

There was nothing to do when he first arrived except seek some minor medical attention for a bite wound on his left leg. The only hostile creature he'd come across after parting ways with Fly and the others was a wild dog. The creature had come barreling out of the marshlands to the north, and took a sneak attack bite at him. As soon as its teeth had hit their mark, it had sped past —until Trent brained it with a shuriken to the back of the skull.

The wound hadn't bled a great deal, but it did burn and seep yellow pus. He didn't want it to get any worse, so he made his way directly to a healer when he got into the city proper.

The healer woman, a Half-Elf, answered the door after only a few seconds when he knocked, and she said nothing to him. Instead, she turned her back and left the door open for him to follow her inside.

The first room he stepped into was a vestibule with a low ceiling and a bench for customers to wait at, with a bead curtain obscuring the view of the next room.

The healer brushed the beads aside and preceded Trent into a smoky room, where several gourds and other trinkets hung from lines of thread tied to the ceiling, which was higher here in her room of business than in the vestibule.

"Pick a seat, young man," she croaked, her voice rough from little use, Trent assumed. "I shall take a look at your injuries."

The Ninja selected the sturdiest looking lounge chair he saw, and set himself down gingerly. His leg throbbed dully, but he didn't mind too terribly, since he was at the healer's home.

The Half-Elf woman crouched on her haunches, and looked at the bite on Trent's leg. She frowned deeply, and shook her head. "This looks like a bite from a swamp dog."

From her croaking voice, Trent's mind's eye saw her whipping out her tongue and snaring a fly. *Disgusting.*

"It was a dog, all right," Trent said.

The healer grabbed his foot and lifted the injured leg, setting off a burning sensation around the afflicted area.

He didn't look down, but he could feel her prodding the open wound with a thin finger.

"Must you poke around like that, woman?" he snarled.

She grunted without verbal comment, and set to mixing some herbs in a pot of water she had hung over the fire in her hearth.

The poultice she eventually brought out looked yellow and waxy, like the dripped leavings of a beehive after a wild animal got at it. It steamed as she ladled it out of the pot and into an earthenware bowl.

She dipped a black brush into the bowl, and then applied the poultice to the wound.

The heat didn't faze Trent, but the sensation of something boiling out of his leg and crawling over the wound stopped his thoughts from wandering. He looked down at the injury.

Small bubbles formed over the waxy substance as it cleaned and disinfected the bite, but he saw nothing crawling around. Sometimes, he thought, Fly's lack of imagination must have been great to have.

Once more his thoughts flickered to the hated Black Draconus and his disciple, Akimaru. Trent couldn't say for certain what exactly it was the white clad Ninja ever learned from Fly. From everything he'd seen of Akimaru's fighting skills and performance, he didn't need much instruction in the arts of the Ninja. True, he often used fighting techniques unfamiliar to Markus Trent, but every good Ninja learned a few moves unique to his preferred method of combat. Trent had a few of his own, but nothing that compared to the destructive power he had seen Akimaru unleash only once on a hostile target. To put it bluntly, it had been terrifying.

The medicine did its work on his leg, and the rest of his body as well, and he found himself ready to lull off to sleep.

The healer woman put a hand gently over his face, and he would have thrown her hand away, had he the strength. He didn't, as it turned out, and so when she brushed his eyes with her fingers, he let them shut and dreamed.

In his dream, he relived one of the most perplexing and confusing days of his life. Three years earlier, before the visit to the healer in Ja-Wen, Thaddeus Fly had given him a task that took him north, into the Dwarven Territories. A part-time agent and contact of the Midnight Suns had discovered ancient ruins deep in the earth when he joined a Dwarven mining crew. The agent's purpose in joining with the miners hadn't been explained, but he had split from the Dwarves, and come upon a strange wooden door in the gut rock of the mountain. The door didn't creak, as the agent had expected it might, and beyond he had found what appeared to be a city buried beneath the ground. How an entire city had become covered by mountain rock, nobody knew, but it wasn't unheard of throughout Tamalaria.

Trent and Akimaru had been dispatched to join the part-timer and plunder the ruins for anything of value. They had been warned against bringing anything back that hinted of ancient mecha, unless they knew at a single glance they could sell it to the Mecha Revitalization Society. That Society consisted largely of a handful of Gnome scientists and Kobold scholars, as well as half a dozen Humans whose obsession with mecha nearly rivaled the Gnomes as a Race.

When the two Midnight Suns operatives arrived outside of Traithrock, three Dwarven guards accosted them. They came not with weapons drawn, but with shouts and bellows that they were on a private road and must return closer to the city.

Trent and Akimaru had slain them swiftly, but with the methods and weapons typical of their class. Nothing out of the ordinary had occurred, except that Trent had clearly seen that Akimaru moved *on top of* the snow instead of through it.

The part-time agent who met with them three hours later was a Human by the name of Victor Solomon, and he had little time to spare for their excursion, or so he said.

Trent smelled the odor of sex on the man, and thought that perhaps his woman was the real reason he was in such a rush to get the job over with.

He led the way down the private road, which did in fact have several signs posted along it claiming that it temporarily belonged to a man named Jeremy Strivenski.

Trent knocked the signs over as he came across them, and Victor Solomon, slender, twitchy frame jumping akimbo as he laughed at Markus's vandalism, continued to lead them to the mine.

He led them inside the mountain, a torch from the entryway in his hand and sputtering flames. Perhaps a hundred yards beneath the earth's surface, they came to the wooden door Solomon had found, and he led them inside.

On the precipice that fronted the city below and around them, Markus Trent marveled at the sheer size and length of the underground city, the lavishness of the buildings. Some stretched perhaps a mile from their bases to their tops, and he could find no words fitting to describe them.

"Pretty amazing, huh?" Solomon asked.

Trent nodded mutely.

Akimaru had already begun to make the climb down, jumping nimbly from rock outcropping to outcropping, dropping down dozens of feet at a time at some points.

Trent prided himself on his agility, but once more found himself in Akimaru's shadow.

"Look," Solomon had said. "I've got a rope ladder and a set of Chimera's wings to make the trip easier. We don't need to go hopping around like animals, like your friend. What do you say?"

Trent tucked the Chimera's wings—a small magical trinket in the form of a pair of crossed feather wings—in his mouth. He let the object get wet, and felt the locked magical power flow over his body, concentrating in his back muscles and shoulder blades.

Two white, powdery wings flashed into being on his back, and he leaped off of the precipice, floating down airily to the ground level of the buried city.

Akimaru had already arrived before him, and gave him a brief bow.

The two Ninjas waited another fifteen minutes while Solomon made his way down with the rope ladder. When the trio reunited, they drew weapons and moved slowly into the city, looking in awe and wonder at the buildings.

Akimaru was the first of them brave enough to open the front door of what appeared to be an old place of business. The white clad Ninja signaled for the two of them to stay put, but Trent wasn't having with that. He shoved Akimaru aside and threw the door open loudly.

Bells jingled overhead when he did so, and he almost laughed. Almost, but not quite—apparently the city wasn't entirely abandoned.

The creature that had been sleeping behind a long counter on the far wall to the door's left side let loose a sound somewhere between a belch and a quiet roar. Sharp, triangular spikes studded its many-limbed body, its flesh bumpy looking and dark gray. Its body, broader than any lycanthrope or Orc Trent had seen, stretched wider as it threw off the last vestiges of slumber. It opened three, red-tinted eyes, set in its chest area. Or at least, Trent thought it was its chest, until his eyes adjusted to the light in the queer shop and he saw that its head protruded not from the top of its body, but from the center of its chest. Its eyes alighted on him, and it screamed now not like a belching child awake from a nap, but a predator ready to take down its next meal.

Trent already had a weapon in his hand, but the glare coming from the creature's eyes hypnotized him into inaction.

The creature leaped over the counter, and Trent saw that it had not three arms, as he had thought, but four. Two arms on its left side, one on its right, and another clawing the air where he supposed reproductive organs should have hung.

It landed heavily on the other side of the counter, and he saw that while its upper body was massive and muscular, its legs were squat and trunk-like— powerful yes, but incapable of projecting it the distance from its sleeping place to him. *Oh gods,* he thought, *someone help me.*

No god answered his silent plea, but as Akimaru sprung into action. The white clad Ninja loosed his sickle at the beast, landing a glancing blow on its hardened carapace.

Blood, thick and black as swamp bile, bubbled out a little, but the creature seemed not to notice. It smiled hideously, showing rows of strange blue teeth just below its eyes.

Several yards disappeared under the creature's churning feet, yet still Trent couldn't move, held by the unflinching glare of those crimson eyes.

When the creature came within five yards of Trent, Akimaru stood directly before it, striking it several times about its body and limbs—quick, darting strikes, leaving no room for counterattack. Trent had seen these maneuvers cripple and kill much larger beings, but this massive monstrosity simply flinched a little with each blow.

It drew back one thick arm, and made a fist. Trent finally managed to move, but it was only his mouth that obeyed. "Akimaru, move! Run!"

The lower arm of the beast swung up, grabbing Akimaru by the crotch, and its fisted hand swung sideways, bashing the Ninja in the head, knocking him through the air to crash into a set of dark boxes set on a counter.

Over he went with a boom, out of Trent's sight.

Here, in his dream, things became a little hazy, because his actual memory of the event seemed strange to him, almost unreal. The creature smiled again, the left side of its mouth curling up higher than even before. Then the room suddenly became cold, chillier than it had any reason to be. He recalled the creature delivering a glancing blow to his head, a blow he'd blocked in part by his outstretched arm with the palm curled up. It was a simple martial arts technique, taught by almost every school of combat, but it had saved his life.

He seemed to recall Akimaru coming around the counter he'd fallen behind, gliding—no, that was wrong, he thought. *Sliding* along. The wooden floor turned into a sheet of ice just in front of his body.

The white clad Ninja stood there, silent and deadly, and as the creature native to the ruins turned to face him.

Akimaru raised one ungloved hand, fingers outstretched.

Cold steam wafted up from his fingertips, and small shards of ice splashed against the creature.

It flailed its mighty limbs, all four of them, and its body slowed to a crawl. Ice spread over its body from the points at which the shards had struck, until it was encased in a thin coating of it.

Akimaru jumped forward and delivered a kick just under the creature's chin.

Its head flew off, jetting blood all over the shop as its body fell, limp and frozen over, to the floor.

Trent, awestruck by this display of supernatural power from the mysterious Ninja, had blacked out then.

His dream was over, and he awoke in the healer's den. She hovered over him, and he motioned her away with a hand. The old, familiar questions resurfaced, but he was pretty sure he had one answer, at least.

And he realized he wanted them all.

* * * *

The next afternoon, Teresa Evergreen contacted while he rested in a hotel room, recovering from the medicine the healer woman had applied to his leg.

It had done its job well enough, and the skin was already scabbing over, but it left him fatigued. The room he had rented was quiet and homely, decorated very much in the recent trend hitting Tamalaria. All of the surfaces that could be wood, were, and every stitch of furniture was crafted by Elven carpenters. The Elven Kingdom was, quite frankly, making a killing during this time period, and none of them complained about the influx of monies from other territories. Trent thought, not with a little contempt, *we'll gladly take your money, but keep your citizens away.*

Trent, Evergreen contacted him through the sutra. *The Hoods and Fly have all been taken inside. They are all captives, and I am inside as well. What should I do?*

"Follow Reynaldi, as I suggested," he said aloud, no longer afraid of being overheard. Nobody in the hotel would know what the hell he was talking about even if they did hear him. "Not too closely, dear heart," he said. "Your powers are extraordinary, but so are his, I'm sure."

Believe me, they are, Evergreen said. *I got within a few yards of him before, and I swear, Mark, he almost looked right AT me.*

Trent chewed a fingernail nervously. Evergreen was an excellent tracker, thanks to her strange power to disappear without any trace. However, she could not engage in combat. Any hostile move on her part shattered her protective invisibility. If Reynaldi had one of the wide radius spells many Paladins had, he could strike her if he even thought someone was in the room that shouldn't be. Then, it would be open combat, and Evergreen wasn't nearly powerful or skilled enough to stand against a Paladin war veteran.

"Be very careful, dear. If you don't think you can get the Glove of Shadows without a fight, don't go for it. If you do get it, I'm in Ja-Wen, a hotel called The Crash Pad. Now, I'm going to get some more sleep."

Trent nodded off easily enough, his dreams still wavering with images of that final kick, the one that had sent the monstrosity's head flying through the air of that ill lighted store underground. The image that lodged itself squarely in his mind, though, the one that kept him shaking and shivering throughout his fitful rest, was not the kick itself.

It was Akimaru's dead, frosted purple-white eyes.

* * * *

Archibald Reynaldi wanted to interrogate the prisoners down in the prison. So much did he want this, he nearly broke his vows, but he held true to his word to the Red Tribe Werewolf.

Ignatious Stockholm, the Elven Paladin thought. "Why do I know that name so well," he whispered aloud as he stared at the Glove of Shadows.

He had it set in his private study in the northwestern tower of the keep, sitting in no sort of protective casing or anything. It just lay on an old card table he'd had dragged up from the barracks belonging to the couple dozen Soldier class troops on the base. The 'good old boys' as he'd often heard them refer to themselves, didn't mind the loss of one card table.

Before Reynaldi and his two most trusted guards left the barracks, another table, identical to the first one, was set in its place.

The Red Tribesman, he thought again. The very idea that he knew someone associated with a thieves' guild made his stomach crawl. All of them were foul, heathen blaggarts who deserved fates worse than death. Yet from Stockholm, he had sensed something almost regal, noble. Great power lay in that man, he knew. Perhaps, before a month went by, he would offer him absolution and a position in the Order.

The man radiated the presence of a Knight. With the proper oaths, he could be made one. For now, though, Reynaldi had to wonder whether anyone from either group had escaped capture.

"Lee Toren!" He fairly shouted the name as he shot up from his chair, darting out of the tower study toward the Soldier barracks. Three days the prisoners had been in his custody, and the one he knew best, whom everyone knew, hadn't been among them. He hadn't even realized that the Gnome Pickpocket, the one man he'd wanted arrested the most of all of them, hadn't been present.

And as soon as he slipped out of the tower, the Glove of Shadows wasn't, either.

* * * *

Lee Toren had waited for perhaps twenty minutes after William Deus, Ignatious Stockholm, and Flint slogged through the snow toward Fort Stone. Then, while Styge and Norman took stock of all of the belongings entrusted to them, he stole back towards Ja-Wen.

Though he hadn't seen the ambush party, he had felt it, felt it in his bones. Years spent as a professional coward had taught him how to sense law enforcement and similar individuals, especially Bounty Hunters. They, in truth, were the worst.

He'd hoofed it about two hours before the snow, his diminutive stature, and his aging body caught up with him. He simply couldn't keep at it, and he remembered suddenly why he preferred spending his winters in the big cities. Big cities had big buildings, and big buildings had big fireplaces. Even some of the less reputable places he used to bed down in, places in Arcade, Suvek, Dorinvale or Cherin Moh, kept the winter chill at bay. Out here, he had nothing to help.

The sound of a wagon bumping along, up ahead of him, on the road, made his heart throb faster than the horse pulling the wagon could run.

Lee tucked his head down, and he plowed through the snowdrifts as best he could, stopping periodically to peer up over the snow. When he'd drawn even with the wagon, but not quite yet with the driver, he made a quick snowball.

Taking careful aim, he hucked the improvised projectile over the wagon top.

He heard a muffled, surprised 'Oomph!', and the horse was reined to a halt.

Lee continued to run, now having real trouble with the snow.

When he finally drew even with the driver's seat, a huge, rot-smelling hand reached down and grabbed him savagely by the hair.

Howling like a dying hound, Lee Toren felt himself hauled up by his scalp.

He stopped howling when he saw the blue, scarred visage of the Jaft looking at him. A thick, black wool coat worn over denim overalls and a checked button shirt, probably flannel, told Lee that he needn't worry any further, despite the flaming pain in his head. The Jaft was clearly a farmer, probably on his way to Ja-Wen with his wagon to sell the last of his autumn harvest.

Before he could introduce himself or ask for a lift, the Jaft brought him around and deposited on the bench beside him. The farmer had long, yellow scars on his face, one that cut across his right cheek raggedly, and one that stretched from the center of his forehead down over his nose, and from there down to his chin. Lee had always been told that Jafts regenerated the fastest of any known Race in Tamalaria, or elsewhere. Then he remembered, staring at the scars, that Aquamancy, or any weapon enchanted with water or ice magic, would leave a scar, or permanently wound members of that race.

"So, little fellow," the Jaft rumbled, his voice soft but loud, full of bass thunder. "Why're you trucking through the snow all on yon lonesome?" The words rolled out slowly, as if the big, stinking farmer had to pause to remember each word's pronunciation before speaking it.

Lee shivered, and didn't answer until the Jaft pulled a blanket from behind him and threw it over his frozen legs.

Nice enough man, he thought, considering most Jafts' natures. The blue-fleshed humanoids were well known, throughout Tamalarian history, as some of the most brutish, violent people in the world. Slow minded, ill tempered, and lacking tact in spades, they often took occupations as troopers and soldiers of fortune, mercenaries and bodyguards. Some few, however, became farmers and animal tenders. Fewer still became mages, practitioners of Pyromancy or Gaiamancy, fire or earthen magic.

"Well, I sort of got separated from me chums, up north," Lee said as the farmer directed his gaze forward and snapped the reins, getting the horse moving again. Lee could see that the horse had a few strange traits, one of which was the fact that its entire body was far more muscular than it should have been.

It would have to be, he supposed, to haul the wagon, its goods and its owner on its own.

"They's all bigger'n me," he continued, "and they sort of lost me in the snow. We was headed up a hill, and I sorta backslid down the slope. Hit me 'ead on a rock, blacked out fer a bit."

"They couldn't find you?" The farmer stared straight ahead, but he grabbed a pair of small paper bags and brought them up front. He offered one to Lee, setting the other in his lap. Lee accepted, looked in, and took out a light green apple.

"Nope. I don't fink they realized I wadn't wiv 'em until they was over the hill. By then, I was buried in the powder."

The farmer made a little noise, as if to indicate that he wasn't surprised. The wagon coach was covered over the driver's bench, the better to keep the elements from bothering the owner. Knowing the farmer's natural dislike of water, and of ice, this seemed sensible.

"So, how much further until Ja-Wen?"

"Oh, we'll get there late evening tonight." The Jaft farmer pulled a small pouch from inside of his overalls, and a packet of rolling papers from a shirt pocket. He rolled a cigarette, and popped it in his mouth.

Lee opened a slender metal case in which he kept his own pre-rolled smokes that he purchased in packets at sundry goods stores. He lit it, inhaled, and blew out a small blue cloud of smoke.

"Come morning, I'll have this wagon uncovered to sell my excess from the harvest. So, what do you do for a living?"

Lee thought for a moment, looking back at the long laundry list of available answers he kept in store for such questions, finally deciding that the farmer deserved his honesty. It might get him kicked off of the wagon and back into the snow, but the Jaft had been willing to pull him up on the wagon, no questions asked. He owed him that much.

"I'm a thief, actually," Lee Toren said.

That little noise escaped the Jaft again, the one that seemed to mean he wasn't at all surprised.

"Look, I know you probably would rather I got down and hoofed it the rest of the way to the city, but I appreciate the ride."

"Oh, I could let you walk, but that wouldn't be very fair, now would it?"

Once more the Jaft's gentler nature left Lee speechless. "

We all do bad things in life, mister." He blew out his own cloud of smoke as the horse started down a slight decline. It picked up a measure of speed, but remained steady and stable, so as not to spill either driver or contents in the wagon. "You think I've always been a farmer?"

Lee considered this a long moment, looking once more at the scars on the blue man's face.

"Used to be a mercenary, mister. I done some bad things in my time, rest assured, but soon's I recalled what I'd been saving for, I bought my land and got out of the business. I hurt some folks, mister, didn't deserve to be hurt. I do what I can to atone. That includes giving rides to shady sorts."

Lee finished his cigarette without further comment, then he leaned back on the bench and fell asleep.

When he was lightly shaken, the farmer had brought his wagon to a stop in the outskirts of the city of Ja-Wen. The sun was partially below the curve of the horizon, the light fanning out into the realm of Tamalaria with a few final sputters.

Lee hopped down off of the wagon, and thanked the farmer, offering him some coin for the ride.

The farmer flatly, silently refused, shaking his big blue head somberly.

They shared a silent smile, and Lee headed off into the city proper, looking for a decent place to spend the night. No dives, no crummy little apartments, he thought. No, he wanted a modest hotel room for tonight. He was even willing to part with honest cash to secure one.

He made his way to Copper Street, and walked its length a while, finally getting too tired to look beyond the establishment he came upon on his right-hand side.

He looked up at the curved wooden sign overhead, and a slight twinge in the back of his skull, a twinge he often called instinct, told him that this was the place.

"The Crash Pad," he whispered to himself.

* * * *

Back to the current day and time.

Rage completed his portion of the escape plan.

Styge listened to Norman Adwar explain his ideas again.

Thaddeus Fly prepared his breath weapon.

Flint and Akimaru stared at each other in studied silence.

Of them all, who would be the first to escape the prison of Fort Stone?

Flint gave in once again, looking away from the white clad Ninja's upsettingly purple-white eyes. "Still no ideas," he said bluntly.

He pulled out his cigarette case and matches, the only concession the guards seemed to have made concerning their belongings, which presented another problem. If they managed a way out, how were they to recover their possessions? Almost everything the Hoods had on them was fully replaceable. *Almost* was the problem, however. Some of their stuff would cost a good amount of money to replace, money that they didn't have on hand, and none of them wanted to have to make a return trip to Desanadron.

The final problem with escape, the one he realized as he had been staring into Akimaru's eyes, was that the Glove of Shadows was here, in Fort Stone. Both Guild groups had come to steal it, and if they escaped entirely, they'd lose their chance at it.

The Ninja must have been contemplating the same problem. "I have a way," Akimaru said suddenly, pulling Flint from his reverie.

"Oh yeah? All right, I'm all ears, pal!" He tugged on one huge, rodent earlobe. "As you can see, that's not too far from true."

"Extract your claws."

Flint stubbed out his cigarette on the cement floor, singing the fur on the bottom of his right foot in the same spot as he had on the previous smokes. A pile of them sat, lamenting in spent silence, under his bed.

He extracted his claws, and held them at his sides as he stood up.

"Excellent. Do they remain roughly the same length if you reduce yourself down to your animus form?"

Again, Flint answered this question with a nod.

"Very good. Now, forget everything you see me do in the next few moments as soon as you can, and ask no questions regarding it. If anyone shall ask questions, it is sensei Fly I shall answer."

Flint shrugged in a non-committed fashion, not expecting much. He had thought about trying to claw his way up the cement wall of the cell toward the grate up near the ceiling, but his claws wouldn't find purchase in the hardened, artificial stone. When he had attempted to go up in rat form with the food platter, he'd proven too heavy, and his animus form snapped the rope.

What Akimaru did after he removed his gloves left more questions in Flint's racing mind than he imagined he'd ever have about any one person again.

Unfortunately, he knew he couldn't ask them, because if he did, the white clad Ninja would probably kill him.

* * * *

During the evening hours of his third day staying at the Crash Pad, Lee Toren heard Markus Trent scream in furious frustration through the thin, slat board wall.

* * * *

"Excellent," Trent had said after Evergreen told him of her successful nabbing of the Glove of Shadows. "Now, you remember where I am, right?"

For a long while, there was no reply.

"Teresa?"

The Glove of Shadows

I remember, Markus, she said in his mind. He felt something tenuous in the air, some disaster on the verge of taking place. *And you know what? I think our relationship, business and personal, is over, dear. This little beauty right here belongs to me now. Good-bye, Trent. Don't worry, I'll make the best of use of it.*

Something in his mind screamed, and there was an explosion of light behind his eyes. She had destroyed the sutra connecting their thoughts.

The primal roar that erupted from his throat could have killed anyone too faint of heart. The traitor had been betrayed.

Chapter Fourteen
Escape, Discovery, and Uncertain Alliances

A sheet of ice covered the wall of Flint and Akimaru's cell. A single rat climbed it with an excited gleam in its eyes.

The tender soil of the earth beyond the cement wall tore apart, easily cast aside by Ignatious Stockholm's claws.

Norman Adwar successfully pried the prison cell door open with his mecha contraptions as Styge prepared spells that would see the two of them safely outside the Fort.

"Don't worry about the others, good Gnome," he'd said when Norman had voiced concerns for his comrades. "They'll make their way out, of that I've little doubt."

Anna and Fly had rethought their strategy.

Since the ceiling of their cell was obviously none too thick, Fly had aimed his mouth upward and let loose wild lightning into the concrete overhead.

The ceiling had come apart quickly, large chunks of gray concrete falling hazardously down toward him.

As Anna had suggested, and already done herself, he darted for the safety under his hardwood bed.

After a minute of rumbling, he and she both stole a quick glance upward, and saw their way out.

He rolled out, and set himself in a crouch, his hands cupped together.

Anna rolled out, stepped up on his hands, and he threw her skyward.

She caught the lip of the hole, and pulled herself up into what looked like a stockroom of some sort.

Fly leaped up through with ease, using the natural leg strength of his people, and helped her fully up through the hole and into the chamber.

"Well, this is where it gets a little tricky, isn't it?" She took in the contents of the stockroom. Weapons were arranged on neat, ash wood racks, and sets of old armor hung on hooks. Under other circumstances, she might have donned some of the armor and a weapon, pretending to be just another guard. However, in the brief description Norman had given her in his notepad, Fort Stone wasn't host to any Draconus. She couldn't pull it off with Fly in tow.

"Not necessarily." Fly eased himself around the hole in the floor, over to the solid oak door.

If anyone had been outside of the storeroom when they blew through it, they would have been staring down at the two thieves when they rolled from safety. He opened the door a crack, and looked out. The hallway the storeroom opened into had large, open windows carved in the stone of the keep. Through the windows he saw an open courtyard, possibly on the northern side of the Fort. Nobody stood between them and escape. Of course, that was part of the dilemma, wasn't it? How could he be certain the others would get free of this place, especially Lain?

He felt a gentle hand on his shoulder.

"Don't worry," Anna said. "Everyone else will get out. I'm sure of it. Now let's get the hell out of here."

Without another moment's hesitation, they burst from the storeroom, out into the hall, through the windows, and across the empty courtyard. Nobody witnessed their escape, save a single woman who stood atop the Fort wall that Fly blasted through with another discharge of electrical power.

She had what they had come for, and they couldn't even see it.

Teresa Evergreen continued north as the heads of the Hoods and the Midnight Suns made their way east around the Fort. They would head back to Ja-Wen, where they would await the others. If the others escaped alive.

* * * *

In his animus form, Flint struggled up the ice. The arctic freeze of the frozen surface flowed through his claws into his body too swiftly for comfort. Finally, however, he made his way through the grille near the ceiling, and into an expansive workroom.

Several furnaces held blazing fires that pumped heat through metal tubes into the main keep, including the prison cells. A pair of Humans, probably Soldiers, were setting food onto several trays and attaching them to thin ropes.

Flint had another advantage over Stockholm in the lycanthrope department, and it was the fact that his particular Race could change shape soundlessly. He did so, and picked up a rolling pin from the counter next to him, creeping up behind the two guards. His padded feet moved him stealthily, cautiously toward their exposed backs as they grumbled and mumbled to one another about the low duty of tending to the prisoners' needs.

Flint assessed the situation briefly. They were only Humans, and thus little threat to him in a physical confrontation. At least, this would have been the case if he were armed with more than a baking instrument, and if they didn't have long swords at their hips and the deadly training to use them appropriately. If he gave them the opportunity, they would slay him without a second's thought. He avoided confrontation where he could, but knew when he couldn't.

Before they could even stand to full height, the preparations of the meals complete, he swung the pin down on the back of the head of the left-hand guard. He almost immediately wrapped the pin up around the throat of the other guard, who clawed and scrabbled at the pin until he lost consciousness. There was a brief, satisfying groan as the men congealed on the floor. "Sorry boys," he whispered to the suddenly still chamber. "If it's going to be you or me, I always choose me."

"Not exactly a bad way to think about it," Akimaru said behind him.

Flint turned and saw that the white clad Ninja had made his way to the grille, and was extending his frost covered surface around it.

A couple of minutes later, Akimaru punched through the iced over area, and pulled himself into the workroom.

"As the Obura say," he offered, dusting himself off. "Survival is never personal. It is natural."

Flint considered this a moment, and then led the way to the only door leading into or out of the chamber.

He focused, concentrated on his ears, thought deeply on the concept of sound. This was a talent he and his Race relied upon heavily.

While all lycanthropes had a few heightened senses, Wererats could literally turn up or down their hearing.

He pressed one large, oval, flap-like ear against the wooden door. He could just make out the sound of footfalls in the hallway.

"Anything?" Akimaru asked.

Flint held up a single finger. A pair of guards rushed past in a hurry, talking in ragged gasps about how impossible it was that someone had stolen 'it'.

Flint's heart dropped into his stomach; had one of the others already gotten a hold of the Glove of Shadows? If so, which Guild had claim over it?

He would hopefully find the answers in Ja-Wen, because that was where he intended to head to with Akimaru. He would be crossing through winter country without equipment, but maybe the white clad Ninja could do something to lessen the harsh conditions.

Flint and Akimaru moved slowly out into the hallway, searching for a way out. They found one without too much hassle, only having to move to the northern hallway at the end of the one they were in. Large, open windows had been cut into the stone of the keep, and a huge hole had been blasted in the outer wall of the Fort. Smoke still filtered up into the air from the hole, and though Flint couldn't tell what exactly it had been from, he had a few suspicions.

They ran through the courtyard, each noticing that nobody stood in their way. They got out of the Fort proper, into the snows of the eastern provinces.

The two Guild members almost ran right into the backs of Anna Deus and Thaddeus Fly.

* * * *

The soil here is getting cold, Stockholm thought. He had been digging up at an angle, so that he and Rage could both climb up through the makeshift tunnel without difficulty. The earth and stones he had now come across held a portion of the dampness and chill of the surface above, and in a few more minutes, his digging claws came in contact with snow and air.

He heard a gasp from behind him.

"We're out, ain't we?" Rage said. "I's can feel da fresh air."

Stockholm smiled back at the Orc Berserker, glad to see the man's mood had changed. Since he had stopped pounding concrete, Rage had been sulky and restless. Now, his face lit up as sunlight, in a thin shaft, broke past Stockholm's shoulder and onto the Orc's face.

With a few more heaves, Stockholm spilled into the snow-strewn fields of Tamalaria.

Exactly where he was remained a mystery for only a few minutes, until Rage came up from behind him and said, "Hey, dere's da Headmaster."

Stockholm let the snow fall off of him and looked over his shoulder. He was perhaps fifty yards away from Anna and Fly, who were dodging Flint and Akimaru's running forms.

Well, well, he thought, *the gang's all here.*

"Come on." He put a furry hand on Rage's shoulder.

Rage nodded and continued to beam at him, happy to be free.

The two warriors approached at speed, but Stockholm didn't need to worry about surprising the four agents with their presence. They made enough noise, crunching through the snow, to make all four heads swivel toward them.

"Stocky!" Anna darted through the snow and would have hugged the big man, but Akimaru and Rage were both present, and neither had a clue that she was, in fact, a woman. She had already let her little 'secret' become ill guarded, and she needed to minimize the damage.

Instead, she stood swaying before him in the arctic winds that blew down from the north. "Good—this is almost everyone. Quickly now, can you smell any of the others?"

Stockholm held his snout up to the air, and took a couple of quick sniffs. He could, in fact, smell a Human and a Gnome moving swiftly south. He could smell many other scents, but these two in particular he knew personally.

"Styge and Norman Adwar are already down and away," he reported, reverting to his role as Chief. "They'll head to Ja-Wen, most likely, waiting for us to regroup. Will, how the hell did these people expect us? Did that preacher you and Flint talked to—"

"No," the Black Draconus cut him off. "I think I know how you were found out, as well as us, Red Tribe. We've come to an agreement, myself and your Headmaster. We'll be working as a single group, for now." He gave Akimaru a slight bow. "At the very least until we get back to Ja-Wen, and question Markus Trent."

"He wasn't with you?" Anna asked.

"He claimed to have business to tend to in the city." Fly clenched and unclenched his fists. "When we get a hold of him, we're going to make him talk. It will be a very violent conversation."

The group moved cautiously down the eastern side of the Fort, stopping after about forty yards, where they saw a pair of slender hands stretch out of a window.

Fly recognized that pale skin at once as Lain McNealy. He sprinted ahead, and stood before the surprised Necromancer woman. "Lain!"

"Thaddeus," she gasped. She had been working slowly at the bars of her window, but wouldn't get free anytime soon. The bars were thick, and set close together. Only because of her natural slenderness had she been able to move her hands through them.

Fly signaled Rage over, and the Orc Berserker planted his feet in the dirt, making certain he got settled in beneath the snow, grabbed the bars, and heaved back on them.

The wall groaned under the pressure, a large section of it finally breaking free.

Lain leaped out, her breath catching in her throat as her powers flowed back through her entire body.

"All right, this should be everybody, aside from the old man and the gearhead," Flint rasped. "We can either stand around congratulating ourselves and twiddling each other's privates, or we can get moving."

Anna looked into the Wererat's face, and saw his hatred for the Midnight Suns. He didn't truck with this alliance, be it temporary or not. Apparently, he had bad blood with Desanadron's other thieves' Guild.

The Wererat led the way south, his anger causing him to move without caution or heed to the fact that the group was largely unarmed.

Would that really matter though, she wondered. In their midst were two Ninjas, a Berserker, a Necromancer, whatever the big crimson Werewolf was, and herself. Flint, while he wouldn't admit it, was a Strong Arm Thug by Class, and though he had a few skills in the brawling arena, he worked best with throwing knives and short swords.

The group followed the Wererat, eventually catching up with him. They stopped at the southeastern corner of the outer wall of the Fort, each hoping to get clear of the Fort without encountering hostile forces.

Stockholm sniffed the air, Flint tuned his hearing up a few notches, and Fly brought his hands together to concentrate. Without his sutras or any other equipment, he would have to rely on the meditation techniques the Obura had taught him.

Anna silently leaned against the concrete wall of the Fort. They were leaving behind the reason they had come to Fort Stone in the first place, or so she thought. If they left now, how could they hope to take the Glove of Shadows later?

Perhaps, she thought, they would get lucky, and Reynaldi wouldn't be able to destroy the artifact here. Hopefully, he'd have to move it again.

"Five or six troopers," Flint said.

"Humans and Jafts, one Elf," Stockholm added. "Moving swiftly south. Styge and Norman will be spotted if they aren't careful."

"They'll be fine," Flint said. "I just heard Norman say something to the old man about making them look like grobvriks. You know, those shelled buggers what only come above ground during the winter?"

They all breathed a slight sigh of relief, except for Fly. He had drifted far into his meditation, and found himself stretching his astral perceptions beyond anything he had in a long while.

His point of view, he discovered, was that of a single crow in a murder, fluttering around some sort of mountainous region. The bird fascinated him, its mind a jumble of meaningless, instinct-driven thoughts. *Food, defecate, eat, defecate, find a corpse, find a corpse.* Such delicate body parts, such fragile bones in this scavenger, he thought.

He realized, with a fright, that he had wandered seriously off course and snapped himself out of the mind of the crow.

The return trip to his own body seemed to take a disturbingly long time, but when his eyes opened, he saw only a few minutes had passed.

He realized as he wobbled back to consciousness, that there had been a *woman* in his field of vision. A woman, he felt certain, that the bird could see, but people could not. Why had she seemed so familiar? For now, he decided, that could wait.

"We've no reason to tarry." He swayed slightly.

Anna gave him a curt nod, and together, Human Rogue and Black Draconus Ninja led the way south. Through the snow they trekked, silently agreeing that the truce between them would hold.

* * * *

For a day and a half, the mixed company of Hoods and Midnight Suns made slow progress. Each was fatigued from lack of exercise and the suddenness of their escape.

They stopped often but slept little, and would have frozen through badly if not for the strange pockets of lowered chill they occasionally passed through. Flint and Fly both had an idea of why that was, but neither Wererat nor Draconus said a word.

The night they spent in the plains did nothing for their tempers, yet none lost it.

Two long hours before the sun rose, they made their way to the outskirts of the city of Ja-Wen, tired, hungry, and chilled to their collective core. Without discussion, Anna and Thaddeus Fly led the company to a large, family-themed restaurant where they all gorged themselves completely and utterly.

Though their equipment had been taken, the guards of Fort Stone hadn't thought that a prisoner would have any good way to use coins in their cells. In that regard, they had all been very lucky to keep their money pouches.

Near the end of their meals, Anna finally asked Fly what he intended to do next.

He held up a claw to stay her a minute before answering. "We find Trent, and beat him senseless. I know for a fact that he betrayed us all. He would have done that eventually, but this journey was the perfect excuse for him to finally make another move."

"Another?" Styge wiped his lips with a napkin.

Fly nodded slowly, thinking back over the three attempts Trent had made over the last twelve years. Two of the attempts had come only a couple of years apart.

"Yes, another." Lain McNealy had seated herself on Fly's left side, and it hadn't escaped Anna's eyes how often she placed her free hand in his lap.

"Three years back, Headmaster Fly went on a mission out of the city, and while he was gone, Markus Trent bent several dozen of our agents to his designs. Upon the Headmaster's return, he had to defend himself against them. Thankfully, Akimaru and Mr. Striker aided him in his combat, but we lost nearly forty men to Trent's scheming. If it were up to me," she said, looking meaningfully at Fly's profile, "I would have had him executed. But the Headmaster is wise, merciful when it serves his purposes better."

"Oh yes, merciful," Flint grumbled. The Black Draconus had almost breathed lightning on Styge and Norman when they had come upon them, not recognizing them for who they were because of the old man's Illusionist spells. Stockholm had turned Fly at the last possible moment, and the explosion of lightning had landed only a few feet from the Wererat Prime. Bastard hadn't even apologized, Flint thought. "You've ordered your people to hunt down our agents so often I forgot how merciful you could be!"

He climbed angrily from his seat and stabbed the table with a fork, shuffling outside without another word.

Anna watched him go, and almost followed. Stockholm put a hand over hers to stay her. "I'll go talk to him," the big man rumbled.

Anna agreed silently, and the Red Tribesman exited the restaurant.

Flint was on an open patio, keeping out of the snowfall that fell gently on the city's streets. Foot trails and wheel ruts stood out in the fresh powder, and a team of Dwarven shovel pushers turned down a busier street, making certain to keep the main ways cleared.

Stockholm put a hand on Flint's shoulder as he stepped out, and gave a little squeeze. "What's on your mind, Prime?"

Flint lit a cigarette and exhaled angrily. He had seen something in Fly's eyes when he had spoken across the table to Anna.

He knows, Flint had thought. "She told him, you know," he said. "She told Thaddeus Fly the one thing that has kept her and I so close."

"She told me too." Stockholm drew level with the Prime. He thought, not for the first time, that if Flint had only been a lycanthrope of a more canine nature, he could have fallen for the man. But certain aspects of Flint's personality grated Stockholm's nerves, and his incessant jealousy was just one of them.

"I don't mind that, Chief," Flint said, using the only nickname he had for Stockholm that the Red Tribesman didn't mind him using. "You're like family, in a way. But *him*." He spit into the snow. "He'll use it against us."

"No, he won't," Stockholm said flatly. "He has a queer sense of honor, like all Ninja. Theirs is a world and lifestyle I only vaguely understand, but I know secrets are sacred to them. They use them as the most precious currency in the world."

The two Hoods stood silently for a while, neither daring to disturb this temporary peace.

After a good twenty minutes, the rest of the Guild members came out of the restaurant, and they all seemed to have agreed on a course of action.

"What now, sir," Flint said to Anna.

"Fly has found Trent through his meditation," she said. "He's at the Crash Pad, a little east and north of here. Lee's there too," she added.

Flint breathed a mental sigh of relief. He knew Lee was a greedy bastard, but he liked the Gnome Pickpocket. Flint had been afraid that Lee might have frozen to death in the plains north of Ja-Wen, traveling without the benefit of the necessary equipment.

"So we're heading over there as a group?" He tossed his spent smoke over his shoulder, where it rebounded off of the helmet of a city guard.

The guard glared murderously up at him, but he took no notice.

"For now, yes. When we get Trent and Lee back, we're going to interrogate Trent, find out what he knows and what he did, precisely. How he set us up. From there, Fly and I have not yet agreed on a course of action."

"So what, I'm taking orders from this skulk now?" The Wererat pointed an accusing claw at the Black Draconus.

Fly said nothing to defend himself from the insult hurled so carelessly at him.

"I pray you're not going to tell me that's so, William, because if it is, I'll wait right here until this little party is over."

"He isn't suggesting anything of the sort." Stockholm once more put a patronizing hand on Flint's shoulder. He felt the tension in the Wererat's bunched muscles, tasted the bile that must be collecting in the back of Flint's throat. *Old hatred*, he thought, *as taught by Remy way back when. Way to go, boss.* "For now, there are no leaders, no orders," the Chief of the Hoods said gravely. "For now, we work as a single unit with the same purpose in mind, the same mission statement. When we have what we need from Trent, we hold council over what to do. Is everyone level with that?"

Quiet whispers of agreement met his statement, and he turned away from the company and descended the patio steps. "Fly, if you would lead the way?"

With the Black Draconus in the lead, the rather motley looking crew from Desanadron shuffled through the snowy streets of Ja-Wen. Everyone pretty much took up their roles of old. Rage kept close to Lain. She had to explain to him that she wasn't actually going to have a baby, though, she thought inwardly, she could always fix that, given time.

Pedestrians, travelers, and even city guards moved out of their way, many clearly terrified of such a nasty looking bunch. They arrived at their destination within fifteen minutes, and much to their surprise, found Lee Toren sitting outside, enjoying the fresh air of the winter day and the polluted air of his cigarette.

His eyes went wide with shock as they approached as a group, but only for a moment. "Come to tan me hide there ol' boss?" he asked Anna.

"Wouldn't dream of it, friend," she replied. "You're a professional, and I know that. I'm only paying you so much, but trust me, a deduction is going to be made in your salary for leaving Styge and Norman to twitch in the wind."

The old Illusionist seemed not to be paying attention, but Lee saw the quick fury in Norman's shining eyes.

"Sorry, mates," was Lee's only reply to that glare. "Simply a matter of my nature."

"Your nature could have gotten us all killed for all you'd have cared," Norman shouted as a steady wind picked up, carrying his voice all the better to Lee's ears.

Fly had an inkling of an idea of what was going to happen next, but he made no move to stop the little Engineer.

Norman sprinted forward, slipping just beneath Stockholm's furry grasp, and was on top of Lee Toren so swiftly that the agile Pickpocket couldn't move out of the way in time. His fists drove hard into Lee's face, and they went tumbling down in a tangled heap of diminutive limbs, each flailing at the other for purchase.

"Should I stop them, sir?"

Anna's mind barely registered Stockholm's quiet question, but she shook her head. Fly and Akimaru stepped around the quarreling Gnomes, heading into the hotel. They had business inside, and would bring Trent out for questioning, though Anna knew that they would ask questions of their own before dragging him out. For now, she wanted to watch this little battle in the snow.

Lee needed to learn a hard lesson in loyalty, she thought, and Norman deserved a chance to finally get in some combat experience that wouldn't prove fatal to him.

Back and forth the Gnomes tumbled, Norman punching as hard as he could wherever he found an opening, Lee trying to block and get at his knives. Twice he rolled Norman off of him, managing to get a hold of a knife handle only long enough to have it knocked away. Norman, Lee quickly found out, had a lot of potential in the area of pugilism. Back and forth his head whipped as Norman punched him, teeth flying free from his darkened gums.

His nose was surely broken, he thought, as he tried to breath through a mouth that was being pummeled over and over again.

Finally, as he tried to punch back, Norman's left fist found purchase against his temple, and Lee's lights dimmed, then totally blanked.

Norman Adwar stood over Lee Toren, a Pickpocket with so many years on the road and in combat that Norm had thought his impulse to attack was lunacy.

A quiet pair of hands clapped as he breathed hard, his breath misting in the winter air.

For the first time in his long life, he had openly attacked someone and come away the victor.

As Anna and the others quietly applauded him, Norman Adwar turned and vomited into the snowy street—his body filled with self-loathing.

* * * *

Markus Trent knew he was in trouble the second he heard approaching footsteps. Those steps held poorly veiled fury and violence. He knew who would be bursting in.

Sure enough, the door flew open, banging harshly on the wall, and rebounding shut right in Thaddeus Fly's face.

Trent barely suppressed a laugh, but felt no humor when the door opened again, slowly. Fly stood in the doorway, with Akimaru slightly behind and to his left.

"Trent," Fly growled, stepping into the room.

Trent had a clear advantage over Fly. He still had his weaponry, while the Headmaster had nothing on him except his uniform. However, with Akimaru now in the room, and Fly's breath weapon twinkling vaguely in the Draconus' mouth, the advantage slipped quickly into the mental filing drawer marked 'Bad Ideas'.

"Headmaster, perhaps I can explain—"

He got no further before Fly's hand seemed to magically transport itself to Trent's throat. The Draconus's other hand whipped into Trent's right-hand pocket, and withdrew the sutra stuffed within.

Trent's heart sank as he realized precisely the sutra's purpose—it hadn't been locked with Chi magic at all. It had been given to him so that Akimaru could read it as he had the bracer in the cottage to the west.

This fear was confirmed as Fly handed the sutra back to the white clad Ninja.

Akimaru removed one glove and took the sutra in hand, reading into its brief history.

"So," Trent managed to gasp. "What is written on that sutra, anyway?"

Fly smiled hideously at him, and let out a bark of a laugh.

"It's the language of my people, Trent. It says, 'traitor'." Akimaru handed the sutra back to Fly, and moved out into the hallway. "Wait right here, Markus. I'm not going to kill you, but punishment is due, rest assured."

As soon as Fly was out in the hall, Trent darted to the window.

The grinning green face held an expression that mirrored the look Fly had given him only a minute before.

Rage followed instructions to a tee, and Trent wasn't sure he could make it past the Greenskin without suffering severe injury.

Out in the hall, Akimaru leaned in close and spoke clearly to his sensei. "Markus Trent instructed Teresa Evergreen, one of our trackers, to follow Lee Toren. She is the one who can become wholly undetectable, sensei."

Fly groaned and nodded. He hated Evergreen but knew she had invaluable talents. Talents, it would appear, that were now being used against him. "She informed the Paladins at Fort Stone of our coming, and the coming of the Hoods. Trent was going to have her bring him the Glove of Shadows, but she has betrayed him. She has the artifact, sensei."

"Terrific." Fly threw up his hands. "How in the seven Hells are we going to track *her* down?" Abruptly, the crow's eye view came back into his mind. The woman had been Teresa Evergreen! The bird had been able to see her, even if he couldn't. "Never mind that. Let's get back in there and drag his ass outside."

Akimaru bowed, and entered Trent's room again.

The Human Ninja was on his feet, his rucksack on his back.

"Are you going to come back to us peacefully?"

"I will." Trent's entire body seemed to sag with defeat. "My plans have failed yet again. However, I have an idea where she'll be heading."

Fly cocked a scaled eyebrow at him.

"She comes from the Dwarven Territories, Traithrock I believe," he said.

"Well, it's a start anyway," Fly muttered. "When we get outside, keep your weapons in their place."

"Why do you say this, Headmaster," Trent asked.

"Because for now, there is a truce between us and William Deus." Fly turned his back on the traitor and moving out into the hall. "Akimaru, bring up the rear. Trent, you stay right behind me."

In single file, the three Midnight Suns, Ninjas all, exited the Crash Pad.

Fly's first sight outside was the Pickpocket Lee Toren laid out in the snow. Then he saw blood on the hands of the other Gnome. "Well, Norman Adwar. I see that victory is yours." His blunted, reptilian snout wrinkling at the smell of vomit in the air.

"Shut it, you," Styge admonished the Draconus harshly. He'd rummaged through his bag for bandages, and he was taping Norman's battered hands. "The youngster isn't exactly proud of what he's done. We're not all savages like you."

Fly stared in wide-eyed astonishment at the Mohawked old man. *For the gods' sake*, he thought, *the man's just an Illusionist! How dare he speak to me that way!* But he kept the temper in check. A truce was on, and he wouldn't be the one to break it. Not yet, at any rate.

He reached behind him, and grabbed Trent by the arm, thrusting him into the middle of the group. "Speak up, and beg for their forgiveness, idiot," Fly growled.

The combined glares of the Hoods and Midnight Suns bored into him, and Trent squirmed inside. His eyes lingered for a long moment on the face of Ignatious Stockholm, a man he had feared for ten years since their first encounter. Nobody, not even Akimaru, scared him as much as the crimson lycanthrope.

"I sold you all out," he said gloomily. "The Glove of Shadows is now in the hands of Teresa Evergreen, and I am to blame. I beg your forgiveness, but accept your punishment." He knelt and hung his head, as was Obura custom.

Also following custom, Akimaru came forward and clutched a large handful of his hair, pulling his face up to look at the surrounding agents.

They all wanted a piece of him, and he knew it.

The first to come forward, surprisingly, wasn't Fly, or Stockholm, or even William Deus. It was the old man, Styge.

He stood before the Ninja, the winter wind flapping his robes about his thin, frail frame. He cupped Trent's chin with one long fingered, gnarled hand. "Young man, you've caused us all a lot of grief." His breath rattled harshly in his chest as he hadn't fully recovered from manifesting his illusions in the prison cell. "Still, I can't find it in me to lash out at you, youngster. After all," he said, letting go of Trent's face to take a step back and throw his arms wide, indicating the whole of the group. "If you hadn't, this sight would not be before me! All these folks, together for a common purpose for once, makes my heart sing with joy! I've never held a grudge agin' you folks. You just don't offer me the perks Will does." He returned to his place in the group.

Next came Flint Ananham, the Wererat who served as the Hoods' Prime. He let the claws of his left hand spring out, and he pushed them up against Trent's throat. He knelt down, and peered into the Ninja's eyes. "The old man may forgive you, but I sure as fuck won't you little punk. You're the worst kind of scum. It's people like you that make a bad name for Ninjas."

He let one claw flicker across Trent's left cheek, letting a thin trickle of blood flow down his face. He too returned to his place.

Now Lain McNealy towered over him. "If I'm around when you die, Trent, I'm going to raise your body and let another zombie rape you with a rusty pipe." She spat in his face, and moved next to Fly.

Nobody moved forward for a moment, until Ignatious Stockholm, huge and menacing, knelt down in front of him.

"Markus Trent," he said.

The Ninja's heart beat faster and faster, near the point of bursting. As the Red Tribesman leaned in closer and closer, he felt the urge to jabber and scream, to writhe free of Akimaru's grasp.

"You have known me, boy. You have known the taste of my claws, the taste of my blade. My weapons are gone now, thanks to you, as are the rest of all of our supplies. You will replace them, tonight, while the rest of us take council with one another. If our two groups remain together, Hoods and Midnight Suns joined in purpose, I shall be your jailer. If we should separate, I feel certain that Akimaru here will take up the task. Either way, you're no longer an ally. You're a prisoner in our midst, and the mobile cell that is the company will hold you in contempt for a long time to come. Yet, you may redeem yourself." He said this last bit very softly. "If you are very, very lucky, and very, very careful."

When Stockholm stepped back from Markus Trent, nobody else came forward. Instead, Akimaru let Trent's head loll forward and put one foot on the Human Ninja's back. He pushed as hard as he could, pitching Trent forward, into the snow.

Trent rolled over, and looked up into the hard, dead eyes of the white-clad Ninja, whose masked face was pressed nose-to-nose with his own.

Akimaru leaned further forward, pressing the place where his mouth should be next to Trent's ear.

"The Red Tribe speaks true, Markus. You must redeem yourself, absolutely and certainly. If you don't, then there will have been no reason for me to save you in the mountains. And if we should have to return to such a place again, and you have not redeemed yourself, I will let you die by the hands of the beasts." Akimaru whispered, letting no one else hear him.

Between the Red Tribesman and Akimaru, he might not live to see his next birthday, Trent thought.

"All right," Anna said after Akimaru helped Trent up. "Let's head to the nearest building big enough for us to hold council. We'll decide what we're going to do now that everyone's here, and the Glove is gone. We may go our separate ways again, or we may continue on as one large group. Either way, we'll decide during our council."

All were in agreement on the matter and they all made their way to the city's largest library for council.

They were not the only ones holding council at this time.

* * * *

Archibald Reynaldi considered the suggestions his highest-ranking officers had given him. After searching for perhaps five hours for signs of the former prisoners, a team of Knights had concluded that the entire group, regardless of Guild allegiance, had gone south, to Ja-Wen. In the process of escaping, two troopers had been slain, in the workroom that connected to the cells from above. How exactly any of them had managed to get into the workroom was still beyond the Elven Paladin, but he wasn't really thinking about the how of it. His concern was only for the aftermath of their escape.

He could accept that any of the escapees had stolen the Glove of Shadows. They scarcely would have had time between the moment of their escape and the hustle and bustle of the troopers of the Fort going about their business. On top of that, he thought, he had issued a general alarm to search for Lee Toren in the area surrounding the Fort. Surely not even the brash William Deus would have been foolish enough to attempt the tower if the entire base was on such high alert.

Could Reynaldi had been double-duped and betrayed by whoever had spoken with the preacher in Ja-Wen? One of Fort Stone's ranking officers, Captain Fillings, had suggested that as a possibility.

"And why not," the Minotaur captain said to the meeting chamber as a whole. "While we concentrated on the prisoners we had, we forgot about the ones we didn't! That Pickpocket probably knew where to go all along. He must have had a way of hiding himself from us, and he tailed Lord Reynaldi to the tower. All he would have to do then was wait for the perfect opportunity!"

"Yes, that does seem very fitting of him," another officer said.

The Dwarven officer scratched his thick, black beard as he knit his eyebrows close together. "Where would he go after taking the artifact? Where could he hope to hide from the Order? We have Forts in almost all lands of Tamalaria!" A number of the officers grunted agreement, and a couple even laughed, as though the idea of escaping the Order of Oun were a ridiculous one indeed. Back in the days before the War of Vandross, one could go days, even weeks, between outposts. After that terrible war, dozens of Forts went up as many Paladins and Knights serving the Order at the time gave up lands and money to spread their influence across the land.

Only two non-commissioned officers were present for Reynaldi's meeting, men he had trusted for years, and neither of them had said a word, or ushered a single chuckle. Now, the Elven Paladin looked to them. On the left stood a Sidalis in a simple cloth uniform, the green camouflage pattern matching his eyes almost perfectly. His physical appearance was highly non-humanoid. A bipedal hornet, his long, translucent wings folded on his back, Corporal Dean Masters took no prisoners and offered no mercy in combat. Two thin antennae stuck out on either side of the square camo cap on his head, and the bulbous black eyes blinked back at Reynaldi as they twitched.

Across from the mutant, Masters, one of the Order's only Lizardmen cleaned his katana on a specially woven rag. Like Masters, the Lizardman wore no armor, and he only wore two weapons on his right hip. He sheathed the katana, and drew the shorter sword set next to it in his red sash, inspecting the edge critically. This man was Sergeant Bergeon, and he was in charge of teaching the proper techniques of caring for one's weapons.

"Corporal," Reynaldi said.

The Sidalis blinked rapidly, and took a step forward. The weapon strapped to his back, a trident, shifted a little between his wings.

"Anything to add to the conversation?"

"Just this, sir." His voice droned high and wheezy, yet devoid of any inflection. "There are two distinct areas where the Order has little or no influence or favor. The Elven Kingdom, and the Dwarven Territories. Of the two regions, I have the distinct feeling that the thief would head to the northern mountains of the Dwarves and Minotaurs, sir."

Reynaldi nodded, and several of the officers muttered among themselves.

"And you, Bergeon?" Reynaldi asked the Lizardman. "Do you concur?"

"Indeed," the sergeant said. "If Dean and I move out now, we may catch up with our quarry before he arrivessss in the mountainssss."

Reynaldi stood at the head of the long conference table, the assembled officers following suit.

"Do it," Reynaldi snapped. "If he gets to the safety of those mountains before you, you'll have to be very discreet in your pursuit. Obey the laws of the territories. Be mindful of the Dwarves' many religious sects. But above all else, get that artifact back here. I'll not let Lee Toren run rampant with something like the Glove of Shadows." He pounded his armored fist on the conference table for emphasis, trying to hide, both from the others and from himself, the temptation that the glove presented even to him. How, he wondered, could an evil being like Lee Toren resist that power? The Sidalis and Lizardman saluted stiffly and left through the creaking double doors. When they were gone, Reynaldi dismissed the rest of the assembled officers, and sat back down at the head of the conference table.

If Toren didn't have the Glove, no matter. He would have whoever took the Glove from the tower study executed immediately upon their return to Fort Stone. Most of the Order had abolished execution, but Reynaldi was an old-fashioned sort, all holy wrath and vengeance. He smiled broadly at the idea of hanging Lee Toren. He would not only volunteer to be the gallows man, he wouldn't bother to wear a mask.

"Oun bless me," he whispered.

* * * *

Two days south of the Elven Paladin, the parties agreed to split. Their styles of command and operation simply differed too greatly. They agreed that if they should run into one another, no weapons would be drawn, no assaults initiated.

The Midnight Suns left with a few parting words to the Hoods, and took themselves to an Alchemy shop, where they could get instant teleportation back to Desanadron. The Hoods would wait two hours, and then follow suit, as had been agreed during their council. How each group approached the situation from there would differ, and Anna wanted to get an idea of how things were going back home.

Fly would contact her three days later, though she did not as yet know this. Anna's mind was filled with concerns for her party members, especially Lee Toren, who'd wanted to be done with her and the Hoods since his harsh beating from Norman Adwar. She didn't know that Akimaru would reveal to Fly the location of Teresa Evergreen's origin, or what it meant. She didn't know that Norman would lock himself in his room and refuse to leave.

She didn't know she was going to have a near death experience.

Chapter Fifteen
Open Wounds

Well, Thaddeus Fly thought as he stormed into the entrance den of the building that served as his base of operations, *at least Deus has men with some discipline.*

The main lobby of the Guildhall was littered with trash, discarded clothes, and slumbering agents.

"What in the names of all gods above is this," he roared, waking nearly a dozen slouching, lazing agents. "I'm gone for a couple of weeks, and this place turns into a total sty. On your feet, maggots!"

"Headmaster," Lain whispered next to him. "I am in dire need of a bath and a change of clothes."

He nodding to her and the others, temporarily dismissing them, including Markus Trent.

The agents in the lobby lined up in front of him, puffing out their chests like military recruits, hands behind their backs.

"Where is Mr. Striker," Fly walked up and down the line, keeping a few feet between himself and these laze-abouts. *Worthless,* he thought, bile rising in the back of his throat. "Would anyone care to answer me?"

"Headmaster," one of the Illeck agents near the right end of the line said.

Fly swooped over in front of him, pressing the end of his blunted snout against the whelp's forehead.

"Have an answer for me, you lazy little prick?"

Cold sweat ran down the Dark Elf's forehead, wetting the end of Fly's face. "I sure hope so, because it might just lessen the severity of your punishment. Now, speak!"

"Sir, he's out in the city, hustling wagon merchants for protection fees," the Illeck said.

A list of the names of the city's more prosperous wagon merchants ran through Fly's head, and on that list, near the bottom, his mind came to a screeching halt—Harold Deus. *Oh shit,* he thought, *please gods don't let him lay a hand on Anna's husband. The truce will be so much used toilet paper if that happens.*

"Akimaru," Fly shouted but he needn't have done so. The white clad Ninja hadn't left when he was dismissed, but now he sped out of the Guildhall so fast he appeared to only be a blur of white cloth.

"Good. Now, what's your name, agent?"

"Sorpalo," the Illeck squeaked.

"All right, Sorpalo," Fly backed away from the Illeck and the line of agents. "You may take yourself to the coroner's office in mid-town Desanadron. Ms. McNealy would probably like a list of the city's most recent dead, along with any files the police department has on the dearly departed. As for the rest of you," he shouted, addressing the rest of the line as the Illeck took off to play gopher. "I want the halls, meeting dens, and my chambers so spotless I could invite the lesser gods over for tea. On the double!"

With no objections, the agents set to work, sweeping, mopping, dusting and rearranging.

"Ah, so good to be home," he whispered to himself.

* * * *

"No," came the muffled reply from the inside of Norman Adwar's personal chambers. The Hoods had returned to their underground base, and Flint wanted to talk with Norman about his altercation with Lee Toren.

The Gnome Pickpocket was furious, and intended to quit helping the Hoods if Norman didn't apologize for beating him down.

"Look, just let me in, Norm," the Wererat pleaded, growing increasingly impatient. All of his petty jealousies had been building up in the back of his mind, as was his nature, along with the frustration of not having been able to lash out at the Midnight Suns. He had been frozen in the snow-strewn plains of the east, beaten by a guard and imprisoned, and had been forced to accept the aid of Akimaru in order to escape. He'd had Markus Trent knelt before him, the opportunity to break his neck right there for the taking. But he knew that Anna wouldn't have let him.

"No," Norman said from the other side of the door. Flint had been given this task mostly because Stockholm had other matters to attend to, foremost among these being reviewing Hollister's reports. Besides, he thought, the Red Tribesman may very well just congratulate Norm, give him a few pointers about where to hit the Pickpocket the next time, and be off to his office.

"You know I can pick this lock and have this door open in less than a minute, Norm. It swings open into the hall, so don't think about trying to barricade the thing." This statement was met with silence from the Engineer, and a moment later Flint heard the satisfying 'snick' of the deadbolt retracting into the door.

He opened the door, stepping lightly past Norm, and taking a seat on the freshly scrubbed floor. Everything smelled like disinfectant and cleansers. One of Norman's little habits, he surmised.

Norm sat down on the floor, his legs hooked in Indian-style, and put his head in his hands.

"I don't know what came over me," the Gnome moaned. His chest twittered up and down with the start of sobs. "I'm just so sick and tired of feeling helpless, useless, and that bastard took off without even warning me or Styge. They clubbed me in the back of the skull without so much as a warning, Flint. Without my machines, I'm nothing."

"I wouldn't say that, precisely." The short bout in the snowy street of Ja-Wen played over in Flint's mind again. It was roughneck, but there was an admirable amount of technique to Norman's punches. "Where'd you learn to fight like that, by the way?"

Norm wiped his left forearm across his face, taking the tears away.

"Oh, that," Norman got to his feet, and absentmindedly grabbed a socket wrench from the shelves beneath the bench, and tightened down a few screws on the odd contraption currently occupying most of the space. "A few years back, I took some leave and went to see me family in Palen. My dad, he's an Aeromancer, and he used to serve as a city guard." Norm finished his work on the large, multi-sectioned device and flipping a switch.

Strange rumbling vibrated through the air from the device, and a chute of some sort opened on the left side. As he continued his story, Norman fed bits of scrap metal into the large machine.

"One of his old guard mates, fellow by the name of Emanuel Topsy, was visiting when I arrived. Human Boxer, and very skilled at his style. Dad set me up with him to do some sparring. It was mostly a joke, and I took a good lickin', but I learn from my mistakes."

"I guess so." Flint drew out his cigarette case and matches. *Getting low*, he thought as he took one of the three remaining sticks of tobacco.

After another minute of feeding scrap metal into the machine, Norm stopped, and put on a thick pair of black rubber gloves. He opened a chute on the right side of the machine, and steam poured out. He flipped a few more switches on the front of the device, and a set of lines of light appeared on a piece of glass he'd installed on the front.

"What is that thing, anyway?"

Now Norman smiled, and puffed out his chest proudly. "It's a machine I built that makes other, smaller machines." He used a set of dials below the screen to alter the picture.

Flint turned his head this way and that, and realized that the picture was a changing depiction of a mecha weapon. *A gun*, Flint thought. *How very quaint.*

"You feed in scraps of metal, input the design you want here on the this screen with the dials, and wait. There's an old power reactor inside that melts the metal. Spokes, cogs, and crane arms inside shape the metals, and when it all cools, the end result comes out of this here chute," Norm indicated the right chute as white smoke billowed out of it.

He lowered his head with a deep sigh, however. "I've been testing it for four months now. Nothing that comes out of it has worked."

"No worries, chum." Flint stubbed out his cigarette on an old grind wheel already half filled with old butts. Norman apparently had the habit too, he thought. "You'll get it right enough. So, you learned a little Boxing from the old boy, eh?"

"A little bit, yes." Norman removed his gloves and set them next to the machine. He saw the question in Flint's eyes, and responded before the Wererat could ask. "Whole thing heats up something fierce when it's operating, dials included. That there screen's a fifth or sixth generation. All the ones 'afore it burst apart from the heat. This one's safety glass." He paused for a moment. "I'm guessing the good master Lee Toren expects an apology?"

"That he does." Flint lit another cigarette and handed Norman his last. "I'd come with you, but I've got to go buy more of these poisonous things. He's at the in-house tavern, along with Will and Styge."

A few agents saluted and greeted him as he left Norman's room, and he returned the salutations with his typically easy smile. Speaking with the Engineer had brought him out of his sour mood, which was very good for him. He didn't like going out in public with a storm cloud over his head, and with the right winning smile, he might convince the girl at the sundry goods store to give him a discount for the smokes.

"Say, Flint?" The Wererat was making his way up an access ladder into the streets when the Engineer called up to him. He looked back down at the white haired Gnome. "Thanks, for the talk."

Flint nodded, and made his way up into the city. Stockholm was great at yelling, he thought, but I'm better at listening. At least I've still got that going for me.

Norman Adwar totted along through the tunnels of the Guild, picking his way between the legs of those larger than him when he could, finally entering the in-house tavern with the last drag of Flint's cigarette on his lips.

He stubbed the end in an ashtray, and walked over to the table at which Lee, Deus and the elderly Illusionist sat, drinking warm ale. He didn't bother sitting, shuffling wordlessly around the table until he stood next to the Gnome Pickpocket.

Lee glared down at him, and Norman got a good look at the results of his Boxing teachings. He wasn't much good at the art of fighting, but he saw he knew enough to pummel someone like Toren.

"Well?" This and nothing more did Lee say to Norm, who stuffed his hands into his jacket pockets.

"I apologize for kicking the living shit out of you—in public yet," Norm said with a broad smile.

Deus and Styge both laughed merrily at the bug-eyed look Lee gave the Engineer.

"I apologize, but make no mistake, I'm not sorry about it. I gave you what you deserved, though I understand why you'd be sore about it."

For a moment, the other patrons in the tavern remained silent, until all at once, Lee Toren joined the laughter of Deus and Styge.

"Well said, Norman," Lee said through swollen lips. He took a swig of his warm beer, and smiled wider, revealing the gaps in his teeth. "No worries about the teeth, mate. I can have a healer grow me back some fresh 'uns. As fer the pride, well, fuck all to it." He signaled the barman that he needed a refresher. "Pride's a double-edged sword that I'm not too keen on anyway. Any road," he said, accepting a new mug of ale. "Sit a spell, and tell us where you learned to fight loik that."

And so Norm sat and shared history with them.

* * * *

"Are you certain, sir?" Hollister asked Stockholm, who had taken his seat in his office once again.

He handed the reports that Hollister had written up to the Sidalis, and smiled.

"Absolutely. We could use an official statement at least once a week, and you'd be just perfect to do it. If you want, that is," Stockholm amended, not wanting to pressure the turtle-like man into anything. "There's no pay raises in it for you, though. You'd be agreeing to do this completely on your own time and effort, Sven."

Sven Hollister smiled broadly, and shook his head a little.

"Oh I wouldn't expect any pay raise, sir. It's just the sort of thing I enjoy doing. So, when are you, the Prime and the Headmaster returning to your posts full time?"

Stockholm pondered this a moment, uncertain of the answer himself.

"You don't know, do you?"

"No, not really," Stockholm admitted. "What it comes down to now is a matter of patience. You've done an excellent job in my stead, Sven, but you need to tear some ass around here." He looked the turtle-man in his large, somber eyes, and wondered about his ability to 'tear ass', as he'd put it. "If you don't, nobody's going to take you seriously."

"Oh, they take me seriously enough," Sven Hollister said. "When I inform them that a few misplaced papers mean no payday for them, they straighten up and call me sir and everything."

Stockholm smiled broadly at this, his face aglow with approval.

"Very good, then." He got up and clapping Hollister on the shoulder. His hand came away a little damp. "Been in the pool?"

"A few hours ago, before I came to see you, sir," Hollister replied. "I like to take care of myself, sir."

Stockholm nodded briefly, and exited the office. Out in the dusky hallways, his mind seemed on fire with revelation. They had left Reynaldi in the dust, but now he thought back on the Elven Paladin's face.

He remembered Archibald Reynaldi—and the Paladin's sister—even if Reynaldi himself had forgotten her.

* * * *

The city of Barfor was in the southeast, not far from the desert known as the Desperation.

A hundred years before Ignatious Stockholm would be called to the deadly confrontation with a crazed gunman, a hundred years before he fell in love with a Cuyotai nearly fourteen years his junior. He was young in his mortal years at this time, and still hadn't trained in the arts of the Knight, and several forms of martial arts still remained unknown to him. However, the ways of the Soldier were already well known to him, and three black belts were his to claim. Fighting was a way of life for him, one he put to good use as a prizefighter in the city's arena stadium every week.

Saturday night again, he thought, glaring around the equipment room at the other hopeful competitors. Just another night to earn his rent, and beat some of the city's 'finest' citizenry stupid.

One of his few friends since arriving in the city, a gray furred Werewolf clothed like a beggar, approached him from among the contestants, though he himself was no brawler. "We've got a new entry tonight, my friend," the gray Werewolf said. "Elven woman, name of Delinda Reynaldi."

Stockholm grunted, tying on his leather gloves.

"Class," he asked without looking away from his hands.

"Best as I can tell, a Knight," the older Werewolf said. "I can't be wholly certain, though. There's magic about her, you can rest assured."

"Magic won't help her," Stockholm grunted. "And tonight's special circumstances, as you'll remember."

Once, perhaps twice a year, the arena held an 'all bets off' night, where the fight only ended only when one contestant pleaded for an end, or couldn't move. On most other Saturday nights, the contest ended when the five official judges called it over, most times before anyone suffered permanent injury. Tonight, somebody might be killed.

"I remember, Ignatious. I'm not foolish, though the girl is. She brought a little brother with her. Boy can't be long out of diapers from the look of him, but he calls her 'sissy'. Parents are nowhere to be found, not by my eye or nose."

"She probably doesn't want them to know how she earns her keep," Stockholm said, getting up.

Several nearby contestants shrank away from him, each silently praying that they didn't draw names alongside him. Stockholm had walked out of the arena the overall victor for three months running, and few were ready to try and claim the title of new champion—especially tonight. All feared that the soil would be their beds tonight.

The competitors were called out into the arena where a makeshift wooden stage had been erected, a single small table situated in the center of the stage, and the arena's proprietor, a bipedal snake-man named Fang Slitherskin, spun an orb atop it.

Inside of the orb, strips of paper with the competitors' names on them shuffled about. He drew two names, called them out, and the first match of the evening began. The rest of the competitors sat or stood along the outside of the arena, watching the first bout without much interest. A Jaft, fresh out of the northern mountains with the first tribes of his people to come into civilized lands, mounted atop a Wererat, pummeling him mercilessly with his short-handled war hammer. Everyone already knew the blue skinned humanoid would be the victor.

Stockholm's first match of the evening was against a Kobold gunslinger, whose reflexes, while impressive, hadn't been fast enough to land a single shot on the blurring streak of crimson violence that was Ignatious Stockholm. Three swift punches later, Stockholm's first match was over. The second round of combat provided little more challenge, with a Human Monk practicing an ancient, outdated kick-based martial art called Tae-kyor-dough. The Werewolf deftly blocked the first kick, and landed a one-two counterattack punch combination to the Human's jaw.

The Monk managed to throw one more kick, a low line strike to Stockholm's shin, which sent a spike of pain through his leg. As soon as the blow struck, however, the big man took advantage of his proximity, grabbing the Human by the head and pulling it down as he drove his knee up into his face.

There was the crunch of the man's faceplate, and a spray of blood as he flew back through the air.

The third bracket of fighters got underway, and Stockholm found himself watching the Reynaldi girl alongside a gruff Lizardman with his left arm now in a sling, and a Khan who stank so mightily that Stockholm's eyes literally teared up.

He watched the Elven girl's movements, the way her sword strikes centered not in her upper body, but from her hips, the interspersed spells lashing out at her opponent. Her opponent was an Illeck Pyromancer. The Illeck's fire spells appeared to be fast and potent, but she was casting while she was backpedaling from the furiously swinging Elf woman. Her flames lashed out without any accuracy, missing their mark every single time.

The Red Tribesman watched with increasing interest as the match played itself out. The spells the Reynaldi woman used didn't appear to have any specific nature to them, so he couldn't figure a good guess as to what school of magic she studied. However, he did take note of three very particular facts. Firstly, all of her spells were cast with a motion from her left hand. Secondly, the spells appeared to be mostly defensive in nature. She put up several warding walls of light blue force, and created a bubble around herself at one point, shielded from the Illeck's Pyromancy as it flowed over the bubble. Third, each spell required an exact count of three seconds to come into full effect.

A loose strategy started to form in his mind as he cleaned the scimitar in his belt. He hadn't yet drawn the weapon for tonight's tournament, but if he faced off with the Reynaldi girl, he'd have to. She hadn't hesitated to swing at the Pyromancer, though the Illeck's only physical weapon was an iron short staff. But competitors started the combat at opposite sides of the arena. *That's a whole lot of space to cross,* he thought mildly. There are only two ways to stop her from using magic—to disable her left hand or cover her mouth. How do I manage this without killing her?

"Ignatious," his older Werewolf acquaintance said, calling his attention.

He looked up into the gray, almost stone-cast face.

"They've drawn your opponent for the round. It's Nathan Quan."

Stockholm's heart skipped a beat. Nathan Quan didn't scare him—instead, he was inherently afraid for the man. Nathan Quan was a thirty-six year old Lizardman with a strange and mysterious illness that wracked his body with muscle spasms. He had once been an accomplished shaman for one of the older tribes living in the southeast. There were only a few tribes still living in the grasslands or towns of the southeast, as most tribes had taken to the desert, which suited them just fine.

Quan's magic and skills with a staff were commendable to say the least, but his illness would kill him if he wasn't careful. A blow delivered with the wrong amount of force could do him in.

"How come I didn't see him in the holding room, or in any of the matches," he asked.

"Same reason you can't see Trogart and Borinero over on the other side of the arena. They're running two matches at a time tonight."

Stockholm thought about this, and realized that the competition was moving along much faster than most weeks. How had he not noticed?

It didn't matter now. He had to tell the judges to disqualify Quan from the competition. Without another word to the aging gray Werewolf, he sprinted around the perimeter of the fighting field, catching Quan's eye as he passed him on the western wide of the waiting/sideline area.

The Lizardman shaman looked pale, and Stockholm knew without asking that he was on the border of Death's territory. He had to get to the judges, and now, before the current matches ended.

The Five Wise Men, they were often called in jest. Each of the elderly businessmen sat at a long oak table on the northern side of the stadium. Two of the five judges used spyglasses to watch the southern bout between Reynaldi and the Illeck, while the other three kept an eye on the northern bout. Stockholm approached them, Humans all, and he stood at the side of their table, panting.

"Honorable judges, I cry your pardon," he said.

None of the judges, who were also the owners of the stadium, made any move to show they had heard him, but he knew they had.

He checked the closer bout, and watched the Minotaur, Borinero, crash his huge right fist into the smaller Sidalis' face. The spiked knuckles on his hand poked holes in the otherwise humanoid face of the mutant, but the holes bled for only a few seconds before strange, black feelers exploded outward, wrapping around Borinero's throat and squeezing until he passed out.

As soon as the Minotaur was down, the judges gave their attention to Ignatious Stockholm.

"Greetings and well-met crimson warrior," Adam Sort said to him. Of all of the judges, he had the largest portion of ownership over the arena, and thus, the largest financial interest. "What can we do for our longest reigning champion?"

"You must stop Quan from fighting." He explained the elderly Lizardman's medical condition. He went on to detail the concept of a 'lawsuit', which was becoming an increasingly popular legal battle system. When he mentioned how much money Quan's family could win if they sued, the judges wasted no time in expelling Quan from the arena.

When the Reynaldi girl stepped into the ring, he stiffened for a moment. Semi-finals, he thought. If I trump her, I move on to the final match, and that'll be that. "Contestants," judge Sort bellowed over the roaring crowd. "Take your positions!" Stockholm unsheathed his scimitar, as did the Reynaldi girl. A loud, boyish voice called out her name, and she turned to wave at her little brother. As soon as she turned back to face Stockholm, he finalized his battle plan. It would be a calculated risk, but it was one he was willing to take, and no rules had been set against it.

"Begin!"

Reynaldi charged at him, closing the gap to fifty yards in a few seconds while Stockholm waited and took careful aim. If she didn't attempt to stop what he was about to do, his scimitar would plunge into the empty box seat next to her little brother. If she flinched, as he expected she would, he would have her where he wanted her.

He hefted the sword up, taking careful aim, and stared her in the eyes, stopping her in her tracks. She looked back over her shoulder, and mouthed a single word at him when she turned back; 'no'.

Stockholm threw, and got only a partial reaction from the Elven girl. She turned to watch the arc of the throw, and sure enough, though it gave the boy a fright, it harmed no one. She heaved a sigh of relief, and a moment later, screamed in horrified agony as Ignatious Stockholm clamped down on her left wrist with his massive, vise-like jaws.

Her blood was sweet to his tongue, and he almost lost control of himself in his enjoyment of its flavor.

With a sharp, short torque of his upper body, the Red Tribe Werewolf came away with the girl's hand in his mouth.

Reynaldi fell the ground, her left arm spouting blood like a fire hydrant. Stockholm hadn't expected the wound to bleed so badly, and his heart quivered as he looked to the judges. They hadn't apparently seen the severity of the injury yet, and the Elf girl was trying to get up, despite the damage. "Don't move, idiot." He picking up the hand he had spit out. He saw, with some regret, that he had chewed the hand unknowingly before spiting it out. Though it could be reattached, he doubted it would ever be the same.

Stockholm pulled a strip of leather from one of his pouches, kneeling down to the crouched girl and tying off the wound to staunch the bleeding. "Judges! Declare this contest over," he cried, looking at Sort. The old man, though looking right at him, shook his head. "You must! She's going to," he cried, his voice turning into a howl of pain as the Reynaldi girl ran her sword through the stomach to the hilt.

Without thinking, he turned to face her, saw the grim smile of satisfaction, and grabbed the sides of her suddenly wide-eyed face.

He wrenched her head to the side in an instant, bloody murder filling his mind instead of reason. There came a crunch, followed by a horrified shriek from the judges and the crowd. She fell from his hands limply, dead as dead can be.

He never saw the boy run to the body, didn't hear young Archibald curse him. He didn't hear the judges declare him the victor. He didn't compete in the final bout of the night. Instead of any of this, he ran from the stadium, from the district, and finally, from the city.

He spent the next year of his life alone in the desert, atoning for his sin.

* * * *

Akimaru kept his hands wrapped around Striker's throat for another minute before dropping him to the ground in the alley. A side door of the restaurant to their back opened, a scrawny black Human coming out to dump the kitchen garbage. Akimaru shot him a look, and the black man threw the bag of trash into the open dumpster across the alley, hurrying back inside as swiftly as he could go.

Striker rubbed his throat and coughed hoarsely, gaining his feet but wobbling heavily. "You can't, do that, ducky," he gasped at the white clad Ninja, who only glared balefully at him.

Striker hunched over, his hands on the dirtied knees of his denim pants. There were no sewer grates in the alley, and the roofs of the restaurant on one side and the items shop on the other connected, so he had no way to leap to a rooftop and be away. Akimaru had him cornered, and unlike most Guild members, Striker didn't do better when backed into a corner. He only did worse. "I was, only doing my job, ducky," he heaved.

Once again, the surprisingly strong hands wrapped around his throat, and he was pushed back into the oak siding of the items shop.

"You will no longer molest Harold Deus at his work, Mr. Striker," Akimaru said quite plainly, his frosted purple and white eyes locked on Striker's. "That is the wish of the Headmaster, sensei Fly. Do you understand?"

The odd agent nodded as best he could, and dropped on his ass, rubbing his frozen throat. Akimaru turned to leave him nursing his pains, but not before Striker could get in the last word.

"Don't think this is over, Akimaru," he growled, gaining his feet. "The next time you come after me, I'm not going to make the mistake of being caught off guard. I'll get you, half-breed," he growled.

Akimaru stiffened visibly, and Striker laughed shrilly as he darted out the other end of the alley.

The Glove of Shadows

Akimaru wondered how Striker would have come upon knowledge of his lineage, but decided that, for the time being, he would let it alone. He had accomplished his task, and would return to his sensei.

* * * *

Harold Deus was having the worst day of his business career. He had been stolen from several times during the morning hours by punk children, and now this strange man, dressed like a pirate, was kicking his wagon and demanding money for 'protection'. The man popped a spider into his mouth, and Harold nearly vomited as he heard it crunch between his teeth. Already in the red for the day, he didn't want to be beaten up for his money, and he wanted this disgusting beast of a man to clear out, and soon. But none of the city guards passing by gave the man so much as a second glance. It was as if they were afraid of him.

Thankfully, a strange young man in all white clothing sped up the road, grabbing the man who called himself Striker by the waist and tossing him with ease across the street into a horse trough.

The two men ran off then, the pirate speeding ahead of the white clad youth, and Harold thought that his troubles for the day were over.

He was wrong, however. One of the officers from the Department of Taxation came by an hour later, and Harold suddenly really was in the red.

He hoped Anna would be home soon.

* * * *

Anna Deus spent her afternoon trying to catch up on Hollister's reports. She had enjoyed her conversation with Lee, Styge and Norman earlier, but now it was down to business. All reports indicated that after their first return home, things had fallen back into place, and all heads were accounted for, save one. One of the younger, fresher agents, a Human youth by the name of Thomas Civil, had been arrested last night whilst breaking into one of the gaming halls in the seventeenth precinct. He would be brought before a judge today for arraignment, and Anna needed to either spring him or have him shut up before he could say anything to save his own skin.

It was one of the less attractive facts of being the Headmaster, but when an agent was captured in the city of Desanadron, measures had to be taken to ensure the safety of the rest of the Guild. Only twice since taking over the Hoods had she ordered the secret murder of imprisoned agents, and she had hoped to keep it that way. One of their secret weapons was an agent who worked in the police department, a Sidalis with the power to erase memories. However, four months ago, he had died in the line of duty while attempting to apprehend a Vampire that had been stalking the city streets at night. Their ability to keep agents quiet had been severely reduced.

She pulled Civil's personnel file from the filing cabinet, and knew immediately that she was had no choice but to order him slain. Civil had formerly been a member of one of the smaller gangs in Desanadron, a group of street thugs called 'The Ones'. He'd been pinched for selling mecha firearms without a license, and he'd rolled over on all of his friends. The gang had quickly been locked up and each member sentenced to fifteen years imprisonment. The nine angry young men were all locked up together in Jorten Penitentiary, near the center of the city.

Anna pulled open one of her drawers, and pulled out an official notice from the Desanadron courthouses. Another of her fine forgeries, she wrote in the necessary blanks that would order that Civil be taken to Jorten to await trial. She would drop the knowledge to his former gang members that he would be joining them in general population soon. Once she had the paper in order, she started to change into a light brown business suit, the sort that lawyers wore in the courthouse.

She made her way swiftly to the seventeenth precinct, walking briskly inside with an air of authority. In the main entrance lobby, signs pointed to the police department, the precinct notary, and the courtroom. She checked the black attaché case she had brought with her, reminding herself of her current false identity before striding right into the police department. She took the corridors down to a set of iron double doors, and walked inside.

A wide oak check-in desk stood immediately before her, and she pulled down the false glasses she was wearing to get her bearings.

Two Dwarves discussed proper axe wielding technique at the check-in desk, each man wearing the three stripes to indicate their rank of sergeant. She brusquely approached the desk, like any good servant of the legal system, and slapped down the internment order on the desk. "Hey, sergeants, need this signed off on before I take it to the judge." She used her best 'I'm in a hurry' tone.

The Dwarves broke off their conversation to look critically at her, and she prayed they weren't checking to see if she was a regular.

"Easy does it, buddy, we'll sign it." The Dwarf on the right shifted uneasily in his chain mail shirt, which he wore over his uniform.

Sleeveless, she thought, *just like Stocky's. Was he a police officer once upon a time?* She resolved to ask him about it once they were on the road again.

The Dwarf on the left skimmed the document, grabbed a quill, and signed his name to it. "Good enough?"

She nodded, and turned on her heel, getting out of the police presence as eagerly and swiftly as she dared. Her heart pounded and she made her way with more confidence to the courtroom. Cops were always on edge, observant, and suspicious of everything. Judges and court officers didn't bother to be suspicious, since the suspicious people were brought to them by the police.

Why am I doing this? she wondered before she opened the doors that would lead her into an indented courtroom. The thought came unbidden, a secret whisper in the chambers of her heart. *Am I really going to send this young man to his death? What's the harm in letting him serve his time? We could just expel him from the Guild, and be done with it.*

But she knew that this was not an option. If the precise location of their underground base were revealed to the police, they would have to up and move, and some of their agents wouldn't escape in time.

She walked into the courtroom, where a moderate number of scruffy men were shackled and chained, all awaiting sentencing or departure to await trial. She hustled up to the judge, a bored looking middle-aged woman of the Human Race, who looked over the document and stamped it, handing it to a court officer. "Thank you for your service Mr. Peach," the judge said to Anna, who turned and left the courthouse. She had done her evil deed for the day, and needed a stiff drink.

She had doomed a promising young man—informant though he was.

* * * *

Evening came and went, and in the morning, Anna had a headache the size of the Elven Kingdom. She had spent most of the evening in the in-house tavern, alternately singing songs with the merry, drunken agents, and crying her eyes out on Flint's shoulder about having Civil killed. She had received word after her second drink that the members of his former gang had shived him as soon as they'd found him in general population, and it had nearly unraveled her completely.

So when she finally fell down from too much drink, the Wererat carried her to her office, cleared off her cot, and laid her down. She bawled a little while longer, smearing his fur with tears, and then passed out, cradled in his arms.

"If only you'd been born a rat," Flint whispered as he laid her head on her pillow. He exited the office into the hallway, where he passed several dozen agents returning from their work. He tucked himself into his own bed, up in the city in a hotel room.

Now, the next morning, he sat across the desk from Anna, who had an icepack pressed against her forehead. "So what's on the agenda for today, Flint," she asked, taking a sip of her coffee. "Ye gods, I can almost chew it this morning," she complained morosely.

Flint chuckled a little at this, picking away at the dirt under his claws with a hunting knife.

"Can't be helped, boss," he said, not looking away from his claws. "As for what's on the agenda, not much. We've got a request from the gaming house on Twenty-Second Street to help fix a few games today. They've got a high roller comin' into town, they don't want him to fleece them like he has the places in Ja-Wen, Torie and Whitewood."

Anna thought it over, and agreed that Flint and a handful of 'riggers' as they were called in the Guild could head on over later.

"Anything else?"

"Just a few items," Flint said. "Fellow by the name of Twitcher wants a word with you. He's an independent agent, wants to join the Guild."

"What're his qualifications?"

The Guild Prime handed her his criminal record. He had a list of warrants out for his arrest nearly as long as Lee Toren, and she immediately signed a form welcoming Twitcher to the Guild. Mostly breaking and entering, she noted, but he had a few cons on his rap-sheet as well. "Next."

"This came in this morning." Flint handed her a copy of the official coroner report regarding Thomas Civil.

Fifty-seven stab wounds, puncturing the kidneys, stomach, intestines, right lung, bladder and spleen. Eighteen random lacerations to the chest, back and throat areas, she read. *Gods almighty, they shredded him apart.*

"I know, it turns the stomach raw, but we've got to do what we've got to do," Flint offered.

It didn't help Anna any with her mood, or her headache.

"Last but not least, there's this." Flint handed over a sealed envelope. It was a purple paper, folded very carefully and scented with an odd, rose-like aroma.

"What's this?" She turned the envelope over and over.

"Not sure," Flint said. "It was lying outside one of our access grates this mornin', though. No idea who it's for, so I thought I'd play it safe."

Anna opened the envelope, which she saw wasn't sealed, thankfully, and pulled out a folded piece of parchment. She almost laughed out loud when she read it. It was a love letter from one of their part-time agents, a Storm Tribe Werewolf, and it was addressed to Stockholm.

Poor girl, she thought. *It's true what they say about the good ones.*

"What's got you grinning like the devil just dropped a treasure chest in your lap?"

"Oh, oh nothing, Flint." She pulled the icepack away from her head. "You needn't worry about this, I'll hang onto it. Nothing else?"

"Not now, boss." The Wererat put the knife away and moving over to the door. He looked back over his shoulder as she chuckled under her breath. "Shall I send word to our friends around the area to watch for Evergreen?"

"Oh, yes, that." Her mind returned to the Glove of Shadows and the tracking agent who had stolen it. "Indeed, do so. If you can, find out if Reynaldi has dispatched any of his own men to hunt for her. We'll want to be armed with as much information as we can get, and I know that's your specialty. Get out there and network, Flint."

He gave her a mocking salute, and left the office of the Headmaster. As soon as he was gone, she pressed the icepack to her forehead again, and pulled out the love letter. She'd received three of these in her time, and her mind wandered back to two beloved memories, and one not so beloved one.

Her first love letter was not so fondly remembered.

* * * *

She is sixteen years old, and has lived in the cottage for four years, giving the landlord an even cut of her earnings, as agreed. She is filling out, though not much in the chest. She is glad of that, because the damned things would just get in the way.

She is enjoying a nice evening off from her work, reading a James Colt novel she has just purchased, fair and square, from the new bookstore up the street. She will not steal from it, because she has seen what stealing from a bookstore can do—it can cause them to shut down, robbing her of her books.

She has not seen her mother in years, and wonders if perhaps, like her hero from the fiction novels, she should go see mama one last time, to apologize and make her peace. She decides that it isn't worth the hassle, at least not now. She has her new book, and she wants to simply enjoy living in the world of James Colt for a few hours.

Near midnight, there is a knock at the door. She dog-ears her page, and heads to the front room.

She opens the door, and there stands the landlord, reeking of drink.

He smiles at her in a disturbing way, a bottle of ale in his hand.

"What can I do for you, sir? Collection isn't for another week."

He places a huge, hairy hand against her forehead, and shoves her inside, knocking her clear to the floor as he pulls the door shut behind him.

"What are you doing?"

He says not a word, flying on top of her and tearing at her clothing like a lecher, hungry for her womanhood.

"I have watched you grow into a fine young woman." His rancid breath is hot on her neck. "This month, I want no prizes, girl. No, not this month." He tears her pants off with reckless abandon.

He is violent and awkward, and she loses her maidenhood to his wildness, shrieking in pain and horror the whole while.

He finishes with her after only a few minutes and passes out on top of her bleeding body. She continues to scream, and in a few minutes, constables burst into the cottage and tear him free of her.

She curls up into a ball, sobbing and bawling harder than ever she has in her life.

One of the officers, is the Jaft who returned her home so many years ago, when she first fell in love with the world of James Colt. His eyes are harder, and there is an extra stripe on his sleeve, but when she looks him right in the eyes, there is recognition.

He puts a gentle blue hand on her shoulder, and she lunges across the wagon into his arms, sobbing heavily. He pats her on the back, and assures her that the Wererat is going to jail for a long time. He will never hurt her again.

She receives healing, but is told that she must stay at the old Lizardman female's hut for three days before she can move again.

Before the Jaft leaves, he hands her the new James Colt book, stroking her hair. "You take care now, girl," he says, and graces her with a smile.

She is grateful, and were it not for the stench of his flesh, she would love him. She does, in a way, but not as she feels she should. He has been there twice now when she needed someone to rely on, and she can offer nothing but her thanks.

The next day, a letter arrives for her. It is from the landlord, and in it he promises to sneak out of jail and come track her down. She decides that one night is enough time for healing. Despite the healer's protestations, she leaves, tossing the love letter in the fireplace of the healer's hut. She needs friends, she decides, and she needs to no longer appear to be a girl.

She joins the Hoods a week later.

* * * *

"You're certain?" Fly and Akimaru sat at his tea table opposite one another, with Trent serving for a change.

He had accepted his punishment well enough, and would try not to get on the Headmaster's bad side again—at least not for a while.

"Yes, sensei. Miss Evergreen joined us on our return trip from the ruins."

"Yeah, she was Solomon's girlfriend." Trent poured a cup for himself and knelt at a third side of the table. "I don't remember much about the whole trip, but I remember that. Akimaru took me to his place to heal up after our little encounter with one of the natives down there. She's apt to come from that area, sir."

Fly nodded, thinking the matter over. He could leave that afternoon with his previous company, head north on horse and be at the southern range of the mountains in a couple of days.

His sutras had aided him greatly when they traveled on foot from Desanadron all the way across the continent to Ja-Wen. They had moved at a normal pace, or so it seemed to the party, but they had in fact moved faster than any horse this side of mortality. He didn't have any more of these sutras prepared, and he'd need the afternoon to properly inscribe them. Aside from this, did he owe it to Deus to tell her they had a lead?

Yes, he decided, he did. *Honor among thieves.* But who will take the Glove if we lay hands on it? Will we have to fight for it?

Considering the fact that Deus had Ignatious Stockholm on her side, he hoped not.

But Deus was only one factor. He sipped his tea. The Paladin would dispatch troopers to track down the Glove, and even if Evergreen did return to the Dwarven Territories, she could be hiding anywhere in those snowy ranges. So he added into the whole equation, 'where do we start'?

"Sensei, if she is in the mountains, she cannot hide from me," Akimaru said.

Fly and Trent looked at each other, and then at Akimaru. Fly had seen the questions lurking in Trent's eyes, and decided that if he ever wanted to have a trusted right hand man again, he'd have to let him in on Akimaru's secret.

"How is it that you can claim that, Akimaru?" Trent asked.

The white clad Ninja looked to his sensei for approval, and Fly nodded his black, scaled head. He sipped of his tea, and shuffled back a little from the table.

Trent seemed to take no notice of this, and a moment later, he wouldn't have needed to. He fell backwards and nearly screamed.

Akimaru removed his head fitted mask, revealing a head that appeared to be carved out of white crystals. The hard, frosted eyes steamed, and the entire room started to drop in temperature.

"I claim this, Markus Trent, because I am born of a Psychic mother, and an Ice Elemental father." The half-breed Ninja pulled his mask back on. Trent sat ready to bolt from the room, but looked over at Thaddeus Fly.

"I hope that answers some questions," was the Headmaster's only reply.

* * * *

On the third morning, Anna awoke from her cot, and decided that a trip up into the city was in order. She wanted some decent food and a change of scenery. She was getting anxious, and Flint's network hadn't yielded any information regarding the tracking agent or the Glove. He had, however, discovered that Reynaldi had dispatched two men to hunt her down, a Sidalis and a Lizardman. They were traveling west, still several days away from the city.

Annoyed at the lack of information regarding the Glove of Shadows, she left the Guild base in a huff. Her dreams had been nightmares, her rape playing itself over and over in her mind, each time the appearance of the landlord that stole her innocence becoming more and more that of a true monster.

She made her way through the dusty streets of Desanadron's fifth district, smiling at the few people keeping early hours. Even the constables, who had no idea what the elusive William Deus might look like, smiled and greeted her with 'good morning sir's. Maybe it wouldn't turn out to be such a bad day after all.

She selected a quaint little mom-and-pop country style diner, and stepped casually inside. The owner of the establishment, an elderly Cuyotai woman, guided her to her seat, pouring her a cup of coffee and handing her a menu before bustling off to greet another customer. Anna took a quick look around, and saw that the new customers numbered six strong, and were all young

Lizardmen, strapped with blunt weapons and looking like trouble. She wondered about the wisdom of coming to one of the more heavily gang populated districts of the city for breakfast.

Most of the small gangs knew who she was, and who the Hoods were, but hot shots like this didn't always care. Unless they were stupid, or suicidal, they left Stockholm alone, and usually Flint could talk his way around them, but they all had a hard-on for her. It would go down as a high mark of honor among punks like the gentlemen being seated behind her if they could claim to have laid out the famous William Deus.

One of the Lizardmen gave the old Cuyotai woman a swift kick to the ass, knocking her over as she turned away to fetch them coffee. They barked their harsh laughter at her, but the old lady did nothing to invite more trouble on herself and the cook in the kitchen, who was her even older husband.

Anna's stomach growled with hunger, but her heart burned with fury. She was a thief, true, but she didn't mess about with the old and infirm. They could have broken her hip with a stunt like that, and at her age, the lycanthrope wouldn't regenerate very fast. "Pricks," she muttered under her breath.

"Excuse me, what was that you toffer." The butt-kicker turned in his seat to glare down at Anna.

Oh boy, she thought, *I'm in trouble here*. Still, she would stand her ground, and hopefully, the owners would have someone in the back on hand to take care of jokers like this. If she could stall them for just long enough, she might be okay.

She got up from her booth, and stood nose to snout with the Lizardman.

He wore no shirt, only long leather pants, heavy combat boots, and a brace of knives in a bandoleer diagonally on his upper torso. His friends were similarly garbed, and they all had a single tattoo on their right forearms of a bull's head with a knife through it, the eyes big, bold 'x's.

Bullock Boys, she thought. *Just great. I had to pick a fight with some of the toughest sons of bitches in this district, didn't I?*

"I called you pricks." She puffed out her chest and got in the Lizardman's face. "Real big men, picking on a little old lady."

That's right girlie, she thought to herself, *bluff them as best you can.*

The reptile looked her up and down, and she took heart in the fact that he didn't seem to know who she was.

"You've got a hell of a mouth on you, boy." The ruffian pressed against her, forcing her back a step. "You have any idea who ye be fuckin' around with? We're Bullock Boys, tenderfoot." He drew the iron mace hanging at his side. "We'll crush you as soon as look at you, boy, and don't you forget it. Now step off, stranger."

The old Cuyotai woman came with the gang's coffee, and before she could hustle away, the punk in front of Anna turned and swung the mace hard into her retreating calf.

She screamed out as the other Lizardmen laughed—and Anna plunged one of her knives as far as she could up into the punk's brain.

There was a whirl of movement then, and Anna tried to escape by running toward the north-facing window of the restaurant.

However, as the wood planks of the floor passed under her feet, another rounded mace struck her hard in the back, and she went down hard, coughing blood. Thick-soled work boots stomped and kicked her all over, reducing her body to an inwardly shrieking bundle of injured muscles and organs. They broke her left knee with a hard stomp, and she tried to scream, but couldn't, as one of the punks had just shoved a wadded up napkin in her mouth as a makeshift gag.

She blacked out then, and didn't see who saved her from certain death.

Ignatious Stockholm, Flint, and Thaddeus Fly wiped their weapons and claws clean, the Black Draconus offering to pay for the damages.

The elderly Cuyotai couple said "no thanks, just get out," and together, the head agents of the Hoods and their unexpected ally carried Anna's injured form to a healer.

* * * *

"So you see," Fly said to Stockholm and Flint as a Sidalis healer worked on Anna's ragged, beaten body. "We've decided to head toward Traithrock. I was looking for Deus to give her the word, but when I finally found her, you two were cleaning house with the Bullock Boys."

Fly looked over at Anna Deus. The mutant healer used his special powers to mend the wounds all the way through, setting the bones back in place in her leg before proceeding.

"I'm surprised you helped us, to be honest." Flint puffed hard on his cigarette.

Stockholm waved the exhaled cloud of smoke out of his face, coughing meaningfully.

"I thought the truce was, you know, temporary and whatlike."

Fly shook his head slowly, looking over again at Deus.

Stockholm's gaze followed, and he hung his head.

"I should have gone with her," he muttered.

Flint put a hand on his shoulder as they stood in the waiting area beyond the bead curtain. *Seems to me every healer has these damned things.*

"Now now, chum, you couldn't have known where she'd be heading. This is a rough city. She just forgot that the gangs rule in some districts, not the Guilds."

"A hard way to be reminded," Fly offered. He too waved a cloud of smoke aside. "Do you mind not poisoning the air with those foul things? They smell horrible."

Flint blew an enormous cloud right in Fly's face, twitching his lips to make the cloud in the shape of a boat of some sort. It parted against Fly's stubbed snout, and he grunted in disgust. "You regenerate, but folks like myself can catch the black rot from those things."

"So don't stand so close to me," Flint snarled, still unhappy with Anna's decision to tell this *klofchet* her secret. *'Klofchet'* was a curse word in the Wererat tongue, roughly translating into 'butt-humper', but much harsher.

Fly took a few steps away, but came right back up as the mutant healer approached the unlikely trio.

"How is she?" Stockholm didn't catch himself in time to refer to Anna as a man.

"She's going to be fine." The healer rubbed his hands together. "I've undone the bindings around her breasts to give her better breathing faculty. The

222

bones are set, and the power is working through them. She'll need to be laid up a full twenty-four hours, but she seems pretty resilient. She'll be just fine, but I have the distinct impression that unless one of you good gentlemen stays here, she'll try to get up and move around before she should."

"I'll stay with her," Flint spouted immediately.

Stockholm gave him a brief nod of approval. "You make preparations for us to leave tomorrow, Stocky. Fly." He extended a hand to the Black Draconus, who accepted it and shook. "We thank you. But make no mistakes, we're still going to do better work than you Suns blokes."

"I welcome the challenge." Fly actually gave Flint a smile. "We'll be heading out this evening, ahead of you. Don't worry, we'll only take enough steeds to take our party north. If we meet up in the mountains, we'll keep the peace, if you will."

"You have our word on it," Stockholm replied. He turned to Flint, and lowered his voice. "Make sure she's comfortable. Don't let the good doctor get too touchy-feely, either. He looks the sort."

Flint nodded, and the Black Draconus and Werewolf took their leave, setting about their business. Flint finished his smoke, stubbed it in the waiting room ashtray, and entered the healing room.

He grabbed a wicker chair and moved it next to the bed she lay upon. He and Stockholm had sprinted after her as soon as they realized she wasn't in her office, afraid that she might go off on her own, as she often did when she had a bad night's sleep. Flint had passed by her room twice in the night, and had heard her moaning within, trapped in her nightmares. He had gone to see Stockholm, who was sitting by the fire in his private chambers, reading a book. Flint had given him warning, and Stockholm had agreed to make sure she didn't leave alone. So great had been his need for sleep during the night, however, that he'd actually slept past Anna, and had failed to follow her.

Flint didn't hold it against the Werewolf, though. He too had slept in, and it had been Stockholm who had woken him up by tossing his bed over on its side. They'd followed Stockholm's nose to her, and arrived only just in time to stop one of the Lizardmen from kicking her skull in. They had taken the Bullock Boys apart, and Fly had entered the diner just in time to stab one of them in the lung before the Lizardman had a chance to bash Flint's brains across the floor with a spiked club. Now, here she lay, healed up, but still looking bruised and beaten.

Her eyes fluttered open an hour later, and he put a hand on her chest, just above her exposed breasts, to keep her from getting up.

"Where, am I," she asked in a dry, cracked voice.

"A healer's hut." Flint took her limp right hand. "You got pretty banged up, boss lady."

Her eyes drooped, and her head lolled to the side to look up at him.

"How, bad was it?"

Flint grumbled, and lit up a smoke with his free hand. The healer looked at him disapprovingly, but he went right on anyway.

"That bad, huh?"

Flint simply nodded.

She cleared her throat, and the healer brought over a glass of water, handing it to Flint.

"Only a little at a time," the mutant said. "You don't want her to gag."

Flint let her take a small sip, which she took graciously.

"I thought, I saw, Fly, before I passed out, all the way," she gasped.

Again, Flint nodded. "I'm so sorry, Flint. I know, that burns your ass."

He stroked her hand, leaving the cigarette in a tin tray next to him to burn a little.

"No worries, missus," he said softly. "You really had us worried, though. What were you thinking, going to the fifth district? The Bullock Boys have had it in for us for a while now. Them and the Blue Fists." He referred to a gang of Jaft youths who mugged people at night, armed only with their knowledge of Boxing. They were brutal, vicious bastards all, but they knew better than to mess with old folks like the Bullock Boys had. On top of that, the Blue Fists let it be public knowledge that they only struck at night, so the daylight hours were safe for anyone to pass through their turf.

"You know, it would have been nice, to have a few of those guys around," Anna managed to croak.

Flint gave her the glass, and she sipped a little more water. She coughed harshly, spraying water. "Could you, put that out, for now?"

He stubbed the cigarette, and took her hand again.

"All right, let's get out of here, my mousy friend."

"Not a chance." He put a bed sheet over her. "I'll cover you for your own peace of mind, but you're not going anywhere for twenty-four hours. Doctor's orders."

"So, what did Fly want, anyway?"

Flint told her the situation, and she nodded, accepting it all. She had no qualms about a truce, but with almost a full day's travel ahead of them, Fly would reach the tracker girl and the mountain territory first.

No biggy, she thought. *We've come back from behind before.*

She held a little talk with her Guild Prime, and dozed slowly back to sleep. Flint slept in the chair next to her cot, and the healer nipped off for a nap himself.

The mutant healer was proud of his power, and looked at the ceiling of his bedroom, only slightly regretting the lingering presence of the Wererat. He had the impression that there was a very special relationship there, though he also sensed that nothing could come of it. The wedding band on the woman's left hand had been sort of a giveaway. "Still," the mutant said aloud, stretching his arms and legs in his bed, all five of them. "Time heals all wounds."

The healer's hut was still with sleep.

The Glove of Shadows

Chapter Sixteen
Five on Two

The same evening, Fly paid for six horses, three to ride and two to pull a wagon, and assembled the team at the northern gates of the city.

Rage rode in the wagon, while Lain McNealy drove them from the seat up front. Fly, Markus Trent, and Akimaru rode the three free chargers.

Rage kept the company's belongings in the back of the wagon with him, in order to let the others be unencumbered, should they run into trouble.

Onward and northward they rode, keeping a mild pace that Lain's two-horse team could match.

They made about ten miles before Fly called a halt for the night, and built a fire with which to make the evening meal.

Lain had kept her come-ons to a minimum since departing from the city again, but she continued to give Fly subtle glances. Now, she inched close to him before the fire.

"So," she whispered in his ear. "You want to use the back of the wagon tonight, just you and I?"

He felt his blood rush to his nether regions, boiling over to the bursting point. But no, he thought, he had to restrain himself, at least for the time being.

"Not tonight, Lain." He felt lame as he tried to think of an excuse. What was it the Human women always said? "I've, um, got a bit of a headache." He looked over at Rage, who seemed in a bit of a funk as Akimaru explained why the gods had to take even the littlest kittens from their mommies sometimes.

During their stay in Desanadron, the big green bruiser had come upon a small family of strays, and one of them had been laid out by illness and fleas. Rage couldn't understand why the gods would kill such a cute little kitty, and he'd brought it back the Guildhall. Lain had admonished him for bringing it into the building, but she'd been understanding. Now, with his teacher distracted with the Headmaster, the dim-witted Berserker sought answers from Akimaru.

"It's not fair." The Orc pounded a huge, gnarled green fist on the ground.

"Got news for you, big guy." Trent picked at his food. "Life isn't fair."

Rage shot him a look full of acid, but Akimaru put one steadying hand on his broad left shoulder.

"Never mind him, Rage-sama," Akimaru said. "I am sure that if you ask the Headmaster nicely, he'll let you get a kitten from a pet shop when we return to the city."

Rage positively beamed, and looked hopefully across the fire at the Black Draconus, who rolled his eyes but shook his head yes, he could have one. The fire burned down some more, and Lain, Rage, and Akimaru all covered themselves in their bedrolls, falling asleep before Fly and Trent. The Human Ninja fed some more small twigs to the fire, intent on talking a little with his Headmaster, who was also presently his jailer.

"Fly?"

"What is it Trent?" He poked at the fire a little himself, but his eyes felt like they were weighted with bricks. He hoped Trent would keep whatever was on his mind brief and to the point.

"What made you do it?" Trent clearly referred to the death of Fly's sensei.

Fly poked the fire with his small stick again before dropping it into the wreath of flames. He looked up to the starry sky above, and heaved a heavy sigh. Perhaps it was time, after all, to explain himself to his right-hand agent. After all, he had promised answers, and hadn't he already spoken of this to Anna Deus?

"Mostly, it was pride, Markus," he began. "It was also a deep desire to truly belong. I wanted to show the elders that I was worthy of being a member of their council, and slaying one of their number seemed just the thing to do. I couldn't say if I really thought it over." He looked ahead into the fire once more. "I don't think so, or I would've realized what sort of fate awaited me when the deed was done."

A strange silence developed between the two former Obura Clan Ninjas, and each added a few twigs to the fire.

"So you wanted to prove yourself by killing an elder?" Trent finally ventured, almost a quarter of an hour later. Fly made no reply, his mind drifting toward sleep. "Not much different really than me trying to kill you, to take command."

Fly's attention snapped back to Markus Trent, and he remembered in an instant why he always waited for Trent to fall asleep first. If he didn't wait, he'd never wake up again.

"No, I suppose not." Fly let the admission hang in the air. "I suppose that's why I haven't killed you in all these years. You may not like me very much, Markus, but you need me around, to better yourself."

He lay on the grass, hands behind his head. "I think some day you'll be good enough to kill me. Until you are, think on this. Do you really want to make the same mistake I made?"

For the first time in many years, he allowed himself to fall asleep first.

He was pleased beyond measure when he woke up the next morning.

* * * *

Morning and early afternoon of that day passed swiftly under the stampeding feet of the Midnight Suns' mounts, until they came to the cooler stretches of the northern plains.

The lands a day or so north of Desanadron on horse were barren, devoid of life, mostly as a result of the illness that seemed to have taken permanent root when Richard Vandross had assailed the city thirty or so years before. Not even the wildest of animals could be seen here, but this was more boon than bane for the Midnight Suns. They could reach the mountains before nightfall if they continued on their mad pace.

However, at around five in the afternoon, Markus Trent exclaimed in surprise from Fly's right.

Thaddeus Fly looked to the east, and spied two strange figures, one riding a stamprous, one of the strange beasts born of the Desperation, and the other flying toward them like a large, horrid insect.

Dean Masters flew through the air swiftly, his hornet's wings buzzing loudly as he sliced through the cold breeze with acrobatic grace, while his companion, Bergeon, rode the tamed stamprous slightly behind him.

226

The Sidalis and Lizardman had spotted the Midnight Suns and knew them as prisoners. Though Reynaldi hadn't ordered them to do so, each felt that justice needed to be dispensed on these heretics and murders. Bergeon's beast, tired from days of stomping ceaselessly west, shuddered beneath him.

"Corporal, you're going to have to stop them or fly me over there." The Lizardman drew his katana from its sheath.

The mutant, Masters, responded by waving his left hand in front of him, creating an invisible barrier around the fleeing Suns, who wanted no trouble until they got into the mountains. "Don't worry, and slow your beast, friend Bergeon." The hornet-man descended to the ground, standing still as the Lizardman brought his beast under control.

The stamprous, an odd hybrid of alligator and ostrich, skidded to a halt about twenty or thirty yards away from the Midnight Suns, watching the spectacle that Masters had provided.

The thieves' Guild members and their mounts charged forward, and when they came in contact with the invisible barrier the mutant had erected north of them, they blinked out of existence, reappearing one hundred yards south of the termination point of the barrier.

"Are they aware of the trap," the Lizardman asked before kneeling to pray for Oun's good grace.

"Not yet," buzzed Masters in his high-pitched drone. He drew the spear from between his translucent wings. "They will be, though, if the one dressed in the gray tunics keeps looking this way," Masters said.

"Hm. Right. Then for honor, for glory, and by the grace of Oun our god, let us go and destroy these heretics," hissed Bergeon.

* * * *

Fly shouted the order to increase their pace, and the Suns drove their horses hard to the north.

After a few minutes, he wondered if perhaps Trent had done something to him in the night after all.

The mountains got closer for a few minutes, and then seemed to shrink back from the company.

A few minutes later, this optical illusion played out before his eyes again, and he shook his head as he tightened his grip on his mount's reins.

The creature beneath him suffered from the hard pace, and if they continued on like this, the beast might just drop to the ground, with him pinned beneath it.

Once more his eyes played tricks on him, and the horse he rode shuddered, whinnying madly and rearing up on its hind legs, almost throwing him to the ground.

He looked around, panic driving a swift steed of its own down the narrow track of his spine. Akimaru's mount had tossed him off, as had Trent's, and Rage and Lain McNealy had abandoned their wagon and mounts. Thankfully, Fly saw, Rage had possessed the presence of mind to grab their travel gear before bailing out of the wagon.

"Everyone, center." He collected the members of his company together. "All right, what the hell is going on around here?"

"I don't know, but those two gentlemen are getting closer with each passing minute." Trent pointed east.

Fly followed Trent's finger. The two approaching figures were both afoot, but one had left a harnessed stamprous behind him. Even at this distance, Fly saw that the two men were a Sidalis and a Lizardman. They didn't appear to be much of a threat to the five Midnight Suns, but as harsh experience had instructed him, looks could be deceiving.

"So they are. Rage, I want you to go give them our warmest regards," Fly said.

When the Orc Berserker detached himself from the group, Fly thought he heard a muffled 'pop' to the south of them. He looked south, and saw to his mounting horror the maddened horses stampeding toward them.

Hadn't they fled north. He screamed out a warning. "Wait, Rage!"

Too late. The Berserker had been given an order that involved violence, and he didn't even turn as the first of the chargers slammed into him, bearing him to the ground with its massive hooves.

"Raaage!" Lain McNealy made to run to the flattened Greenskin, but Akimaru had her by the wrist, keeping her clear of the path of the other horses as they ran right over the bulky form of the Orc Berserker.

Fly's eyes were not watching this gruesome spectacle—they were locked on the Lizardman with the katana.

Had the reptilian warrior created the trap they were so neatly ensnared in?

No, Fly thought, *he appears to be a mere swordsma*n. The mutant, however, could be capable of it. The Sidalis all had their own brand of powers, granted to them by their strange, freakish nature.

He smiled a wicked, half-moon sickle of a smile. He wondered if these hostile strangers had any idea what sort of powers they themselves were up against?

* * * *

"Oh my, I think that must have hurt very badly," Masters whispered over at Bergeon. His buzzing, droning voice took on a hint of cruel pleasure as the last of the horses trampled over the Greenskin warrior. "Don't you think so, Bergeon?"

The Sidalis looked over at his companion, but the swordsman was locked in a staring contest with the Black Draconus who was still astride his mount.

"Hello? Earth to Bergeon," the mutant chided, waving the head of his trident-headed spear up and down in Bergeon's field of vision.

The Lizardman seemed to snap out of his trance, and looked into the bulbous, insect eyes of the corporal.

"Sorry, Dean. I was just wondering what sort of trouble we just got ourselves in." The reptilian swordsman took a few cautious steps backward.

Dean Masters had never been afraid of any mortal man in his life, and the Order of Oun was only too glad to have him on board, though he didn't worship their deity. So why was his friend worried about a band of thieves?

When he looked from Bergeon's face back to the west, he watched the Orc Berserker rise from the ground, bloodied and battered, but smiling as evilly as any warlock in history ever could.

When the first of the panicked horses came toward him again, having passed into the cycle barrier to the north, the Orc let out a howl of primal fury and stuck a meaty arm out, letting the horse clothesline itself.

It toppled end over end to the ground, where the Orc decapitated it with a swift blow from his steel war axe. Blood dribbling down his forehead and his axe, Rage of the Orc clan Porag stalked toward the Order of Oun agents, smiling that horrible smile.

Dean Masters had finally met a man to fear.

* * * *

"I thought he was dead for sure," Lain McNealy breathed softly, her mouth a surprised O.

Fly guttered harsh laughter and shook his head. "Hardly, my dear Ms. McNealy."

The remaining horses had calmed, mostly due to exhaustion. Having witnessed one of their kindred be slain by a creature they had tried to trample to death, they agreed to be docile.

The wagon had come apart during the mad, looping retreat to nowhere, but Fly didn't really worry too much about it. Rage would just have to pack mule for them, a function he was used to serving.

"A few horses stomping him into the ground isn't going to keep Rage down." Fly dismounted, and gave his steed a warning stare.

"Maybe not, but those two don't look like amateurs, sir." Trent grimaced as their green companion closed to within ten yards of the strangers.

"You may be right, Markus Trent." Akimaru squinted his frosted eyes to better see the confrontation that would soon take place. "Perhaps one of us should go help him."

"No," Lain said. "He's on the brink of a Berserker fury, and he'll just as soon attack us as let us help him. A Berserker has no allies, and cares only about killing everything in sight. It often doesn't end there, either."

"How do you mean?" Trent realized that he knew little of the Midnight Suns' heavyweight enforcer, and found that he actually wanted to know more. *Perhaps he isn't so useless after all,* he thought as Rage began the combat with the strangers.

A fast, deadly blow of his axe was deftly knocked askance by the Lizardman's katana.

"Well," Lain said. "There's two kinds of warriors that Necromancers like me don't care much for following. First off, there's Paladins, and that's for obvious religious reasons. But secondly, there's Berserkers. It's difficult to raise an undead servant if the main body has been diced into more pieces than a man can count on all of his digits."

Markus Trent turned to look at the combat, and pray for the outcome to be in Rage's favor.

* * * *

Bergeon had seen the angle of the initial attack at the last possible second, deflecting the path of the war axe with his katana and stepping aside. Loose soil flew in all directions, bits of blasted soil striking Dean Masters in the side of his face. No sooner had he kept a rock from his eye than he was whirling his spear in a swift circle in front of him, warding off several hard, fast blows from the Orc.

Ye gods, Masters thought, *he's fast*. Far faster than any Greenskin, be it Orc, Goblin, Ogre or Hobgoblin should be. But the speed and strength of the attacks didn't disturb his usually cool demeanor so much as the widening smile on the man's face. How could he be so enthusiastic about a two on one battle?

"Masters! Your barrier," Bergeon cried.

The mutant flicked his left wrist, tearing down the barrier that held the Midnight Suns from getting further north.

Another flick of the wrist, and the barrier became smaller, more focused, right in front of him. He eased back, holding his spear at the ready, as Rage attacked again.

The Orc seemed to bounce away from the barrier, but he continued to hack away blindly at it.

Bergeon, meanwhile, had positioned himself on the Orc's left flank, trying to get in his peripheral vision. Bergeon's code of warrior conduct disallowed backstabbing, and he would not disgrace himself for the sake of the Order.

"Face me, Orc! I am your opponent now!"

Rage stopped mid-swing, shifting his feet and pivoting his hips, bearing down on the Lizardman swordsman with an ease that made Bergeon quiver. However, saw the angle of the attack much earlier than the first strike, and he ducked and rolled forward, coming up against Rage as he stabbed the Orc in the stomach, driving his sword in to the hilt.

The bloodlust should have gone out of this Orc, Dean Masters thought as Rage grabbed his companion by the snubbed snout and tossed him aside like a child's plaything.

Rage pulled the katana free from his body, and tossed it aside like a twig, taking no notice of the dark, crimson blood flowing down his stomach. The Orc pounced toward Masters, who flapped his wings as he darted aside, the axe barely missing his left wing.

He buzzed over to Bergeon, who had reclaimed his katana and sheathed it.

"Come on, sergeant, we've got to regroup." The mutant put an arm under the stunned Lizardman and carried him back toward the stamprous.

Rage made no move to follow, and when the agents of the Order of Oun disappeared to the north, in the very direction the Suns would be heading, the Greenskin warrior passed out.

* * * *

The world came back into focus, slowly but surely.

When the Orc Berserker tried to sit up, but was gently held down by the coldest hands he'd ever felt.

"Geez, where'd you guys get the icepacks," he asked groggily.

Akimaru looked up at Trent, who actually graced him with a sardonic grin.

"No icepack, Rage-san," the white clad Ninja said. "Ask no questions, for a time. Ms. McNealy is preparing bandages for your stab wound."

Rage tenderly moved his right hand over the wound, and it came away bloody and wet.

"Ah, this is just a flesh wound," the Berserker said, though he knew full well this was a lie. His body felt sore and battered, like he'd been dropped down the side of a mountain. "Why do I feel so bad?"

"Well," he heard the voice of the Headmaster say. A moment later, Fly's upside down face blocked the noon sun.

"There's the matter of the horses trampling you, combined with the stab wound and the exertion you put yourself through on our behalf. We are very thankful to have you along, Rage-san." Fly walked away from the wounded Orc as Akimaru and Lain saw to him, and Trent joined the Black Draconus, only moving about seventy yards north. Fly had decided to ride his mount in all directions as soon as the mutant and the Lizardman had fled, and discovered that the queer barrier the mutant had used before was back in place.

This time, however, the Midnight Suns appeared to be trapped within a bubble of the Sidalis' force. No matter where he rode, he found himself coming back on the company from the south. When he rode south, he found himself turned around without his notice, completing the trap.

"We're in trouble, Headmaster," Trent said bluntly. "This is the mutant's power—to create barriers that can hold things within it or without. We know not the range of his powers, and they may be miles away before this barrier fails him. They are only two men! How did they hold Rage at bay?"

"They're skilled, Markus." Fly decided to make himself useful and collect scraps of wood from the wreckage of the wagon to build a cooking fire. "Did you see the way the Lizardman stood, how he held his blade to the side, horizontally?"

Trent nodded, and took a seat on the brown, dried out grass.

"He's a true swordsman, that one. As for the mutant, I think if you strip him of his powers, he's just a pikeman."

"With wings," Trent added with a derisive chuckle. He looked over to Lain, Akimaru and Rage. "It was a little frightening, seeing him like that again. I've only seen him go off like that twice, but never with that much expectation. You knew we'd need him, didn't you?"

Fly didn't meet Trent's stare, but he nodded as he took an iron pot from the travel gear and set it over the fresh fire he'd struck with his flint and steel.

"To deal with Stockholm, or something like those two strangers?" Trent continued.

"Yes." Fly's stomach growled for food. "You may think it cruel of me, but I brought him along basically as a tool. When someone or something faces Rage, they leave themselves bare for reading. I think I know exactly how to combat the swordsman at this point, and I'm pretty sure I know how to deal with the mutant."

Trent sat and stared at Fly expectantly, waiting for an explanation.

"Be a good little prisoner and fetch me Lain," the Draconus said levelly.

Trent groaned, but moved to do as he was asked.

Lain McNealy and Trent swapped places, and she hunkered down on her haunches, adding a few spices and herbs to the stew that Fly was cooking for the company.

Fly looked over at Rage, who had fallen back to sleep. "How's he holding up?"

Lain just shook her head, her lips set in a tight, grim line.

"It's not good, Headmaster," she said softly. "Akimaru laid hands on him, and explored his wounds with his chi, I believe you call it."

Oh, if only you knew, Fly thought.

"The sword didn't go all the way through his body, but it pierced his stomach and may have ruptured his spleen. He's bleeding inside, and badly."

Fly nodded, his mind acknowledging that they might lose the Berserker before this trip was through.

"Akimaru says he can heal him, but he needs a great deal of time to do it. The Hoods may stumble upon us if we don't get free of this bubble before long. So, do we give Akimaru his time?"

"Yes," Fly replied without a moment's hesitation. "We cannot lose him if it's avoidable." He knelt before the cooking pot, and Lain inched closer to him, wrapping an arm around one of his.

For once, he didn't pull away.

* * * *

That same morning, Anna Deus led her company of Hoods agents out of Desanadron.

Fly had kept his promise, leaving enough horses in the northern stables for them to purchase, and the six of them rode north on five horses.

Stockholm's mount had been the largest stallion available for sale, but it still labored beneath his massive frame. They made poor time, and by noon had only traveled an eighth of the distance Fly and the Midnight Suns had.

They broke for lunch a little after later, each member of the company refreshed from their time in the Guildhall.

Norman and Lee had resolved their differences, a fact Anna was most grateful of, and rode together on the smallest charger. Now, gathered around the fire, they appeared to be all smiles, with the exception of the Chief.

She decided to get all tensions and doubts out in the open.

"All right everyone, listen up." She stood and addressed the group as a whole. "This whole business of the Glove of Shadows has gotten us harassed, attacked, arrested, and frustrated. So let's get all of our issues out of the way, right now. We'll go around round robin, and you can all lay down your problems and doubts concerning this journey. Let's start with age before beauty, with Styge."

All eyes turned to the elderly Illusionist, who was busying himself with a sketch.

"No worries here, young man." He didn't look away from his drawing. "I only wish I had an extra pillow for my saddle. That thing's chaffing my old behind something fierce."

Anna hadn't figured Styge would complain much, because he only griped about the little things.

"Still can't figure why you've got me along on this goose chase, though. Can't see what good I'll be to you all. I'm just an old man, after all," he said.

"You've already proven yourself," Norman offered. "Without your magic, you and I'd still be enjoying the hospitality of Fort Stone."

"Okay, you're next, Lee," Anna said.

The Pickpocket looked up from his whittling, and just beamed a smile at her.

"Oh, no complaints here, though your bill for my services is gettin' up inta triple digits bucko," he said.

Ah, dependable, greedy Lee Toren, she thought.

"Very well. Norman?"

The Gnome Engineer was watching Stockholm ladle out food into earthenware bowls with hungry greed in his eyes. He looked up at Anna after she cleared her throat noisily.

"Oh, well, just a few issues I suppose." He took a bowl from the Red Tribesman. "I'm sort of useless in most confrontations. Plus, we're heading into the mountains, right?"

She confirmed this briefly

"I hate the cold. That's just a minor complaint, though. Otherwise, I guess I just wonder what we need the Glove for."

"Are you kidding?" Flint spewed soup on the ground at his feet. "It's the Glove of Shadows! We could steal anything we wanted if we had it, right out from under people's noses yet! It's like a dream come true!"

"Sure, fer folk loik you an' me," Lee said around a mouth full of broth. "But Norman's got no use fer it, since it doesn't beep or boop or anyfin' loik that."

From Flint's response to Norman's statement, she decided to skip over him, and go on to Stockholm.

"What about you, Chief? Any issues to get out in the open?" She expected Ignatious to remain mostly silent, as he often kept his thoughts closed to those around him. Instead, he spoke, and at great length.

"The Glove of Shadows is an artifact of another age," he began, chewing his food and letting his thoughts linger on the past. "I first laid eyes upon it when I was studying the arts of a Knight, many centuries ago. This was before the Fall of Mecha," he said, once again confirming Anna and Flint's suspicions regarding his general age. "I was learning the path of Knighthood from an aged Half-Elven Knight, in the city of Povernham."

"Where's that," Lee asked, taking a sip from his hip flask.

"It no longer exists on any map," Stockholm said, shaking his head. "What is left of it lies in ruins in the south, near the shore. The city thrived on technology, you see. There was a weapon of massive power kept deep underground. When the world's mecha started to malfunction and fall apart, the weapon ignited itself, and blew most of the city and its inhabitants into the ocean," he said softly, shaking his shaggy head. The company looked at him with great respect and awe in their hearts. "But that's a tale for another time.

"The Glove of Shadows came into the possession then of a man named Clinton Murdock, a Gnome collector of such artifacts. He had no idea what the Glove was, or what purposes it could be set to, but one of his collector friends did. A Wererat, named Shadrack Tulane." He finished his soup and sett aside his bowl. "I had been in the company of my instructor several times when Murdock invited him over to view his new purchases. On one such visit, I noticed that the Glove of Shadows had gone missing.

"Tulane turned out to be the thief, we learned, and he had taken it with him to the southwest, deep into the forest of the Elven Kingdom. He and other bandits he kept company with had a lair underground in the Kingdom, though few ever discovered where exactly it was. We searched, my instructor and I, for their hideout, but never did we find them, or hear from them again. Nobody is certain what happened, but during those days, the Elven Kingdom was rife with the seeds of the coming civil war that would leave the dark Elves as a separate people, the Illeck."

On this note, Flint thought back to all of the history books he had read. That civil war had taken place approximately two hundred and twenty years before the Fall of Mecha. If what Stockholm said was true, then the Red Tribesman was somewhere in the range of a thousand years old. *Cripes*, Flint thought, *he looks good for his age*,

Stockholm continued his narration, capturing their attention again.

"It is suspected that the Illeck, in their attempts to find a home for themselves, came upon the hideout, and thus slaughtered the Wererat and his friends, taking up permanent residence. The Glove of Shadows became something in tales told by one thief to another. But let me tell you this." Stockholm looked into the face of every person around him. "That Glove is a cursed thing. When we returned to the Gnome Murdock, his home had been set on fire by wild Pyromancers. My instructor and I followed the path of ownership back to a tradesman who lived in Arcade, who had owned the Glove as a showpiece for a year. Shortly after he had sold it to Murdock, his wife slit his throat in the night. She claimed to not know why she had done it.

"Before the tradesman, the Glove had been in the possession of the great Pickpocket, Toby Samson. One night, while he was out on the town with some friends, he picked up a prostitute, who took money from his pouch after he had fallen asleep."

"That doesn't sound so bad." Flint puffed away on a cigarette.

Stockholm gave him a creepy, gentle smile. "She replaced the money with a copperhead snake. It bit him the moment he fished in his pouch for money. The woman took the Glove of Shadows as well, and was found the next week with a spear through her head, pinning her to her headboard."

"So you're suggesting we leave it be," Anna said, not making it a question, but a matter of fact.

Stockholm grunted, but said nothing otherwise in response to her statement. "Chief, is that what you're suggesting?"

"No," he said, laughing a little. "I'm suggesting that if we get a hold of it, we lock it away someplace where nobody can get at it. It's cursed, Will, like I said. We don't want to go using it."

"Is that the secret, though?" Flint lit another cigarette with the end of his previous one. "Do you have to use it for it to curse you?"

"It would appear that way. I didn't remember all of this when Lee brought us his information. I had to drudge up several of my old journals from my old storage unit in the city. When you've been around as long as I have, you tend to forget some things until they rear their ugly heads. I would have said something before, but as I've said, I couldn't quite remember."

"Hell of a thing to have to remember," groaned Lee.

Stockholm hitched up and got ready to move out again. "Each owner who has tested it out, and wound up dead for their troubles. The only owner my instructor and I came upon who had owned it and not suffered such a horrid fate was a Minotaur from the northern mountains. He had come upon it completely by accident, he told us. He had found it on the outstretched hand of someone crushed by an avalanche."

The company rode north again, but now they looked forward not to owning the Glove of Shadows, but to sealing it away, perhaps forever.

We should have left it to the Paladins, Anna thought bitterly as they rode along.

* * * *

Evening fell upon them, but still Thaddeus Fly could not get free of the barrier around them. He did, however, learn the dimensions of the trap, and could estimate how much room they had to work with.

Akimaru finished healing Rage, and promptly fell over on his side, limp and seemingly lifeless. But Lain checked his pulse and reported that he was simply drained from the effort.

Rage remained in a deep sleep, and the two men were covered with wool blankets for the cool night.

Probably an empty gesture for Aki, Fly thought.

On Fly's orders, Markus Trent rode a horse through the cycle of the barrier trap, letting the animal canter along at a slight jog to reserve its energy.

He brought the horse up short and dismounted a few feet away from the Headmaster and Necromancer, his face screwed up in barely controlled anger. "It's no good! Either they're still very close, or the barrier can be left on its own."

"They'll have to sleep some time," Lain offered. She had a loose plan forming in her mind, but the plan required an expenditure of magic that would render her feeble, like Akimaru. Still, she decided, it's better than rotting here. "There is something I can try," she said.

Fly and Trent looked to one another, and then back at her.

Fly made a hand motion, telling her to get on with it.

"Well, you know the dimensions of our imprisonment, Headmaster. Direct me to the edge of the barrier to the north, and I can raise a body from the soil outside of the barrier. I have sensed the dead here, and I can hear their moaning in the soil."

A brief shiver to ran up Trent's spine. Like Akimaru, the woman gave him the heebie jeebies.

"Once raised, I may place my consciousness in the creature, and take control of its body. It will be awkward, but it may be that through its eyes and ears, I can find the strangers who attacked and trapped us here."

Fly knew there was something she wasn't telling him, and he worried that they might finally get free of the barrier, only to find three of their five members incapacitated. However, it was a course of action, and he didn't want to sit around and do nothing. "Very well. Make it so, Lain, but hear me well. Only do what you must. Take no unwarranted risks. If you find anything, return to your body and inform me. I'm going to tuck in for now. I'd suggest you do the same, Markus."

Trent unfurled his bedroll, and tucked in, fully aware that Fly wouldn't actually go to sleep.

Fly led Lain to the northern border of the barrier, and left her there to her work. She was frightened of the consequences of leaving her physical body behind—animals could prey on her if the barrier dropped, the weather could become inclement, or a host of other evils could beset her deserted body. "Got things to do," she whispered to herself.

She steeled her nerves, sat on the ground, and focused her power.

She wove a complex set of hand movements through the air, almost separate from her own thoughts. She had memorized these motions so thoroughly that she didn't even pause to think about them. She had also performed this ritual several times, which helped facilitate the process.

She sent her consciousness wandering through the earth, searching for a suitable and, preferably, freshly buried body. Murder victims constituted the majority of her findings out in areas like this, but sometimes she got lucky and found an old battlefield. This was no such case, however. After a few minutes' searching, she found a reasonable specimen—the corpse of a freshly buried timber wolf.

Someone had crushed its skull, she could see, and attempted a decent grave out of respect for the animal. She decided a probe of the creature's brain and memories would be in order once she raised it.

"*Kalatos mansos, kalatos mansos, kalatos mansos,*" she chanted, over and over again for five minutes.

Humanoids typically offered less resistance than animals, particularly when the head was damaged to slay the formerly living host. Animals, however, were hardwired differently, and damage to the brain couldn't necessarily leave her an easy path to control. Instincts for an animal weren't always seated in the gray matter in their skulls, and instincts could live on for many years after death. *Time to see how useful this beast might be,* she thought. "*Kalatos, lupino servantes,*" she said.

The ground rumbled slightly, and her mind brushed against the undead wolf's.

Muscles stretched as the animal dug its way free of its grave, bones popping back into place for the first time in nearly a year.

Yes, Lain thought, *a year dead.*

The undead wolf burst from the ground, snarling and snapping at the air as maggots and worms spilled out of their former meal. It looked in her direction, and she felt the malevolence of the animal locked inside the dead body.

This will do beautifully, she thought.

She stared into the one remaining eye in the creature's head, and it bowed low on its front legs.

"Good boy," she whispered, closing her eyes once more.

A moment of concentration, and she felt her body go limp. Her field of vision blurred, twisted, and came back into focus from the undead wolf's point of view. Only the right eye could see, and the world was bathed in shades of gray instead of color. Her nose, however, seemed capable of identifying a thousand different odors, each cycling through her newly acquired mind.

Interesting, she thought, trying to mouth the words but finding that firstly, the lungs had decomposed. Secondly, a wolf's mouth really wasn't shaped to allow for speech. How did the Werewolves manage?

She looked at her own limp form, sprawled forward in a half-kneeling position. Her one working eye could just make out the aura of the barrier, the power unlike any magic she'd ever seen in corporeal manifestation. Sidalis powers tended to be like this, however, magic-like but not quite really magic.

How do I proceed? She sniffed the air with her servant's nose.

Hmm, she caught a familiar scent, something the wolf had smelled often in life.

Hornets. She caught the mental image of a swarm of the stinger-bearing insects flying toward the wolf. The image dissipated, and she took a moment to pour over the creature's mind in search of its final memories.

Its mind was a horrible mess, thanks mostly to the caved-in skull and brain damage suffered in its final moments of life. There were glimpses of rolling grasslands passing either side of the wolf as it ran along with its pack. Brief olfactory memories brushed through her Human mind like a pulse of force she never knew existed in the world. The timber wolf had several thousand words to describe these odors, and each scent was overwhelmingly vivid, even in memory. No terms regarding color co-related to her Human language, but that was just fine for her.

As soon as she turned the wolf's body toward the north, Lain McNealy knew it had been an alpha male of a large pack. Even after a full year in the ground, the beast was physically sleek and powerful, and probably faster than any zombie she could raise from a humanoid corpse.

She considered keeping the creature around after she was done here with it, but wondered if its current power was a result of her abilities as a Necromancer, or the fact that her own mind was sharing space with its own.

Never mind, she thought, running on all fours to the north, sniffing at the air.

The mutant was still relatively close, within olfactory range.

After a full ten-minute sprint north toward the mountains, it became clear to her that she and the wolf varied widely in their ability to gauge distance with their noses. It was another fifteen minutes before the odor of the hornet-man became so overpowering that the wolf's one eye started to dart around on its own, trying to seek out the source of the smell.

As soon as that one eye fell upon the Sidalis, the memory of the wolf's death played out in her mind. It had led its pack into the woods that skirted the mountains to find fresh food. Lain had never smelled deer before, but now she knew the scent as easily as she knew her own name. The sound of the thrush and bushes being trampled and forced aside only slightly ahead of her long snout filled her ears along with the jackhammering of the wolf's heart, pounding rapidly in her temples. On it ran, faster and faster, until suddenly its pack mates had been left in the dust.

Turning sharply to its left, the wolf caught sight of the deer, or rather, what it had thought was a deer. As soon as it came in sight of the animal, the wolf stopped, watching with a mixture of confusion and fear as the animal before it stretched out and changed shape, the sound of snapping bones and rearranging bodily fluids filling its ears. Before it now stood a creature covered with scales and coarse, black fur.

Lain knew of the wild, vicious shape shifters—Troke, they were called, a Race that were capable of civility and culture. Most, however, were still wild. They had existed in the mountains and the Allenian Hills for hundreds of years, and the origin of their species was widely unknown.

The Troke smiled and barked harsh laughter just before bringing its right hand, metamorphed into the shape of a mace, down on the wolf's skull.

Before the beast could devour the wolf's limp form, however, a pack of Werewolves, who had also followed the scent of deer, sprang on the Troke, stabbing and slashing it to bloody shreds with short pikes and spears.

The lycanthropes, respectful of their kindred species, had buried the wolf in the open plains. A ceremony of sorts had been performed to set its spirit at ease.

Fat lot of good it did, Lain thought bitterly, her own emotions beginning to blend with the instincts of the beast she inhabited.

The Sidalis, along with its companion, came back into focus up ahead. Apparently, neither had yet seen the rotting wolf, and so Lain stalked slightly closer, using a rock outcropping as cover.

There she listened in on the two strangers.

"—need to rest," she heard, tuning into the conversation part way through.

"If I do that the barrier around them will falter." This second voice was high pitched and droning, a buzzing monotone.

The Sidalis, she thought.

"We should push on into the mountains tonight, make sure we leave those criminals in our dust."

"Lord Reynaldi ordered us to find the thief and the Glove of Shadows, Dean," the Lizardman, rasped. "We shouldn't even have concerned ourselves with those murders. We keep ourselves tucked in here, we wait for sunlight, and then we move out.

Lain heard the low moaning of a beast, most likely the stamprous she had seen earlier. She risked a quick look around the rocks, keeping the wolf's head low, and saw the strange animal. The Lizardman was stroking its head gently, like a loving owner.

"You rest, then, Bergeon." The Sidalis poked the ashes of a fire with his spear. "I'll not give those criminals the chance to get ahead of us or find us."

The Lizardman shrugged his shoulders, and tucked himself into a bedroll.

The mutant stared straight ahead, into the fire.

So, Lain thought, *he needs to remain conscious to keep the barrier up.* There had to be another way to disrupt the power, of that she was certain. Perhaps if the barrier had a larger number of occupants, it could be forced to burst.

Running the wolf back toward the company, she decided that more work yet had to be done this night. Onward and onward she ran, with no extent of stamina to worry about, since the creature she inhabited required no air or food to keep moving. As soon as the wolf saw her limp form with its one good eye, she left its mind and body, returning to herself.

Lain yawned and stretched, relaxing the muscles in her arms and legs. They felt stiff and overused, lingering sensations from having taken the undead wolf with her own mind.

Lain McNealy started to raise the dead en masse.

* * * *

Morning came, and with it, the release of rain from the skies above.

Anna's company had made poor progress the day before, with Stockholm's steed being overtaxed from carrying his heavy frame.

Today, he took the animus form of a long, sleek red wolf, and ran alongside the company.

Despite the rain and the muddy ground, the Hoods made much swifter progress, with Stockholm's free mount charging at the head of the group.

Upon Flint's suggestion, Anna and the others took their group slightly west of the course they had set for themselves the day before, opting not to follow the exact same path the Midnight Suns had. The Wererat's reasoning for this change of plans had been sound. "Don't want to run into any of the same trouble they might, boss," he'd said at dawn. Anna had agreed wholeheartedly.

Their two respective styles of command, she and Fly, meant they were more apt to handle situations differently. An issue that Fly might deal with swiftly with violence might take many hours of her diplomatic reasoning to get past, and though a truce was on, she didn't want to clean up the Draconus' messes. *Besides,* she thought, *the truce just means we aren't going to attack each other. We never agreed not to set traps for one another.*

They traveled north by northwest until noon, when they stopped for a brief meal and to rest the horses.

As soon as the company had dismounted, Norm set to work with one of his strange contraptions, scrutinizing some sort of readout on its glass display.

Anna smoked one of Flint's cigarettes and stretched her legs, which eventually led her to the Gnome Engineer. "What's on your mind, Norm?"

"Well, for starters, I was hoping you could get one of those off the Prime for me," Norm said with a smile.

Anna bummed another smoke off of the Wererat, who grumbled under his breath that it was a good thing he'd brought two extra packs with him.

He handed her one, and one of the spare packs.

She stuffed the pack into her denim jacket pocket, and handed the spare cigarette to Norman, who struck a match and inhaled deeply.

"I really should have stopped cold turkey on these things," he commented before returning to his device. "William, there appears to have been several dozen plots of disturbed soil here last night." He waved the device over the ground.

"Zombies?"

Norman shrugged, unsure of what to make of his readings.

"Or perhaps skeleton warriors?"

"Can't be sure for certain, boss," he said. "I know this, though. If the critters had just come up on their own, without assistance from a Necromancer, the ground would have been torn apart all around us. I think we may have a spot of trouble if we run into a Necro who could raise so many so easily."

Anna thought about Lain McNealy, the pale Human woman whom they had rescued from Fort Stone. One of the Midnight Suns, Anna knew, but Stockholm and Flint had both reported no signs of the Suns along their route. Was it possible that she could raise the dead from such a distance?

"Well, give it no mind, Norman, but keep an eye out just the same. There's a lot of Necromancers who live outside of cities like Desanadron, and there's the Tivursky brothers to the east." The Tivursky brothers were a trio of Vampires who lived in the woods to the north of Desanadron, a strange bunch who weren't actually brothers. They were three independent Vampires who had vowed to never drink from the throats of the living, and often raised corpses to keep guard over their squat cottage in the woods. Peaceful though they might be, crusaders from all over still tried to stake them.

"You think those blokes would really call guards up from all this way away," Norm asked.

"Probably not, but it's something to keep in mind."

Anna sauntered over to Styge, who was once again deeply involved in his sketchbook, adding the smallest of details to a picture of a Blue Dragon he'd been working on since the company had first left Desanadron. She stood behind him being careful to stay out of what little light he had.

Tarps had been stretched across tent poles they had packed with them, keeping each member of the company and their cooking fire out of the rain's direct downpour.

"Whatcha working on, old timer?"

Styge looked up and gave her a wicked grin. His Mohawk stood up stiff and straight, gelled to the hardness of cardboard. "Just something I've been holding in reserve, sort of a last ditch weapon, young William." He held the pad up to her, and she took it cautiously, looking over the fine lines of the scales of the dragon. Styge had created an incredibly realistic depiction of a Blue Dragon— one of the kinder breeds of dragon in the known lands. They mostly inhabited the mountains they were about to head into, keeping to cold or cooler environs. Peaceful creatures though they were, if angered, they became volatile, hostile casters of magic—mostly water and ice-based spells.

She handed the pad back, and Styge continued drawing in the scales and spines on the whip-like tail. If Styge were forced to conjure this drawing into a physical manifestation, they'd all have to take cover, because the creature's countenance was pure rage and fury. She shuddered to think of the old Illusionist bringing that drawing to life. Not only would it pose a risk to everyone around him, bringing it into a manifested force might kill him. Norman's machines had been enough to render him weak and feeble—what amount of magic would be required to do the same with a dragon?

Anna made a decision lightning-quick; she would have to have Flint or Lee steal the sketchpad away before they entered the mountains. Before the old man had a chance to kill himself trying to protect the company. Unfortunately, she would forget about that before entering the Dwarven territories.

* * * *

The previous night, perhaps five miles east of the Hoods' lunch spot in the rain, Lain McNealy had focused all of her considerable force into raising undead minions from miles around.

And so for miles around, she felt the draw of the undead creatures she raised as they came to see their new master, their creator. The first moans could be heard after only a minute or two, and Fly, Trent, and Akimaru all awoke to find their company surrounded by dozens, possibly scores, of shuffling zombies and skeletons. Trent immediately drew two throwing knives, and Akimaru started making motions with his ungloved hands, but Thaddeus Fly put up a hand to stay them.

"What the hell is she doing, holding a convention," Trent spat as he approached the Headmaster.

Fly looked at the pale Human girl. Despite his awkwardness, he could come to enjoy her company, perhaps even in the capacity she wished for.

"I think she's got a plan, Markus," Fly said.

Akimaru had strapped his gloves back on, and was moving Rage's massive body away from a pair of undead dogs sniffing too close for comfort.

"Don't make a move unless you have to. And for the gods' sakes, Trent, get over there and help Akimaru." Fly pointed to the struggling white clad Ninja.

When they'd dragged Rage a safe distance away from the dogs, Fly looked around, and tallied the total number of undead entering the barrier trap.

After ten minutes, the total was somewhere around sixty-seven.

Ye gods, he thought, *how many can she summon? How far is her power reaching?* The number continued to climb, until an hour after she had begun, nearly two hundred shuffling, moaning zombies and skeletal warriors milled nearby.

There was a sudden, audible explosion of force around them, and Fly, Trent and Akimaru all covered their ears and dropped to the ground.

When Fly opened one eye to look over at Lain McNealy, he saw she was smiling. She stood and walked to where the barrier should have flipped her back to the barrier's southern edge.

She stepped through empty space, and laughed.

* * * *

Just before dawn, Dean Masters shoved on Sergeant Bergeon's shoulder, hard and quick. "Come on, sergeant, we've got to move."

"Dean, calm down! What's the matter?" The Lizardman rolled out of his blankets and splashed water from a tin cup on his scaled face.

Then he stared straight ahead, shaking his head and rubbing his eyes. What he saw before him, stretched out in uneven ranks for about two hundred yards to the south, almost made him scream.

"*That's* what's the matter." Dean Masters got his wings beating.

Bergeon looked over at his faithful steed, and knew he would have to leave it behind. He swiftly strapped his swords on, and was lifted up and away from the campsite. Below him, rapidly fading from view, a hundred or more undead creatures fell upon his stamprous and the remains of their camp, clawing at everything they could. His steed let out one final, anguished cry as the zombies tore greedily at its throat and face, searching for fresh meat to feed on.

The Necromancer woman *had* to die, he decided.

Chapter Seventeen
End of the Trail

Teresa Evergreen had expected pursuit. It stood to reason that as soon as she betrayed her beloved Markus Trent, the Midnight Suns would be hot on her trail. She just hadn't expected them to take so long to come after her.

She crouched atop a rock spire along the first of the footpaths into the northern mountains, looking down at the Midnight Suns. She'd been waiting in a nearby cave for two full days.

Earlier this very morning, before the sun had fully come into view, she had seen a strange mutant flying past, a hybrid of man and hornet, with a Lizardman gripped in its hands. They appeared to be working together, and if her instincts were still to be trusted, they too were looking for her. "Well, well, the game gets more interesting all the time," she'd whispered to herself.

Now, however, looking down at the Midnight Suns, she realized that the game wasn't all that fair. After all, they had no way of finding her, so long as she kept her wits about her and her powers active.

Her heart skipped a beat, however, when the white clad Ninja, Akimaru, looked up toward her. Had her cover wavered slightly?

But no, Akimaru looked away from her and up the trail again, following just behind a groggy Rage.

Teresa followed after, leaping from stone spire to stone spire, nimble and agile as ever. When the footpath the Suns followed turned west, she continued north, navigating and negotiating steep inclines and jutting mountain faces.

She had left marks of her passage, but unless Akimaru was inspired to leap up onto a rock spire, nobody would find them. Trent, however, just might, she realized, and increased her pace. She had to find someplace to hide, and she had less and less time to do so. If the Midnight Suns had arrived finally in the mountains, then the Hoods wouldn't be too far behind.

Though her powers nearly rendered her untraceable, she knew one of the Hoods could find her. Not Stockholm, no, and not the Wererat either.

But that damned Illusionist might be able to see right through her veil of invisibility. On top of that, she had to worry about the mutant and his Lizardman friend. She had no idea if they could successfully track her down, but she didn't want to take any chances.

Where could she go, in the mountains, where she could successfully take refuge? Certainly not with Solomon, she thought, he'd want to wring her neck for leaving him for Markus Trent.

But the ruins, she thought. Those ruins could make do.

* * * *

"Remember, head straight back," Stockholm said in a low voice to the horses as the rest of the company headed into the mouth of the hills that lead up into the mountains proper. Stockholm released the bridle of one of the chargers, and it led the other horses south and east again, toward the city of Desanadron.

Finished with their purpose, the Red Tribesman hadn't wanted to risk them being slain by wild creatures waiting for them at the foot of the hills.

"That was real noice of you, mate, real noice," Lee grumbled, walking along next to Norman Adwar at the rear of the ascending company. "Now how the hell are we gonna git home?"

"The gods gave us each two legs, Lee," Stockholm's replied before heading up toward Anna.

Flint leaned back toward the two Gnomes from his spot in the middle of the company.

"Four sometimes," the Wererat said with a grin. He coughed harshly, and lit another cigarette.

"Sure, loit another one 'ere my ducky," Lee said. "You sound roit as rain me mousy friend."

"Piss off," was the only reply.

The Hoods made their way up the footpaths, the rain left behind them in the flatlands of the northern plains. Here, in the hills fronting the Dwarven Territories, the air felt cool and clammy, damp with the snow they would soon be passing into. Knowing that the Dwarven Territories never experienced anything but wintry conditions, everyone from the company had brought their snow gear, and started to strap it on at around midday, when the elevation started to rise greatly. They were in the Territories now, without a doubt, and the first of the snows could be seen up the trail.

The Hoods didn't break for a meal at noon, choosing instead to push onward. Anna had guided them to one of the easier climbs up into Dwarven lands, the slopes gentle enough that even Norman Adwar and Styge could make their ways up without too much trouble.

Stockholm fell back several times from his position up near the front, each time offering to carry the old Illusionist, but Styge refused him politely.

His attention kept darting off to the east, where he thought he could just barely discern someone hopping around the higher spires of rock like a frog or grasshopper. Nimble, he thought, whoever that was.

In this fashion they marched throughout the daylight hours, the old Illusionist finally taking up the Red Tribesman's offer as late afternoon shifted into early evening. Flint let Norman ride on his back for a little while as well, Lee complaining about not getting so much as an offer of a ride.

Anna laughed at the expert Pickpocket, whom she knew to be more than sturdy enough to handle the wintry conditions of the mountainous Dwarven Territories.

As the sun set in the east, the company found a small alcove set in the side of the mountain and made a temporary shelter there for the night.

No plant life had been seen in the last hour of their travel, snow blanketing the area eternally. This told Anna that they had made excellent time. The Hoods would be atop this particular mountain in another half a day, so long as they continued to follow the twisting, circling path they were on, and then they could make an easy trip north, to Traithrock. In the Dwarven capital they would hunt down information where they could, and try to figure out their next move in the comfort of Dwarven hospitality. Gruff, hard working, and often combative people though they were, the Dwarves also knew a thing or two about how to treat travelers.

The Rogue wondered if Stockholm had spent any time here, among the Dwarves, and after everyone else had gone to sleep, except for her, Flint and the Red Tribesman, she asked.

"Yes, I have lived in these mountains, though not in Traithrock. The people there know me, but not so well as the Monks of the Kento temple in the far west. Their temple sits on a cliff face, with a long drop to the ocean on its back side."

"That'd be one hell of a drop if someone used the wrong door to duck out for a squat," Flint joked.

Anna and Stockholm both laughed for a moment before Stockholm turned serious again.

"You know, we had one young apprentice make that mistake," he said evenly. "Luckily for him, the masters were able to save him. They tossed him a sutra scroll that allowed him to float down to the water, gentle as a feather. He had to swim around for a while, but they got him back up to the temple."

"So, did he finish his training all right," Anna asked.

Stockholm grunted a harsh laugh. "He was expelled a month later for laying with one of the chambermaids. Sex was not allowed in the temple grounds, you see."

Flint balked at this. "You mean to tell me that the whole time you're there, you can't have any romping around? Well, no offense, my fine furry friend, but it's a good thing you've got a strong willpower." Flint puffed on his smoke. "I never would've lasted a month!"

Anna punched him in the arm, and took a sip off her aleskin.

"What? I'm serious boss. Life of celibacy just isn't my style!"

"Really?" She felt slightly tipsy from the ale she'd consumed throughout the evening. "Just when was the last time you got lucky, mouse?"

Flint rolled his eyes and thought back. "Four months," he said. "She was a fine piece of…" he stopped when he saw their faces.

They each tucked in for the night then, unaware that the Midnight Suns were camped less than a mile away, on another of the mountains.

* * * *

"Good thing we're both cold-blooded," Bergeon said to Dean Masters as they surveyed their surroundings. "Did you notice those footprints on the taller spires when we were flying past?"

"I did." The Sidalis cleaned the tip of his spear with some of the snow on the ground and a rag. "I don't think any of the thieves we're after could have done that. You know, Lee Toren wasn't with those prisoners. Perhaps you were right before."

"What do you mean," Bergeon said, licking the air with his tongue to get a good whiff of the air around them.

"I mean perhaps we should leave them alone. That Orc was no laughing matter, friend, and the Necromancer woman apparently has a good deal of power at her disposal.. They're beyond our skills to deal with, just the two of us."

"Nobody is beyond our skills, Dean," Bergeon snapped. He was a devout swordsman without a specified Class, and his love of his steed had been greater than any Knight might have for their horse or griffin. Only Beastmasters had a fonder relationship with their animals than Bergeon had had for his stamprous. He had raised the animal from birth, naming it Talon, running with it in the fields, and training it in combat. Yet a legion of undead had been brought down on it, and he'd been forced to leave it to its fate. *No,* he thought angrily, *we'll not leave them go.* "That woman took Talon from me, and I shall have her head for it."

"Oh for heaven's sake, it was just an animal."

A moment later, one of Bergeon's swords was at his throat. "And you and I aren't much more than that, Dean Masters! You just remember that!" The Lizardman glared at Masters a moment longer, and sheathed his weapon. "We are not under the eye of Reynaldi right now. His orders can wait. Lee Toren can't go far with the Glove of Shadows—not in these mountains. We'll find him, but not before we slay the Necromancer woman. And if the Orc survived his injuries, we'll finish him off as well. Nobody escapes the death of my swords."

The two agents of the Order of Oun walked a while, periodically stopping to check for signs of people's passing. They found the small, heavy tracks of Dwarven patrols here and there, but discovered nothing to indicate the passage of the thieves.

Although the sun had set long before, another two hours passed before Bergeon agreed to set camp in an outcropping of rocks that fronted a cave set in the mountain. He didn't want to go in the cave and disturb anything living there, so instead, he and Dean Masters took turns keeping watch throughout the night.

The next morning, they found the Midnight Suns again.

* * * *

Akimaru went around the company, shaking everyone awake. Fly had told him to wake them just before sunrise, since he would have the last watch of the night.

"Oh man," Markus Trent said, shivering. "This weather up here sucks."

"Get used to it." Fly hitched up his rucksack. "We're heading for Traithrock, and we'll need another full day, maybe day and a half on these mountain paths. As long as we don't come across any Dwarven patrols, we'll be just fine."

Everyone got up, getting their things together. "How are you feeling today, Rage?"

"Better, sir." The lumbering Greenskin stretched his massive frame lazily, working his limbs awake. "Still not up to, ah, you know, um, what's the word?"

"Snuff, Rage-san," Fly said. "The term is, up to snuff."

"What's snuff?" the Orc Berserker asked seriously.

Fly chuckled at his ignorance, but smiled gently at the man. "Lain can explain it better than I, my fine green friend. For now, let's just get going."

The Midnight Suns moved out into the snowy day. The sun shone brightly in the mountains, but imparted little of its warmth on the snow-covered mountains.

They continued on up the mountain, keeping to the paths they knew, avoiding the broader ones that Dwarven patrols would surely watch.

Then, around one turn in their mountain path, they saw the two strangers who'd attacked them, weapons at the ready.

The two groups stared at one another menacingly.

Atop the slope, the Sidalis and the Lizardman swordsman stood, feet apart, battle ready.

Trying to fight on the slope would be madness, Fly realized, but the mutant had wings. All he had to do was hover out away from the slope, and pick them off with his spear from a distance. Being at a higher elevation, the pair of strangers also had the advantage over Fly and his company. How would he deal with them appropriately?

"Sensei, please step aside," Akimaru whispered into Fly's ear.

The Black Draconus did as Akimaru asked, and stood near the edge of the slope. He risked a brief glance downward, and saw that if he slipped wrong and fell, he would plummet a good six or seven hundred feet before he struck another footpath. He would be killed for sure.

"We will let you pass, murderers," Bergeon said, pointing his katana right at Lain McNealy. "If you give up the Necromancer. I shall have her head in exchange for the life of my steed."

"You attacked and trapped us, swordsman," Fly shouted up past Akimaru, who was steadily walking up toward the soldiers.

Bergeon didn't hear a word of what Thaddeus Fly yelled. His eyes were locked on the Necromancer, his blood boiling with hatred.

Dean Masters only heard Fly vaguely as well, but for different reasons. He had seen the Orc, who had survived his wounds, but looked ill, weakened. But his bulbous, insect eyes were locked on the feet of the white clad Ninja approaching them. The man didn't walk through the snow, but atop it. No sign of Akimaru's passage could be seen.

"Sergeant, look." The corporal pointed at Akimaru.

Bergeon tore his eyes away from the Necromancer, and was shocked by the same observation Masters had made. "What the hell are we dealing with here?"

"I don't know, Dean, but you'd better use one of your barriers, and be quick about it," Bergeon said, as Fly let loose a shuriken.

The metal projectile split the mutant's left hand up the middle, and he let out a horrendous, high-pitched wail of agony as Akimaru made his move.

The white clad Ninja shifted his feet, and threw his hands forward, releasing a cone of force at Bergeon.

The Lizardman saw that the cone was actually thousands of minute shards of ice, and he drew his shorter sword, weaving his blades back and forth before him. Only a handful of the shards struck him, piercing his body like arrowheads without wooden shafts. His arms and legs bled openly on the snowy slope, but he was largely unharmed.

Bergeon's training alone saved him from the next attack, as Thaddeus Fly came through the air at him, a jump kick just glancing Bergeon's shoulder as he spun to the side.

The Lizardman looked to his right, and saw that another Ninja, a Human clad in gray tunics, sat astride his ally, Dean Masters, stabbing the mutant over and over in the arms.

Masters managed to throw Trent off, squaring off with him and lunging with his spear. He missed the stab, but tore it back around, cutting open Markus Trent's left leg and spraying the snow with blood.

Fly drew one of his short swords, and engaged in a fast-paced duel with the Lizardman. Back and forth they went, exchanging blow for blow, neither making much progress. Fly knew the level of skill of the swordsman was high, probably much higher than his own. However, he had watched Bergeon, fight against Rage, and had watched his movements when Akimaru had flung his cone of frost at him. He had a pattern, and Fly waited for the opening that would help him finish this battle.

Trent, meanwhile, was backpedaling, being forced against the side of the mountain by Dean Masters's continued assault. The mutant had lost his ability to put up his barriers when the shuriken damaged his left hand, but his skills with a spear hadn't been much diminished. Over and over again he came at the gray-clad man who had tried to take advantage of his injury, landing one more slash on Trent's face—before he was slammed by a huge, green fist.

Rage loomed over Masters as the mutant fell to the snow, sending up clouds of snow as he flapped his wings to get away.

He just got away from a stab to his back, Trent's knife landing hard in his right calf.

Masters groaned in pain and rubbed the left side of his face where Rage had punched him.

The Sidalis floated out over the side of the slope, out of their attacking range. "What good are your weapons now, fools?" He cocked his right arm back, securing a chain at his hip to the blunt end of his spear. He would throw the spear and haul it back, hopefully landing it in one of them and pulling them over the edge, down to their death.

Which one, which one, he thought. That was when he noticed Akimaru again—too late.

Masters saw a shining surface jutting from the slope—a walkway made entirely of ice. Upon the walkway, which led right up beside him, stood Akimaru, the white clad Ninja.

"What the hell," was all he managed before the grinning apparition, with its ice stalactite-covered head, breathed a freezing mist over his wings.

Dean Masters plummeted out of the sky, screaming all the way down.

After a full two minutes of screams, there was stunted silence, with only the clash of swords to break it.

Akimaru put his mask back over his head.

Fly looked for that opening, missing his opportunity only by a half a second each time it showed up.

The pattern was getting tighter as he struggled against the swordsman, each passing moment lending him seemingly greater speed.

While Fly flagged and slowed, this Lizardman, this inferior creature, gained the advantage.

Now or never, he decided, and opened his snout.

Bergeon's eyes went wide, but he managed to tuck and roll away from the blast of lightning just before Fly let it erupt out of his mouth.

The mountain shook as the blast struck empty air.

Bergeon took advantage of this slip-up on the Draconus' part and pelted down the slope toward the still Necromancer woman.

The gray clad Ninja was on the ground, tending his bleeding wounds, and the white clad freak was still walking back slaying Bergeon's companion, leaving the Necromancer wide open to attack.

Screaming for blood and vengeance, Bergeon bore down on her. Lain McNealy didn't move, couldn't seem to move if she had wanted to. He had her dead to rights.

A few yards away from the woman, a huge, meaty fist reached out from behind a jutting segment of rock in the mountain, grabbing him by the throat.

In all of his years of training, Bergeon had never let his anger get the better of him, and now, he had let himself make the error that cost him his life. He darted his eyes to the right, and found himself looking into that wide, shining smile he had seen a few days before.

The Orc he had stabbed in the stomach knocked his sword out of his right hand with ease as he crushed the breath from his neck. "Remember me?" Rage asked before he threw Bergeon over the edge of the slope.

* * * *

Anna Deus and her band of Hoods experienced no such trouble on their way to Traithrock, which they reached just after noon that same day. The Dwarves on duty at the city gates had recognized Ignatious Stockholm, and palavered with him before letting the company into the city proper.

Traithrock spread before them, smoke rising out of chimneys everywhere they looked, guards standing about and holding friendly conversations with the townspeople. Crime was not much of a factor in daily life here, so guards were closer to the meaning of civil servant in the Dwarven Territories. If a shop owner needed something taken home, or brought to the shop from his abode, he needed only ask a passing guard to do him the favor, and it was done. Anna envied these people their peaceful existence, devoid of the fear of gangs and Guilds.

"All right people, let's split up," Anna said to the group as a whole. "We'll meet up back here by the gates at nightfall. That goes for everybody, Lee," she said meaningfully. "I don't want you taking advantage of these people's trust and getting us in trouble."

"No worries, mate." Lee inhaled the lovely aroma of home-cooked food from nearby. "I never cause trouble when I'm here. I prefer ta have me 'ead on its shoulders, know what I mean?"

The Hoods split into teams, heading out into the city of Traithrock.

Styge and Flint headed west, toward the business district. Anna and Stockholm headed north, toward the government buildings and the mines. Norman and Lee, being Gnomes, who were often considered a cousin Race to the Dwarves, headed east, toward the taverns and the first of the residential districts. Each team had a single purpose—find anything relevant to their search, particularly where a fugitive might hole up.

As they had agreed, they met back up by the gates as the sun started to set on the day. There, each team revealed what little they had learned.

* * * *

Styge and Flint made their way to the shopping district in the southern region of the city of Traithrock, slumping along at a leisurely pace, enjoying the hustle and bustle all around them. The Dwarves were busy folk, and had no use for nonsense or tomfoolery until after dark.

Flint watched a team of Dwarven carpenters work on the siding of a new tavern, no foreman in plain sight. Only by the difference in work clothes was Flint able to finally identify the man as they passed by, because even the foreman was getting his hands dirty, hammering huge support spikes into the wood siding.

"Very industrious people, Dwarves," Styge observed, puffing on a tobacco pipe. "Hard workers, hard drinkers, hard people. But they're very respectful, very law abiding folk."

"Yeah, I'll give you that, old man." Flint slowed as they passed by an elaborate stone cathedral. "But how can you tell a male from a female around here? They all look the same to me."

"Oh, that's easy." Styge approached a trio of Dwarves who were seated before the cathedral, sipping coffee in tureens from a thermos.

He stood there a moment silently, until they acknowledged him, then he turned his eyes to one in particular. "Excuse me, ma'am, but would you happen to have.the time?" He kept his hands folded behind his back.

"T'is half past five hours in the afternoon."

To Flint, the Dwarf woman's deep husky voice sounded no different than any Dwarven man's.

Styge shuffled back to him, and together, they walked down the street further, ducking into a sundry goods store after a few minutes.

"So, how do you do it old man? I've lived much longer than you, but I can't tell the difference."

"It's easy, when you know what to look for." Styge ordered a box of matches and a half-pound of pipe tobacco from the clerk.

The counter was low, as was the ceiling, and Flint had to duck a little to fit in the store's main room. He wondered what sort of trouble Stockholm was having, seeing as he had a good foot on the Wererat, and a good deal more width.

"And what exactly does one look for?" Flint wrote down an order for six packs of rolled cigarettes and handed it to another clerk, this one a teenaged Human boy. The store was lit with tubes of glass hung in brackets set in the wall, orange swamp gas glowing inside of the tubes. This was a strange new form of lighting, discovered and developed by the Dwarves of the hill regions to the east of the mountains. The swamp gas could be collected by simply holding a glass container over one of the many natural ground vents in any of the swamps found throughout Tamalaria. Then, it was filtered through rubber tubing into the light tubes of a building, and a match was struck against the access hole of the rubber tube. The swamp gas burned slow and bright, lighting a room quite well and for a long period.

"Well," Styge said, thanking the Dwarven clerk for his purchases. "Take a look at this man's left ear."

The Dwarf gave him a queer look, and pulled the scruffy red hair back from the side of his face.

Flint saw a plain ear.

"What do you see?"

"I see an organ that aids in hearing," Flint said sarcastically. "What the hell else should I see?"

"No earrings, right?"

Flint shook his head.

"Very good. That means this fellow is a man. Also, there's the matter of the beard. See this gentleman's beard?"

Flint took a good long look at the long, crimson beard. It was braided on the two sides near the edge of the long, flat chin.

The Dwarf tipped his head back and grinned, pleased that someone was admiring his facial hair.

"Now, what one thing stands out about it?"

"Aside from the typical Dwarven length? No offense, sir," Flint said.

"None taken." The clerk watched these strangers' conversation about Dwarven ears and beards with interest.

"Dwarven women braid their beards in the middle." Styge lit his pipe. "That's the easiest way to spot a woman in the crowd." Styge turned his disarming smile on the store clerk. "Now then, could I ask you a few questions, sir?"

Nice transition, Flint thought. *Compliment the man, then start asking questions. Too bad he's not a Rogue. He'd make a good con man.*

* * * *

Norman Adwar and Lee Toren walked through the city streets of Traithrock, and in order to keep suspicions low, did what most civilized Gnomes did in strange cities—they held hands. It made Lee sick to do it, and Norman wasn't too fond of not having his hands free, but they knew that they'd stick out like sore thumbs if they didn't among these Dwarves. In Traithrock, two kinds of Gnomes let their hands be empty around each other. Thieves, for one, and Alchemists for another. Neither of these sorts was trusted in the Dwarven Territories, and so the pair of Gnomes from Desanadron walked hand in hand down the busy streets of the tavern-infested area of Traithrock.

When they picked a less than seedy tavern, they found the publican of the establishment locked in an arm wrestling contest with a Jaft man, another of the Races prone to living in the mountainous and dangerous regions of the lands. As soon as Norman and Lee took in the sight of the blue fleshed humanoid gaining a slight advantage, the owner/bartender of the tavern shifted the pressure on his elbow and slammed the Jaft's arm down on the bar counter.

Uproarious shouts of praise and disbelief filled the air, along with the natural stench of several of the contest loser's kinsmen. Five Jafts in all stood about the pub, all huddled together to laugh and jeer at their companion's failure to best a 'wee man' at a test of strength.

"Anybody ever tell you you've got a knack for getting people into the worst possible places and situations?" Norman asked Lee.

"Certainly, lad," he replied. "You isn't the first, and you won't be the last, I'll wager. Now buck up, lad, and let's get us some drinks." Lee Toren's eyes naturally lingered on each loose stringed money pouch he saw. "This is one sort of bar where we won't have ta say a word to anyone to learn of current, local news."

The two Gnomes let go of one another's hand, approaching the low countertop with Lee in the lead, two fingers up.

The Dwarven publican nodded evenly at the Gnome Pickpocket, and poured two clean mugs of ale.

Norman eyed his glass with suspicion before sampling the beverage, which, much to his surprise, was slightly sweet.

"Excuse me, sir," he said to the publican, who looked away from the current Jaft challenger for a moment. "What's this made with?"

The Dwarf laughed merrily for a moment, and shook his head. "It's honey ale, lad. Brewed and distilled with mountain snow and honey. Careful you don't drink it too quick, master Gnome. It may taste kind enough, but there's a bear's bite behind every swig. Not exactly for the casual Gnome customer."

Norman thanked him for the information, and took a seat at the bar, settling in to watch the next contest.

Lee Toren, meanwhile, set his eyes on a man with whom he had worked a few independent jobs years back. The man was a Tanner Cuyotai, a member of the most common tribe of werecoyote. Artemis Lane, the man had called himself, although Lee figured that had to be a played up name. Most performers of the fine art of confidence man took on several names a year, or kept an arsenal of readily assumable identities on hand for repeated use.

Lee strode over slowly, savoring the sweet sense of a victory already at hand. Lane, if that indeed was his name was now, was engaged in conversation with a pair of respectable looking Dwarven gentlemen. He wore the fine black and white tunics of a nobleman. Tufted collar and cuffs flowed out over his furry neck and wrists, and lent a subtle grace to his movements as they ruffled.

"And that, my fine sirs," Lee heard as he approached, "is how you could literally triple your profit margin over the course of only a month."

Lane held up a long, slender finger to stay the Dwarves. "If you kind sirs would excuse me, one of my investors would like a word with me right now. Isn't that so, Mr. Orten?" The crafty Cuyotai looked Lee dead in the face.

"That's roit, moi ducky." Lee realized wouldn't have the immediate advantage to press, as the two Dwarven businessmen clearly wanted to linger, untrusting of such a smooth transition in the Cuyotai's speech with them to this newcomer. "Timothy Orten, gennelmen," Lee offered the Dwarves a friendly hand. "I should just loik to say that you'd be makin' a foin investment wiv the good sir here, if'n you's opt to invest."

The Dwarves muttered to one another for a moment, and then asked Lane to excuse them while they talked over his proposal in private.

No sooner had the two Dwarven investors exited the tavern than a pair of hairy, gnarled hands wrapped themselves in the front of Lee's tunic and hauled him forward, spilling a good quantity of his ale to the wooden floor.

"What the hell do you think you're doing, Lee?" Foam forming at the corners of Lane's mouth. His eyes were wide and wild, and the Gnome Pickpocket gathered that his con had already seen some rough spots along the way. "I've been working those two stunted fools for three whole days."

"Calm down now Artie." Lee pushed away from the Cuyotai Rogue with his free hand. "And be mindful of the beer. I paid good coin fer this drink."

Lane grunted and motioned Lee to take one of the empty seats across for him, but the way he did so made it clear that Lee only had a couple of minutes to ask him any questions.

"All right, you little braggart," Lane whispered, keeping his voice low and a fake smile plastered to his broad, canine lips. "What do you want?"

"Answers, Mr. Lane." Lee took a swig of his honey brew. "Just a few. First off, you seen any strange folks passing through the city? Stranger than normal, I should say," Lee amended before Lane could give him a smartass reply.

"Nothing too bad, not really. There's a tribe of Jafts in the city for trade and booze, maybe a few loose women if they can find a compatible species. That's about all." Lee finished his beer with a quick chug, and wiped his mouth with a sleeve.

"Roit. Good enough, then. One more question."

Lane raised a suspicious eyebrow. "That's it? Two questions? You're usually much more full of inquiry, Lee. Old age finally catching up to you?"

"Never mind my age and answer my question. Is Solomon still hanging about? You know, the old part-timer? Mister 'I'll work fer anyone what pays me enough'?"

"Oh, he's still kicking about. Skulks around a ways from the city a lot, near the old mines what got shut down last year." Lane smiled and waved at the two Dwarven businessmen he'd marked before. "You have your answers, Lee. Now get out of here before you ruin my deal."

Lee offered his hand, which Lane shook, and he was off the seat and away.

When he got back over to Norman, the Engineer was three quarters into his third honey ale, and well beyond the path of mere drunken happiness. He had to sling Norman over his shoulder and carry him out of the bar, moving awkwardly back through the city streets to where he would rendezvous with the rest of the Hoods.

The mines seemed a safe enough bet, if he could get anything useful out of Solomon. Then again, he thought as he laid Norman down in the snowy street to sober up, assuring the guards nearby that his friend had simply taken too much honey ale too quick, perhaps he wouldn't have to drag anything out of Solomon. Not when blokes like Stockholm and Flint were readily available.

* * * *

"If someone was going to hole up nice and tight around here, it'd be in those mines," Morek Rockmight said to Ignatious Stockholm.

Anna had let the big Red Tribesman lead the way toward the government buildings, and Stocky hadn't even wavered slightly in his path to the councilor's abode. A quaint, three story house, built on a scale to accommodate Humans and Elves with ease, Morek's home was open to all those he considered friends. This list included some of Tamalaria's finest, and its worst. He'd never been quite sure where to lump in Ignatious Stockholm.

"So why were the mines abandoned?" Anna asked after thanking the Kobold house servant for her tea.

The Glove of Shadows

The three of them sat on the covered patio of Morek's home, drinking hot tea and enjoying the cheese-filled biscuits the hired help whipped up for them on the pinch. Morek tried to apologize for the quality of the food available on short notice, but Anna waved the apology off. If she could eat like this every day, she thought, she'd be as squat as the Dwarven Boxer.

"Last year," Morek said, "a team of diggers was headed in for a routine day on the job. Only one of them was soused as all get out, and stumbling around loik an idiot. He seemed to fall through a crack in the wall, as 'is mates says it. When they followed him through it, they found this door. Well, you know us Dwarves—we're not naturally curious folks, but this was just something too weird for comfort, you know? We'd been pulling iron and gold and copper out of those mines fer years now, and suddenly there's a door up near the higher levels? Didn't ride well with the lads, and so they came back and told the council about it.

"We all talked it over, me and the other six councilors, and we agreed to send in an exploration team. Five men, heavily armed, with some good fighting skills and a few of the machine weapons we've scrounged up from other hidden ruins over the years. Never know what you're up agin when goin' under the ground anymore. Um, do we 'ave any of those chicken things left, Travis?" This last question Morek directed at the Kobold butler, who smiled his polite smile and nodded.

"Cor, heat those up and bring 'em out. You'll find these a treat, big man," he said to Stockholm. "Good stuff, good stuff. Kobolds is really very good at three things, I've found. One is magic. They've got a nat'ral talent fer it. Another's cleaning, which they've got an even better knack for. And the last is cooking, because believe you me, I'd never find the patience to sit around the kitchen and concoct half the stuff ol' Trevor there comes up with."

"The mines," Anna tried to get the aging Boxer back on track.

"Oh, right." Morek looked surprised at himself for digressing. "So we sent in a group of five able men. Not the *very* best, but mind you, these blokes had been around since Tanarak of Sidius. Very reliable, capable in a pinch. Five went down into the ruins beneath the mines, and only two came back alive." Morek's voice lowered to a threatening whisper. "The creatures they described are freaks of nature, demons almost for sure. Blighted, black-skinned things wide as an Ogre and fast as a leopard." His voice filled with a terrible awe. "Three or four arms, strong as an ox to each limb. And there were other monstrosities down there, my friends. Things the two survivors couldn't even bear to talk about. Weird animal hybrids, and even a few things they could only describe as men made of mecha and steel. No, if anyone wanted to take refuge down there, they'd have to be able to make themselves totally invisible to survive."

Invisible, Anna thought. *Like Teresa Evergreen.*

* * * *

The city of Traithrock finally hovered into plain view below the Midnight Suns. Though they were all beaten, bloodied and bandaged, they were glad for the sight of it. The Dwarven people wouldn't exactly welcome them, Thaddeus Fly knew. Theirs was a motley crew to be sure, and among them was an Orc, one of the few species in Tamalaria that the Dwarves openly hated.

As the company got closer to the city, Fly noticed that Akimaru exuded more and more of an air of impatience, anxiety. Had he been here before? Fly thought a few years back. He had sent Aki and Trent on an excursion up here to a set of discovered ruins. The part-timer, Solomon, probably still lived in Traithrock. He might be able to provide them with ideas on where she might be hidden.

The Midnight Suns arrived before the city's open gates a little after the sun had set, only a few hours behind the Hoods, who had already held council and moved on.

As soon as Fly stepped through the gates, two-dozen Dwarven guards surrounded the company.

Axes, short spears and war hammers at the ready, the city's guards held a safe distance from Fly's group. One of the stout troopers, wearing heavy banded chain mail with a single plate of metal over his right breast, approached the Black Draconus. Upon the plate was emblazoned a diagonal blue line, apparently some sort of rank signifier Fly had never laid eyes upon.

"Hail and hold, outsiders." The Dwarf hollered in harsh, guttural tones, though Fly was only a few feet away. "Most who come to Traithrock through the open and public roads are welcome, but not all. We would know your names, and your Class. If you belong to any army, give us your rank and your nation as well."

Well, Fly thought, *may as well get this tricky business over with by playing it honestly.*

"I am Thaddeus Fly, Ninja. I am the Headmaster of the Midnight Suns." The Black Draconus called back just as loudly as the Dwarf. He looked around at the assembled guards, and saw the blissfully unaware looks they gave each other. Good, he thought, they've never heard of me. "With me are," he said.

"No, Thaddeus Fly, Headmaster of the Midnight Suns," the captain of the guards said, putting up a staying hand. "We shall hear from your compatriots themselves. You there, Human." The captain pointed at Trent. "Name, class and status." Trent gave the captain a low, mocking bow, grinning like a court jester at play for his king.

"I am Markus Oliver Trent." H stood to full height. "Ninja, and second in command of the Midnight Suns, though this is often a point of dispute among our Guild."

Nice, good little public jab, Fly growled in his mind.

"Good. You, woman," the captain spat.

"I am Lain McNealy, Necromancer, member of the Midnight Suns. I have no official rank."

There came some mixed, apprehensive murmuring after her introduction, but the captain made no comment, insisting only that the Orc go next.

"Um, I'm not really sure what to do Ms. McNealy," he whispered to the Necromancer.

She whispered something briefly in his ear, and he grinned. "Oh, dat's not so hard. Okay, um, my name is Rage. I'm a Berserker. I'm in da Midnight Suns. Was dat okay?" He whispered the last, seeking the Necromancer's approval.

Oh boy, Fly thought, here comes the really hard part. "You there, white one," the captain said, pointing an accusing finger at Akimaru. "Name, class, status. Now!"

"I am called Akimaru. I am Ninja, and am also a Midnight Sun," Akimaru offered evenly. "Nothing more shall I say to you, honorable captain." He offered the Dwarf a deep bow from the waist.

This seemed to have a calming effect on the captain of the guards, and that calm spread from him to his kinsmen.

"It is well," the captain said, giving a curt hand signal to his men, who lowered their weapons and slowly returned to their posts. "You may pass into this our city, but be warned. Any shenanigans on your parts will be sorely and swiftly dealt with. Understood?"

The company as a whole agreed, and the captain of the guards sauntered away. They had finally made it to Traithrock, and with only the strange mutant and the swordsman Lizardman to deal with along the way. Those two had been a tremendous pain in their collective ass, but at least they had been the last obstacle between themselves and Traithrock.

Now, to find Solomon, Fly thought, *and beat whatever info out of him that we can.*

* * * *

Two hours prior to the exchange between the guards and the Midnight Suns, the Hoods all came together at that same spot. No Dwarven guards bothered them. The city's denizens recognized Stockholm, and the Gnomes were their cousins in spirit, so the group was left to hold their brief council. This particular council began with Flint giving Lee a small, blue pill to force feed to Norman.

"It'll sober him up in about five minutes flat," the Wererat explained.

"You sure it isn't some sort of poison?"

"I save those pills for your coffee." Flint gave a dubious smile.

Flint and Styge went first, telling Anna that they hadn't found out much, except that the mines northeast of the city had been shut down a year back for reasons unknown to the shopkeepers.

On this subject, Lee and Norman, now sober and suffering a huge headache, had little more to offer.

When Anna retold Morek Rockmight's account, things took a serious turn for the better. They all had a rough idea of what Teresa Evergreen was capable of. However, they all agreed that the group could do little without good food and rest, and so they all headed, as a group, to the only hotel in the city that catered specially to 'big people', as the mountainous Dwarves called them.

The accommodations were comfortable, if nothing else. The company split into three rooms, keeping the same partners as they had for the collection of information. When Anna and Stockholm entered their room, they had both been pleased to see that the housekeeping staff took their jobs seriously.

"So, left or right?" Stockholm eyed up the two available beds.

Neither would be a good fit for his massive frame, Anna saw, but if he curled up in his animus form, either would be perfect.

She opted for the one on the left, and tucked herself under the covers. She lay there, quite still, for a long while, waiting for the soft snore of her crimson companion.

After an hour and a half, she rolled over, and saw him sitting on the edge of his bed, staring at nothing.

"Stocky?"

He gave her no answer. Instead, he stood up, a glassy, unfocused look in his eyes, and shuffled out of the room like a zombie.

"Stocky," she said, only slightly louder, praying he'd snap out of whatever trance he was in. She didn't want to be alone, here, in this foreign territory. She knew that Flint would already be fast asleep in his rented chambers, and though she liked them all, none of the others seemed fitting company at this late hour. She rolled back over, and waited quietly for Stockholm to return.

A half an hour later, the Red Tribe Werewolf came back into the room, looking haggard, but smiling.

Anna sprang from her bed and jumped at him, wrapping her arms as best she could around his huge upper body.

He patted her comfortingly on the head, and she suddenly found herself crying, wishing she could be back home, in bed with her husband, Harold. "Don't leave me alone like that, Stocky," she said, pounding a limp fist against his barrel chest. "Never again, you hear me?" She looked up into his huge, cavernous eyes. "Where have you been, anyway?"

She sniffed the air around him, particularly the odor coming from his left hand. "And what's that smell on you?"

"Oh, nothing much," Stockholm said with a grin. "I just had to take care of some business with a fish."

Before Anna could protest or ask any more questions, he scooped her up, laid her back on her bed, covered her up, and gently kissed her forehead. "Good night, Annabelle Deus. Rest well, and think no more on this matter. Soon, we will all head home, and live a while without William Deus in our lives."

She smiled warmly at him, and found that his kiss had made her drowsy, as Harold's always had. Within minutes, she was restfully, peacefully asleep.

* * * *

Markus Trent hadn't felt so good in a long, long time as he ran the cheese grater along Solomon's leg for a third time.

Oh, what beautiful, gorgeous shrieks Solomon makes. To think that Fly granted me this delicious playtime.

The Midnight Suns had wasted no time following the direct path through the center of the city that Markus carved for them. He was anxious to be done with this whole business, anxious to be back in Desanadron, going about his usual tasks and daily habits. The road was no place for him, and pent up frustrations were on the verge of breaking him apart when Fly had suggested that he 'tune Solomon up' to get the information they needed.

Trent had opened the front door of Solomon's cottage with ease, picking the lock so fast he might as well have had a spare key. He and Fly had barged through the door, falling upon a half-sleeping Solomon as he had headed for his door to see who was trying to call on him at this late hour.

The two Ninjas had quickly incapacitated him, and Fly had helped Trent bind him and gag him in a straight-backed oak chair in his own bedroom.

The prostitute in the bed hadn't even woken up from a drunken sleep that would take a massive explosion to wake her.

Fly had instructed Trent to get the information they needed, and then had exited the cottage to wait with the others.

"Isn't it marvelous, Solomon," Trent asked the part-time agent and freelancer. "If you survive to see another sunrise, it shall be the most glorious sight of your long, meaningless life."

Trent raked the grater across the exposed bone of Solomon's left leg again, coaxing another hiss of agony from the bound man.

"No whore will ever be able to satisfy you as much as the fresh morning air being drawn into your lungs. Don't you see, Solomon? I am setting you free. And you don't even have the stomach to thank me for it!"

Another scrape of the bone, and though the muffled screams were gratifying, the cheese grater had become boring.

Trent left Solomon to wallow in his misery for a few minutes, while he searched his cottage for more goodies to work with.

He came across a glass bottle of vinegar, popped the stopper, and took a whiff. It was strong stuff, and he instantly liked it. However, this wouldn't be good for more than a few minutes of fun so he scrounged about for more goodies.

"Ah, isn't this convenient," he whispered, feeling the front of his pants swell out from his growing erection. What he had come across was another glass vial, this one filled with a thick, greasy lamp oil.

His hands flew over the drawers of the kitchen he had found the oil in, and his fingers found purchase on a book of matches moments after throwing the silverware drawer to the floor. "Perfect."

Back to Solomon, who was now crying and sobbing. Trent danced in front of him, cackling like a hyena as he poured the vinegar on the bleeding leg wound.

Solomon screamed with renewed vigor, thrashing about like a nightmare marionette.

"That's right, that's right, scream for me sissy boy." Trent danced behind the chair, pouring a small portion of the lamp oil into Solomon's greasy black hair. He struck a match, and let it fall onto the damp scalp, reveling in the screams and the thick, black smoke of the burning flesh atop Solomon's head.

When Trent finally doused Solomon's head with water from his kitchen pump, the man was teetering on the brink of death.

Trent undid the gag in his mouth, and crouched down next to him, all business and false concern.

"You know, if you just tell me what I want to know, we won't have to continue this all. I've got a healing sutra right in my pocket that can fix you up just fine, friend."

Solomon still moaned a little, though his voice had been strained so badly that he couldn't make a noise louder than a kitten's mewl.

"Now, has Teresa been by to see you?"

A silent nod, and nothing more.

"Good, excellent. How long ago did she drop in?"

"Yes… terday," Solomon managed, licking his cracked lips. "She… wanted, to know, if… the mines, were… still being… worked… on."

"Okay, good. We know they aren't." Trent pulled a sutra from his pocket. The writing on it would be completely foreign and unreadable by Solomon, but he knew Trent would tell him how to activate it before he left.

"Is she heading there?"

"Yes," Solomon croaked. "To, the, ruins." The part-timer confirmed Trent's fear that Evergreen would be confident enough in her powers to try to hide among the monstrosities living therein.

Trent patted him gently, warmly, on one bound arm.

"You've done well, Solomon. I'm sorry I had to put you through all of this, but I figured it was the only way to get you to talk. After all, old flames have a way of making men keep their mouths shut. Now, you can use this sutra to heal yourself once I'm gone. Not before, or I'll have to split your eye with a shuriken, okay?"

Solomon nodded, and Trent placed the sutra in his hand. "Very good. Now, I'm going to leave. Remember, shuriken to the eye." He left the cottage bedroom, and then the house.

Outside, Fly and the others turned to face him.

"The ruins, Headmaster," Trent said with a satisfied smile. "You know, I didn't think you'd let me have any fun on this whole trip. Thanks for proving me wrong."

The Midnight Suns left the city behind them an hour later, navigating through the city streets and out through the east gates.

In the cottage that Trent had used as a romper room of torture, Solomon unleashed the chi magic locked in the sutra.

There was a brief, hot flash of yellow light, as from a hundred candles flickering to life. So raw was his throat that he didn't even scream when the lights turned out to be flesh-eating scorpions, which crawled into his open leg wound and mouth, devouring him from the inside out.

The Glove of Shadows

Chapter Eighteen
Test of Strength

Anna's eyes fluttered open as the sunlight dribbled in through the slats of the window near her bed. She hadn't meant to sleep so late, but she and the others needed the rest. For reasons she couldn't readily put her finger on, she didn't think the Hoods would be left in the dust.

She rolled out of the bed, stretching her arms and legs and rubbing feeling back into them. She strolled over to the door, secured the deadbolt, and took off her shirts and wraps, getting in one last breather for her lungs and breasts.

She walked over to the bathroom, admired the Dwarven plumbing design, and drew herself a bath. The tub was too large, even for someone like Stockholm, but Jafts and Minotaurs could grow to ridiculous heights, and they were probably the hotel's most frequent guests.

She stripped and slipped down into the warm water, letting it soak through her skin and into her sore muscles. *Too much time on the road.* She closed her eyes briefly.

There was a disturbance of the water, and when she opened her eyes, she nearly shrieked when she saw that Stockholm had joined her in the tub. He had a washcloth over his privates, but she felt awkward and distressed nonetheless.

"What," he said gruffly. "You haven't got anything I'm interested in, remember?"

For a moment, she couldn't think of anything to respond with, and she erupted with coarse laughter. She splashed the water at him playfully, but he didn't return the gesture. Instead, he took the soaked cloth and draped it over his snout.

"Gods almighty you gave me a scare," she said. She draped her arms over the sides of the enormous tub, making herself comfy. "You know, you and I have spent a lot of time together on this whole journey. I feel like I'm getting to really know you."

"That's because you pal around with Flint all the time," Stockholm said through the washcloth.

Anna's eyes wandered southward through the clear water, and quickly spun away when she caught the slightest glimpse of his manhood. *Cripes*, she thought, if he were straight, *he'd give some lucky girl a run for her money.*

"I like the Prime well enough," he said, "don't get me wrong. But he and I simply lead much different lives. You and I, too, but I think you and I needed to get better acquainted. Especially since I'm going to be gone for a while next year."

"What do you mean you'll be gone? How can you know that, big guy?"

"Just trust me on this, boss lady." He pulled the cloth off and rubbed soap on it. "I'll be gone for quite a while, possibly up to a full month or two. I'll put in appearances where and when I can, though."

"Stocky," Anna said, hesitating a little. "Um, there's a few things I know I'll never understand about you. Ever. But one thing I have to ask is this—how long have you been living like this?"

Stockholm stopped halfway through rubbing under his left arm with the cloth, and looking at her with the most serious cast in his eyes he could manage. "How long have you been drifting the lands of Tamalaria?"

Thick silence settled in the bathroom, almost taking on a visible hue of a barrier between the two of them. Finally, he gave her a partial answer, which for now, was good enough. "If it's a question of how old I am, I'll answer you as honestly as I know how; I'm twenty-two-hundred and forty-three years old. Much older than those of my species, even my long living tribe, live to. As for the how or why of that, I cannot remember. Something happened a very long time ago to me. It involves a handful of the gods, that much I know." While he wasn't giving her the whole truth, he figured this much was better than nothing.

"The wandering. Yes, I've drifted a lot over the last six hundred years." Stockholm went back to scrubbing his underarms. "I learned all of the combative arts I could, as early as I could, so that I could handle every situation I came across. But I haven't really had a clear purpose for a long time, boss lady." He now splashed water on himself. "Now, I do. I make things work for a while, until next year. Then, I do as the gods council me to do," he said.

"I never figured you for a holy man." Anna raised an eyebrow as she grabbed a washcloth of her own and set to work scrubbing clean.

"I'm not." The Red Tribesman appeared thoughtful for a moment, and then stood up in the tub, turned around, and stepped out. He shook himself off like a dog, his hair poofing out in large tufts like a cartoon character. "By the way, Anna?"

"Yes?" she asked, as a tsunami in miniature smashed into her, breaking over her upper body with a wet 'smack'. "Oh, you bastard! I'll get you back." She exited herself, drying off and selecting a new outfit for the day's work ahead of them. It would be the last day of this long, hard trip. *And in the end*, she thought, *we won't even do what we've been trying so hard to do, not if what Stocky says about the Glove is true.* What then would they do with the artifact if they gained possession of it? Would they warn Thaddeus Fly about the curse upon it, since it seemed fated that they would run into the Midnight Suns again in those forsaken ruins? She didn't know, and as long as all of her companions stayed safe and free of injury, she didn't care.

* * * *

As Anna and Stockholm were getting out of the bath, Thaddeus Fly and his band of Midnight Suns stomped up the snowy trail toward the mines. Several signs, each written in a different language, warned of the closed mine ahead. Nobody in the company could read the ones written in Dwarven, but Trent could decipher the signs written in the rough scrawl of the Jafts. The signs left for the blue-fleshed humanoids not only had writing on them, but little pictures of stick figures falling from cliffs, skulls and crossbones, and one picture depicting a group of lawman stick figures beating a central figure about the head with sticks with nails in them.

The Minotaur warnings Rage could interpret, since their language was so closely akin to that of the Greenskins as a whole. "Pass, at own, risk," he read aloud. "Hey boss, I tink it's dangerous around here."

Fly rolled his eyes and moved ahead.

The company came upon the entrance to the mines a couple of hours before noon. Large wooden gates, painted gold and black to warn against entry, stood between two natural rock formations. A sign behind the gates, written in the common tongue, read, 'This mine closed due to hazardous conditions, to include: sudden drops, instability of shafts, and dangerous, hostile creatures of unknown origin and/or nature. Thank you for staying out. This means you!'

Rage grabbed one of the gate doors and ripped it from its moorings, tossing it aside like so much driftwood. "Da way is clear, boss."

Fly instructed everyone to take a last stock of their belongings before they entered the mines. As they set about securing their gear and pulling weapons out, or in Lain's case, raising a few corpses from the snowdrifts and the hard packed ground, Fly took Trent and Akimaru aside.

"All right, you two." He put a hand on each man's shoulder. "You've both been down there before, and I recall you telling me about the freaks that guard the ruins. Remind me what we're up against if we go down there now."

Trent's mind reeled at the memory of the multi-limbed guardian that had nearly killed him. Other monstrosities dwelled in those ruins, but this time, he wasn't going in ignorant of them, and Akimaru was not his only reliable companion. Together, the five of them should be able to take care of business, but what if there was a whole community of the creatures down there? What then?

"Well, Headmaster," the Human Ninja began. "I'll not sugarcoat it, sir. It's going to be horrific. The one creature I recall with any clarity nearly killed me. If not for Akimaru, I wouldn't be here right now."

Fly considered this for a moment before looking to Akimaru, the half-breed elemental and Psychic.

"Aki? Anything to add?"

"Yes, sensei," Akimaru said. "The creature which Trent mentioned is not unique. There are likely several dozen of them down there, along with others I sensed and saw when we were in those ruins before. I took Markus-san and Solomon back to the surface, and returned there when they were away to Solomon's home, that Markus Trent could receive healing."

This was news to both Fly and Trent, and so they listened more intently to the white clad Ninja.

"There are wild Sidalis down there, along with the monsters that lurk about. In addition, there are men made of mecha, long since rusted over, but still dangerous to us.

"The mutants live and hunt in packs, though *what* exactly they hunt for food, I do not know. The abominations, like the one Trent and I saw, are primarily solitary creatures who lurk and stalk alone, picking at the mutants unfortunate enough to fall to them. In addition, a handful of earth elementals are holed up in one of the larger buildings."

"The mecha men—" Fly was concerned more with artificial drones than with the mutants or elementals. He had little working knowledge of technology. "What did you observe about them? Are they dangerous like the other inhabitants of the underground city?"

"Yes, Headmaster," Akimaru said. "They are dangerous. They hunt as well, but they seem to do it out of habit, out of nature. They use mecha weapons both carried in hand and embedded in their bodies."

As soon as Akimaru said this to him, Fly realized what the Midnight Suns would have to do to survive.

"Everybody, make camp," the Black Draconus said. "We're going to wait here for a while."

Rage and Lain made no sign of surprise, and made a basic camp along with Akimaru and Trent.

When they were settled in, Fly sat in the snow and waited. Norman Adwar, he thought, would be a great addition to the excursion. "We wait for William Deus and the Hoods. We keep the truce, and we work together to find Evergreen. We can use their muscle and their unique skills. Above all, we can use a distraction for the mutants and monsters," he said.

* * * *

When Flint reported that he could see campfire smoke, Anna knew that Thaddeus Fly waited for her. The Black Draconus Ninja would want Anna and the Hoods along for the ride as well. She was all too happy to agree—for the time being.

"You want I should send up a white flag, William?" Flint asked. "You know, the whole 'we come in peace' thing?"

"No, Flint, that won't be necessary. If he's waiting for us, Fly has serious doubts about the safety of entering the ruins alone. We'll help the Suns out as far as we can, or as far as we dare. Remember, we're both after the same thing here." She addressed everyone in the group. "Help keep each other safe, but by no means let one of the Suns get his hands on the Glove first. We'll find Evergreen and cut her hand off if it's required. But we'll not let Fly have it. No curse is going to rid us of them, damn it! We'll run them out of Desanadron ourselves.

Mutters of agreement rose from the Hoods and Lee Toren, and the company continued up the path in the face of the falling snow.

Forty minutes later, at sharp incline in the path, they veered slightly right and came within eye- and earshot of the Midnight Suns.

Fly's company sat in a loose semi-circle, a few undead Minotaurs and Dwarves milling about under Lain McNealy's command.

Anna saw the Headmaster's broad back, and when the white clad Ninja, Akimaru, pointed in her direction, Fly rose and turned to face them, one empty hand up in the air. "Hail and well met," he called to the Hoods.

"Hail and well met." Anna sprinted ahead of the group, her feet slipping and sloshing about in the fresh fallen snow. She finally made her way up to Fly, sucking air. The mountains were no good for her lungs, she decided, no good at all. She learned over the last few days how the Dwarves, such stout fellows all, could be such good marathon runners out in the plains and forests of Tamalaria. When you worked for most of your life in a region like this, it did wonders for your stamina. "So, what's the situation?" she asked.

"We aren't entirely certain," Fly said. "We decided to wait for you and yours," he said, nodding at the Hoods as they gathered up behind Anna. "In particular, we've been waiting for Norman Adwar, so we could ask him a few questions."

This caught Anna's interest, and she beckoned the Gnome Engineer forward with a wave of her hand.

Looking abashed, Norm waddled up through the deepening snow.

Fly gave him a perfunctory bow of respect. "Good Master Adwar."

"Um, yeah, hullo there," Norm said. "Uh, what exactly do you need me for? I'm just an Engineer." His left hand patting the heavy metal object tucked into his waistband, reassuring himself that it was still there.

"Akimaru, come here," Fly said.

The white clad half-breed stood and stalked over, the soles of his boots never sinking beneath the powder. He stood next to his sensei, his hands hanging loosely at his sides.

"Describe to master Adwar here the mecha men you spied in the ruins on your previous trip here."

"You've been here before?" Anna's suspicions of Fly's motives grew. If he already had an idea of what was down in the ruins, why wait for the Hoods? Could the beings lurking down there be *that* dangerous?

"Yes, I have been here before, along with Markus Trent," Akimaru said flatly. "I have laid eyes upon more of the inhabitants of the underground city." Akimaru turned his focus on Norman, who shivered when he saw those frosted, glassy eyes.

If he turned on his Identifier, he wondered, what would the readout display say? Or would the device simply implode in on itself?

"Master Adwar," Akimaru said, "there are men who are composed of machinery down in the ruins, armed with mecha weapons that they both carry, and have as parts of their body. I spied no flesh on their bodies, though I could not get close enough to be certain."

Norm's memory flooded through his mind's eye—lines and lines of text from ancient technology guides he'd read over the years laying before his mind. Portraits of technology of the Third and Fourth Age scrolled past, dozens, scores of them, and he had to shut his eyes to bring the images into full focus.

Two groups waited silently while Norm considered the newest batch of images in his head.

Heads, he thought suddenly, *that's the ticket*. "The heads, Akimaru, what did they look like?"

The half-breed considered this for only a second.

"Their heads were shaped like curved tubes. Like the metal items they fire from their carried weapons," he said.

"Bullets," Norm said. "The heads are shaped like bullets. Okay. I think I remember seeing one of those in a workshop in Palen." He drew out his pad of paper, and did a swift, crude sketch of the mechanical man he'd seen. "This looks like crud. Any artistic talent, Aki me boy?"

Instead of answering, Akimaru brushed gently past the Engineer and over to Styge, who was finishing his drawing's last minute detail. Akimaru ripped the pad from Styge's hand, turned it over to a blank page, and handed it back.

When Styge had his hands on the pad again, Akimaru clutched the old man's shoulders gently, and sent the image of the mechanical men to Styge's mind directly.

There came a flurry of pencil strokes.

After only a handful of minutes passed, Styge handed the finished drawing to Akimaru, who returned to Anna and Norman, holding the torn sheet to them.

"This is what I saw, master Adwar. By the way, Master Styge, very nice work you do here."

Styge gave him his gap-toothed smile, and rubbed his Mohawk roughly.

"Yup, that's as I guessed." Norman took the picture. "It's an old model of security droid." He dropped the obscure word into his sentence as though anyone would know it aside from him and Stockholm. "From the middle of the Third Age, I'd wager. They're equipped with a long-lasting battery that only powers their bodies when a warm-blooded creature comes within three hundred yards," he said. "If they've been moving around at all like you say, Akimaru, they haven't got but a few years left in the ol' fuel cells. Course, that's a little beyond the scope of our time frame, isn't it?"

Anna, Fly and Akimaru said nothing in reply.

"Of course. Now, here's how we go about dealing with them," Norman said.

The entire group, Hoods and Midnight Suns alike, gathered around the Gnome Engineer.

"Don't forget there's other things down there to worry about, Norm ol' chum," Lee advised.

"I haven't forgotten," Norm spat irritably. "Now listen." He pointed fixedly at the drawing. His finger rested on the stomach of the machine drawn on the paper. "This here is where the battery is housed. A direct blow to the chassis will dislodge the battery and take them out of commission."

"Simple as that?" Flint was frankly surprised that anything technology related could be so easy to deal with.

"Should be." Norm's voice slightly clouded with doubt. "There's another model, came out not too long after the first run of these, that had a sturdier battery housing inside. A simple blow to the stomach wasn't enough with them. You had to shatter the housing completely to shut them down. Just bear in mind, though, that these things may be rusted and old, but they're bound to still be deadly accurate."

"Wait a minute," Fly said, raising a finger. "You said they react to anything warm blooded, right?"

Norman nodded, a smile alighting his face when he realized what Fly was about to suggest.

"Not a problem then. I'm cold blooded, as I'm sure Akimaru is," he said, to which the half-breed nodded. "We'll personally deal with the mecha men then. Will they even detect us?"

"Nope," Norm said. "They only react to warm blooded threats, like I said. Their targeting systems were developed by the Dwarves during their Third Age border skirmishes with wild Minotaur tribes. You two won't even register."

That much at least settled, the group looked to Akimaru concerning the other creatures in the ruins.

"The many-limbed creatures of black flesh showed little fear of magic and are immensely powerful, physically. However, they are slow, as their legs are very stout. Swift maneuvers, hit and run, will work best. As for the mutants, I cannot say what tactics would work best. They will, as a result, be our largest problem."

With nothing more to hold council over, the ensemble from Desanadron headed into the mines, uncertain of how many of their members would come back to the surface alive.

* * * *

The Guild members stood crowded together atop the steep cliff that dropped down to the outskirts of the buried city and took in their surroundings with true awe. Other than Akimaru and Trent, had never seen such an enormous unpopulated area, or buildings so tall.

Even Lee Toren, who'd seen an amazing sight or two in his time, sucked in air through his teeth and whistled, the sound echoing out over the city. "That's some scenery, eh? Now, how the hell do we get down from here?"

Lain McNealy moved back into the mineshaft, summoning a few agents with her.

When there was enough room on the ledge to move about, Lain sent several of her zombies through, giving them orders with words lost to the majority of lands.

The Minotaur and Dwarven corpses shuffled toward the lip of the ledge, and crouched.

One large Minotaur, only a few weeks dead from the look of him, clung to the ledge. Another Minotaur cadaver climbed down and grasped its ankles. On and on this went, with Lain summoning up more corpses from the mineshaft itself to join the 'human' chain that would serve as the group's ladder.

Anna eyeballed the horrific structure critically, and asked Lain if it would hold Rage or Stockholm's weight.

"Certainly," Lain replied. "When a person is dead, their arms don't get tired."

Twenty minutes later, the proof was in the pudding as they say, as the Orc descended the ladder of corpses to the floor of the ruins. Stockholm didn't bother with the ladder, opting instead to leap from several hundred feet up. He landed in a crouch, thudding against the ground with a discernable tremor.

"Real subtle there big fellah," Flint moaned. "Nobody in this creepy cavern's gonna notice a huge Red Tribe Werewolf leaping out of the sky. Dolt," he added, trying to keep his voice inaudible.

Stockholm, though, clouted him one upside his head.

Flint rubbed his head, and tuned up his hearing. Something was breathing heavily, and not too far away. "Heads up and eyes open, folks, I hear trouble."

The two groups spread out, the Hoods keeping to the north of the main road heading into the city while the Suns took the south.

They stayed roughly twenty-five yards apart, all brandishing what weapons they had on hand.

Anna looked over at Norman. "Um, Norm? What is that?" She indicated his weapon.

"Oh, this?" Norm gave a satisfied smile. "It's called a revolver. Forty-four caliber. Packs one hell of a kick, but I made a few adjustments to compensate for recoil."

His words were all gibberish so far as she could tell, but he seemed pleased, and she knew from the sound of it that it was a weapon. That was good enough.

The first monstrosity leaped from around the corner of the first building they approached.

Huge and lumbering, it stampeded toward the Midnight Suns, loosing a horrid battle cry as it charged.

Trent, his memories of the monster's kinsmen resurfacing, searched for the crimson eyes that would be found in its upper torso.

He spotted them, wide and bloodthirsty, pathetic almost in their primal need and hurled three shuriken in rapid succession, striking the eyes with deadly accuracy.

The lumbering behemoth went down in a twitching heap, grappling at its impaled eyes and shrieking its final death throes.

Anna's spine stiffened at the sight of the beast, all muscle and sinew stretched as tall as she and as broad as Stockholm or Rage. A shiver ran the course of her body, and she set her focus forward now, making certain to sweep the interiors of the buildings they passed.

None of the structures seemed unstable at a passing glance, but with her usual eye for detail, Anna saw the signs of decay. Crumbling bricks, loose molding, and strange, thick roots wrapping around the foundations of the smaller structures. These telltale signs informed Anna that this marvelous, forgotten metropolis would be nothing but mortar and dust in a few decades.

Up ahead, she spotted Lee Toren ducking into what appeared to be a storefront. "Flint, go retrieve our wayward hired hand," she called to the Wererat, who saluted and sprinted into the shop after the Pickpocket.

The interior of the store was littered with a thick layer of dust, dozens, perhaps hundreds of old cobwebs, and the footprints of Lee Toren. The Gnome stood before a shelving unit caked with dirt and grime. Something shiny must have caught Lee's eyes, because the Pickpocket stared vacantly.

"Oi, what have you found, Lee?" Flint asked a second before he pulled the Pickpocket back from certain death.

A thick, winged serpent slithered before the Wererat and Gnome, and Flint barely tugged Lee out of the path of its venomous fangs.

Flint was about to stab the creature in the head when it turned its gaze upon him. His arms went slack at his sides, and only Lee's quick recovery saved Flint from the fate he'd prevented the Pickpocket from suffering.

The Gnome struck the serpent through the head with one of his daggers, pinning it to the floor as it thrashed under his hand. When the creature fell still, Lee pulled his weapon out, and looked Flint up and down.

"Sorry about putting you through that." Lee shook his head. "I just glanced in and that thing had me, mind and all. We really have to tread lightly…. Hey, what's this?" He plucked up an object from the shelf, turning it over in his hand this way and that. "Any ideas?"

He handed the object to Flint, who sniffed it a moment, and then turned it this way and that. It was a thin, rectangular container of some sort, with something rattling around inside. He grasped the edge of the container, and it opened with ease, revealing a shining, circular disk. The words 'The Roving Tramps' were imprinted on the disk like a declaration.

"No idea," Flint said, tossing the container and its disk aside without interest. "Come on, we're wasting time here. Remember, we're not treasure hunting, Lee. We have a purpose."

"Oh, yeah, I forgot, we're down here in these godsforsaken ruins, looking for a woman who can make herself totally undetectable. Sorry for being greedy."

Anna and the rest of the Hoods stood outside, arms folded with looks of disapproval. They continued on down the main avenue in silence, keeping themselves razor sharp.

The two groups pulled slightly tighter together as they went, the buildings crowding in around them. Harsh barks and growls sounded around them, the denizens of the city coming out of their hiding places to look at these new intruders, or as most of them thought of the mixed companies, meals.

Only two miles away, atop a three-story building labeled 'Chet's Hardware', Teresa Evergreen looked at the sudden activity down the avenue. Her pursuers had come for her.

Ten minutes passed, and the Midnight Suns and Hoods made little progress, trying to stay well away from any open buildings and resisting the urge to branch out onto intersecting streets. "This is taking too long," Fly called over to Anna, who simply nodded. "We need to find the woman quickly, before our hosts decide to take action against us *en masse*."

"I agree, but we have little choice. We don't exactly know how we're going to find her." Anna stopped in her tracks, and all of her agents, with the exception of Norman, followed suit.

The Gnome Engineer was using another of his gadgets, staring at it as he crept along with the revolver in his right hand.

"Two streets south of us, we've got droids." Norman finally came to a halt twenty yards beyond Anna.

Stockholm stiffened, his nostrils flaring haywire.

"Fly, Aki, you two want to,,," Norm got no further as a mutant crashed through the window of a nearby residence, flying at Norman with one long, leathery arm extended.

"Norman, no!" Stockholm gauged the speed of the creature and his own movements, terror ripping through his heart as he concluded that Norman would be flayed alive before he could intercept the wild Sidalis.

Its entire body was ropy and thrashing with anticipation, its flat, board-like face a mask of hideous boils that swelled as it closed on Norman Adwar.

Norman, either out of fear or instinctive reflex, brought the barrel of his revolver up, aiming straight at the creature's face, and pulled the trigger twice.

Two hollow, booming reports echoed through the cavern ruins as gaping, bloody holes tore open in the mutant's face. It fell mere inches short of Norman, twitching and its head bleeding. A smoldering, bloody mess decorated the back of its skull as brain matter sizzled and popped around the wound.

Norman vomited explosively, much more than he had after beating on Lee Toren in Ja-Wen, the foul reek of his stomach's contents filling the air as they splashed over the back of the dead mutant.

"Well played, Norm, well played," Flint said, rushing past the stunned Stockholm to pat Norm on the back, which triggered another burst of vomit.

"Come now, it's not so bad. It was you or him, right?"

Hands on knees, crouched over to stay on his feet, Norman Adwar nodded a very little bit.

The reports of the firearm had scared off most of the group's visitors, and Fly and Akimaru took full advantage of this, acting on Norman's previous statement and moving toward the droids south of their position.

When they came upon a group of six rusted mecha men shuffling aimlessly about, the two Ninjas stabbed them in their frail stomach chassis.

With whirs and buzzing noises, they fell limply to the ground, their artificial lives snuffed.

The Ninjas returned to the larger group, and everyone seemed to take in a large sigh of relief.

"Well, that's dealt with," Anna said.

She had no idea what was about to fall upon them, and neither did anyone else, perhaps excepting of Akimaru. The half-breed knew all too well the sound of the creature that bellowed from the far end of the city. It was the primary reason he had ceased his exploration of the ruins. Despite his considerable powers and skills, he would never be able to defeat that particular foe.

The true Guardian of the underground city had awakened.

* * * *

Teresa Evergreen heard the reports of the Gnome's revolver, and knew that the mixed company of Hoods and Midnight Suns would make swift progress now that most of the city's inhabitants were scared off.

Having the advantage of freedom of movement, she took off west, toward the far end of the city.

Teresa explored the ruins when she had first arrived. At the far end of the city, several miles from the ledge that led back to the ruins, she had found a creature that could only be described one way. It was Death given a host body and a license to dispense of the pleasantry of waiting for a mortal's true end. The construct appeared to be a Half-Giant, grafted here and there with dozens of mecha implements and armed to the teeth with gigantic weapons.

An aura of magic hung about the construct, though Evergreen had never met a Giant that could perform spells of any kind. It stood stock still in some sort of constraints set into the wall of the iron cage that enclosed it.

A lever set into the wall next to it drew her attention, and when she flipped it down, the construct's eyes flew open, and the constraints retracted into the wall, releasing the Guardian. It stretched its massive arms and legs slowly, laboriously, and groaned. Yet beyond this, it made no move.

The construct's left arm, she saw as she stood beside it, was encased in an artificial housing of some sort, with the words 'Technos Corporation Unit D-4' stamped into the metal. That housing, she realized, was where the flow of magic was coming from.

Artificial magic, she thought. *How fascinating the era this thing was from must have been.*

When the creature let out a low, rumbling moan, she felt a little pang of fear. When it roared like a one-man army, she nearly urinated in her pants. The Guardian sensed a threat, and marched off to meet it, breaking down the cage wall in front of it by simply walking into it. Teresa Evergreen smiled despite her fear. She'd like to see her pursuers get past this monstrosity.

* * * *

When the nearby mutants and beasts fled in a panic, Fly, Anna, and every other agent with them knew they were in deep shit. If the freakish inhabitants were afraid of whatever was coming down the main road toward them, they didn't stand a chance.

"Options, everybody," Anna shouted as the ground beneath them rippled with tremors.

"Scatter and run like all get out," Lee Toren shouted above the din of stalactites in the cavern ceiling falling all around them.

This was exactly what they did, with Akimaru lagging a little behind with Stockholm and Rage.

The three of them served as a rearguard until a huge chunk of the cavern ceiling came down in front of them, severing them from the others.

Anna turned back and shouted for them.

"Go on ahead," Stockholm called back. "We'll find a way around." He turned to Rage and Akimaru. "All right, gentlemen. We can either go around and find the others, or we can stand here and fight whatever it is that's going to be bearing down on us."

"I vote we run," Akimaru said without hesitation.

Stockholm peered into the half-breed's eyes, and saw genuine terror. If a creature such as Akimaru was worried, then he should be too.

"All right, point taken. You've seen it before, haven't you?"

Akimaru nodded hurriedly, and led the trio down a side street. Rage plunged a heavy fist into the face of one of the monstrosities that had first threatened the company, or at least one of its kinsmen, breaking its face and sending it flying ahead of him. As it fell heavily to the cavern floor, he ran over it, crushing several vital organs under his sheer weight.

"Nice, very nice," Stockholm commented as he took in labored breaths.

"T'anks," Rage replied.

The trio turned again, running up a road parallel to the main road. After a few minutes they made their way back to the main company, who had only moved about a hundred yards back toward the city's entrance.

They'd gathered in a circle around Styge, who Stockholm saw was seated on the ground, chanting and waving his hands in mysterious motions.

"What's de old guy doing?" Rage inquired.

"The only thing that matters right now," Stockholm said with a wicked, murderous smile. He looked at Rage and put a heavy hand on his shoulder companionably. "He's saving our asses."

* * * *

As soon as the company separated from Stockholm, Akimaru and Rage, the others ran up the street a little way, and waited for their safe.

Styge took an immediate seat, pulling out his sketchbook, and the others l watched as the denizens of the ruins came flying at them from all directions. They appeared to be set on getting one last meal before going into hiding from whatever creature scared them so badly.

Flint, Fly, Trent and Lee Toren defended them, knives and shuriken flying with deadly accuracy.

Norman fired into the oncoming assailants seemingly at random.

His shots weren't, however, as random as they appeared—several more mecha soldiers had come lumbering from their hidden posts, and he took them down as priority number one.

The mutants of the ruins were wild and unskilled at the use of their powers, and so they came bodily at the company—they could be dealt with by the others. The mecha men acted purely on programming, and had to be put down quickly.

Anna had little battle prowess, and backed herself up against Lain McNealy, who was reviving fallen mutants and monsters as soon as they perished from their wounds.

It was a stalemate at best, but everyone knew they had to protect Styge. The old man was up to something, and from the sound of the words escaping his mouth and the hand motions he was making over his drawing of the Blue Dragon, it was something on a scale beyond grand.

The last of their assailants scattered as another bellow from the Guardian sent shockwaves through the air and ground.

Anna looked south, and saw Stockholm, Rage and Akimaru running toward them, rejoining the group just in time to be of no help.

Flint, who had suffered a few scrapes and cuts, was breathing heavily as Stockholm approached. "Fat lot of good you did," he mocked, smiling at the Red Tribesman. "I know you and Akimaru could both have jumped over that boulder in the road."

"True enough, but we weren't about to leave Rage behind." Stockholm looked not at Flint but at Styge. "He's really going to manifest a Blue Dragon in here, isn't he?"

Flint merely nodded, and sank down to one knee.

"Flint, are you all right?"

"I think one of those buggers had venom." The Wererat held his left arm up for Stockholm to inspect.

Sure enough, one of the slash wounds had swelled up and turned a bright, vibrant orange.

"It won't kill me, but it's going to be hell going to the bathroom I think, ha ha." He dropped his rear end on the ground.

The entire company as a whole looked up then, responding to another loud, ominous growl from directly above them.

A Blue Dragon hovered in the air, snarling violently as it floated westward, down the road toward the city's Guardian.

* * * *

Teresa told herself to stay put. However, curiosity was a hard thing to conquer, and she wanted to leave nothing to chance. If the Hoods and Midnight Suns managed to steal a victory over the construct, she could slip past them while they licked their collective wounds.

Up the main road she sprinted, barely able to keep stride with the Half-Giant.

A few miles later, she spied the Blue Dragon, snarling and snapping at the air, shimmer into existence.

"Styge," she whispered aloud.

In her surprise, she let her cover slip for just a moment.

The Half-Giant construct wheeled on her with uncanny speed, raising the artificial left arm toward her.

"No, wait, I'm not what you're after! Look, look at that Dragon."

A burst of lightning force erupted from the end of the mecha arm, ripping through her body, sending currents of force and agony through her muscles, her bones, her very soul. She tried to cry out, but found her lungs melted to liquid in her chest. The construct stood still for a moment, its face devoid of any emotion or interest.

As Teresa Evergreen fell dead to the ground, the construct loomed over her a moment, and spoke its first words in over a millennium. "Target neutralized," it said in a half humanoid, half mechanical voice.

It turned back toward the east, and stomped steadily down the road, the Blue Dragon coming into full view now.

"Target acquired."

* * * *

Flint slapped Styge's cheek, shook him by the shoulders, and hollered in his face.

Nothing worked—and Styge remained motionless on the cavern floor.

Though the Wererat didn't know it, Styge was still very much alive and awake. The continued physical existence of the Blue Dragon took a large toll on Styge, but it was a price he could afford to pay—for now. Too long at it, though, and it would be lights out, permanently.

The Blue Dragon floated downward toward the ground and its oncoming attacker.

The construct Guardian pounded forth, bound to the restraints of gravity despite its full complement of otherworldly powers.

As the two colossal opponents closed on one another, the Blue Dragon brought swirling lightning to bear, and the construct aimed its mechanical left arm at the Dragon's zig-zagging chest and underbelly.

The Blue Dragon, as a creature purely of Illusion magic and only temporary physical presence, didn't have to wait as long to summon its power as a real Blue Dragon would. A bright starburst of power erupted with a thunderclap from its throat, searing into the Guardian's chest, hurling it back through the air.

"I could have done that," Fly said without much enthusiasm.

With their feared Guardian locked in combat with a Dragon, the city's freakish residents felt safe enough to explore out into the streets to see who would live, and whether or not their earlier prospective meals had left the ruins. Seeing that they hadn't, several abominations made their way toward the company, who turned to face them.

From having squared off with one another on many occasions, the Hoods and Midnight Suns moved around one another with a strangely fluid grace, agents from one Guild aiding those of the other with expertly times cooperative attacks.

Norman's revolver ran out of ammunition, and he fell back toward Styge so that he could reload.

Anna stepped into his place, pulling her short sword and deftly dodging and rolling aside from the multiple heavy limbs of the mutants, monsters and hybrid animals.

She struck out at them where she could, but she was getting winded again, and wouldn't be able to keep up the pace for too long.

Norman returned to her side, his revolver cracking off reports even louder than the Blue Dragon's breath weapon, sending bullets tearing through the creatures' heads and chests.

He wasn't exactly a marksman, but Norman had found his niche all right, she thought.

Akimaru sprayed shards of ice at the oncoming assailants, and tapped a few on the forehead with his bare hands. Those unfortunate few didn't even live long enough to feel their heads burst apart when Rage or Stockholm took their cue from the white clad Ninja and punched or kicked through the skulls that had become cold as ice, and as fragile as glass.

These three, of all of those assembled, worked together with the seemingly least amount of forethought or effort. The battlefield was the kingdom to which each had been born, the closed fist was their scepter, the body count their proof of heritage. The only crowns upon their heads were Stockholm's matted, bloody fur, Akimaru's ice spikes covered by his mask, and Rage's thick sheets of sweat.

Flint, Norman and Anna moved with similar grace, though they had Markus Trent alongside them. While Anna wasn't very skilled at melee or missile combat, she was a Rogue, and knew a thing or two about dirty fighting —which Trent and Flint were all about.

Kicks aimed at what they thought, and often rightly so, were genitals. One of them led a freak away from the others while Trent sneaked up behind it and slit its throat.

Norman was able to use these loosely formed tactics to reload when he needed to, and thankfully, he'd brought a whole load of bullets along for the trip, in case the revolver worked. If it hadn't, he'd probably be dead by now.

Fly worked in conjunction with Lain's many undead servants, nearly two dozen of whom she had summoned from the corpse ladder that would let them out of the city. Accompanied by the falling mutants and monsters, these lurking, shambling combatants served mostly as decoys, but a few were very freshly dead, and more than worthy allies under her command.

Together they cut down a large number of the residents of the ruins.

Styge, meanwhile, stayed focused on keeping the Blue Dragon image solid. He only had a few minutes left to work with.

Whatever the Guardian was, it was terrifying, going blow for blow with the Blue Dragon. When Styge floated the Dragon over it, seemingly out of reach, the Half-Giant grabbed large chunks of debris from the fallen stalactites around him, and hurled it into the chest or broad side of the illusion made real.

The Blue Dragon would fan a little, wisps of smoke billowing out from around its mostly ethereal body as Styge prepared it for another gust of lightning, letting it circle a little of its own free will.

The Glove of Shadows

The Blue Dragon swooped down sharply at the construct, releasing its thundering fury full force into the Guardian's upper body.

It flew not straight back, but down to the packed granite floor.

Styge motioned the Dragon down atop it, and could feel the construct's ragged breathing beneath the hard scaled talons of the blue reptile.

Perhaps he could defeat it after all. *Wouldn't that just beat all*, he thought.

The Guardian had other ideas, however. It jerked to the right, grabbing the Dragon by the throat.

Styge's drawing, while beautiful, had been too entirely accurate—Blue Dragons were among the smallest of the legendary wyrms, and the construct's enormous hands clamped fully around its throat, squeezing down suddenly and violently on its windpipe.

With an audible snap and moan, the image of the Blue Dragon shimmered into nothingness.

The construct looked around, confusion clearly reflected in its analytical face.

This apparently did not compute, or something like that, Norman observed as he fired off his last round in his current load.

The Half-Giant came at the group again as their straggling assailants fled.

"Scatter and retreat," Anna called out.

Apparently, though, there wasn't too much of a hurry.

After a few hurried steps, the Guardian stumbled, severely injured by the Blue Dragon.

Stockholm slung the old Illusionist over one shoulder and was making away with him, but the Red Tribesman looked over his shoulder at the Guardian.

It had halted a dozen yards away from Lain McNealy and Thaddeus Fly, and slowly pointed its mecha arm at them.

Black fire belched out at them, and both Headmaster and Necromancer fell to the ground screaming and on fire.

"Come on," Flint tried to tear Anna away from the scene of carnage, but she would not be budged—not this time.

Every reasonable synapse in her mind beat on her to turn, take the Wererat's advice, leave this tomb of death and freaks. But she cannot—not so long as those two still screamed, because that means they're still alive.

"You want to save them, don't you?" Flint was incredulous.

"I'll draw its attention," Anna said.

Flint pointed with one long, narrow finger at the changing scene.

Akimaru was wrapping Rage's right hand with a thick layer of mystic ice as the Orc Berserker waited patiently, showing no signs of discomfort or pain.

Meanwhile, Trent danced around like a jester, keeping the Guardian busy with his feints and lunges. The Human Ninja even landed a few shallow stabs to the creature's legs.

Anna watched in fascinated horror as the plan struck her mind's eye.

The scene in her head played out only a few seconds ahead of the physical events, and it went something like this.

Rage, right hand covered with magical frost and ice, lumbered toward the Guardian as it wheeled about, trying to get Trent in the sights of the mecha weapon on its left arm.

As Trent slowed, he back-flipped high over Rage, who roared as loudly as the construct, thrusting his fist into the end of the barrel arm of the construct.

A huge conflagration and a wave of concussion force sent everybody, including Lee Toren, sprawling to the ground.

And what has everyone's favorite wise-ass, amoral and cravenly Pickpocket been doing since the battle between the Guardian and the Blue Dragon had begun? Just what he had always done best.

He secured the object the Hoods had hired him to help them seek out, and waited atop the ledge leading into/out of the ruins.

The Glove of Shadows hung loosely tucked into a vest pocket as he sat and pulled out a cigarette, lighting it as the concussion wave struck the entire city.

* * * *

Smoke and dust clung to the air around them as the Hoods and Midnight Suns pulled themselves into sitting positions. The blast had blown the entire left arm off of the Guardian, they saw, looking up and west to where it lay still, looking shattered and lifeless.

The bloody, spent meat of the severed appendage lay only a few yards away from Rage, who was also very badly off.

The Orc Berserker's face was shredded, the broad, flat green nose torn open to reveal bare nasal passages, the fleshy lid of his left eye completely ripped off. A small piece of metal shrapnel was deeply imbedded in the eye itself, and several dozen other pieces of ancient metal littered his chest and stomach. His right arm was a mess of gore, the flesh and much of the muscle burned to the raw, bleached bone. All of this Anna, Stockholm, Flint and Fly took in at a glance.

Akimaru and Trent had also been very close to the source of the wave of force, and had been knocked hard into nearby storefronts, the glass shattered into thousands of shards.

Trent, still nearly unconscious was losing the feeling in his broken left leg. Sweat and tiny tendrils of blood matted his hair to his head. Even had he been fully awake, he couldn't have seen the carnage, because he lay in a heap behind a store counter.

Akimaru suffered far less injury than Markus Trent, but that was mostly due to his unique physical and magical make-up. When Rage-san had thrust his fist into the cylindrical tube at the end of the Guardian's left arm, Akimaru had thrown up a wall of ice shielding in front of him. This barrier had absorbed the brunt of the concussion wave. However, the explosion had been too much contained fire, and Akimaru had been tossed like a twig in a tornado through the window of the shop opposite Trent, and subsequently through the wooden counter itself inside.

He was bruised, certainly, but not in any way broken or seriously threatened.

Thaddeus Fly had felt the least impact from the concussion wave, because the force of his breath weapon was so much like the force of the wave. He had only been pushed backward a dozen or so yards, and would have stayed on his feet if the Wererat hadn't been hurled bodily into him. The two had gone down in a tangle of angry, panicked limbs, each grappling for the other's throat, certain that they had been set upon by creatures of the ruins again.

When they had one another by the windpipe, they looked into one another's eyes, and shared a silent laugh.

Stockholm had experienced a brief moment of clarity just before the explosion. He had grabbed Norman Adwar and tucked him against his broad chest, crouching forward and keeping his back to the oncoming blast.

The two Hoods flew through the air, Stockholm letting his body go limp at the precise moment of the strike, and tensing up again as Norman shrieked like a banshee in his arms.

Stockholm managed a nearly impossible mid-air turn, and landed heavily on his back, with Norman safely propped seated on his stomach.

"Get, off," was all the Red Tribesman managed after recovering his senses.

Lain McNealy had been completely taken by surprise by the concussion wave. Thankfully for her, her undead minions had stood before her in a line of sacrificial lambs. She had only been knocked a few feet, and was dusting herself off.

When she looked over at Rage, she let out a high-pitched, horrified moan of fear. "Rage! No, Rage." She flew to his side and knelt next to him. "Say something, green meanie, tell me how you feel."

Anna stood next to Lain, and placed a consoling hand on her shoulder.

Lain didn't object, but didn't pay much heed either.

Rage's lips pursed suddenly, and he coughed, a harsh, strangled noise. "I feel like *boigra*, teacher," he muttered through bloody lips. "Can I skip class today? I t'ink dat's only fair." He tried to sit up.

Fly joined them, as did Flint, Norman, Stockholm and finally, Akimaru and Trent, the white clad Ninja supporting Trent under the arm like a walking crutch.

As they all gathered around Rage, who had now successfully sat up, they heard another low, primal roar issue from the Guardian.

"Oh shut it." Norman lanced his gun hand out to his right and pulling the trigger four times in rapid sequence.

Four ragged flaps of flesh burst apart in the Guardian's forehead. To conclude the ordeal, Stockholm leaped through the air and landed with a devastating kick to the construct's organic throat.

Brains blown apart, bled nearly to death, and with no more fresh oxygen coming down its windpipe, the construct fell dead as fast as it had come to life.

Anna looked around the company, and spotted Styge's limp form where Stockholm had been forced to set him down in order to protect Norman Adwar. He easily could have protected them both, so why set down the old Illusionist?

Anna bent over Styge.

His eyes were wide open, and a satisfied smile graced his dry, cracked lips.

She guessed Stockholm's motive for leaving him on the ground, and then took Styge's wrist between her fingers. Her guess was confirmed—she found no trace of a pulse.

Chapter Nineteen
Shortly Thereafter....

Two full days later, traveling slowly due to their numerous injuries, and carrying Styge's body with regard and respect, the Hoods and Midnight Suns arrived back in Traithrock, where they all practically collapsed at the gates.

The following morning, Anna found herself being shaken gently awake by Flint, who had nearly broken a Dwarven healing attendant's arms for trying to remove her clothes.

"Nobody tends to this man but me," he had yelled at them. "He needs his own room for healing, and I'll tend to him with your guidance only."

"I still can't believe he did it anyway," Anna said to her Prime and best friend. She had come to miss him over the course of the journey, though they were rarely more than a few yards apart at any given time. But this journey, she realized, was her opportunity to get to know her trusted Chief, become aware of what he was capable of. And she had also come to know Thaddeus Fly, a man who had once been so intent on becoming a member of an elite, family-like team of elders, that he had gotten himself purged from that team's records entirely. Most importantly, she had come to respect Fly.

"I know," Flint said. Styge had been officially pronounced dead the night before, when Anna had come fitfully awake from a nightmare in which the ashen-faced Half-Giant construct had chased her alone through the ancient, underground city, never once stopping in its pursuit of her. "But you know what, boss," he said, looking at Anna gravely. "I think he knew his time was coming."

"What makes you say that?" She sat up, wincing at the sharp pain in her spine. She'd been through a lot of hiking, battering, running and fighting in the last couple of weeks, perhaps more than she had in years. Maybe a few excursions a year would be in order, just to keep her up to speed.

"Well, he started on that dragon picture a good month before Lee came to us about the Glove of Shadows. He's still got it, by the way. Says he wants you and Fly to come to a mutual decision about what to do with it. Says he heard the stories about it from Stocky, and now he won't even try the thing on."

Flint laughed, but Anna did not join him in his mirth.

He gave her a worried look after her long, studied silence. "What's wrong, boss?"

"It is cursed, though," she whispered, putting her head on her knees, which she pulled up against her chest. "Styge is dead and Rage's eye can never be healed. Any word on Norman?"

As when they had returned to Desanadron after Ja-Wen, the Gnome Engineer had found a hotel room in town, and locked himself in. This time, he didn't even talk to anyone through the door. His quiet musings could be barely discerned when Flint propped his ear against the hotel room door.

"Nothing, Anna, sorry." Flint shook his head. "What do you figure's got him so shook up this time around? I mean, you saw how easily he shot that freaky Giant-thingy at the end, so what's his deal?"

On this, at least, Anna thought she might have an answer. She pulled her head up off of her knees, and looked past Flint's twitching whiskers on his snout, past the ratty teeth, seeking out his inner mind in his eyes.

"Think about it, Flint. Gnomes make great thieves and better scientists, and we had one of each in our company along the road. Yet one thing separates Lee Toren from most Gnome thieves—something that Norman has in common with every Gnome scientist, something important to his current mindset."

"What's that?" Flint handed her a cigarette as he lit another of his own.

She accepted, inhaled off of the same match as he, and let in a long drag.

"Violence, Flint. Killing, the death of another living being at one's own hands. How many of those mutants and freaks did he shoot? Did you keep count, because I certainly couldn't." She waved her cigarette around almost wildly.

Flint's eyes went wide, and she could see that revelation had struck a nerve in the Wererat.

"You understand now, don't you? Gnomes, as a rule, detest the idea of taking another sentient being's life. Even their mages use mostly non-lethal spells. So, how many did he bring down with his own two hands, Flint?"

The door of her room opened a crack, and the Hoods' Headmaster stiffened slightly before seeing the tuft of red fur through the crack in the door.

"He's okay, let him in," she called out to the Dwarf guarding her room, on orders from the Wererat.

Stockholm brought a tray of steaming hot food with him as he was admitted.

"Something from the kitchen, or did you whip this up yourself?" Anna asked.

"Myself." The Red Tribesman handed bowls to Anna and Flint, a sandwich to each as well. "Norman still won't budge, and the Midnight Suns are going to see an Alchemist tomorrow morning for transport back to Desanadron. They are tired of traveling in these mountains and in the snow, as I imagine you both are."

The Headmaster and Prime of the Hoods were both shoving food greedily into their mouths, closing off discussion for the moment.

Stockholm took a seat in one of the available sturdy rockers, squeezing into it with just enough room to breath. "Fly told me he'd have council with you regarding what should be done with the Glove of Shadows once we get back home."

"Stocky, ol' buddy ol' pal," Flint said around a mouthful of assorted meats and buttered bread. "How many of those things you figure Norm topped off?"

Stockholm rolled his eyes back in his head remembering each kill he had witnessed, and trying to remember the total number of bullet reports. He knew that when they had left the ruins, Norman had left the revolver behind, because the barrel and the chambers had become so heated from firing that the metal had become molten.

"Near as I can estimate, somewhere in the region of forty to fifty kills for Norman Adwar," Stockholm said evenly.

Anna nearly choked on her own sandwich, her eyes wide as saucers at the high number.

"Indeed, his mecha weapon was deadly, and he was a fairly accurate shot. However, someday a gun will always get you killed by not functioning properly," Stockholm said, walking away from the Prime and Headmaster. "With a sword or your own body, you've only got yourself to blame for failure."

* * * *

The next morning, Anna Deus, Ignatious Stockholm, Flint Ananham, Lee Toren and Norman Adwar, who wouldn't deny the departed this last unspoken request, stood in silence as Styge was interred in the earth of the cemetery just west of Traithrock. Of all of the company's members, he had been the quietest, the least intrusive, and it seemed at least to himself most of the time, the least useful. However, every Hood there knew that without Styge's Blue Dragon, the Guardian would have slain them all. They, and the Midnight Suns as well, owed him a great debt.

Perhaps that was why Thaddeus Fly had delayed their departure until after the funeral.

Few words were exchanged between the Hoods and the Suns—all members with their own scars to heal, their own harsh dealings with the environment, the ruins, and the Elven Paladin Archibald Reynaldi to remember. And there, Anna speculated, they might yet find an answer.

Each group had also gained something critical to their own members' lives through the whole experience.

Yes, Anna wept as a Dwarven preacher, a tallow-faced young Dwarf named Kurik Dudzick, delivered the final prayers for Styge's soul. Yet out of all of this messy business, she had gained something far more valuable than an artifact like the Glove of Shadows. She had obtained a greater, deeper understanding of those who had survived the journey, including the Midnight Suns.

As the congregation was dismissed from the cemetery (Dwarves believe that only the gravediggers should bear witness to the casket being lowered into the ground. They are a superstitious lot, to this very day.), Anna spotted Fly holding hands with Lain McNealy, and thought that perhaps, with any luck, the Black Draconus Ninja had found something he had long sought as well. The Glove of Shadows had been a tempting prize, but it had become a means to an end. It had been a grand excuse for all of them to get out of the city.

As the two companies left the gated and fenced cemetery, Anna drifted over to Fly. "We'll talk when we get back to Desanadron, Thaddeus Fly," she whispered. "But I think I already have an idea what I want to do with the Glove of Shadows."

The Glove of Shadows

Epilogue

And so life returned to normal for the residents of Desanadron, or at least, for those brave souls who had set out on a quest to retrieve the Glove of Shadows.

Lee Toren collected his twenty-five hundred gold pieces for his troubles, shared a few drinks with Norman Adwar, who still remained strangely quiet, before departing from Desanadron to find new suckers to swindle.

Borshev and Hollister were informed that in the event that the Headmaster and his Prime or his Chief ever left together on a journey again, they would once again be entrusted with the running of the Guild.

Anna decided that after young Mr. Civil and his ugly business, no more secret executions would be carried out in the name of keeping their base of operations a secret.

"No secret is worth a man's life," she had told them earnestly before departing again, leaving the Guild in Flint's capable hands.

The Wererat had learned a great deal from observing Stockholm over the last few weeks. His own style of command curved a little towards Stocky's own, and Stockholm tried not to be too harsh with the agents his first few days back. He even smiled and shared a few drinks and laughs with the regulars once he was back in his groove. Yes, these two gents had certainly learned a lot out on the road.

Norman Adwar got his lab cleaned up, and produced one more revolver on his weapon-making machine before he tore it apart, bolt by bolt and screw by screw. He took his time, being methodical about it. If he ever decided to look past the horror of the numerous lives he had taken in the ruins, he would put the machine back together again. For now, he left the one revolver he made in a heavy chest that required two hands to open. If there ever came a time when he couldn't open the chest, he would leave the contents inside forever. *End of story, end of game*, he thought.

He had learned one of the most important lessons of anyone in the Hoods —monsters take many forms, and some are in our own hearts and minds.

Across the city, in the warehouse that is home to the Midnight Suns, Markus Trent took at least half of his torture devices down off of the walls of his chambers. He had come to understand that Fly had done he had done honestly, but without a solid understanding of the consequences. He really couldn't hold Fly's misjudgment against him anymore. The Black Draconus had admitted his mistakes, and for the first time in Trent's life, he accepted someone's apologies without condition.

Several floors below, in Fly's locked chambers, well, let us just move on and say that the headmaster finally accepted Lain McNealy's come-ons. He finally forgave himself for his earlier transgressions in life, and found a way to obtain that sensation of truly belonging—in a familial sense.

Yet when they were finished, both of them, along with Trent, wondered once more about poor Rage, blind in one eye.

What they didn't know was that one of the shards of metal that had pierced Rage's eye had found a nice spot in his brain.

Though the Dwarven healers had been able to remove it. They did not release it before the shard had done its work; it freed a group of neural receptors in his brain, and Rage would soon find he was able to grasp Lain's teachings almost as easily as any normal Human or Elven child might.

What of Akimaru, the half-breed elemental and partial Psychic? The white clad Ninja requested one whole month of free time as soon as the company had returned to the Guildhall.

Fly had granted him his request, and Akimaru hadn't even stuck around to say good-bye.

So what had the white clad Ninja learned?

Something very simple, actually, he thought as he lounged in a snowy woodland path southeast of Ja-Wen. He loved the snow and the cold of winter. But then again, that was only natural, now wasn't it? However, his trip out east had served a double purpose, one to which Deus and sensei Fly had agreed upon.

They had given Akimaru the Glove of Shadows, since he had assured them both that he had a friend in the eastern lands who could deliver it where it was going without raising too much suspicion.

Akimaru now sat on the crest of a hill, watching his friend approach from the north on the back of a huge, black stallion. Even with his own discerning eyes, Akimaru still couldn't have guessed what his friend was if he hadn't been told outright.

The rider skidded to a halt in the snowdrifts, and called down softly, "Hail and well met, Akimaru, half-breed Ninja."

"Hail and well met, Grigory Molis, half-breed Knight." Akimaru smiled devilishly beneath his concealing white mask. He handed the wrapped Glove of Shadows up to Molis, who undid the wrapping, looked at the Glove, and shuddered.

"You know what is asked?" Akimaru said.

"Yes-yes. No need to mother hen me about it, my friend," the half-demon Molis said. "I'll be sure this gets to the right hands straight away. Stay well, my frosty friend."

"Go well, my damned friend," Akimaru replied, and lay back down in the soft, comfortable snow. He starts to chuckle, and then roars with horrific cackling. How ironic, he thinks, that it should come so perfectly full circle.

To the north, Archibald Reynaldi was getting impatient with the long wait without word from the Sidalis corporal, Dean Masters, or the Lizardman sergeant, Bergeon.

As he washed his face in his private lavatory sink, he wondered if perhaps they had been bested, slain in combat with a bunch of thieves.

No, he decided. *Not those two.*

Late that evening, the Elven Paladin was called down to the front gates of the Fort, where he was greeted by a remarkably noble-looking young Human, possibly a Knight, possibly a very noble Soldier.

With a heavy heart, the man told Reynaldi that Masters and Bergeon had been slain, but they had brought him from Fort Flag for backup.

He had managed to take the Glove of Shadows from Lee Toren after beating him and throwing him in stocks. Now that artifact was rightfully Lord Reynaldi's to deal with as he saw fit.

The Glove of Shadows

"You know," the young Knight said, leaning in close. "I do believe there is one way for the Order to use this thieves' tool for a divine purpose."

Reynaldi pricked up his ears, unwrapping the Glove of Shadows, still perfectly intact. It had drawn him since he'd discovered it—and he'd delayed his original intention to destroy it.

"Do you have any heretics who won't confess their crimes against the Order down in the cells?" the Knight asked

Reynaldi nodded his head.

"My good Lord Reynaldi, the Glove of Shadows can be used to steal *anything* from a man. That includes the truth."

Had Reynaldi been a vulgar, crass or baser being, he might have felt an erection form from the sheer excitement of such an idea. However, he was pure of heart, and would take the Knight's suggestion as soon as he went back down to question the heretics against the Order in the morning.

When morning came, he put the Glove on, asked the heretics his questions, and wiped the Glove over their chests.

Two of the three accused heretics immediately confessed to demon worship, and were put to death.

The third man confessed to the sin against the Order of adultery against his wife, for which he was whipped and then released.

How glorious is this, Reynaldi thought with glee. *I can go to each Fort, and we will no longer have to play around about getting the truth from the accused. I can take the truth from them with this. In no time, I'll become the greatest man of the Order.*

That night, a freak accident of nature occurred. The southwestern tower of the keep inside of Fort Stone was struck by not one, not two, but three bolts of lightning.

Only one person had been present when the tower was struck.

Archibald Reynaldi fell victim to the curse of the Glove of Shadows. Where this mysterious artifact is now, is anyone's guess.

The End

www.ingramcontent.com/pod-product-compliance
Lightning Source LLC
Chambersburg PA
CBHW070852260626
47170CB00007B/2587